RETURN *to* ROME

MARK MUNRO

Published in Australia by Sid Harta Books & Print Pty Ltd,
ABN: 34632585293
23 Stirling Crescent, Glen Waverley, Victoria 3150 Australia
Telephone: +61 3 9560 9920, Facsimile: +61 3 9545 1742
E-mail: author@sidharta.com.au

First published in Australia 2022
This edition published 2022
Copyright © Mark Munro 2022
Cover design, typesetting: WorkingType (www.workingtype.com.au)

Mark Munro
Return to Rome
ISBN: 978-1-922958-05-1
pp372

Mark Munro is a Queensland-based writer, musician, tropical gardener, amateur historian, and father of four. Born in Canada, he grew up in the forests of Manitoba before migrating to Australia in 1987. He has worked in IT for over 30 years and lives with his wife Suan on the Brisbane city fringe.

This novel would never have been completed without the support and love of my wife Suan. I thank you for our many late-night brainstorming and editing sessions that helped Return to Rome get over the line. Thanks to Daniela Bertua for her brilliant cover art, and all the team at Sid Harta for believing in the concept.

Mark Munro, Brisbane 2022

lease gods! Don't let me die today. I thrash about madly in my iron chains. It's so dark in this cell, I can barely see. Above, in the great Roman Colosseum, I can hear the roar of the crowd.

'Occidite eum!' Kill him, they shout in Latin. Another roar, even louder. 'Kill him!' The crowd pauses, gasps as one, and it is done. 'Victor!' they shout. 'Victor!' The cheering fades to a murmur. I pull again at the chains around my ankles, desperately. My skin tears and bleeds, but they won't come off. I am next. I am going to die here.

I've been in this cramped brick chamber, beneath the floor of the amphitheatre, for hours. The heat is unbearable. My throat is dry. The place stinks of rot and animals and death. In my cell, three other men are chained up as I am. One, an Illyrian, sits with his eyes closed, mumbling prayers to his god over and over. A great, bearded Gaul thrashes about in his chains like an animal, beating himself against the wall, bleeding from arms and legs, crying out in the tongue of the Gauls. The third man, a fellow Roman, calls out to me.

'Marcus! Hoc est quomodo desinit?' he wails. Is this how it ends? 'At least we die before the emperor himself, in Rome. The centre of the world.' He pauses. I can see the anguish in his face even in the dim light. 'Do you think they'll send the lot of us to fight one another?'

'I know not, Lucius,' I reply. 'Perhaps they'll pit us against each other to fight to the death. But we'll not stand a chance against him.' I nod towards the Gaul, who could tear me in half in an instant. 'If the three of us fought him together we might overpower him.'

'I doubt it. Hoy! Illyrian!' shouts Lucius. 'Quo nomen?' We don't even know his name. The Illyrian stares at Lucius, his eyes uncomprehending and wide with fear. He goes back to his prayers.

'We might have a shot at the Gaul, if we unite against him, Lucius. But what would be the good of it? We would have to slay each other next! You know as well as I, there can be but one winner. And even the victor of our contest will doubtless be torn to pieces by a wild beast or a gladiator.'

'Aye Marcus, I fear you speak the truth. I pray the gods grant us a swift and painless death. It is past noon, no? It won't be long now.' It's true, our end is near. We have but minutes to live. My breath is laboured. I feel as if to pass out. Didn't my mother tell me the gods will protect the innocent? Will they let me die today?

Sitting with my back to the wall I close my eyes as if not

to see the hell I am in. Is this all I get? Nineteen years of life. In my mind's eye I see my home, our little farm, only a day's wagon ride from the city of Neapolis. When I was taken, only a few weeks ago, the hills were already green with the first rains of winter. Our plot was a good size and the richness of the soil allowed us to make a good living on it.

I see our horses grazing peacefully, the line of the Italian mountains in the distance, the peak of Vesuvius visible on a clear day. The little pond in front of the house, with the big willow tree next to it. The stone bench that my father built right by it, inlaid with blue marble – the perfect haven from the hot summer sun.

I miss my father, who never saw me taken away. He had travelled to the city that day, transporting horses to a patron. I last saw him the evening before, sitting as he always did in the cooler weather, before the fireplace with my mother. They talked quietly of the affairs of the farm, the town, of me and my sister. He always took my mother's hand as they spoke, gently caressing it. Though married twenty years, he never lost his affection for my mother. I recall the warmth in her face, in the soft light of the fire. Looking beautiful as always, with her hair tied up tightly and greying at the edges, she laughed at my father's jokes no matter how many times she heard them. I would rest, half-asleep on the old couch nearby, our cat Cicero purring on my lap. How I ache to see them all again.

That morning, that horrible morning! I had just finished walking Phoenix, the new colt my father had given me for my birthday. I heard horses, not our own, but strangers' horses galloping at speed towards our gate. A trio of the emperor's soldiers armed with short swords pounded on the front door.

'Gaius Junius Corvus!' they shouted, demanding my father show himself in the name of the emperor, Tiberius Augustus. My mother met them and stood defiantly in the doorway.

'What are you doing here? What do you want with my husband?'

The leader of the three stepped forward. 'We have a warrant for his arrest, for crimes against the Roman state.'

'What crimes? This is absurd!' she shouted. 'I'll go to the magistrate at once. By whom is he accused?' But they ignored her, pushing past her into our atrium where I sat at the table, too frightened to move.

'Where is your husband, woman? We will arrest you too if you shelter him!' the captain demanded.

'Not here. He is in the city attending to business.'

'Search the place,' he barked at his underlings. They worked their way through the rooms, kicking open doors and rushing about with deadly seriousness.

'Not here, sir,' said one.

'Then check the grounds. The barn, the sheds. He could well be hiding. Tipped off, I suppose.' The captain glared at my mother.

'I speak truthfully,' my mother pleaded, 'he went to Neapolis before sunrise with four horses for a gentleman there.'

The captain seemed to accept this but was clearly annoyed.

'When will he return? Honestly now, good lady.' His voice had softened a little.

'He stays two or three days most times. He will canvass the markets for foals sometimes.'

The captain looked about our house with a calculating stare. Then straight at me, as though he hadn't seen me before.

'Boy! Does your mother speak forthrightly? Where is your father?' He approached me with his hand on his sword hilt. I backed away in fright, nearly toppling my chair.

'It … it is as my mother says. He went to the city early with the cart and horses to sell. For a friend of the governor, I think.'

The two other soldiers returned to the house, empty handed. 'He is not here. There is no wagon in the barn.'

'So, it seems the lady speaks the truth.' The captain pounded the table with his fist. 'By Jupiter, we are too late!' He drew his sword and flourished it in my mother's face. She held her ground, but her hands trembled. 'Well, let us hope so. We wouldn't want to be in contempt of the emperor's officers would we, Lady Corvus?'

She shook her head and stared at the floor, unable to speak. 'It is such a pity, that you and your husband had a chance to do the right thing by selling this dust heap to the Prefect. You have made a very foolish decision.'

'There is another way, sir.' One of the soldiers grinned and nodded his head in my direction.

'I like your thinking, Cornelius. Take the boy.'

My mother shrieked. 'No! He is an innocent child. He has harmed no one!'

'Master Corvus. Get up. Come with us.' I stood and looked at my mother, unsure what to do.

'Please, sir. He is a boy, in only his nineteenth year!'

'Man enough already, lady. Tie him, Cornelius.' My hands were bound tightly in front of me with a leather thong. 'We will take him to the city. This will no doubt guarantee your husband's reporting to face the charges.'

'What charges? I beg you, tell me!'

'The warrant comes from Rome with the seal of the emperor's own office. Conspiracy in a plot against Drusus Caesar, the emperor's son.'

'What? What would a horse farmer of Campania know of intrigue in the capital? My husband is a righteous citizen, as you yourselves are!'

'That is the charge. Our warrant is from the Prefect Sejanus himself.' My mother gasped. Sejanus is the head of the emperor's guard and the most feared man in Rome. Those who come in his name, come with the emperor's authority, and those he comes for are never seen again.

'You can retrieve your son in Neapolis. If your husband reports to the garrison there within three days, the boy will be released unharmed. If not, he could well be fodder for the gladiatorial games in Rome.'

'Of course he will report. My husband is a man of honour!'

'Let's get out of here.' A soldier took my arm and dragged me to the door.

'At least let him wear his cloak. Think of the weather!' My mother grabbed a woollen cloak from the hook by the door and threw it over me. At the same time, she pressed something into my hand, hidden by the folds of the cloak. It was a handful of coins; I quickly pocketed them.

'Out of our way, woman. There's nothing you can do for him now.' I was hauled outside and ordered to mount one of the horses. As I did so, the cloak fell to the ground. I reached for it, but they shouted at me to leave it. The soldiers mounted, and as they turned their mounts the coat was trampled in the mud.

'Fear not, Marcus. The gods will protect the innocent!' my mother cried out. 'You have done naught, and by the gods you will be freed!' I turned and saw her small figure in the doorway. That was the last I saw of her.

The days after are but a cloudy recollection: starved in a filthy jail in Neapolis for many days, interrogated by corrupt officers of the Prefect, kicked and beaten when they were not happy with my answers to their questions about my father. I was then taken to Rome in a prison convoy with murderers and robbers. I was cast into a prison wagon, my three companions thrown on top of me, then suffered the humiliation of being paraded through the streets of Rome being abused, laughed at, and spat on. All for a crime I didn't commit.

'I am innocent!' I shouted, as if anyone cared. I can still see the face of a young boy looking down from his second-floor window, hooting and throwing garbage on us, his father grinning beside him.

'Memento mori!' the boy shrieked with glee. Don't worry child, I will die. If only you knew, I am as innocent as you.

On we rode through the cobblestone streets until the great bulk of the Colosseum rose before us. From our cage we looked up in awe and terror. How could such a vast building exist? The greatest arena in the world, in the heart of the capital. Its three rows of stone arches glistened white in the sun. Marble statues adorned the upper archways and banners flew from the roof. Was this the last time I will ever see such a sight? Before I could take it all in, our prison wagon descended a short ramp and entered the shadowy tunnels beneath. Games keepers and imperial soldiers met the convoy at a great iron gate. With much shouting, checking and signing of tablets, the wagons were emptied one by one. Soldiers in iron helmets, and shoulder armour approached, short swords in hand, to fling the door of our cage open.

'Captivis, exite!' they shouted from all sides, beating the iron bars with the sides of their swords. Out, out! The four of us were dragged out, beaten, and pushed down the stairs to the gloomy dungeons below the arena. The soldiers shoved us into a stinking cell with a cold, earthen floor. They clapped even colder iron chains on our wrists and ankles before slamming the metal door shut and locking it.

We are still here hours later, half dead with thirst and scarcely able to breathe. *I shouldn't be here. I am an innocent man,* I think for the thousandth time. But it's no good; innocent or not, I am a prisoner here, condemned to die before the sun sets for Roman justice and for the amusement of the crowds.

I, Marcus Junius Corvus, am the son of a farmer not a gladiator or a swordsman! What chance have I in the gladiator games? Death is my sentence—death for treason against the emperor. And justice in Rome, in the fifth year of the reign of Tiberius Caesar, demands I die today.

Startled by the shouts of men nearby, I peer into the dark corridor. Our time is close. The knot in my stomach tightens. All morning the opening acts of the Games have played out above us. I have never been to Rome, but I know how the Games will unfold. On my last birthday, I was taken to see them in the amphitheatre in Neapolis by my father. A lesser spectacle certainly, but no less bloody than the Games in Rome.

It was not men, but beasts, that died first before the crowd this morning. We heard them from our cell, their unworldly growls and whines echoing through the dungeons. Caged animals, fearful for their lives, as we are. According to Lucius, they came from every corner of the Empire, shipped to Rome at great expense. One by one their cages were thrown open, the animals dragged out with hook and whip, then hoisted by elevators to the arena floor above. There, they became sport for hungry wolves or great cats, who would run them down and kill them. Then, it was the turn of the predators to be slain, fighting for their own lives against armed gladiators. It shames me that we Romans, a civilised nation, take lustful pleasure from the death of the gods' beautiful creatures. One by one they were slain, we heard their awful death cries, and heard their butchers hailed as heroes. Sport indeed.

It has gone quiet above us. I suppose food sellers will be hawking their wares, and children skipping up and down the staircases begging their parents for treats. The poor will sit in the cheap seats, high in the third tier, many with free tickets handed out by politicians. In the middle seats will sit the merchants and well-to-do citizens, paying good money for a better view than the rabble. In front are the marble-lined terraces where the rich and powerful sit: senators and patricians surrounded by their families, slaves and hangers-on, their names inscribed into the marble so that all will know who they are.

I look across the dark cell to Lucius. He is a young man like me, perhaps a few years older, slender built, with soft brown curls that fall to his shoulders.

'Where do you make your home, Lucius?'

'My family is from Ostia. We are traders in olive oil.'

'Is business good?'

'We have done very well these past years. My family has two acres of warehouses near the harbour. We export the finest oil – 20,000 amphora per year. All was going well until we crossed paths with Sejanus.'

'Sejanus? What happened?' Lucius too was a victim of this evil man.

'We refused to sell our business to one of his criminal friends. So, he forged a charge of treason against my family.'

'Treason! How could this be? Is it treason to refuse the advances of extortionists?'

'Treason it was. Something absurd about conspiring against the emperor's son.'

'Et tu Lucius! Why, that is the very charge laid against my father! One would think half the citizens in the Empire were in this imaginary plot! Why did they bring you here?'

'It was horrible. They came at night, three weeks back. They took my father away in his night-clothes, and returned him a day later, beaten senseless. A few days later they came to our house, saying I was to be torn apart in the Colosseum, and my wife sold in the slave market because of my father's lack of co-operation.'

'An outrage! Is there no recourse? Did your family have well-placed friends in Rome? Could they not appeal to the Senate?'

'The Senate, indeed. Half our noble senators are in the pay of Sejanus, the others live in terror of crossing him. Fearing for their lives and their properties, should they speak out.' Lucius utters a curse and spits.

Next to me, the Gaul comes to his feet and howls some unintelligible words towards the ceiling. Dressed in little more than animal skins, he is a frightening sight. He gestures with bare arms towards the three of us, trying to tell us something, but I can't understand him. He slips to the floor, speaking softly to himself.

Lucius looks at me. 'Marcus if you live, you must promise me you will give my wife and parents word of my fate. Tell them I died bravely.'

'I will Lucius. I will go to Ostia. What is your family name?'

'We are of the Sufinius clan. Look for our warehouses near the pier of Agrippa.'

'I swear to you, I'll go. And I beg you too, if you live, send to Abellinum to tell my father, Gaius Junius Corvus, how I died. And tell my mother and sister, that I never failed to think of them until the end.'

'I will, Marcus. You can count on me.' I feel better for a moment, sealing our pact. But I know neither of us have a chance of living beyond the next hour. Above us, we hear trumpets.

'Caesar has arrived,' Lucius says.

'Hail Caesar!' shout the criers.

The crowd answers in unison, 'Hail Caesar!' Twice more they call out, and the throng responds. I hear the clanging of metal gates opening nearby and jump up in fear.

'Our time is near, Marcus,' whispers Lucius. It is now men who are the hunted; time for us condemned prisoners to meet our fate. In groups or pairs, lesser criminals, forgers, and thieves are thrown in the arena to receive sentence. Defenceless and stupefied at the vast crowd, few have time to think before being run down by a hungry beast. The flash of teeth, and the spurting of blood, means another sentence has been carried out. A dozen times we hear the cries of the condemned, a dozen times we hear the crowd cheer.

'And we call ourselves civilised men!' curses Lucius. 'How did our people become such a brutal race? Taking sport from the cruel death of men.'

'And pleasure from the butchering of innocent beasts,' I reply. 'One would have thought that in our eight hundred years we Romans would have learnt to treasure life, and regard as precious the mortal men and beasts the gods have put on this earth.'

'Maybe in another thousand years, Marcus. Or two thousand—' It is abruptly quiet above. We look at the door anxiously. Have they come for us?

'Taking out the corpses,' says Lucius. This task takes too long. The crowd begins to clap their hands impatiently and sing bawdy songs, eager for the grand finale of the carnival of death. Now, it is man against man, released in pairs or small groups, to fight to the death in the cruellest game of all. Murderers, traitors, and rapists will carry out each other's sentences. If by muscle alone they fail to kill one another, short swords, or spiked clubs are thrown in, that the killing may be expedited. And when all prisoners but one are slain, the victor may win his freedom courtesy of the emperor's thumb if he pleased the crowd. If not, he will die with the others, dispatched by a gladiator.

Cages are flung open all around us. Men are taken away, some crying out in terror, others stupefied with fear. I cover my ears, but I cannot keep out the screams of the victims and the shouting of the crowd. Fear eats at my heart like a worm devouring my insides. Tugging on my chains one more time, I feel nothing but pain. Lucius and the others jump to their feet. A games official with a slate stops before our cell, and peers in.

'Fourteen! Bring them all to the east lift,' he tells a group of guards. Even the Gaul is silent and fearful. We press our backs to the wall, cold fear on our faces. The door is flung open and two guards enter to unchain us. First the Illyrian, then Lucius. In seconds they are hauled down the corridor without even a chance to say farewell. But the guards return in a minute for me and the Gaul. The size of him causes them to hesitate.

'Titus! Two more men,' shouts one of them to the games

keeper with the slate, who disappears. The guards wait, but no extra men arrive. Finally, he returns without any helpers.

'Get on with it. Take them to the east lift. Now!' he barks.

The two guards approach the Gaul cautiously. He lunges at them, but the chains hold him back, and they stay just out of reach of his big hairy arms. He lunges again, and a guard swings a heavy truncheon hard into the Gaul's chest to wind him. But he greatly underestimates the resistance of the giant. In an instant the Gaul has the guard in a headlock, choking him with his enormous arms. The guard's eyes look to spring from their sockets as he gasps for air. The other guard brings the butt of his sword hard down on the Gaul's head and he falls, senseless. Released, the injured guard falls to his knees, clutching at his throat. Two other guards arrive.

A heavy strap is put around the Gaul's neck and his chains are undone. Three guards drag him in a stupor down the dark corridor. The last guard approaches me, sword drawn.

'Well, Campanian, how's it going to be?' I hold my arms out meekly, and he unchains me. I am thrown out into the corridor. The guard pushes me first left, then right, then on towards the lift. We catch up to my companions as we pass through an open gate with heavy iron bars. Above us is a trapdoor, closed, but its outline visible as sunlight shines through narrow gaps. Before us is a large wooden platform, fixed with ropes on its corners. A pair of slaves man a set of ropes and pulleys nearby; they stare at us with cold, unfeeling eyes.

We are about to be hoisted up to the arena floor, where the final act of our lives will be played out. I tremble uncontrollably, hearing nothing. My vision grows cloudy as though seeing through a dark tunnel. This is it. It will be over soon. A games official holds us up for a minute, waiting for some unseen signal. Then, it's time. Ropes are pulled and the trap door falls open above us in a cloud of dust. Having been in the dark all day the sunlight in the opening blinds us. I am pushed onto the platform, flat on my back. Lucius and the Illyrian are thrown on top of me, pinning me down. I struggle to move, for they are crushing me and I can barely breath. I don't want to die on my back but I can't free myself.

The Gaul, recovering from his stupor, finally understands what is happening. Two of the guards struggle to pull him by the leather strap onto the platform. But he catches hold of the strap, wraps it around a guard's neck and pulls with all his might. We hear the crack of breaking bones and the guard falls, clearly dead.

'Titus, Paulus!' shouts his companion. One charges with his body in an effort to knock the giant onto the platform. The Gaul grabs one of the hanging ropes and tries to wrap it around the guard's neck, but his luck has run out. A sword flashes, the giant pulls back to avoid the thrust, but the rope in his hand is cut along with two of his fingers. The guard strikes again. The Gaul screams in pain and holds up his arm, staring at it in amazement as blood pours out in a crimson fountain. The guards charge him again as one, and he falls onto the platform. I am crushed under his weight, and I feel his warm blood on my leg.

'Pull up, now!' cries a guard. The slaves tug on the ropes

with a will. The platform lifts, and we lurch upwards. But the severed rope has caused the platform to become unbalanced, and when we are nearly up to the arena floor it tips, spilling all four of us back onto the ground. This time, I am on the top of the heap of humans, and this is my chance. The descending platform has knocked over one the guards who stood below. I push past him and run down the corridor.

I run through the maze of passageways, past the empty beast cages, past the cells of men, a few still containing prisoners. I cannot remember how to get out of here, for every way looks the same. I run without looking back, for I can already hear footsteps of someone pursuing. Right, and right and left again through the maze. My followers are almost upon me and I realise this corridor is a dead end. I turn to face my attacker, but it's Lucius, thank the gods!

'I thought you knew the way, Marcus,' he shouts at me, half laughing. He must have fled the same time as me and was wise enough to pry a short sword from the fallen guard's hand.

'Are they after us?'

'What do you think? Of course they are! This way.' We turn back and hear the shouting of guards calling out to each other as they search for us. By now, the handful of remaining prisoners have worked out that we are free. They begin hooting encouragement and banging on the bars of their cells. Above, the crowd has witnessed the accident at the lift, and they too are jeering, adding to the chaos.

After finding several locked gates we reach a large passageway. In one direction, we can see the broken lift, brightly lit. The opposite way is surely our only hope. I push Lucius ahead of me and run for my life. Sure enough, we reach the entrance to the dungeons at the western wall of the amphitheatre, where we first entered hours ago. But the exit is blocked by a heavy gate. Outside, stand a small group of officials and attendants, oblivious to the commotion.

The two gatekeepers, hearing the crowd's jeers within the arena, have climbed up the stairway leading to the stands to see what is going on. We rush past them and fling our weight against the gate, but it will not budge. It is locked and too tall to climb over. The gatekeepers hear the commotion and come running back down.

'What in Jupiter's name are you doing?' one shouts. In an instant, Lucius runs his sword through the man's shoulder, and he falls. The other, unarmed, backs away towards the gate with arms outstretched.

'Spare me! I have eight children.'

'Open the gate!' Lucius puts his sword to the man's throat. His hands trembling, he takes out a large metal key and opens the latch.

'Juno blesses you,' is all I can think to say while Lucius strikes him hard in the chest with the sword hilt, felling him. We dash out into the sunlight. *We are free.*

In the forecourt are empty prison wagons; their drivers resting on top and the oxen standing in dumb silence. We thread our way through them. I can't help looking back at the stupendous bulk of the Colosseum.

'Stop them!' I hear shouts behind us. Which way to go?

Getting lost in the crowds of the city is our only hope. I take off down the road leading away from the Colosseum. It is densely lined with shops and crowded with people making their way to and from the amphitheatre. *This* crowd will save me, not cheer for my death.

Not as swift as I, behind me Lucius has been caught up by a pair of guards. He turns to fight them with his sword, but he is no match for trained soldiers. I see the flash of steel and the spurt of blood as he falls. I close my eyes and clench my fists. Poor Lucius. *May the gods take you to heaven and look kindly upon you. I knew you but a short while, and you've laid down your life for me.* For he has given me precious seconds to get away. I sprint down the narrow streets of the market, turning one way then another. No one here knows my face. I slow down to avoid suspicion, and try to act normal, avoiding eye contact with anyone. I am not home free yet.

I reach the end of the street of shops, and suddenly come to a vast open square. I halt, stunned at the vision before me. A plaza of immense colonnaded buildings stretches into the distance, all built of glistening white stone. The great Forum of Rome. The most magnificent sight and the holiest place in the world. Perhaps I could find sanctuary in one of the Forum temples! I cautiously walk through a great bronze gate into what must be the Via Sacre, the sacred way, the main avenue of the Forum. There are few people about, for commoners have no business here.

I approach a compact circular temple, ringed by stone columns. On the pediment above the entrance are the words

"DIVA VESTA". The sacred temple of the Vestal Virgins. The priestesses will surely give me sanctuary. But as I try to enter, I am rudely pushed away by two men in black robes.

'How dare you! A filthy commoner, seeking to enter the temple of Vesta!' one says.

'But I was just …' I back down the steps and continue down the avenue. On the left is a huge colonnaded temple of white marble. Fire burns from two vast bronze cauldrons on pedestals outside it. It is the temple of Castor and Pollux. Its gates are closed and there is no one in the forecourt.

I regret entering the Forum, for in my dirty garments I stand out like a beggar at a banquet. I look back towards the gate at the Forum entrance. Four praetorian guards in their black leather armour are conferring with the gatekeeper, who must have absented himself temporarily from his post when I passed. He points in my direction. The guards look up and run towards me.

I bound up the steps of the temple to the Divine Twins and pull open the golden doors. A row of marble columns stretches down each side, so tall their tops can scarcely be seen. In the middle of the temple, the golden walls of a large shrine hide the inner sanctuary. What stunning grandeur. If I could find the high priest, I could ask for his protection. *The gods will protect the innocent,* did not my mother say when I was torn from her? And the sacred twins are the patron gods of horsemen. Surely Castor and Pollux will save me.

I edge slowly past the golden walls of the sanctuary, my head bowed low, in awe of where I am. Emblems of the sun and the gods are etched in the gilded walls of the shrine. A gap reveals the sanctuary at the very centre of the temple. There are two colossal statues of Castor and Pollux seated, looking forward with sightless eyes. About them, priests are making offerings, smoke from their sacrificial fires and incense obscures the light from a few torches. The bronze statues glisten and seem alive as the light flickers on them. All about is the smell of burning animal flesh and the sweet scent of incense. I dare not interrupt the ceremony. I kneel facing the great images and pray in a whisper.

'Sanctuary. Save me, Divine Castor. Divine Pollux,' I whisper over and over. I look up, but the ceremony continues. I rise slowly, and steal away, accidentally backing into a small table. On it are various implements of the priesthood and a small silver shrine. The doors of the shrine have come ajar. Inside, on its shelves rest several painted wooden idols. One of them I recognise—Juno, the protector. I pick it up. Juno will surely keep me safe.

'You there, wretch! Leave this sanctuary!' a priest calls out. He moves towards me, but I can't see his hooded face. I palm the idol and hope he hasn't seen it. I drop to my knees.

'I am sorry, Master. Forgiveness!'

'Who are you? How dare you interrupt divine sacrifice.' Fear takes over, and I can say nothing. I turn and flee the temple, springing down the broad steps. Thankfully, I am not followed.

Next to the temple, I notice a shallow pool, walled in stone. A trickle of water falls into it from an ancient pipe. I pause to drink, scooping the water with my hands. This must be the Fountain of Juturna where the twins themselves watered their horses in ancient times, when the gods still walked the earth. Good luck for a horseman like me. I drink my fill. As I stand, I feel a sudden gust of wind. The sky darkens instantly as a cloud crosses the face of the sun. It makes me uneasy. I must move on.

I pass carefully between the great temples, avoiding the avenue where surely soldiers are searching for me. I come to the greatest temple of all, that of Jupiter Optimus Maximus, king of all the gods. I creep up the steps. Either Jupiter will strike me dead or save me, it must be one fate or the other.

I thread my way through the mighty columns of stone, into the heart of the sanctum. My heart pounds in fear, for I should not be in such a holy place. Grand frescoes adorn the walls: paintings of Jupiter, his divine wives and children. A fire burns in a colossal, raised, gilded cauldron. I kneel before it. *Divine Jupiter, King of gods, ruler of the heavens and earth, save me.*

A powerful wind blows through the temple and extinguishes the sacred fire. What have I done? Jupiter is angry with me! I drop to the floor and press my face against the stone. The fire flares up and lights again. I realise I am still holding the statue of Juno and pray to the great trio of gods. Jupiter, lord of all the gods. Juno, goddess of mercy. Minerva, goddess of wisdom. Give me strength, and courage. Preserve me! Another icy blast blows through the temple. I get up and shuffle my way backwards out of the temple, my head bowed low.

Outside, a storm is forming. Lightning flashes and thunder

rumbles. Have I offended the gods? I turn and spy a group of soldiers in the distance, spreading out to search the Forum. I feel an icy numbness. I am surely finished. Won't the gods help me! A soldier spots me and shouts to his companions. He runs towards me, sword drawn.

I run down the narrow passage beside Jupiter's Temple. A great crash of thunder almost knocks me off my feet. I find myself in a clump of cypress trees, before a short gilded column. It appears to be covered with a map of some sort. The Milliarius Aureum, the golden milestone- I learnt of this as a child. This marker is the very centre of Rome; the point from which all distances in the empire are measured.

Standing before it, I clutch the idol of Juno. *Jupiter, Juno, Minerva, hear my prayers!* Another blast of wind blows the cypress trees about, showering me with leaves. Streaks of lightning fill the sky. *Gods of Rome, take me away from here!* The deafening onslaught of thunder shakes the very ground on which I stand. A cold rain lashes my face as I look to the heavens. *Take me to the other end of the world. Take me away from this barbaric time, take me a thousand thousand years from now!* I fall to my knees but slip on the wet marble. A flash of blinding light envelopes me.

CHAPTER II

I t is dark when I come to my senses. My entire body is paralysed, my head pulsating with unbearable pain. I drift in and out of consciousness, barely able to think. I am face down on the ground. With difficulty I roll my head to one side and lift my eyelids. It is night, and pleasantly cool. I drag myself up. I am alive. *I am alive.* I can see I am far from the city, for there are no lights anywhere. I rub my aching head and bruised limbs. Where am I? How did I get here?

I try to remember the last minutes before I blacked out. Imprisoned in the dungeons of the Colosseum, *that* I remember too well. The fight at the lift, the flight with soldiers at my heels through the tunnels and the Forum. The immense temples, white marble glistening against the blue Italian sky. The temples of Gemini, and Jupiter. The soldiers coming towards me with swords drawn. So, my escape is real. But how did I get here in this wilderness?

The soldiers must have taken me. They must have caught

me in the Forum, delivered me a good beating and left me for dead here in a dusty plain outside of Rome. Well, I am alive, and the gods be thanked for it! I am still grasping the little statue of Juno. In the moonlight I kneel, hold it out before me, and thank her. I thank the Divine Twins for the blessed waters at the Juturna fountain, and I thank Jupiter, king of the gods and the whole world, for delivering me. The gods decided I would not die in the arena today. They have spared me for something, for what, I do not know.

I get to my feet and try to walk, but stumble over the rocky ground in the darkness. My head pounds again, as though to burst open. Better to rest until sunrise. No point wandering into a soldier's encampment and getting caught. I lie down on my aching back, fold my arms over my face, and close my eyes.

I awaken to the faint glow of dawn. It is so cold. How can it be this cold in October? The birds are already awake. I hear their raucous screeching in the distance, sounding almost like eagles, yet not like any bird I know. As the day brightens, I take in the landscape. The land here is exceedingly dry. The soil, a curious red colour. Not cultivated but wild land. Low, dull-green shrubs sparsely cover the landscape. Here and there, gnarled, white-trunked trees with tattered bark and blue-green leaves stand tall and alone. There must be some signs of how I got here, yet I see footprints of neither men nor horses, nor any wagon tracks. I must have wandered off the road and collapsed here sometime in the night, but I remember nothing.

Louder now the birds shriek; the flock approaches and roosts in the nearby trees. One perches on a branch above my head, folds its large wings and peers down at me. It is as large as an eagle, pure white, with a golden crest on its head. It inspects me carefully first with one eye, then the other, before flying off to the west, calling loudly. The others fly after it, screeching too, and they are answered by more distant calls of their species.

I know little of religion, but I know that priests in the temples take great heed of the flights and habits of birds, for they alone among earth's creatures, visit the heavens above, and take their direction from the gods themselves. These golden crested birds with white plumage remind me of the veiled priestesses, the Vestal virgins, attending the temple of Vesta in the Forum. They must be telling me something. To the west they flew and to the west I shall go. I tighten my sandals. Besides the image of Juno in my pocket, I have nothing save the handful of coins my mother gave me when I was taken from my home. They are snug in the inside pocket of my tunic. Little enough, but I will find my way back home, gods willing.

I walk westwards with the sun already warming my back. I set my bearings on a line of low hills in the distance some miles away. Perhaps there is a stream or waterhole at the foot of them, or if I am in luck I'll come to a farmhouse. It is going to be hot later, and these stunted trees provide little shade, so I quicken my pace.

An hour passes, then two. I rest in the meagre shade of one of the ghostly trees. I pick a handful of its leaves and chew on them for moisture, but they taste oily so I spit them out. Nevertheless, they have a pleasant, cooling fragrance. I breathe in the oil deeply and find it soothing. The tree trunk is oozing a dark golden gum. But there is nothing to eat here. Thirst soon overtakes all my thoughts. My throat is raw, my breathing laboured. There must be water here somewhere. I lean against the tree to rest, for it is foolish to walk any further in the midday sun.

I awaken hours later, my throat aching for water. There are ants all over my legs. I flick them off, but one bites me hard. I crush it in my fingertips, but the sting smarts for several minutes. The sun is not so high now, yet I am confused—the sun is in the north. How is this possible? I scan the horizon. The line of hills is still there, larger now than when I set out, and the tallest peak is plainly visible. It is as though the world is upside down. No, I could have mistaken east for west when I saw the birds this morning. That's it, I must have been confused with my head half in a dream.

I must find water. I set off again to the west, the sun is now in my face, but not so strong. In the late afternoon I finally reach the rocky hills, almost dead from thirst. There are a few green trees here, but on close inspection they are just scrawny acacias. I climb a little up the nearest slope and see nothing but rocky ridges and scrub. Higher up I am finally able to survey the country. Away to the north and south, the land is flat and barren. Back the way I came from, there is nothing but flat dry plains to the horizon. Will I die of thirst here, in the middle of nowhere? My family will never know my fate. The jackals will come and devour me. My bones will lie here bleaching in the sun.

My head grows dizzy, I fear I am going mad with thirst. I sit on the bare rock, close my eyes, and see a bearded man with a lightning bolt in his hand. I call to him.

'Jupiter! What is my destiny? Why did you save me from the arena only to die of thirst?' Jupiter smiles as if to say something. Then the vision vanishes. *I am losing my mind.*

I climb further in the darkening twilight. With my last strength I reach the top of the ridge. I look down into the gulch below, and in the dying light I see green plants! There is water here. I slide down on my backside, too tired to care about my legs as they are scratched and scraped. At the bottom, there is a patch of reedy grass, and the sandy ground is damp. I pull out the reeds and dig with my hands. Nothing. I dig further into the sand, and a tiny trickle of water seeps into the pit I've made. I dip the reeds into the water and lick a few precious drops from them.

There must be more water here. I scramble out of the gulch and search further on among the rocky ridges. At last, in a deep depression in the rock is a much larger bed of reeds, and on its edge, a small pool, scarcely a few inches deep, but it is fresh water. I drink my fill and roll onto my back. I will live for another day or two. I feel a little life returning. I need to rest for the night. To press on in this uneven terrain is to invite a crippling fall. A few bunches of reeds make a pillow. Tonight, I sleep a free man in my own bed, even if it be a bed of stone in a red desert miles from home. Mother, Father, Sister, I am alive! If only I could reach out and tell you.

How will I ever get back home? If I could get to Ostia, the

port of Rome, I could take a ship for the south. If I keep my head low, no one will recognise me there. With the stars and the gods as my witnesses, I vow to make my way home, no matter what it takes.

I look up at the stars, seeking the familiar constellations. It is late October, when the Bull is high in the sky, and the Hunter rises shortly after sunset. Yet the stars do not look right. Is it the wound in my head? I see the Hunter rising in the east as he should, but he is upside down, the three stars of his belt pointing straight up. And the Bull, and the star of the North are nowhere to be seen. Directly overhead, the great milky river gradually becomes visible, but the shapes of the stars are unfamiliar. While trying to understand this puzzle, sleep overcomes me.

I awake before dawn, the eastern sky just beginning to glow. I feel the pangs of hunger, for it is two days since my last meal. And it was a foul one at that, in the dungeons of the capital.

I get up and explore my little gully. I have no weapons and my chances of catching game are slim. Opposite the pool of reeds, stands a trio of palm trees, their crown of weeping fan leaves pretty against the red rock and blue sky. I pick up a dead palm frond. The blade is covered in spines, and I drop it quickly, having drawn blood. Even flora attacks me. I pick up another frond more carefully and strip off the dry leaflets. I scrape the blade with a sharp stone. It is thick and woody, and I carve it to a point. A poor spear, if ever there was one. Could I even catch a rat? Perhaps a blind one.

My belly growls with hunger. At the pool, I pull out one of the water plants by the roots. I wash off the mud; the base is thick like an onion. I take a few sniffs. No, I'll not eat this. I look out beyond the hills, at the dry parched earth. Nothing but rock, dry grass and the gum bearing trees as far as I can see. I close my eyes and bite into the root. It is starchy and foul tasting. But edible. I choke down a few more mouthfuls and throw the rest away.

I decide to keep heading westward, over the rocky hills, as there is nothing but wilderness the way I came. I walk up and over the gently sloping rocky ridges, heading towards the high point I had seen yesterday. As I get closer, its appearance is striking: a slender pinnacle of crenellated stone, like the tower of a fortress. I reach it in an hour and stop for a rest at its foot. I climb part way up, but the rock is crumbly and dangerous. The sun begins to burn the land, and the air plays tricks. Wavy lines of turbid air mean I can barely see a mile or two. I slide back down and decide it's time to sleep away the noon day heat.

I wake with a start. I hear voices. Or am I dreaming? My heart starts to pound. I listen, frozen with fear. Again, I hear voices and a man laughs, closer this time. Hunters? Soldiers? I look around for a weapon, but I threw down my little spear long ago. Again, I hear them, much closer this time, coming straight towards me. It sounds like there are two men, speaking in a tongue I do not recognise. They appear over a little rise before I can think what to do, and I jump up in fright.

They see me too and stop. They are tall, finely built young men clothed in strange garments: long blue leggings, leather boots, and bare chests. On their heads are broad straw hats. Their skin is black as coal. One of them calls out to me.

'Mate, are you lost?' They look at each other and grin. 'Tourist, long way off the track, eh.' I don't understand their words. My father had taught me common phrases in many languages but not this one. I raise my right hand in the Roman greeting and tell them I am a friend.

'Salve! Amicus!' They are carrying packs on their backs. Each bears a curious iron club with a wooden handle over his shoulder. I greet them again, asking if they live nearby. 'Salve! Prope habitas?'

'Salve to you too, mate, whatever that means. Are you lost?' the taller one asks. I shrug my shoulders.

'Non comprendus,' I say slowly.

'I think he's sayin' he don't understand. Sounds a bit like Spanish talk to me. He looks harmless. Dem clothes is kinda funny though.'

'Well, you know them backpacker types and their hippie clothes,' says the other. They look at my sandals. 'Yah, hippie shoes too.' They notice my scratches and scrapes.

'You fall off a cliff, buddy?' says the shorter man. I rub my wounds gently, still not sure what they are saying. The taller one sighs.

'We can't leave him here. I mean, look at him.'

'Let's take him back to the road at least. He can hitch from there.'

'Yeah, don't wanna lose a whole day's hunting coza him,' says the other.

The taller man approaches me and asks slowly and deliberately, 'What's-your-name?'

The other repeats, 'Name. Name?' They must be asking for my nomen. I touch my chest.

'Marcus.'

They nod and grin together. 'G'day Marcus! I'm Bardo, this is Mick.'

'Salve, Mick,' I bow slightly to the shorter man. Bardo takes my hand and shakes it warmly. Mick follows suit. They are friendly. They are not going to kill me.

'You thirsty, mate?' says Bardo. He motions with his arm, as though drinking.

'Thirsty mate.' I repeat, making the same motion. Bardo pulls out a metal drinking vessel from his pack, twists off the top, and hands it to me. It has cool, sweet water, and I drink and drink. He grimaces; I realise I may have taken too much. I hand the vessel back to him. He turns it over and the last few drops trickle out.

'Gratias,' I say, 'gratias!'

'I think he's saying thanks,' says Mick.

'No worries, mate,' says Bardo, and slaps me on the back.

'No worries mate,' I repeat with a little hesitation. They laugh.

'He's probably hungry too,' Bardo says.

'Well, don't give him too much tucker, we won't be back at camp 'til tomorrow.'

'Hey, you hungry?' asks Mick, and hands me a small pouch made of strange crinkly material. I don't know what to do with it; he takes it back and tears the top off. Inside are triangular chips of baked corn, covered with salt and pounded cheese. They are excellent, and I devour several handfuls.

'Good tucker, eh?' Mick asks. I have forgotten my manners.

'Good tucker. Delectamenti!' I reply then hand the bag around to my new friends. We soon finish it off.

'Come on, let's get a move on.' The two men start off the way they came and beckon me to follow.

'This way, buddy. We'll take you to the road. You can hitch into town.'

I follow. Whoever these magnanimous men are, they are kind to strangers and I admire them for that. I close my eyes for a moment and whisper thanks to the heavens. Mick and Bardo walk swiftly westward, and we soon leave the hills and return to the scrub below. They talk among themselves, with me not understanding a word. Occasionally I hear the word 'hippie', usually followed by laughter. Perhaps they think I am from the land of Hippie, wherever that is.

As we leave the hills a walking track becomes apparent. We continue along this, and after half an hour or so come to what is clearly a road, raised a little above the surrounding plain. It is covered with loose gravel instead of paving stones, as good Roman roads are. There are wide grooves in the roadway, but they don't look like cart tracks.

'Marcus, you can hitch into Quilpie from here,' says Bardo. I don't know what this means, but it is clear they intend to leave me here.

'Stay put, road train come 'long soon. You hitch into town,' says Mick. Seeing the puzzled look on my face, they point down the road. 'Quilpie. Quilpie, that way.'

'Don't go ta other way, it's a thousand K's to anywhere!' They motion me to stay put. 'Wait here. Hitch into Quilpie.'

I repeat their words, 'Hitch into Quilpie.'

'He's got it now. Good luck, mate,' they call out. Bardo and Mick head back towards the hills. I wave, and soon they are out of sight. At least I have found a road. Where there's a road, there'll be a village every few miles, for all of Italy is the same. But am I in Italy? I must be in Calabria, the hot south, for I have never seen such a dry place before. Yet this time of year the winter rains should have turned even the Calabrian countryside green. The language the men spoke – it was unlike any from the Latin provinces of the empire, even the Greek lands, and I have heard many tongues in the markets at Neapolis.

Perhaps I am in Egypt? Yet how did I remain unconscious for so long? I had heard of soldiers falling in battle and being knocked into a sleep-like stupor for days or even weeks before reviving. Maybe I took such a head wound in the Forum?

The day advances, and I regret being out here with no shade. The road is arrow-straight, running to the horizon in both directions. I am getting hungry again, the baked corn was scarcely a meal. I sit on a stone in the ditch beside the road, the sun burning the back of my neck. Though I fight it, I begin to doze off.

I am awakened by a deep tremor that I can feel in the earth itself. I step up onto the road. In the distance a cloud of dust appears. It grows larger and larger. It must be a whole cohort of cavalry, by the speed of their approach and the vast size of the dust cloud.

It gets closer and louder. To avoid being trampled, I leap onto the embankment. The noise is deafening now, but it is no cohort of cavalry. It roars like a vast waterfall, but louder and deeper. Out of the dust cloud appears a great machine. It is a huge, wheeled carriage made of iron and glass, as high as a house and running on enormous black wheels. It is pulling three long trailers, yet I see no horses. What is making this monster move with such swiftness?

As it approaches, I glimpse a man through its front window. He holds up his arm in greeting as the machine approaches. On the front of the machine a timber board reads "Road Train". I wave too as it passes at speed. The great cloud of dust sweeps over me, blinding and choking. I pull my shirt over my face.

Down the road, the great machine slows down, its many wheels whining and screeching. The noise dies down to a steady rumble. As the dust settles, I can see it has stopped a quarter mile down the road. Smoke pours from an iron chimney on its roof. It must be driven by fire! Four lanterns on the rear wagon flash on and off. From a side window, the man beckons me to approach.

I walk towards it, torn between dread and curiosity. On the covered trailers are written in Roman letters: "Western Queensland Trucking Co" and "Mt Isa – Roma – Townsville". I am relieved to find I am still in Roman territory. If they are using Latin letters in this country, surely my people rule here. "Roma", it reads. Could this man in the thunder-wagon take me back to the city?

As I reach the front of the machine, the driver opens a door and leaps down to the dusty road. He is heavy set, his skin fair, his face and right arm burned by the sun. He wears a vest dyed a brilliant orange, and short pants. 'Where you headed pal?' he asks as he beckons down the road.

'Roma?' I say questioningly.

'Roma, eh? No, not going that far. I can take you to Quilpie, then I'm heading over to Mount Isa.' Quilpie, I remember the young black men telling me several times.

'Quilpie, Quilpie,' I repeat.

'Too right! Hop in,' he says, and climbs back up. He seems friendly enough. What choice do I have but to trust him? I will surely die of thirst or starvation alone out here. I approach the door where he got in. He waves me around.

'Other side, mate.' He pushes open the door. I climb up and sit in the big leather seat. A great wheel is mounted in front of him, and there are many levers and switches. 'Door,' he says, and points to the door. *Ah, the porta,* I think as I pull it shut. The man pulls a harness over his body and fixes it to a buckle. He beckons me to do the same.

'Better belt up, buddy.' I do as he asks. I introduce myself. 'Marcus.'

'How ya going, Marcus. I'm Jono,' he says. He holds out his hand.

'Salve, Jono,' I say, and he grins. He pulls at the levers in front of him. The great machine roars to life, and we lurch forward. I watch as he pushes the pedals with his feet and turns the wheel with his hands to control the wagon. I grip the seat with both hands. We are picking up speed. How *does* this machine move? There are no horses or slaves to pull it. It is as though this man has tamed fire itself to drive this beast. It rumbles and rattles, louder and faster. To the side, the rocks and trees move so swiftly they start to blur. I feel dizzy and close my eyes. I have ridden chariots pulled by fast well-bred horses, yet they were not as swift as this machine. Jono glances at me from time to time. 'Ever been in a big rig before, Marcus?' he asks. I open my eyes and shrug, not knowing what he is asking. Ahead, the road rushes towards us, but I find looking forward lessens my dizziness.

He tries again to converse. 'So, where you headed? Here on holiday? You coming back from Birdsville?' he asks.

'Non comprendus,' I tell him.

He looks at my shoes. 'Backpacker eh. Where you from? German? Swedish? Italian?'

'Italia,' I blurt out, pleased that he knows my home country.

'Italian eh. Rome? Milan?'

'No, Campania. Abellinum,' I reply.

'Ah. Haven't heard of that one, Abell—something. Me daughter married an Italian. Wish I could speak the lingo.' He falls silent.

Jono sighs heavily from time to time and concentrates his gaze on the road ahead. His brawny arms are covered with tattoos of unicorns and other beasts. I feel obliged to break the long silence. I ask him what I need to know above all else: where are we?

'Ubi sumus?'

He laughs. 'No capish. Can't speak a word of Italian.' Evidently, he doesn't understand Latin. Curious, as the words on the sides of these wagons are in Latin letters. We both fall silent.

After a time, he asks, 'Ya thirsty, mate?' I know this question from the men I met this morning.

'Thirsty mate,' I reply.

'Great, I'll get us a couple of stubbies.' From behind my seat, he pulls out a bottle from a small blue chest and hands it to me. Surprisingly, it is quite cold. He takes one for himself, pulls the top off, and takes a long drink.

He notices my difficulty removing the metal cap. 'Twist it,' he says, motioning with his hand. I manage to get the cap off. 'Cheers,' Jono says and clinks his bottle to mine.

'Cheers!' I repeat and take a drink. It is fine, smooth ale, as good as I have ever tasted. I moan in delight.

'Beauty, eh? Nothing like it on a scorcher. Not supposed to drink on the road, the boss'd kill me if he knew. But hey, how many coppers you see out here? I only have one stubbie in the arvo, to keep under the limit.' I nod knowingly. I examine the bottle, it reads "XXXX Gold". I tilt it back again.

'Beauty,' I repeat.

Some miles later my anxiety has been dulled by the drink. In the distance I spot another cloud of dust. Another of these great machines must be approaching. As the gap closes, panic sets in. How will these two giants pass on this narrow road?

Jono scarcely slows the machine, but pulls over to the left. My terrified gaze shifts between the oncoming machine and Jono. I grip my knees. The other moves across to its left also. Jono waves his hand out the window at the other driver, who salutes in return. The other machine passes within a few inches and disappears behind us. It takes considerable time to emerge from the dust cloud.

I drain the rest of the bottle; Jono takes it and throws it into a basket behind his seat. Gods, let this journey be over! On we travel, at double the speed of the swiftest horse. Outside, the landscape passes unchanging for mile after mile, just low, dull-green shrubs, rock and red sand in all directions. I feel lightheaded and doze a little.

I awake abruptly when Jono jerks back with his feet. His hands work the levers, the machine roars and spews smoke, then it slows. The gravel road changes to a kind of smooth, black concrete. We pass a sign; in large letters it announces, "Quilpie POP 562". We have arrived in a town.

Small, neat houses appear at intervals along the road, fashioned of timber with iron roofs. Jono pulls the machine to the side of the road.

'Here's Quilpie, Marcus. I recommend the pub for counter meals—great tucker there. Say hello to Lucy for me. Best of luck, mate,' he says and shakes my hand. It is evident he wants me to get out here.

'Gratias, Jono. Gratias,' I tell him, and climb down. The great beast moves on, leaving me in peace. I make my way into the village. I know where I am at last; a little town called Quilpie. This is little help however, as I've not heard of it, nor do I know what province this is. I hear a noise behind me. Another of the great machines? I turn, but it is much smaller, the size of an ox cart, built of painted metal with wheels of black tar. Yet another comes from the village, this one painted black, with an iron tray filled with bales of hay. Horseless wagons. What incredible magic! Or is it? Perhaps they are powered by fire, for I can smell fumes. Yet scarcely any smoke emerges from them. The people of this land are either fantastic magicians or gifted with great genius to create such things. Others drive by, and soon I become used to them. Oddly, they pass each other on the left.

I walk on, and the houses become more numerous. Most are raised on timber piles, like seaside houses in Italy. Many have wide verandas and are decorated with pretty iron lattice work. A few have seen better days, the paint is fading, the roof rusting. Several have a horseless cart parked in front. Behind the houses are expanses of dry fields.

A horse grazes peacefully in a paddock beside a well-kept house painted a pale yellow. I approach the fence, whistle, and he trots over slowly. He is a dark chestnut colour, a sleek and athletic stallion. I stroke his nose, he nods and snorts happily, but alas I have no treats for him.

A woman calls out, 'Morning.' I turn to greet her. 'G'day,' she says as she approaches, looking me up and down.

'G'day mate,' I reply. I suppose 'mate' to mean 'friend'. She is a handsome woman of about forty years, slender with long brown hair tied behind. She wears the same blue leggings and leather boots as the men I saw in the morning, along with a colourful red and white shirt.

'Do you ride?' she asks. I cock my head, not understanding. 'You ride? Horses?' She points at the animal. Ah, horse must mean equus. I love horses, and I tell her so.

'Amo equorum.' I stroke the stallion's nose. 'Pulchram,' I say, as he is beautiful.

'Okay. His name is Futura,' she says.

'Futura?' The woman nods.

'Yes.' She strokes the horse's shoulder lovingly. I admire a country woman. They are not like those of the city, who know nothing of horses and are frightened even by the bleat of a sheep.

'Are you in town for the races? Here in Quilpie.' Confused, I don't answer. 'Tourist, eh? We don't get many backpackers out this way.' She opens her handbag and pulls out a sheath of small papers, handing me one. 'This has all the details. It's a lot of fun. People come from all over the state.' I nod. She holds out her hand. 'I'm Shirley, by the way.'

'Marcus.'

She takes my hand and gives it a pump, as is their custom. 'Pleased to make your acquaintance, Marcus. Might see you down at the track.' She turns towards her house.

I head for the road, glancing back to call out, 'Gratias, Shirley.'

She waves, then shouts, 'Car. Car!' while pointing wildly to the road behind me. I am nearly struck by one of the horseless carts that I hadn't seen approach. It swerves to avoid me, and the driver yells something which I am sure is uncomplimentary.

'That car nearly got you. Better keep an eye open. We drive on the left here,' Shirley says. So, these horseless carriages are *cars*.

I continue into the village. I examine the paper Shirley gave me. Beneath a drawing of galloping horses, it reads "Quilpie

Country Races, 19–20 October". There must be racing in town today. A map shows how to reach the circuit. I fold it and stuff it in my pocket.

It is past noon. I am famished, parched, and grimy. There must be some sort of eatery or tavern here. I continue towards the town centre. Cars pass from time to time, their passengers taking no notice of me. I come to a two-storey timber building with elegant iron lattice work. There are many cars parked in front. Atop, a big yellow sign reads "Imperial Hotel XXXX". On wide verandas along the front and sides of the building a handful of people are seated at tables, eating and drinking. I remember "XXXX" from the bottle of ale the driver gave me. I have found a tavern.

I take out a few coins from my pocket. I can only guess the price of a meal here, but it could not be more than a few sestertii. I take a deep breath to gather my courage. Please, let the strangers here be as friendly as those I've met so far! Adjacent to the tavern is a large water tank. I wash the dust, dirt and dried blood from my face, arms, and legs, to at least try to make myself look like a respectable Roman, not a beggar.

I cautiously head up the steps and go inside. It smells a little of stale beer, but the aroma of cooking fires my hunger. There are a few men drinking ales at the bar, but the tables are mostly empty. A young woman with raven hair is working behind the bar.

'G'day stranger,' she calls out.

'G'day,' I nod back.

'We're serving for lunch 'til two,' she says. I approach the bar. 'What can I get you?' she asks. Seeing me hesitate, she points to a signboard covered with chalk writing. 'Lunch menu on the board, sir.' It is decorated with drawings of fowls, cattle, corn, and wheat. I tell her I want the first item in the list and point at it.

'Hoc unum,' I say.

'That one?' she points, and I nod. 'Number one it is,' she says. 'That comes with chips or salad.' She meets my blank stare. 'Chips or salad, darl? Chips?'

'Chips?' I repeat.

She turns around and shouts through a little window to the kitchen, 'Number one, Billy, with chips.' Then she turns back to me. 'Anything to drink?' I give her a blank look. 'Drink?' she says, and motions with her hand. I point to a glass of ale the man at the bar is drinking. 'Pint of four X?' she asks. I nod in agreement. She hands over the glass, and I reach to hand her some coins.

'No, pay when you're ready to shoot through.' She points to one of the tables. 'Have a seat.'

I blow a deep breath. At least taverns in this province hold no surprises. I will not starve here, as long as my money holds out. I relax a little, sipping my drink. The tavern doesn't differ too greatly from those at home; the bar is solidly built of ancient timber, richly coloured from age and years of polishing. Oddly, they don't store their spirits in amphora, but in iron drums that I see stacked near the rear door.

The serving girl rushes about her work, taking orders, cleaning glasses, serving drinks. People come and go, mostly men, some old with grizzled beards, others barely boys. Nearly all wear broad-brimmed hats of felt or straw. I wish I had one. I learn the raven-haired bar girl's name is Lucilla, but many patrons call her Lucy.

I overhear two men at a table nearby mention 'races' several times. I pull out the paper the woman gave me. *Quilpie Races.* I will certainly attend. The races are an important festival in a small village like this, as significant to the locals as the Games are in the city. I have little doubt everyone will be there. Perhaps I could meet some of my countrymen. Or people who trade horses. People who may know my father or the way back to Rome.

My meal arrives with a smile, complete with a knife and a miniature trident, rolled in a paper napkin. The dish is sort of pastry, hot and smelling heavenly of cooked meat. I tear it open with my hands, but it is steaming hot and I scald my fingers. Observing the manners of others, I pick up the knife and little trident, and begin eating with them. Within the pastry is chicken and various vegetables in a beautiful gravy. A fine meal! Served with it is a sort of tuber, shredded and cooked in hot oil. This must be the 'chips' Lucy spoke of. It doesn't take me long to finish it off. I push back my chair and empty my glass. For the first time in weeks, I have a full belly.

I wonder how I will pay the tariff. The menu board isn't of much assistance. "Chicken Pie Chips/Salad $10.40". What does this mean? The man at the adjoining table finishes his meal and approaches the bar where there is a small money box, curiously adorned with tiny lights. Lucy accepts his money and thanks him. Following his lead, I retrieve some coins from my pocket and go up to the counter.

'How was it?' asks Lucy.

'Good tucker!' I tell her, which pleases her. She glances at my table and turns her attention to the money box. It has a little panel, with small buttons on it. She pushes several of them with her fingertips, and the little machine clicks and beeps.

'Fourteen forty, love.' Being ignorant of how much this is, I hand her a silver denarius. Surely, it's enough, being a day's wage for Roman workman.

She takes it and studies it for a moment before putting it back in my hand. 'You're going to need more than that, sir. Fourteen forty,' she repeats. Seeing my lack of comprehension, she pulls out a paper and writes "14.40" on it. I don't know what these characters mean. Why can't she write it in normal Roman numerals? Perhaps I have underestimated the price. I pull out another denarius and hand it to her. Surely *this* is enough.

She is about to say something, then looks over the coins carefully. 'You tourists! No, mate, you gotta' use Aussie dollars here.' She leans over the counter and says firmly, 'Australian dollars.' She then reaches into the money box and pulls out some small paper notes with figures and images on them. 'Aussie money, you understand? You can change money at the bank. You go to the bank, change money,' she says slowly. She rolls her eyes, and mutters again, 'Tourists …' She comes around the counter, takes my arm and leads me out onto the veranda.

She points up the road. 'Bank. Two blocks over.' She reaches into her pocket, writes a note and hands it to me. "Westpac Bank. Change money to A$", it reads. She beckons again. 'Go to bank, then come back here, and pay your bill proper. I trust ya.' She mutters to herself, 'don't have much choice,' as she returns inside.

Embarrassed and confused, I head down the steps and walk in the direction she indicated. I would need to find this "bank".

It is busier here in the centre of town. People young and old pass, going about their business, all curiously dressed. Many give me a funny look, some smile and say the inevitable 'G'day.'

I give them a cheerful 'G'day' back. On this side of the street is a block of brick buildings, occupied by merchants. One is signed "Australia Post", another, "Quilpie Florist". The last, by name and scent, obviously a flower merchant.

Across the street, standing prominently on the corner, is a substantial building of sandstone. Four stone columns flank the front entrance, which hint of Roman architecture. My people could be here!

Above the columns, engraved in stone, "Bank of New South Wales – Anno Domini MCMXXXII". I have found the bank the waitress spoke of. And the inscription? The Year of Our Lord 1932. What does that mean? Surely no Lord could rule for nineteen hundred years! But there it is, inscribed in stone. Rome itself was founded 800 years ago, what gods or lords ruled a thousand years before that? The Egyptian gods? They were ancient when Rome was still a swamp.

A sign on the wall of the building reads "Westpac Banking Corp" in red and white letters. This is where Lucy said I should go. A grand building such as this, occupied by money changers—I should not be surprised. A profitable business. Just before I reach the darkened glass door, it parts and slides open all by itself. I peer inside to see who might have pulled the glass panels aside but see no one. The doors again close, nearly catching me in their grip. I move back a little and again they open, as though unseen hands are working some magic. I venture inside. It is surprisingly cool and lit by cleverly shielded lanterns embedded in the ceiling. Men and women, dressed in white and tan uniforms, sit at desks. Others are rushing about. Many sit at little machines with buttons which they are furiously stroking with their fingers.

A young man approaches. 'May I help you, sir?' he asks.

I greet him with a 'G'day,' as I have learnt to say.

'Would you like to make a deposit or withdrawal? Or talk to someone about a loan?'

'Change money,' I tell him, handing him the server girl's note.

'Change money? Certainly sir. Please follow me.' I follow him to his desk, and he beckons me to sit before it. 'What currency have you got? USD? Euro? Sterling?' Thinking it wise to obtain enough money to last for a time, I pull out an aureus and hand the small gold coin to him. 'Oh!' he says, 'You want precious metals. I'm sorry, but we don't normally change gold here, you'll have to go into Brisbane for that.'

'Change money,' I repeat. I lay all the money I have on the

desk: five gold, ten silver and a few copper coins. 'Change money,' I tell him, waving my hands over the coins.

He shakes his head. 'Wait here a minute.' He motions me to remain seated as he goes to talk to one of his co-workers. 'Julie, could I see you for a minute?' he asks a young woman softly.

'Yes, Dave?'

'This customer would like to change gold. I told him he has to go to the city, but he is quite insistent. I don't think he speaks English.'

The woman comes over and greets me with exaggerated kindness, I guess she is his superior. Noticing my coins, she asks if she may examine one. Picking up a gold piece, she seems puzzled. She feels it in her hand for weight, like any moneychanger.

'It's not Australian. Not Krugerrand either. Too small. Probably 22 carat, though.' She looks at the coin carefully and mouths the letters of the inscription. 'C-A-E-S-A-R–why this is an old Roman coin!' she exclaims. 'I'm sure of it. See there. A-V-G, short for Augustus. I think Mark collects this stuff. One moment, Dave. One moment, sir.' Julie leaves to seek yet another colleague. In the awkward silence, Dave smiles at me.

'So, where are you from, sir?' he asks.

'Italia.'

'Ah.' Not knowing what to say, he pretends to examine a sheaf of papers on his desk, and anxiously looks up several times.

After a minute, Julie brings over an older, well-dressed, bespectacled man. He is carrying my gold coin and a small balance. He pulls up a chair next to me while Julie stands behind him, arms folded.

'This is ancient Roman gold, quite rare and valuable,' the older man tells us in the manner of an expert. 'A beautiful piece, in near mint condition. Extraordinary! Would be a fine acquisition for any collection.' He cannot hide his excitement.

'Are you willing to buy it from him, Mark?' asks Julie. 'He appears to want to change this stuff for dollars.'

'I will certainly try tempting him to part with it.' Mark turns to me. 'I gather you don't speak English?' Seeing my blank reply, he nods patiently.

'Are you from Italy?'

'Italia.' I nod. 'Campania.'

'I thought so,' he tells the others. 'He is indeed Italian. But back to this coinage. It is truly remarkable. Recent metal detector find, I suspect. This grade of antiquity wouldn't be out of place at a Christie's auction. I wonder why he's selling it?' He peers over his spectacles, looking me over.

Dave speaks softly to the others, 'Probably a backpacker. Must have spent all his dough on grog and babes. Hell, that's what I'd be doing if I were backpacking around the world.'

'I bet *you* would,' says Julie.

Mark looks again at the coin and sets it on the balance. Now we are getting somewhere. This man *is* a money changer. 'Eight grams. Gold value alone, a quarter troy ounce, about 600 bucks,' he says. He looks at the coin, then me, as though weighing up both. He takes a deep breath. 'How much do you want for it?' he asks.

I take his meaning. I am not familiar with the coinage of this province, and don't know what to ask for. I shrug and hold my palms up towards him, as if to ask *him* to name a price. He strokes his chin nervously.

He tells the others softly, 'You know, collector's value of *any* Roman Imperial gold coin is at least a grand.' He looks at me, craftily. 'Will you take five hundred?' He holds up five fingers. Now we are in the bargaining game, for certain! Whatever his offer, his first price will be low, like any trader in the market. I hold up ten fingers.

'Ha, he wants a grand!' Dave says, stifling a laugh.

Now Mark holds up six fingers and smiles. I hold up eight and meet his smile calmly. He stammers and runs his hand through his hair repeatedly. It's obvious he wants my coin. He holds up eight fingers, 'Okay sir. Eight hundred it is.'

'Eight hundred,' I repeat.

'Good man. A deal it is.' He offers his hand, and I shake it.

'Dave, get 800 from my savings account, please,' he says as he hands the man a small card. Dave returns shortly with a sheaf of the shiny notes I had seen at the tavern.

He counts them out in front of me. 'Fifty, one hundred, fifty, two hundred … There we are. Eight hundred Aussie dollars.' He takes the coin from the balance and puts it in an envelope. I pick up the notes. How curious, these colourful pieces of greasy paper are of value here. Aussie dollars. That's just what the waitress said. I put them and the rest of my coins back in my inside pocket.

I stand and give them all a hearty 'Thanks, mate'. They rise and smile, obviously pleased.

'Thank you! Good afternoon, sir.' Julie leads me to the door.

As I am leaving, the spectacled man calls out, 'I could be interested in some of those denarii too—'

Out in the hot sun again, I make my way back to the Imperial tavern. Lucy greets me with a smile at the bar. 'Did you find the bank okay?' I pull out my roll of notes. 'So you did. Well done.'

She plucks one from my hand, puts it in the cash drawer, and gives me more of the notes and a couple of coins in change. I am relieved to have solved the problem of money. Good to know my Aussie dollars are as valuable as gold or silver in this land. I certainly have enough money to keep me in food and drink for some time.

I take a table outside on the veranda. Making sure no one is watching, I draw out the strange money and examine it closely. What could possibly make these things valuable? True I have never seen this material before, but wouldn't a shopkeeper prefer *real* money? Gold, silver, bronze, as the whole world does? These paper dollars are in different sizes, on their faces, images of people and places. In each corner, a symbol. The smallest note "5" is coloured pink. A slightly bigger, blue note, has "10" in the corner. The "20" is red, and the large yellow notes of which I still have fifteen, read "50". I must learn these numbers. Why they don't use good Roman numerals is beyond understanding.

I examine one of the coins I was given in change. It is

large, octagonal, and despite its appearance is not silver but an inferior metal, probably copper alloy. It bears the legend "50 cents" and a crest, with the words "AUSTRALIA 2014". Is this the name of this nation? Australia? The South Land.

On the back of the coin is a portrait of a middle-aged woman. It reads "Elizabeth II DG Regina". By the grace of God, Elizabeth, Queen. So, Caesar is a woman here! An empress rules over this land of Australia.

'Elizabeth,' I say to myself, turning the coin over and over in my hand.

My thoughts turn to the horse races that Shirley spoke of. Not wanting to miss them, yet not knowing what hour they run, it would be unwise to tarry too long in town. I have nothing better to do in any case. I examine the handbill, and from the rough map determine the racecourse to be a half mile north of the town. I set off. Soon the land turns to cultivated fields and paddocks. A car passes, pulling a sort of wagon. I glance back at it and see a horse inside. How odd to see a wagon carrying a horse, instead of the other way around. I am on the right path.

The track is set among fenced paddocks of various sizes, some with horses grazing peacefully. The track itself is a little different than our Italian courses. The surface is soft dirt, but is much broader, with gentler turns than our hippodromes. It appears to be about a mile and a quarter around. Tiers of timber benches under a large awning run along one side, but there are only a handful of people there.

I climb into the stands and take a seat a few rows up to survey the scene. On the track itself, some horses are being walked by their owners to shake the kinks out of their legs. Knots of people chat under the few trees nearby. It is warm, and I am weary. I fold my arms over my chest and can't help drifting off.

'You made it!' calls out a woman, whom I recognise as Shirley from the town.

'Salve, Shirley,' I mumble as I rub my eyes. The sun is low now, we are in the soft glow of twilight.

'Taking a little break, I see?' she asks cheerfully. I nod, not comprehending. I stretch my arms and try to stifle a yawn.

'Say Marcus, my daughter was supposed to help me unload but she hasn't shown up. Teenagers! I wonder if you could give me a hand with Futura? You seem to be familiar with horses.'

Futura, the stallion I met in the paddock when I first came into town. I knew he was a racing animal. So, he will run in tonight's program. She seems to be alone, and I guess she needs assistance. Perhaps she is a widow. 'Futura. Bene.' I climb down to join her.

'Thanks so much! Very good of you. This way.' There are many cars now in the lot next to the track. Shirley's is here, with her stallion still within the wagon. She unlocks a side door and enters, speaking softly to the horse to reassure it. I follow. The animal is nervous at my presence. She offers me the lead rope. 'Hold him while I get the back gate,' Shirley says. The gate drops, and I slowly back the horse out. He stamps and snorts indignantly but is happy to be free. I stroke his neck to calm him.

'This way,' calls out Shirley. I lead Futura through a pair of gates and release him into a small paddock. We return to her car. 'Thanks, Marcus. You're a good man. I've got a few things in the ute too, do you mind?' She points to the back of her car, laden with a saddle and other leather gear.

'Porto?' I ask.

'Yes, please.' I grab the saddle and sling it over my shoulder, pick up some of the other gear and haul it to the paddock where Futura stands. He is agitated, whinnying constantly, his ears pricked. Other riders are gathering too. Around us horses are being brushed, saddled, and walked. I can sense their nervousness; they know they are about to race and are jittery. The smell of horses is strong here. This is a place I can feel at home! I set the gear down, and stroke the stallion, holding it while Shirley saddles him.

'Mum!' a young woman shouts as she runs up. The horse is momentarily startled; his eyes widen and he shifts his body away from the girl.

'Easy, you'll frighten him,' says Shirley.

'Sorry I'm late, I was at Angie's. We were doing her hair and we were going to braid it, but she decided not to then her boyfriend called and—'

'Never mind. Honestly! It's almost post time. You'd best be getting this horse ready.' Shirley introduces me. 'This is Marcus, he's been giving me a hand. You know, since you were *far* too busy.'

'Hey Marcus, I'm Sabina.' She offers her hand, and I shake it.

'Salve, Sabina.' A fine Roman name. She is perhaps a little younger than me, around seventeen years, slim and pretty. She has long dark hair, tied behind in a ponytail. She must be Shirley's daughter, she is the image of her mother. 'Fillia?' I ask Shirley, indicating the girl.

She laughs. 'Yes, she's my filly all right. My youngest.' She turns to Sabina. 'He doesn't say much, but he knows his way around horses. His get up is a little far-fetched too, probably a uni student up for the races.'

'Or a backpacker,' Sabina says as she looks me up and down, without any shyness. 'Where are you from, Marcus?' She has a small stature, her eyes are bright and brown. She wears riding boots and a white shirt buttoned to the collar. Over her arm she carries a jacket patterned in red and white check.

'Italia. Campania.' My usual line.

'Buongiorno! That's about all the Italian I know. Have you been to Rome? I'd *love* to go to Rome, I was thinking after I graduate, maybe. Well, if we can afford it.' She is bursting with youthful energy, and did I mention she is very pretty.

'All right Sabbie, save the flirting for after the races. Let's get Futura prepped. Marcus, you'd best take a seat now,' Shirley says, pointing her thumb to the seating. 'Futura runs in the third race. He's got a good chance; the field looks pretty weak. I reckon you'd do well to put a wager on. Horse number six.'

'Six,' she repeats, and holds up six fingers.

'Six.' I nod.

'Sabina will be riding him. If that girl can remember half the things her father taught her, she just might have a chance. Hoping you'll cheer her on.'

I make my way back to the stands and find a good perch on the top row. The track is instantly lit up with brilliant white light. At intervals around the track, great lamps are mounted on tall poles, which have all been lit simultaneously by some means. More patrons are arriving, on foot and by car, which they park in a field nearby. A young man with a torch directs them. I had heard of night racing at Rome. On feast days the emperor would sponsor torchlight races at the Great Hippodrome below the Palatine Hill. A breathtaking sight, so I was told.

Families and couples take their seats in the stands. The hard wooden benches are not comfortable, but it doesn't seem to bother anyone. It seems the whole town is here. I have a great view and am pleased to have arrived early to get a choice seat. In the centre of the track, opposite the finish line, a wooden hut sits atop a tower. It is lit within and several men mill about inside. Behind me, outside the stands, is a larger timber building. Its windows are open and people start to line up in front of them. Placing wagers, no doubt. Nearby, several food wagons are setting up, the smell of woodsmoke and grilling meat comes from their direction.

'Goood evening ladies and gentlemen!' A loud voice calls from the tower. A silver-haired man is speaking. I don't know how he projects his voice in so loud a manner.

'Welcome to the Quilpie Spring racing carnival. Country

racing at its finest. We may not be the biggest in Queensland, but we're certainly the best!' On and on he rambles. At last he stops, and I hear music coming from the booth. Oddly, I can't see any musicians. The crowd starts to clap and sing in unison. I feel like joining in, but hesitate, not wanting to draw attention to myself.

The silver-haired man resumes his patter. Down below, horses are led towards the starting barriers. Their riders are mounted now, crouched in the saddle, each in a colourful jacket and cap. The horses carry a numbered flag on their flank. On a signal from the steward, the horses enter the starting gates. One by one they are pushed in, assisted by a pair of attendants who must take care to avoid being kicked. Some refuse to enter, and there is much stamping and head tossing. It takes some time to coax them all in.

The group of spectators that were at the wagering booth have moved to the railing next to the track. Everyone feels the anticipation; the people cheer and clap. At last, the final horse is pushed into its box. In an instant a horn sounds, the gates fly open, and the horses bolt along the track.

'They're off!' shouts silver-hair.

What a glorious sight! The horses thunder past my vantage point, dirt flying. The people shout and wave. I count fifteen horses on the field. I look eagerly for Shirley's horse, but don't see it. I admire the horsemanship of the riders, these steeds are very swift indeed, they could easily challenge the best Italian horses. They approach the first turn. Silver-hair calls the race at the top of his lungs.

'Purple Velvet leading from Garden State by a length with Maroon Shadow a nose behind.' Down the back stretch now at full gallop, the field begins to spread out. A horse whose rider bears a bright yellow jacket has a clear lead, and it lengthens as they approach the final turn. In the stands, everyone rises to their feet, and shouts for their favourites.

'Come on Shadow!' a woman in front of me screams, and her children shout likewise. The riders use their whips now. The horses strain and fly towards the finish. The cheers around me crescendo as they cross the line. The rider in the yellow jacket has won by a generous margin. What a spectacle!

The rest of the field finish. The riders stand in their stirrups to slow their charges then turn and one by one make their way back. At the finish line, the winning horse pauses, the rider accepts handshakes from some well-dressed people, probably the stallion's owner. I imagine they are handing over the prize purse. I wonder how much he has won. Back home, one could earn 500 sestertii at a country meeting, with the jockey retaining a fourth part of the winnings.

Soon the horses are off the track, and the crowd quiets. Winners are lined up at the wagering booth waving their tickets in their hands, and I feel happy for them. How good it feels to be at the races again. I feel a kinship with these people of Quilpie. I feel homesick too. I think of the many times our family would attend the races in the afternoon in Abellinum, picnicking under a tree, cheering our favourites at the rail.

My father and I would visit Naples in the spring, looking to buy promising yearlings for our patron, Gaius Aemelianus.

We owe a great deal to Aemelianus and his family; they have bought horses from us for years and place a great trust in my father's eye for picking the swiftest animals. Aside from visiting the markets and races, we would sometimes visit Aemelianus at his magnificent villa. While the elders talked business, I played in the garden with his many children while slaves brought us treats. Just last year, I got to sit at the big table in the atrium with Father, Aemelianus and his bookkeepers.

After a few minutes another race begins to form. Like the first, it starts to a great shout and cheer. This contest is much closer; the early leader appeared to have the victory, but two others surged ahead on the home stretch, each overtaking the leader, neck and neck. Everyone comes to their feet as one just noses out the other to win. Could there be any better entertainment! A celebration of the beauty and strength of these magnificent animals, and the skill of their riders. Who needs the bloody Roman Games, where innocent creatures from the corners of the earth are slaughtered for amusement? Surely the gods gave them life, as they gave man life, not for man to destroy but to marvel in it.

The third race begins to form. Among the riders is a petite figure in a red and white check patterned jacket. Sabina. Her riding helmet is close over her eyes, and her ponytail falls behind in a neat plait. She rides Futura and takes a few slow turns on the track while waiting for the start.

I must put a wager on her. A winner for sure. For the gods led me to meet this girl and her mother this day – hardly an accident. Her horse's banner carries a "6" in the red circle.

Horse number six, Shirley had said. I climb down through the crowd which is not easy as many people are sitting on the stairs. I join the line at the wagering hut.

'You right?' the bookmaker asks when I reach the counter. I pull out one of the red coloured notes and hold out six fingers.

'Twenty bucks, race three, horse number six?' says the young woman behind the counter. I nod. 'Win, place or show, mate?' she asks. Not understanding, I shrug. She frowns. 'I'll take that bet to win then.' She writes it out efficiently on a little chit of paper and thrusts it to me. 'Next, thanks!' I make my way back to the grandstand.

Again, it takes some time to get all the horses into the barrier stalls, as several are too nervous to enter. Sabina steers Futura into the sixth chute. One by one the remaining horses enter. The horn sounds, and they spring out at full gallop. I spot Sabina in the middle of the pack as they approach the first turn.

'Godspeed,' I whisper and clench my ticket tightly. I follow them on the back stretch, my eyes fixed on Futura. He runs with a smooth, long stride. Sabina runs down one horse, then another. As they approach the final turn, she is in third place. The crowd jumps to their feet, and I join them. 'Citius, Sabina!' I shout. Around me everyone screams for their favourite. They are on the home stretch now. But she is blocked in by the two horses in front of her. She pulls Futura to the outside. Bold move! On they ride, and Futura surges ahead. She has passed one of the leading pair and is in second place. Silver-hair is carried away by the excitement too.

'Night Star by half a length. Futura coming on hard on the outside!' he shouts.

They rush towards the finish, and the thundering hooves make the stands shake. The shouts of the crowd are deafening. Both riders and horses strain for the finish. Futura draws closer and closer to the leader, and just pulls even as they fly past the line. Who has won? I hold my breath. I could not be sure if Sabina overtook in time or not. Everyone is still on their feet, talking excitedly as they wait for the decision.

A minute passes, then silver-hair announces. 'Photo finish folks, and it's Futura by a nose!' I hear 'Futura' and I know he's won the race. I can't help but leap up and clap my hands over my head. The crowd settles, and resumes their seats, talking excitedly about the race. Below, the horses have come back around and left the track. I bound down the steps to find Sabina, but I don't see her in the pack of horses and people. I join the queue of betters at the wagering shed, and hand in my ticket. The young woman hands me seven red notes. Easy money!

I return to the rail and wait for Sabina. I wonder if she is married. Unlikely, for surely her husband would be here helping with the horses, not her mother. I wonder if she is from Sicily which is famous for strong, energetic, dark-haired women.

The next race is already underway when at last I see her. She is holding Futura's bridle, her jacket is unbuttoned and her helmet in her hand. A group of friends greet her, congratulating her excitedly. She graciously accepts their embraces.

I call out to her. 'Salut, Sabina! Victoria. Magnfiico!' She smiles in recognition and gives me a mock bow. 'Mirabilis es,' I tell her. *You are amazing.*

'Why thank you, Marcus. I'll take that as a compliment, whatever it means.'

'Futura est Equum celere.' I make the motion of a galloping horse with my fingers and pump my fist.

'He's amazing, hey! I've had him since he was a yearling. Might make us few bucks if he keeps this up.' She pauses to draw breath. 'He is a great finisher isn't he. When I was boxed in, I knew I had to go outside. And he knew just what to do! Once he sees daylight, he's unstoppable.'

'Bene.' My reply is drowned out as the race in progress comes tearing around the turn. We both look back down the track and watch the finish. Sabina's mother approaches.

'Salut Shirley.'

'Hello Marcus. Did you see Sabina ride? Impressive, eh!'

'Magnifiico,' I reply and wish I could say her praises in her language. I hold up my winning betting ticket.

'Well done, Marcus. It's your lucky day. Good on you.'

Sabina turns to Shirley. 'Mum, do we have to stay 'til the end?'

'Why darling, it's a big night, don't you want to watch the rest of the races?'

'I'm so tired, Mum.' She pauses, then adds, 'Can Marcus join us for dinner?'

Shirley smiles. 'Why not, he seems harmless enough. He doesn't talk much though. He sounds a bit like an Italian.

Maybe Dad can sound him out. Still, he knows his way around a horse so he can't be all bad.' She turns to me. 'Marcus, would you like to join us for dinner at our place? Pasta, nothing special.' She makes an eating motion with her hand, and I catch on.

'Vero.' I nod enthusiastically. 'Hungry, mate,' I tell them and rub my belly. They laugh.

'Marcus, how about you meet us at the car in say fifteen minutes, and we'll bring you with us. You know our car?' Shirley points to the parking area.

'Car,' I repeat.

'Sabina, walk Futura around for at least ten minutes and make sure you give him a good hose down. Then we'll head off.'

'Yes, Mum.'

They head off with Futura. The races continue, I half-heartedly watch them from the rail. After a time, I spot Shirley with Sabina leading the horse out, and go over to join them. He is quickly loaded into the wagon.

'Hop in.' Sabina beckons me into the car's rear seat. 'Coming through. Shove over, Marcus.' Sabina pushes in beside me. She is unexpectedly close. I'm aware of her warmth and the scent of her hair. I feel embarrassed in my filthy clothes.

Shirley starts the car and we drive off. It carries startlingly bright torches to light the way ahead. Soon we are back at their house on the edge of town, the same place I met Shirley this morning.

I help Sabina unload the horse, throw him a biscuit of

hay, and release him into the paddock. Shirley heads for the house. 'I'll check how Dad's getting on with dinner, we're all starving. Sabbie, you get that gear stowed before you come in, no nonsense. I'm sure Marcus will give you a hand.'

'*Yes*, Mum,' Sabina says, with exaggerated exasperation. 'Come on, Marcus.' We unload the riding gear into the large shed. Along one wall are iron hooks carrying the trappings and tools a horseman needs: straps, blankets, stirrups. Bales of hay line the back wall. The sweet scent of hay instantly reminds me of home. Soon everything is stowed away, and we head to the house.

Sabina pulls off her boots and tosses them in the hallway. 'I'll get Dad. I reckon he'll like meeting you.' I take off my shoes too, adding them to the pile in the hallway. I peer into the parlour, it is softly lit by a lamp embedded in the ceiling. Like all their lanterns it emits no smoke. Along one wall is a small table with fresh flowers and portraits of family members. They are extraordinarily realistic and must have been painted by a gifted artist. I see several pictures of a younger Sabina, her hair in long braids.

'That's Sabbie when she was little. Cute little possum, wasn't she?' I turn to meet her father. 'I'm Antony. A pleasure to meet you. You can call me Tony.'

'Marcus.' I reach to shake his hand. He grips my hand firmly. He is not a tall man, but handsome with soft features, a face darkened by the sun, and greying hair.

'I hear you're Italian. Would you be here on holiday?'

'On holiday.'

'He doesn't speak much English, Dad,' says Sabina, appearing behind him. 'But he loves racing and he's great with horses. He helped Mum unload at the track.'

'And why didn't *you* help?'

'Well, I was a bit late. I was at Angie's and uh …'

'Spare me child. Go wash up now, we're almost ready to eat,' says Tony. Shirley has appeared and gives her husband a kiss on the cheek. 'Almost ready, Shirl. I'll open a bottle of wine in honour of our guest.' He leaves, presumably heading to the kitchen.

'You look like you've had a long day, Marcus. Probably want to have a bit of a wash, eh? Sabbie, get him a towel from the laundry.'

Sabina takes me to the bathing room. She hands me a towel. 'Here you go. You have a quick shower. I'll see you in a few minutes.'

I strip off and climb into the bath. There are taps for both hot and cold water, which is very civilized. It is rare to see hot water outside of the public baths, other than in rich men's villas. I let the warm water run over me. It's been days since I have had a proper bath. I scrub off the filth of my prison, of the arena, and of the desert. I stand under the water for ages, closing my eyes and savouring the warmth.

I hear a knock on the door.

'Hey, Aquarius, save some hot water for us!' It is Sabina's voice. I quickly dress and follow the sounds to the kitchen. Plates and cutlery are being laid out. Tony enters. I notice his walk is rather laboured, perhaps from an old back injury. He takes a seat and beckons me to do the same.

Sabina sits across from me. 'That's where my brother usually sits. He's away at uni.' Shirley sets down a large platter and takes a seat next to Tony. A basket of warm bread is passed around, fragrant with garlic. In the centre of the table sits a steaming cauldron of stew.

'Rigatoni. Hope you like it, Marcus,' says Shirley as she ladles out a serving for each of us.

'He should Mum, he is Italian,' says Sabina. Shirley serves out a big helping of noodles, ground meat, vegetables and herbs, with cheese sprinkled on the top. Tony opens a bottle of wine.

'Wine, darling?' Tony asks Shirley. She nods, and he fills her glass. 'Marcus?' I nod too and hold out my glass. We tuck into our meal with relish. The stew is delicious, I devour it like a man starved, along with a generous helping of bread. I notice the others' eyes on me.

'I dare say he hasn't had a decent meal in some time,' says Shirley, obviously pleased.

'Delectamenti,' I tell her.

The family talk little during the meal, but as they finish, they speak of the races. Sabina tells her father of her victorious ride; he listens intently with his knife and little trident held by his plate. 'Well done, cara mia. Well done.' He turns to me. 'So, Marcus, you can pick a winner when you see one, no?' I look at him blankly. Tony pushes aside his plate and pushes back his chair a little. 'I expect he has an eye for a good horse.' He turns to me and speaks slowly and deliberately. 'Marcus. Tell me about yourself. I hear you're a horseman.'

There is an uncomfortable silence, as I don't comprehend.

'Do you work on a station round here?' He seems to genuinely want to know more about me.

Sabina frowns. 'I don't think he speaks English, Dad.'

'Perhaps, darling.' Tony patiently asks again, 'Lavori in una fattoria vicina?' His words sound familiar, yet unfamiliar at the same time. They sound like a peculiar form of Latin, strongly accented. I believe he's asking if I work on a nearby farm.

I answer in simple Latin words. 'No, in Italia habito.'

'Now we're getting somewhere.' Tony turns to the women, who are watching with anticipation. 'He says his home is in Italy.'

'Familia mea in Campania habitat. Laboro cum equis,' I tell them, and Tony translates.

'His family is in Campania, the province where Naples is, you know. His accent is quite odd, it sounds more like old Latin than Italian. Perhaps he grew up in a monastery.'

I continue, 'Cum patre vivo in villam. Nos equos vendere.'

'He says his family works a farm, raising horses.'

Sabina jumps in. 'I knew it!"

Shirley smiles. 'I could have told you that too.'

Tony ponders my words thoughtfully and shakes his head. 'He calls horses equus, like in Latin, instead of cavallo, as we say in Italy. He breeds horses with his father, as far as I can tell.'

'Dad, ask him if he's in Quilpie for the races.'

'Vieni a Quilpie per le gare?'

I don't know how to answer. How could I explain to these gentle people I was in an imperial prison just a few days ago?

They would be mortified.

'Yes. Races,' I tell them.

'Well, good for you. We might be only a country town, but we put on the best racing festival in the state of Queensland.'

'Ask him where he's staying tonight, Tony,' says Shirley.

'Dove alloggi?' I don't understand his words. He tries again. 'Dovi … dormirai?' he asks and folds his hands to his face as if sleeping. I don't want them to think I am a travelling beggar, so I make up a plausible answer.

'Taverna. Imperial.'

'Ah, taverna.' Antony nods knowingly. 'He's staying at the Imperial.'

'Good choice. Lucy and Ben will take care of him. But it might be a little rowdy there on a race night.'

They converse among themselves. I try to follow their conversation, but it is not easy to make out anything save a word or two. I stifle a yawn.

'It *is* getting late, darlings,' says Shirley. 'I think we all best be getting to bed.'

Tony gets to his feet, and we follow. He takes me by the arm.

'It's been a pleasure meeting you, son. We would be pleased to have you as a guest in our home again. I imagine Sabina has taken your number down?' I give him the blank stare. 'Telephono? Numero?' He grins. 'È un piacere conoscerti. Buona notte.'

'Buona notte,' I repeat, as he shakes my hand firmly.

He departs for the back veranda. I turn to Shirley and thank her. 'Gratias, Shirley.' I take her hand and kiss it gently. 'Cibus erat delectamenti.'

'Charmer,' says Sabina.

'You're very welcome, Marcus, but Tony did most of the cooking. We're happy to have you over any time. Sabina, show him to the door please, like a proper host.'

Sabina leads me to the entry hall. I don't know what to say to this charming girl. I tell her she is very kind, 'Facis amice—'

She interrupts, 'Sorry Marcus, I don't know much Italian.'

'Gratias, Sabina,' I tell her, as I take her hand to kiss it.

'Ooh you are a sweetie, aren't you. I can't say I've met a boy like you before.' She looks into my eyes intensely, then abruptly leans over and kisses me on the cheek. She turns to the little table by the door, picks up a paper and writes.

'This is my number. Call me tomorrow, maybe we can go out. There's a carnival in town, at the show grounds. We could have a look. If you want to, I mean.'

I tell her I want to visit her again, 'Volo enim vos visitare.'

'I'll take that to mean you'll call me. Goodnight, Marcus.'

'Bunom nocte,' I repeat.

'I know that one. Buona notte to you too.' Her words are not exactly Latin, but similar enough and I take her meaning.

I retreat down the steps, almost falling over backwards. She giggles and shuts the door. I head back towards the town centre, a bounce in my step.

Long before I reach the tavern, I can hear the ruckus. There are many cars here and dozens of people milling around outside. There is music, singing, and shouting. I'm uneasy staying here. I don't care to get into a brawl with the locals, about my clothes, my language or my manners, but I am tired to my very bones.

I turn back towards Sabina's house. I feel an urge to ask if I can lodge with them for the night but lack the courage. Who am I, but a stranger with strange ways. They surely would be afraid to let me spend the night in their home.

I pause and lean on their fence for a moment. I can see the lights of the house are mostly out now. A car or two passes, but soon there are no more. It is getting cool now. The last light goes out and the house falls silent. All is quiet in this country town, there is only the crickets and the sound of a distant dog barking.

Across the road from her house are farmer's fields, with a couple of sheds in the distance. I cross the road, slip over the fence, and push through the long grass to the largest shed. I pull open the timber door. It takes a minute before I can make out anything in the darkness. From the smell, it is a disused animal barn. I slip inside. On the wall are some rusting tools and an old blanket on a hook; on the floor is a little straw. I take down the blanket, make a rough bed from the straw, and curl up to sleep.

Sleep doesn't come easy. My mind races with all that's happened today. Did it really happen? The kind young men who gave me water and helped me back to the road. Jono, the truck driver who gave me a ride into this town in the great machine. The races! And Sabina and her family, down-to-earth country people who welcomed me into their home. They are good people here in this land called Australia. How different to those in Rome who treated me like an animal.

A little moonlight filters in the dust-streaked window. I take out the little paper that Sabina had given me. I can just make it out. "Sabina 0491 573 770" and a little circle like a smiling face. Sabina. What a pretty name. But I don't know what the numbers mean.

What to do tomorrow? How am I going to get home? I could do worse than to stay in this town, to get to know these people, to learn their language and their customs. Above all, to find out where I am. Who are these Australian people? They use Roman letters, yet they don't speak Latin. Except for Tony, who speaks a strange variant I can barely understand. And their odd machines! Their vehicles that move without a horse, and lanterns that light without fire. A wonderful, ingenious people.

I know I cannot remain here. I must get home. My mother and father's anguish at my being carried away must be unbearable. They could know nothing of my fate. What of my father—what dark business did he become mired in? How did he cross paths with Sejanus, Rome's cruel Prefect? Perhaps my father is in one of Rome's dungeons, as I was. The thought horrifies me.

How to get home? Perhaps Sabina and her father could help. They could take me to a port, where I could take a ship for Italy. Yet, I fear moving around in a busy port full of soldiers and the emperor's men. As an escaped criminal, I would be worth many denarii to a bounty hunter.

I will need to go to the capital of this province. Perhaps I could get an audience with the governor, or one of the representatives of the Queen Elizabeth. I could tell them my story, the truth. Yes, perhaps Sabina and her parents could help me. I drift off, thinking of her smile.

73

CHAPTER V

'Get up!' I feel a man's boot in my side. 'Get up! You're trespassing.' A large man with a black beard is glaring at me. He holds an iron bar. 'You bloody city bums. Get out of my shed!'

I sit up and try to apologise. 'Paenitet me!'

'Damn foreigners.' He looks about the shed. 'Have you stolen anything? Huh?' He yanks the blanket off me and throws it aside. He must think I am a thief. He pulls out a slim black slab from his pocket. He touches it delicately with his fingers, then holds it to his ear. He speaks loudly into it. I look about, but there is no one else here. Who is he talking to?

'Rick! Yeah good, mate. Well, not so good. Can you come round to my place? Caught a bloody trespasser in my shed. Don't know what he's stolen.' Is this man insane? Why does he speak to this little box? 'Yeah, right away. No, no weapons. He seems harmless enough. Don't think he speaks English.

Probably a hungover backpacker. Yeah, I'll keep an eye on him until you get here.'

He puts it back in his pocket. It must be his household god, that he carries about with him. I feel in my shirt pocket for the idol of Juno and cradle it in my fingers. I pray silently for protection. But in this land, so far from home, I doubt the Roman gods have any power.

He barks, 'Outside, pal!' and motions at me with the iron bar. I stagger to my feet and go outside where the sunlight blinds me. 'Sit right there. Don't move. I said sit!' He points to the ground, and I obediently squat down.

In trouble again. Maybe I can run past him. The man has a large belly and doesn't look as though he could outrun a lame ox. After a moment, he addresses me. 'Where you from? Backpacker?' he asks.

'Italia,' I reply, hoping this is what he asked.

'Ah. Had a little too much to drink last night, I'm guessing? Too many beers at the track?' He motions as though drinking.

'Thirsty mate,' I tell him. He laughs. I feel the tension easing.

'I bet you are. And at eight o'clock in the morning.' I look down, embarrassed. He continues to stand over me. He again takes the black slab from his pocket and fondles it some more.

A car drives up to the shed. Unlike the other cars in town, this one is painted blue and white, with a rack of red and blue squares on its roof. A young man gets out, smartly dressed in a neat uniform and leather cap.

'Rick,' my captor calls to him.

'Morning, Syd.' He looks at me. 'This your unwanted guest, I assume?'

'Yeah, found him sleeping in the shed. Probably scared him a bit.'

'Did he steal anything? Any property damage?'

'Nah, don't think so.'

The uniformed man beckons me to get up. 'On your feet, sir. What's your name?'

'Marcus,' I answer.

'Marcus what?'

'Marcus Junius Corvus.' The two look at each other and shake their heads.

'So, you speak English then?' I look dumbly at them. 'Didn't think so. Look buddy, you're trespassing. I know you've been partying a little hard last night, but you can't just crash in someone's shed.'

The big man says, 'I dunno, Rick, maybe just let him off with a warning.'

'You don't want to press charges?'

'Nah. Just a kid having fun. Remember when we were young?'

'Yeah! Like that time we went on that pub crawl in Townsville? How you ended up in that tree, I'll never know.' Both men laugh heartily and shake their heads.

'Get in the car,' directs the officer. He opens the rear door and beckons me to take a seat in the back. He slams the door shut. There is a wire cage separating the seats. So, I am a prisoner again. I silently curse my carelessness.

'Take care, Syd. Say hello to Jacquie for me.' The two men shake hands and slap each other on the shoulder. The officer gets in and we drive off, back to the town centre.

'I know you think this is funny. But trespassing could get you a record. You don't want that, do you?' He glances at me in a mirror suspended above the front window. I put on a submissive look, and gaze at my feet.

We turn into a broad tree-lined street, and arrive at a low building, probably the town's guard post and jail. There's a blue and white chequered sign out front, impressively lettered, "Queensland Police Service". Inside, a young woman is seated at a desk. Her uniform identical to Rick's. She casts her eyes over me.

'Whatcha got this time Rick? Drunk and disorder?'

'Nah, trespass. Was sleeping in Syd Knight's shed.' She goes back to her paperwork. The officer goes to his own desk and beckons me to take a seat before him.

'Now I need to ask you a few questions. Answer me straight, it will save us both a lot of time. I need your full name.'

Nomen—easy. 'Marcus. Marcus Junius Corvus.'

'That's a mouthful. You got any ID on you?' He says again, very slowly and loudly, 'I-dent-i-fi-ca-tion.'

I don't know what he wants. I try, 'Italia. Campania.' This line usually works.

'Okay, you're an Italian on holiday. Where are you staying? Where's your luggage? Where is your passport?' To each question, I offer nothing but a blank look. He puts his palm on his forehead and sighs loudly. 'All right. Let's try this. Do you have any money? Money?' He reaches into his pocket and pulls out some Aussie dollars. Ah, I see what is happening here. He is asking for a bribe to let me go. I smile and give him a knowing nod. I pull out my roll of money. I don't know his price, so I place the notes on the table, one at a time, each time pausing, to see if he calls enough.

'Well, at least you aren't a vagrant. Put that back in your pocket.' He pushes the money away. He doesn't want it, I must have mistaken his meaning. Now I will be in more trouble than ever! But he continues his questioning, unfazed by my attempted bribe.

'If you're going to stay in Quilpie, I want to you to book into a hotel.' He pauses. 'You ought to stay at the Imperial. You know, the tavern in town?'

'Ah, taverna,' I say.

'Yes, you got it. The taverna. You sleep there tonight.' He folds his hands as though sleeping.

'Sleep, taverna, tonight,' I repeat.

'Now get out of here.' He points to the door with his thumb.

I make my way down the steps, quickening my pace when I realise I am free and out of trouble again. The sun is strong now, the day is going to be a hot one. I walk back to the tavern. Its doors are open, but I don't see any patrons yet. Just the staff, busy cleaning and bringing in supplies for the day. I'm already hungry, I might as well get something to eat. But the counter is unattended.

'Sorry sir, not open yet. Lunch from eleven,' advises a young man hauling in fresh bread on large trays. It seems it will be a while before any meals will be served. If I'm going to get something to eat, it will have to be in town.

Along the main street, the locals are busy going about their business. I spot a group of people carrying food in paper packets, and drinks in paper cups. I enter the establishment. It is packed with customers lined up at the counter and standing at some tall narrow tables. I join the queue, and listen carefully to what the people are ordering, but all I can work out is that the drink they all seem to want is "coffee". When my turn comes, the serving woman calls out cheerfully, 'You right, sir?'

I point to a roll of bread behind the glass and call out 'hoc'.

'One cinnamon scroll? Anything else?'

'Coffee.'

'Flat white?' the girl asks. I nod slowly, pretending I know what this means, and she accepts my answer. I pay with a few coins. Soon I have my breakfast and head outside.

Needing a bit of peace after the morning's incident, I try a side street, and soon reach the edge of town. I am pleased to find a small park situated next to a small stream, where murky brown water flows silently. There are a few decrepit wooden tables, and no one else is here. I sit with my back against a big, old willow tree, its soft foliage nearly touching the ground. I finish my meal and rest in the shady spot. It is a beautiful sunny day. The sky is a brilliant blue, and there are many birds about, singing happily. I welcome the tranquillity that envelopes me.

The sun rises higher. It must be nearly noon. I hear a car approaching. It pulls into the little park; a young man and woman have come for a picnic. They lay out their meal on the table and sit together on the same side. The way they eye each other and laugh together, I can tell they are young lovers. I don't think they see me, but I am not hiding either.

I think of Sabina and of her confident, cheeky smile. Such a sweet, energetic young woman. Would she see anything in me? I think not! Who am I, but a lost Roman in ragged clothes. Still, I *should* visit her again. Her father, with his confident manner and his determination to speak to me, made me trust him. Yes, I will speak to him again and find out where I am and how to get to a port. I resolve to call in after the evening meal, for I don't want to impose on them.

The lovers leave the park after a time, arm in arm, kissing and laughing. I am envious, for here am I, lost and alone in a world away from home. I turn back for the town and soon reach the Imperial. There are diners here now, having their midday meal, some drinking ale. I spot Lucy behind the bar, unpacking bottles. She sees me and grins.

'Marcus! Back for lunch again?'

'Salve Lucy.'

'Did you catch the races last night?'

'Races. Bene!'

'Bene indeed. So, what can I get you?'

I must try to hire a bed for the night. 'Locus ad Somnum?' I ask. She looks puzzled. 'Dormire?' I fold my hands to my head as if sleeping.

'You want a room for the night? No worries. I think we have a single left. Shared bathroom though. Come with me.'

She beckons me to follow. We go through a little door, to the foyer of the inn.

At the desk she hands me a card and a writing tool. I fill in my full name.

'Put your car rego here,' she says pointing to the card. 'You have a car?'

'No car,' I shrug.

'That's okay. Leave it blank then. How many nights, love?' After struggling with words and signs, I work out her question. I decide to stay a week.

'It's forty dollars per night. Pay the first night now, the rest when you check out. Who knows, you may not hang around here a week. A lot of folks don't.'

'Forty dollars,' she repeats. I reach for my roll of money and pull out a large note marked "50" which is sufficient. She takes a key from a row of brass hooks behind her. 'Room five. Up the stairs, about halfway down. Bathroom at the end of the corridor. Numero cinque. Pop down if you need anything.'

'Gratias,' I tell her. I find my way to the room and enter with the little key. It is small, but tidy with ancient timber floorboards, and a small bed with a bright orange cover. At the window is a little table. The view is of the street in front of the inn. The sun is bright, so I draw the curtains. I sit on the bed with my back to the wall. It is past noon and I'm hungry.

Back in the bar, I try to decipher the menu board. Lucy returns to the counter. 'What are you having today?' I point at the second item on the board.

'Barra and chips. Good choice.' She calls out the order to the kitchen, and I pay.

I take my meal outside on the veranda. I feel awkward, and aware of being alone in a strange town with no one to talk to. 'Barra', I soon learn, is a fine white fleshed fish. The lunch crowd drifts away, and I head back up to my room. I lie on the bed, staring at the ceiling with its ornamental patterns.

Where on earth am I? And how am I going to get out of here? This place is unlike any I know in the Roman world. The sunbaked land, the gnarled gum trees, the bluish hue of the vegetation. Soil that is red instead of black. And the people with their strange manners and wonderful inventions are so different from Roman men. I must surely be a vast distance from home. The great truck that Jono gave me a ride in—did it not have "Roma" written on its side? In Latin letters, I saw it with my own eyes. Perhaps this distant province pays tribute to Rome, yet I have seen no Romans, no soldiers or officials of the imperial state.

I remind myself to go tonight to converse with Sabina's father. He seemed an honest man. Surely I can confide in him and his gentle family. He will help me find my way back to Rome, I know it. I feel better having decided on a plan. I sprawl out on the bed to sleep off the heavy meal.

It is dark when I wake to the muffled sound of shouting from the bar below. Fiddling with the lantern on the desk, I soon learn how to operate it. It casts a dim yellow light. I look in the small mirror hanging behind the door and am shocked at the sight. Marcus, you look like a ragged beggar! Your clothes are filthy and your beard long. I wash my clothes as best I can in the basin in the room. I wash myself in the bathing room down the hall, and regret having no blade for shaving. I must find a tailor's shop tomorrow.

Downstairs, I take a seat at the end of the bar. It is full of patrons tonight and a good deal of drink is flowing. The place is absurdly loud. Every customer shouts to be heard by his companions. There is a young man behind the bar tonight, and I order an ale. Four young men sit around a small table near me, drinking tall glasses of ale, their conversation loud and animated. I raise my glass and smile at them, but they just laugh to each other and ignore me.

In a corner of the tavern, on a little platform, a troupe of musicians is setting up. A young man with a short, black beard draws a stringed instrument from its case. Another man, tall and very slim, sets up a drum kit. Both have broad, black felt hats and close-fitting shirts fashioned from chequered cloth. A young woman with long yellow hair joins them. She is dressed alluringly in a short skirt, a form fitting pink top and short leather boots. It is not only my eyes she catches; there are hoots and whistles from many of the patrons as she takes to the little stage. The guitar player tunes and strums his instrument.

The lights dim. From behind the bar, a man I had seen yesterday steps onto the little platform and addresses the patrons.

'Good evening Quilpie. How is everyone tonight?'

Everyone gives a happy cheer in reply. 'Ladies and gentlemen, the Imperial Hotel is very proud to welcome back to the stage Western Queensland's finest trio. You all know Camilla, Ian, and Isaac. Let's hear it for the Quolls!' To more cheering, the drummer starts up a lively beat, the guitar player joins in. The instrument is sweet, well-tuned, and very loud.

'Any girls ready to party?' the young woman shouts. Which brings a big cheer from all the women in the tavern. They play a lively song and many patrons sing along. For their next song, the young woman performs a soulful ballad. Almost everyone in the bar looks at her longingly. She is very pretty, and a skilled singer. Some spirited dance numbers follow, which draw some patrons to the dance floor. They appear to be somewhat drunk; their dancing is random and not the slightest bit coordinated, but very amusing.

Finally, the band pauses for a break. The bar goers return to their drinks and shouted conversations. Some are ordering meals. I get up to do the same.

'Hey, look at this weirdo.' One of the young men from the table near me, a beardless youth with his hair cropped short, looks at me.

His companion, a redheaded youth with the barest of hair above his lip, yells loud enough for me to hear, 'Look at those stupid gypsy clothes.' The two other boys at their table, not as bold as their companions, blush and snicker.

'Looks like a Paddo yuppy, a long way from home,' says the brush-head.

'Hey, dickhead. Are you from Paddington? Why you

wearin' that crap?' the redhead shouts at me, then laughs with his buddies. By their tone, they are in the mood for trouble. I try to attract the waiter's attention to order a drink, but there are many people crowding close to the bar.

Having got my drink at last, I return to my spot at the end of the bar, but my chair has been taken. The red-haired boy has his boots spread across it. This one, obviously the leader of these ne'er-do-wells, looks at me defiantly with a stupid grin on his face.

'Seat's taken, partner.' He looks at his buddies, who giggle like foolish schoolboys.

'Looks like you'll have to sit someplace else, mate,' says brush-head.

I pick up my drink, give him a big smile and put on a gentle demeanour, even though I'd like to teach him some manners with my fists. I hold out my palm and ask if I may sit down.

'Possum sedere?'

Redhead's tone turns mean. 'What kind of talk is that! This is Australia, boy. Speak Australian.' I try to take the chair, but he won't move his legs. I know this kind of boy. Foolish know-it-alls, cowards who put down others weaker than themselves. He is emboldened by the tittering boys in his gang and strengthened with false courage of drink.

I lean over towards the redhead and whisper something into his ear, too quiet for him to hear. I tip half my drink into his lap which brings him to his feet abruptly.

'What the hell!'

In an instant I take my chair back, wheel it around to the

bar and set my drink down. I turn my head a little, to give myself warning of what might be coming.

'Son of a bitch, I'll kick your ass,' the thug shouts as he comes towards me threateningly. It's my turn to grin, and I point to the big stain on his lap. Redhead looks dumbly at himself, his mouth open. The other three stare at their leader, unsure whether to laugh or not.

'No, you won't, Nathan.' A large man in a black uniform has stepped in front of him. He is well-muscled and has a name badge on his chest. He must be employed to keep order in the bar. The red-haired kid, his face flushed with embarrassment and rage, stands speechless. Half of the bar is now looking at him and laughing at his expense.

'That son of a bitch poured his drink on me!'

'I saw the whole thing. It was an accident. I've been watching you all night, bothering people. If he did it deliberately, hell, you deserved it.' He stands towering over the redhead. 'I think you're done for the night, Nathan.' He points his thumb to the door. 'Outside. *Now.*' He turns to the other youths at the table. 'Get out and learn some manners or you won't be drinking here again.' They file out slowly. There is much hooting from the bar patrons as they exit.

'Sorry, sir,' the big man says. 'Dumb punks giving strangers a hard time, it's not right. Queenslanders aren't like that. Well, most of us. Anyway, it's bad for business. I'll get you another pint, on the house.'

I realise my fists are clenched and I am sweating. A close call. The last thing I need is to get into a fight and end up in the town dungeon. Around me, the drinkers have returned to their conversations, the incident forgotten. A young waitress brings me a large glass of ale and pats me on the shoulders.

'On the house, sir.'

'Gratias.' I nod.

A short while later, the guitar player returns. He sings and plays solo for a time, first a slow ballad, then a lively tune that sets toes taping and hands clapping. The audience applauds at length and he acknowledges them by tipping his hat. The young woman joins him on the stage.

The beer does its work, soothing my frayed nerves. The music is mesmerising. Entranced by the beautiful singer, swaying sensuously in the soft light, my troubles fade away. All about me, the people of Quilpie seem to be happy, enjoying their night out with friends, drink, and music. This could be a scene from a tavern back in my home province. People are not so different after all. There are both gentleman and bullies in every town.

My meal comes after a long delay, but I am not so hungry and only finish part of it. On the musicians play. A group of women get up to dance among themselves, slapping each other's hands and bumping their rear ends together. Only one other patron sits alone, an elderly man at the other end of the bar. He watches the singer, glassy-eyed, nursing a drink that he never sips. He is here to be around people, as I am. I wish I could speak to him, to learn his story.

The musicians break again. A few patrons drain their glasses and make for the door. Mine is empty too. I get up and head out for some fresh air. Out on the veranda, a few knots of people are standing about. Several hold little sticks of smouldering paper in their fingers, from which sweet smoke rises. It is rich, oily, and quite intoxicating. They hold the sticks to their mouths to inhale the smoke. What an odd custom. It is a pleasing smell; I wonder what herb they burn. I watch, fascinated, trying not to stare.

'There he is!' someone shouts. I turn abruptly.

'Get him, Nate!' The red-haired youth from the bar is coming at me and lands a punch in my chest before I have time to react. I drop to my knees and turn away so he can't give me another. He kicks me hard in the back, again and again. I ask for mercy.

'Miserere frater!'

'Take that, you wog punk!' He lays a hand on my shoulder to swing me around. But I grew up in the south of Italy and know how to fight. I yank his arm hard and pull him over my shoulder with a jerk. He lands flat on his back. I set my foot firmly on his chest. He struggles and calls to his fellow jackals. 'Josh! Dan! Belt the bastard. What you are you waiting for?'

I turn to face them with my fist raised and ask if they want some too. 'Hey! Quidam vultis?' They circle me, and one of them jumps on my back. This fool is easily dealt with. I turn and back up hard into the wall. He drops to the ground with a thud and a groan. The two other youths back away slowly and run off. But Nate is not done. He is back on his feet and has a blade in his hand. There is shouting from the patrons on the veranda.

'He's got a knife, mate. Watch yourself,' they warn. I face him and advance. He backs away a little, obviously a novice at this sort of combat. I fain a lunge at him as though to punch, but instead I kick the blade from his hand. He utters an oath and raises his fists.

The air is shattered by an ear-splitting whine. It is coming from a car that has just pulled up, with powerful red and blue lights blinking on its roof. From the car bursts a uniformed man. At the same time, the tavern owner and his burly security guard emerge from the bar. Nate turns to flee.

'Hold it!' shouts the big man. 'Nate, get your chicken ass back here! Don't make me tackle you.' But Nate has vanished into the night.

'You again,' says the man from the car, turning to me. It's Rick, the patrolman who took me in earlier. Great. 'Marcus, I thought I told you to stay out of trouble.' He turns to the big man, 'So Ben, what have we got here tonight?' He explains to the officer what transpired and makes a motion like he's holding a knife.

Rick takes me by the arm. 'Are you hurt, son?' He turns me around and looks me over. 'I reckon he's all right. Marcus, you go on up to bed now. Best not to take on punks like that. Just give the word to big Dave,' he points to the giant man, 'and he'll straighten them out.'

It seems I'm free to go. I blow out a deep breath and climb the stairs up to my room. Greatly disturbed by the fight, it takes a long time to fall asleep. I see the young toughs coming at me over and over. I have got to get out of here. Back to my people. Back to my home. To get away from this desert land. If only I could communicate with these people! I have learnt a few words and phrases of their language; this may be of use in the tavern, but how can I have a serious conversation with anyone. I must get to the sea, to a port. I'll talk to Sabina's father. I can understand him, though with some difficulty. He will help me take a ship for Italy. I'll do it first thing in the morning.

I wake as the early morning sun paints orange and yellow streaks on the ceiling. I rise. Outside, the warmth of the sun on my face is comforting. After a simple breakfast at the bakery, I follow the dusty streets to Sabina's house. She answers my tap at the door, barefoot, dressed in her sleeping gown. I have come too early. I try not to stare at her. I ask to speak to her father.

'Antonio? Parles Antonio?' I try to ask her help, but I can only stammer. Grasping my filthy shirt, I ask her where I may buy clothing. 'Ubi emere vestimentum?' I pull my ragged beard. 'Tonsorem?'

'I'm not sure what you're after, Marcus. Do you like, need a laundry?' She motions as though washing clothes.

'No, no. Emere. Tabernam.'

Scratching her head, Sabina turns her head to shout into the house, 'Dad! Can you come here for a minute?' She turns to me. 'Just calling my Dad.'

He comes to the door. 'Sabbie! Put something on. My goodness, you young people. Who have you got there? Oh, it's young Marcus.' He joins me on the porch and shakes my hand. 'Buongiorno, Marcus. Come stai?'

'Bene, bene.' I nod. He asks how I am enjoying my stay at the Imperial. Before I can construct a reply Sabina re-emerges clad in a pink robe, tied at her waist.

'Dad, did you find out what he wants? I think he's lost his clothes or something.'

'Perche stai visitando, Marcus?'

With gestures and broken Latin, I convey my need for clothing and a shave.

'He is asking where he may buy clothes. And he's desperate for a shave.'

'Oh! I bet his luggage was stolen. Ask him if that's what happened to his stuff.'

Antony asks if I was the victim of a robbery.

'Yes,' I reply without elaborating.

'I knew it. Oh Dad, I could take him shopping! Could I, Dad? Please?'

'Sabina, my darling,' Antony replies with patient exasperation, 'you may take the young man to the shops. After you've finished your breakfast and brushed your hair.'

'Yay! I'll be right out, Marcus,' she squeals and disappears inside.

'Sabina ti porterà a fare shopping. Lei uscirà a breve,' Tony says. Great! Sabina has volunteered to escort me shopping. 'Caffè?' he asks.

'Coffee? No, I eat already. Gratias, Tony.'

I'm offered a seat on the porch, and Tony sits next to me. He tells me there are few clothing shops in town for men, but they are of good quality. I nod and try to tell the real reason I have come here. I ask him if it is far to the sea here. 'Tony, ad mare, longene?' He looks at me.

'Ad mare? L'oceano? Molto lontano da qui. Very far.'

'Dies iter? Quem portum proximum Quilpie?'

Before he can tell me where the nearest port to Quilpie is, Sabina bursts out with half a slice of bread in her mouth, a handbag on her arm, and pushing her feet into her shoes. She looks charming in a simple floral print dress.

'Come on, Marcus. Bye Dad!' She pulls my arm and we fly down the steps.

'Don't I get a kiss?' calls out her father. She runs back and kisses him on the cheek. 'You be back for lunch, you hear.'

It is a bright sunny morning. There is a gentle breeze, very welcoming as the heat builds. It brings the scent of the bush with it: dry earth, and gum trees. Sabina is bubbling with excitement. She talks rapidly with scarcely a breath between her words. Which is both cute and convenient since I understand nothing she says.

'I'll take you to Jill and Suzanne's—they have great stuff there, but maybe not so much for men's clothes. Oh! You should get some western wear, so you fit in better. Of course, Brooks! They can set you up there. Then we'll have to go to the chemist to get you shaving stuff. This will be fun! I've never gone shopping with a guy before. Well, except my brother. But he doesn't count.'

On she chatters. I can do little more than nod and agree with her every second or third sentence. She is so full of youthful energy. We enter the shop of a clothing merchant, called Brooks. It is quite sizeable but a little musty and ill-lit.

'Let's get you some jeans first. Here, this way.' On the wall are shelves stretching to the ceiling, bearing the blue leggings that nearly every man in this town seems to wear.

'What's your size, Marcus? I'm guessing you're a thirty-four.' She pulls out several pairs of trousers, which they call 'jeans', and hands them to me. Working her way down the aisle, she piles more and more onto my arms. 'Okay that should do it. One of these is bound to fit. Shirts next. Over here.' On shiny metal racks are dozens of shirts, some plain, some in colourful patterns. The girl flips through them, weighing up their merits. 'No. No. Maybe. Yuk! No, no ...' At length she pulls one out and throws it over my arms. Onto the next rack, she continues to flick through the racks of shirts. 'And this is gorgeous! What size are you? You're probably a large. Wait, here's a large.'

Soon I am struggling under the weight of a dozen garments. When I protest, she finally gives in. I'm led to a tiny, mirrored cubicle, where I'm evidently meant to try them for fit. I find the shirts close-fitting for my liking, but they are cut from fine, soft cloth, and feel good on the skin. I emerge wearing each piece in turn, to face Sabina's thoughtful judgement. A pair of jeans, and three shirts are found to be satisfactory. When I reach for my old clothing, she stops me.

'You don't need to wear those old things. What you've got

on, you can wear out.' Before I can argue, she looks at my feet. 'Oh my God, those sandals! We'll get you some new ones. Let's get you some boots. Wait, I don't know what your budget is. Maybe we should get some regular shoes first.'

At the other end of the shop, we browse through the vast selection of shoes in styles I have never seen before. Eventually we agree on a pair that meets her fashion sense, and that I can walk in without pain. Finally, we are done. Or so I thought. Near the serving counter, a rack of fine leather coats draws me over.

'Oh Marcus! You should *so* get a leather jacket. Like this one. No wait, this one!' She pulls out a tan coloured jacket with rows of little leather tassels decorating it along the back, chest, and sleeves. 'This is western style. It's so you! You *have* to get this one.' I must admit, it is very smart and well cut.

'Beautiful is jacket. I buy,' I tell her.

'It's very cowboy. Wear it anywhere in country Queensland and you'll fit right in.'

At last, we bring our purchases to the serving counter, and the young woman counts it out for us. 'Two hundred eighty-four dollars, sir.'

'You *do* have money, don't you?' asks Sabina anxiously.

'Yes, money. Aussie dollar.' I produce my roll. Sabina picks out six of the large yellow bills. The clothing is wrapped in paper, the bag handed over, and at last the shopping ordeal is over. Back on the street, I feel awkward in these clothes and am certain everyone I meet will ridicule me. I look down at my clothes, and struggle to put together a few English words I've learnt.

'Sabina, I am, how you say, stultis.'

'Huh? You don't like your clothes? You look perfect. You fit right in. When in Rome,' she says.

'When in Rome?'

'Do as the Romans do! Surely you've heard that expression.' I shake my head. 'Anyway, you look great. You are a true Aussie boy now.' She looks at my face thoughtfully. 'But you do look a bit, you know, *yeti*. We must find you a razor. To the pharmacy.'

Down the road, we enter a sort of apothecary. It is lit with harsh white light, its shelves full of strange little jars and boxes. At the rear of the shop, men and women move about in white robes. It is beyond Sabina's ability to explain what all these things are for. She sees me puzzling over a rack of little boxes, each bearing the picture of a woman in all manner of hair colours. With words and gestures she explains these are potions for dyeing one's hair. If the women back home only knew of these concoctions. What a fortune could be made if this secret could be brought back home! With help from an assistant, I obtain a packet of blades and soap, then our expedition is complete.

'Thank you, Sabina,' I tell her, using one of the few phrases I have mastered.

She takes my hands in hers. 'It was my pleasure, Marcus. I had fun. Besides, you're no stranger.' I kiss her on the cheek, which takes her by surprise. 'Cheeky boy, aren't you! I gotta go, Dad gets angry if I miss lunch. Would you join us for dinner tonight? Say, about six?'

I cock my head, trying to understand her. 'Dinner? We eat?'

'Yes, that's it! Dinner.' She motions as if eating. 'Six o'clock. Okay?' I nod, stupidly. 'Great. See you tonight.' She bounds away. A happy warmth fills me. I *knew* she likes me. Didn't she say 'beautiful' many times? And to take me around town marketing? She must like me.

That evening, I reach Sabina's house just after dusk. She is standing on the porch waiting for me, her arms folded. She is barefoot and still wearing the pretty print dress.

'Marcus! I was worried you weren't coming. Didn't we say six? Or don't you have a watch? Or a phone? It's a dinner date, not breakfast.'

'Sabina, bonum nocte.'

'Oh, look at you.' She looks me up and down, then caresses the leather of my new jacket. 'Obviously, someone with taste picked these out.' She turns and shouts into the house, 'He's here, Mum!'

Shirley greets me at the front door. 'Marcus, don't you look nice! Love the jacket. Please come in.'

The meal is already prepared, and we take our places at the table directly. Shirley brings out a fine joint of lamb, exquisitely seasoned with rosemary and mint, with vegetables on the side. We tuck in with a will. In the middle of the meal, a burst of strange noises comes from Sabina's lap. She pulls out a small black slab, just like the one the farmer had used. She begins speaking into it.

'Sabina! No phones at the table,' admonishes her father.

After gazing at its face for a moment, she returns it to her pocket. What are these things? Does everyone carry one?

Her father compliments me on my new garments. I tell him Sabina is to thank for the tasteful choices. She happily recounts every minute of our excursion, pausing only briefly to take a mouthful of food. Tony raises his hand to interrupt her. He asks me politely how I came to lose all my possessions.

'Tony! Don't ask him that,' says Shirley. 'Not entirely our business, dear.'

'It's all right, darling. I'm just curious. I imagine he was robbed. Marcus, immagino che tu sei stato derubato?'

'Si. Derubato. In Roma.'

'He says he lost everything in Roma. Maybe he was working on a cattle station there or something. I'll ask him. Marcus, lavorando in Roma?'

'No.' I want to tell these good people the truth, but they wouldn't believe me.

Sabina notices my discomfort. 'Don't press him, Dad. There's no need to be nosy.'

Over dinner, I learn from her father that their family has been in Quilpie for three generations. Sabina's grandfather first came to the area from Italy to raise horses, 'in the fifties'. I learn Sabina has a brother Alessandro, studying law at a university in a city called Sydney, far away to the south. A lucrative profession, though according to my father, a lawyer is merely a hired gentleman who rescues your estate from your enemies and keeps it for himself.

We push our chairs back, comfortably full. I ask Sabina to

teach me the words, in her language, for items on the table. Some I find are not dissimilar to our Latin words. Butyrum, here is called butter. Plate is the same in Latin and in their language, which I learn is called English. The whole family joins in, eager to teach me more. They are very amused at my attempts to pronounce the more difficult words.

Sabina is quick to pick up many Latin words as well, and Tony sometimes helps when we are at an impasse on a particular word. It is not difficult to pick up the words for objects, but their grammar remains baffling. Still, the family is pleased when I use a few English words. My rendering of 'please pass the milk' attracts a little cheer from everyone around the table.

'His head is full now, too many new words will give him a headache,' says Tony, as he rises from the table. Shirley begins to clear away the dishes. Sabina asks me to visit her in her room.

'Get those dishes cleared away first, young lady,' her mother says firmly.

'And mind you keep the door open,' calls out her father.

'Tony!' says her mother. 'Yes, listen to your father.'

'You're drying,' says Sabina, throwing me a towel.

As we wash up the dishes, we continue the language lesson. She hands me a cup or a knife to dry and I try to name the object correctly in English, while she names it in Latin. I am better at this game than she is, and she playfully splashes dishwater on me. I flick the water from a spoon on her, which makes her shriek.

'Are you nearly done there, children?' asks her mother from some unseen place in the house. We grin at each other and resume our chore. Soon the job is done, and she leads me to her bedchamber.

Along one wall is a simple desk, against the other her bed is covered by a white blanket embroidered with butterflies. At the back of the room is a large window through which I can hear crickets chirping in the still night air. On the walls are prints of horses, and a faded picture of some hairy young men.

'Gladiators?' I ask.

'No, silly. They're a band. You know, singers?' She sings a few bars of an incomprehensible song. I take it they are musicians of some repute. 'Hold on, Marcus. Gotta call Lynn. One sec.' She draws the little slab from her pocket and fondles it with her fingers. She speaks into it as though she is having a conversation with it, just as I had seen others do. She talks for several minutes, then falls silent. She continues to fondle the device for some time.

I point to the little slab, and ask, 'What is thing?'

'Iphone 8. What do you have? Do you have Nokia or something?' I shrug my shoulders, not understanding. 'It's my mobile. Cellphone? Huh? You've *got* to be kidding! You don't know what a mobile phone is?' She covers her mouth with her hand. 'Wait, you're pulling my leg, aren't you?' She grips her left leg. 'Oww, my leg, my leg!' Seeing I don't respond, she rolls her eyes. 'I'm pretty sure they have phones in Italy. Don't you?' Before I can answer she jumps up. 'Wait, I have an idea. I'm going to use the translate app to ask you stuff! Why didn't I think of this before.' She taps her fingers furiously on the phone. 'I'll just test it out. Wait, I'll put it on speaker.' She speaks slowly into it, 'Your name is?' And the box speaks back!

'Il tuo nome è?' it says, mimicking a woman's voice. How amazing! Another of these people's astonishing gadgets! It appears to be asking my name. Sabina looks at me expectantly.

'Marcus,' I tell her.

She taps the box, again it asks 'Il tuo nome è?'

'Marcus,' I reply again, patiently.

She says triumphantly, 'It works. It works!'

She asks me simple questions like 'where do I live' and 'how old am I', by speaking into the box, and having it translate her question into a crude form of accented Latin, the same sort that Tony speaks. After a time, she asks if I want to ask *her* a question. What I'd really like to know, is are there are any people here who can speak my language.

'Quis enim Latine loqui?'

'Say it into my phone.' She holds it next to my mouth and I repeat the words. The box speaks.

'I'm sorry, I don't understand. Please rephrase or try simpler words.'

'So much for that idea. Stupid app. It doesn't understand your accent.' She fiddles with it for a minute. She asks me again to speak into it, but it does not understand any of my words. She flings it on the bed and gets to her feet. 'Anyway, I had *such* a fun day, Marcus.'

I take it this is my cue to depart. 'Thank you, Sabina. You … good woman.'

'Well, thank you too, Marcus.' After an awkward silence, I get up and take my leave. Passing the parlour, I convey my thanks to her mother and father, and they bid me good night. Out on the porch, Sabina says her farewells.

'Good night, Marcus. Loved having you over. See you soon, I hope?'

'Good night, Sabina. Yes, you see I soon.' She laughs and gives me a little kiss.

'Good night, funny man.'

Startled, all I can say is, 'Good night. Sabina.' She closes the door, and I slip into the night.

A week passes, then another. Summer is approaching, which baffles me, as it must be November by now, when it ought to be getting cooler. Each day is a little warmer, but the nights are still pleasantly cool. I spend my time exploring the town and its surrounds, talking to people at the tavern and in the eateries, learning their language as best I can. I truly admire these people, their kindness, their outgoing nature, lack of formality, and their fabulous technology.

Their phones, I eventually learn, are used to speak to another person at a distance. Sabina showed me many more of their incredible gadgets. A radio that produces music from thin air, and a box that shows moving pictures! It left me quite astonished; it is beyond my capacity to understand how these things work.

I visit Sabina on a few occasions in the late afternoon after her lessons, sometimes taking a meal at her home. I feel they are growing fond of me. On the weekend, Sabina and I have lunch together in the town; we take in such amusements as the little town offers.

One hot afternoon I surprise her by meeting her at the school gate. She is slowly walking with two of her classmates, all garbed in school uniforms. They are gossiping animatedly, and she doesn't see me until they are almost upon me.

'Marcus!' she shouts, giving me a warm hug. Noticing her wide-eyed companions, she straightens. 'What are you doing here?'

'I give to you, surprise.'

'Well, you certainly did.' One of her friends, a petite girl with reddish hair, looks from me to her, and holds out her palms.

'Well?' she asks impatiently.

'Sorry. Bec, Alisha, this is my friend, Marcus. Marcus, this is Bec and Alisha.'

'Hey, Marcus,' they say in unison, looking me over.

'Hello. I am happy meeting with you young womens.' They hold back giggles.

'Young *women*,' Sabina corrects.

'Soo, is this your cousin or what?' Bec asks.

'No, he's not. He's a, a friend. We met at the races.'

'Ah.' Bec and Alisha look at each other, nodding.

'He's from Italy. He's staying in town for a while.'

'Oh really?' says Alisha.

'Perhaps, Sabina, I could walk you to your home?' I ask.

'Of course, Marcus. That's decent of you.' She waves to her

friends. 'Gotta go, girlfriends. Later.'

'Ciao, Sabina,' says Alisha, still studying me.

'*We* should take up riding,' says Bec.

The sun is hot, and we try to keep to what little shade there is.

'Would you like to carry my books?' she asks.

'Yes. Yes. I carry.' I should have thought to ask. *Dumb, Marcus.*

I swing her backpack over my shoulder. We talk of her day in school, and her lessons. We arrive at her home. Looking into the distance, she asks, 'Say Marcus, have you been to up Baldy Top?'

'Baldy Top?'

'It's a mountain just outside of town. Well, not really a mountain, just a big rocky hill. Great spot to watch the sunset.'

'I not understand.'

'We go for walk. Up mountain. Yes?'

'Yes, angel. I walk with you.'

'Great. It will be fun. But it's a bit hot now. Let's wait a while. Have a seat, I'll get some drinks.' She takes the backpack and disappears inside the house. I take a seat on the porch. A moment later she returns with tall glasses of a sort of sweetened lemon juice, which is very refreshing.

'What name, this drink?' I ask.

'Lemonade. Nice, eh? Especially when it's hot. Which is like pretty much all the time in Quilpie.'

We chat for a time, then fall silent. I have the urge to take her hand in mine, and do so. She looks up at me and kisses me on the cheek. We while away the next hour, chatting in broken sentences, resting, and holding hands.

'Let's go,' she says. 'Sun's not so hot now.' She ducks inside to get a bottle of water. We set off in a direction I have not been before. We leave the town behind and follow a dirt track to the west. After a half mile, a rocky outcrop comes into view, rising steeply from the flat. 'That's it there. Pretty, isn't it?'

With the late afternoon sun drawing shadows on the red landscape, the rock is indeed beautiful against the deep blue sky. We reach the foot of the hill and begin to ascend a marked trail. It follows a gentle slope, winding its way around the rock. A few gum trees have found a footing. We pause under one for a drink. We resume the climb, and soon reach the top.

'We made it! How about that view!' Sabina says.

I take in the panorama. To the east, the town is visible, the streetlights just starting to come on. Nearby is another rocky hill, larger than the one we're on. Away to the west, nothing but scrawny trees and red dirt as far as the eye can see.

'Quilpie, is very far from other place,' I say.

'You got that right. Up here, seems like ours is the only town in all of Oz. I wish … well, I wish we lived in the city. It's so dead here.'

I shake my head. 'No, no. City bad. Dirt, noise. Thieves!' She looks up at me but doesn't reply. At the summit are a few timber tables and viewpoints marked with iron railings. There are a handful of other people here, mostly couples and a few teens, like Sabina, in their school clothes. Sabina sits on the railing and beckons me to sit beside her. After a long silence,

I ask her about her school friends. 'Your *amico*—friends, I mean, they seem to be quite, um, curious.'

She smiles at last. 'Yeah, you could say that. I hadn't told them about you yet.'

We sit in silence. The sun is getting lower; the softening light turns the rocky crags a warm orange. The trees on the plain turn a dark olive and their shadows lengthen. The sun sinks into a thin layer of cloud.

'Wow,' I say. A useful word I learnt recently.

'Wow is right,' says Sabina softly, staring at the sunset. We watch in silence as the sun turns into a flaming red ball. The clouds turn pink, then yellow, then grey in turn. Suddenly the sun is gone and twilight is upon us.

'Come, Marcus. I'll show you something.' Sabina leads me to one end of the summit, and clambers down into a shallow gulch. There is an aged tree, its leaves sparse on its twisted branches. 'Here, come around this side. See?' She points up at the trunk, where letters have been engraved. They are just visible, obviously having been carved years ago. "Tony + Shirley" it reads.

'Your mother and father?'

'Yep. Dad showed it to me. He carved it there when he and Mum were dating. A long time ago. Like, last century. He told me there would never be anyone else but Mum. Isn't that sweet?' I nod.

'They love each other still,' I say.

'Yeah, I guess they do.' She pauses. 'I'll show you something else. Look down here.' She points to another inscription, just legible. 'See there. S-a-b-'

'Sabina! Your name.'

'Look closer.'

'Sabina and—there is no other name.'

'Yep. I carved my name and left a space. For the man I will fall in love with. Foolish, eh?'

'No! Non stultis. Not foolish at all. You are … romantic.'

'Yeah, I guess. I doubt I'll ever find someone to love. I mean, here, in Quilpie?' She closes her eyes and shakes her head.

'But you will! There is someone for you. Someone, somewhere.'

She smiles. 'Really?'

I take her hand. 'Of that I am certain, by the gods.'

'I hope you're right.' She looks intently into my eyes. I move towards her and our lips meet. 'Marcus …' she says, holding me close.

I kiss her passionately. 'Sabina, I—'

She smiles and kisses me again. We look away, awkwardly.

'Let's go, we gotta be back by dark.' I follow her back to the main path, and we join the other people making their way down. We reach town just as darkness falls. Sabina takes my hand in hers. I look at her and smile. We walk to her house in silence, hand in hand. When we arrive, Tony is there watering the garden. Sabina quickly lets my hand go.

'Hi Dad,' she calls.

'Hi darling. Marcus, come stai?'

'Very good, Tony.' He nods and continues his chore.

'Well, bye Marcus.' She gives me a quick kiss, hurries

inside. Her father looks at the door then at me. I wave and hurry home.

A few days later, Sabina tells me, with joy, that school is nearly finished for the year. She also tells me that her brother Alessandro will be returning home from university soon. Their parents long to see him and speak of him often. He arrives on the appointed day, and I am invited to dine with the family.

He is tall, bony, long haired, and badly dressed with trousers full of ragged holes. He is close to my age, but cocky and pays me little attention. I was introduced as Sabina's boyfriend, which amuses him.

'A little kid like you! A boyfriend! Sick,' were his only comments.

Later that week, I am permitted to take Sabina to the town in the evening with Alessandro and his friends. Alessandro, whom they call Alex for short, soon grows tired of our company. Aware we are keen to be alone together, he leaves us.

'Pick you two up at nine, from Kelly's. Keep out of trouble.'

Kelly's is a small restaurant on the edge of town, whose specialty is deep fried fish. We wait for our order of fish and chips at a table outside on the footpath. Sabina tells me that she too will be leaving Quilpie soon in February, to begin her university studies at a town called Toowoomba. She will be learning animal husbandry at the college there. I am very pleased. She will make a fine farmer. I tell her I admire her courage, in studying in a faraway town.

'Do many women attend universities, in this province?'

'Of course we do! Equal opportunity. Well, in the cities, there are often separate boys and girls schools for younger kids. But not in the outback. How about in Italy?'

'In Italia, very few girls go away to study. Only, how you say, rich peoples. Many girls learn their letters, but little more.'

'How backwards. That's not fair at all.'

Her coming departure reminds me that I too must move on from this place. I remind myself I still have no idea how to get to the sea, to a port. When will I start my trek home, across the sea? The thought fills me with as much dread as hope.

CHAPTER VII

Over the next weeks, I live in reasonable comfort in the sleepy town. My new clothing lets me move about as a local, and my money is holding out. My English is improving. I know the words for a great many things. One day Sabina will teach me the names of animals; another day, the colours; another, the parts of the body. It pleases me that many words come from Latin, though they pronounce them differently. But constructing sentences in English still gives me difficulty. Their language is plagued with silent letters, irregular verbs, and a vast number of synonyms – for half a dozen words can convey the same meaning or nearly the same, and the subtle differences escape me.

It is quite incredible, that the language spoken by the people of Britannia has spread to this far corner of the world. Sabina tells me that Australia was first peopled by black men, like those I met on my first day in the desert. And that British people came to Australia in sailing ships, 200 years ago, to these shores, to establish colonies. Who would guess the barbarians of Britannia could colonise faraway lands! Just as Rome spread its colonies around the inland sea. She tells me that many of the first ships carried convicts, transported here for hard labour.

Sabina is eager to learn of my family and presses me often for details. She wants to meet my sister Valeria, and hopes she will come to Australia soon. Yet, I must remain vague on how I came to be in Quilpie.

One Sunday I am invited to dinner at Sabina's. I wash, shave, and put on one of my new shirts in my little hotel room. I must admit, the clothing is well tailored. In the mirror, I no longer resemble an unwashed barbarian. I could pass for an Australian. My wounds have long healed, and with the generous meals I've been taking, I have put on weight and look like a man again.

I putter about the room in the afternoon, watching through the narrow window the people coming and going. The sun sinks in the sky, and soon I hear clattering from the kitchen downstairs along with the smell of cooking. I wish to return Tony and Shirley's hospitality, so purchase a bottle of good red wine at the bar.

On the way to her house, I pass a second-hand goods shop, "Bric a Brac", the sign reads. The window is filled with old books, curios, clothing and costume jewellery. I really must get something for Sabina. I study each piece of jewellery. On a little shelf there is a bronze friendship ring, the sort with two clasping hands around the band. It is almost the same as one my mother had for years, though this is worn and tarnished.

The shop door bursts open and a woman emerges. She reaches for a paper sign hanging in the window and flips it over to read "Closed".

'I'm sorry, just closing up,' she says. A set of keys jingles in her hand.

'Please. I buy that ring. I give you money now?' I quickly pull out a wad of notes, the sight of which causes her to hesitate.

'What are you after?'

I point to the rusty old ring.

'That one?' she asks.

'Yes, that one. With hands.'

'It's unique, isn't it? I've never had one like that before. A man from Perth came through last year with a tin of old jewellery. Sold me the whole box for a song. Anyway, if you want it, twenty dollars.' I hand over the money. She quickly ducks inside, and in a moment brings out the ring, packed in a little cloth bag. 'Cheers. Have a nice evening.' She locks up and disappears down the street.

At Sabina's, a large joint of meat has been roasted, as is their habit on a Sunday. I can smell grilling beef before I even enter the house. My gift of wine is warmly accepted by Shirley, and we pass an agreeable evening.

After Sabina and I wash up, we sit outside on the porch on the tattered old couch. I reach into my pocket and draw out the little cloth bag.

'Ooh, what's this Marcus? A present?'

'Yes, sweet one. A gift for you.'

She pulls out the ring. 'Oh, it's gorgeous!' She slips it on her little finger. It fits snugly there.

'It is a ring, for friendship. I bought at the town, but I am sure it was made by a Roman. It is our style.' She examines it closely.

'It's two hands holding each other. Aw, that's so cute! Thank you.' She reaches out and gives me a long tender kiss. I am suddenly tongue-tied. *Say something, Marcus.*

She holds her hand out and admires it on her finger. 'Oh, but I haven't got you anything, sweetie.'

'It is not necessary. Being with you, time together, is gift enough.' *Good one, Marcus.*

'Ah, aren't you Joe Poet. You're starting to grow on me.' She moves towards me, and we kiss passionately again. Although it is wonderful, it leaves us both at a loss for words. We look away awkwardly. I begin to fidget. I feel a need to change the subject. I take out a coin and show it to Sabina.

'Answer me this, Sabina. This empress Elizabeth, who's portrait adorns your coin. Is she Caesar now in your capital? Or a ruler in times past?'

She laughs. 'Caesar! Well, you *could* call her that. We just call her Queen Elizabeth.'

'Queen Elizabeth,' I repeat. 'She rules still?'

'Yep, she sure does.' I learn she has ruled for more than sixty years. I ask if she is a fair and just ruler.

'I guess so. But she lives so far away, we don't *really* get ruled by her. She lives in Britain.'

'Britannia?'

'Yes, Britannia. She is queen of Australia, officially. But we are ruled by a parliament now. You know, democracy?'

'Yes, democracy. An invention of the Greeks. Not proven to be a stable form of government, in any nation, according to my teacher. Does the queen has many sons?'

'*Have* many sons. Two I think, Charles and Andrew. Wait, and Edward too.'

'Are they great warriors? Have they proven themselves in battle?'

'I don't know! I think Prince Andrew was in the air force. Or was that Prince Edward? I'm not sure.'

'I am sorry. I ask too many questions.'

'It's fine. I know you're just curious. Marcus, so what about Italy? Who's the prime minister there these days?'

'I don't understand, prime minister?'

'Okay, who is Caesar in Italy now?' she rephrases.

'Tiberius, of course.'

'I thought it was Conti – wait, he went a while ago, didn't he?'

'Conti? Is he of the house of Claudius?' I ask. She shrugs. The conversation having run its course, I think about what I *really* wanted to ask her. I draw a deep breath and take her hand in mine. I ask what I need to know, more than anything else. 'Where are we?' She is puzzled by the question. 'Where is Quilpie? To what nation or province does it belong?' I repeat.

'You want to know where Quilpie is? You're in Queensland. Didn't you know that?'

'Queensland? Is this in Africa? Is it a great nation?'

'No, dopey, we're not in Africa! It's a state of Australia. I guess *you* failed geography. Come with me, I'll get the atlas.'

I follow her into her bedroom where she pulls out a small bound volume from the shelf above her desk. She leafs through it while I sit on the bed beside her. It is a collection of maps.

'Here's Australia.' She points to a map of an island, indeed labelled "Australia" in broad letters.

'So, Australia is island?'

'It sure is. The island continent. And look, there's Queensland.' She points to the north-eastern portion of the island. 'And this is Brisbane, so Quilpie is about here,' she points her finger near the centre of the page.

I have always loved maps. My father has an old map of the Mediterranean Sea and the surrounding lands, which I know by heart. I study her map keenly. Quilpie is certainly nowhere near the sea. But how big is this island, Australia? And which sea surrounds it?

'How far to go the sea?' I ask.

'To go *to* the sea,' she answers. 'Well from here, a long bloody way! About 900 kilometres, an all-day drive.'

'Kilometres?'

'You don't know kilometres? Surely Italy went metric long ago.'

'Metric?'

'Okay, okay. Mmm, about six hundred miles by the old measure.'

'Six hundred miles. Such a distance! So, this island where we stand is vast. Why in Italy, there no place more than seventy-five miles from the sea.'

'It sure is. Australia is the biggest island in the world. Or so they taught us in school. So, show me where's *your* home, Marcus.'

She hands me the volume and I flick through it, trying to find a map of any familiar place. At last, I find a page entitled "Europe". In the centre I clearly see the boot-like shape of Italy. Around it, the nearby lands have unfamiliar names. Gaul is now called France, and Hispania is called Spain. I see Britannia and its neighbour island, Hibernia, named Ireland now.

I trace my finger over Italy. Aquilea. Roma. Napoli. Sicily. Familiar names, thank the gods. Across the Adriatic, the land of the Greeks. And down here, Egypt. But where is this island of Australia?

'Where is Australia?' I ask, pointing at the page.

'I'll show you. It's not on this map. Hang on, there's probably a world map at the front.' She turns to the first page of the atlas. 'There. But it's too tiny. Wait, my brother's got a world map on his wall. Come with me.' She leads me into the adjacent bedroom. It is unoccupied, but clearly a boy lives here, judging by the clothes strewn about, the unmade bed, and the print of a partially dressed woman on the closet door. On one wall, a large map stretches nearly the width of the room.

'Here. A map of the whole world.' The whole world. I look it over carefully. 'There's Australia.' She points out Australia in the lower right-hand corner. 'And Quilpie is about here. And way over here, is Italy.' She points at a spot on the other side of the map. I draw closer to it. Just there, lies Italy, a tiny finger of land, but a hundredth the size of Australia!

I struggle to comprehend. If Italy is so insignificant, then Australia must be an immense island. If that is so, Italy must be *thousands* of miles away! Between myself and home is not a few days sail, but oceans and continents. Why, to return to Rome will take years of voyaging. I feel a choking feeling deep in my throat. I press both hands to the map, moving them over the vast distances. "Australia. Indian Ocean. Arabia. Rome."

'Marcus, are you alright?' I feel as though a noose is being drawn around my neck. At last, I know where I am. On the other side of the world! This can't be. How is this possible?

'No. No, it can't be true! How can I be so far from home?'

'Australia's a long way from anywhere, didn't you know that?'

'No, I was in Rome, just a few weeks ago. It can't be!'

'What? Are you okay, Marcus?'

'No. No! I will never get home now!' I try to control my breathing, but I cannot suppress the choking feeling. 'Perditus.'

'Huh? What's a perditus?'

'Lost. Lost! PERDITUS!' I repeat, over and over.

'Marcus, you're scaring me. What's the matter?'

'I have to get out of here.' I push past Sabina, into the hallway. Her father has come to see what the commotion is.

'Marcus, what are you doing?'

'He's just acting a little crazy, Dad,' says Sabina.

'LOST! I am lost!' I wail. I push Tony aside, rush through the open door and out into the night. I stop out in the street in the dark, gasping for air. I look up. The stars stare back at me, familiar shapes, but there is something wrong with them too. I *am* on the other side of the earth. Just as I prayed in the temple in the Forum. Could it be so? Why, the gods answered my prayers, by delivering me here! That is why the stars are upside down! And the sun—the first day, didn't I see the sun in the north? The world is upside down, and I am on the wrong side of it.

'Marcus?' I hear Sabina calling from her doorstep. 'Marcus, please come back inside.'

'I am sorry, Sabina. I must go.'

I run down the road leading away from the town centre. A truck suddenly appears on the highway, its lights blind me. I stagger off the road and cross an empty field. The dry scrub scratches at my legs. As I reach a large tree, an owl screeches at me. I drop to the earth and cower on the ground. It takes flight, circling above me for a moment, then takes off into the night, its huge wings beating the air.

I am never going to get home. The tears come, and I cannot stop them. *I'll never see my family again.* I fall to my knees. *Jupiter, Juno, and Minerva, I pray to you. Deorum mihi. Help me gods. Help me gods.*

I don't remember how I get back to the inn. Up in my room, I tear off my strange, foreign clothes. I lie awake in the darkness, unable to think of anything but my wretched state. That map of the world, just a sheet of paper, but what awful truth it holds. I am *thousands* of miles, oceans, and continents away from my home. And what of the owl that I startled? Was it bearing a message from the gods, telling me to go?

I spend a very uneasy night, in and out of sleep. I feel bad for leaving Sabina so suddenly. To run away, when she has been so sweet and kind to me, was an act of unforgivable rudeness. At first light, I dress, and I head for Sabina's house. I hesitate at the gate, which is still open from when I left it. What will they think of me? Will she refuse to see me? Will she accept an apology? *Stop it, Marcus. You cannot see the future.* With deliberation I knock on her door. Her mother answers.

'Marcus! Are you alright? When you ran off last night, we thought … We were worried about you.'

Her father pushes past Shirley to the porch. 'It might be time you moved on, son. I mean it.' He stands with his arms folded across his chest, his anger undisguised. Sabina hears the commotion, and comes to the doorway, in her nightdress.

'Marcus, meet me at the cafe at noon.' I nod.

'Goodbye, son.' Her father gently pushes the women inside and closes the door.

Later, true to her word, Sabina comes to the cafe. She is in her jeans and her favourite white lacy shirt.

'You look beautiful today, angel.'

'Just today?' she says cheekily.

'And every day.' I offer to buy her a coffee.

'I'd love one.' I am so relieved she is not angry with me. I ask her if we can go somewhere quieter. 'We go to river? Talk there?'

'Lead on, kind sir,' she says. I bring her to the little park with the willow trees, where I had seen the lovers meet that day. I sit atop one of the timber tables. She sits beside me and takes my hand. 'Marcus, what happened last night? Why did you run away? Were you sick?'

'No, I am not ill.'

I see the pain in her face. 'Did I say something? Are you angry at me?'

'No, no, not angry at you, Sabina. Just afraid. When you showed me the map, I learn how far I am from home. So very, very far!'

'Is that all! So, you are just homesick, then?'

'Yes, homesick.'

'Well, you know, they don't call Australia the land down under for nothing. We *are* a long way from anywhere, that's the truth.'

It is time to tell her. 'Sabina. I must tell you something. I must go home soon. To Italy.'

'You're going home? Oh, that is tragic! But if it's your home.' There is genuine sadness in her voice.

'Italy, my home. Domus meus.'

'Your home, of course. I knew you must go back *some* time. I understand that. Not that I like the idea. So, your visa is expiring soon? When are you thinking of flying?'

'Flying? What do you mean?'

'You know, taking a plane? A nice, cushy triple seven?'

'Triple seven?'

'Boeing? Surely you know about jet travel?'

'Jet? Nullo intelego.'

She eyes me suspiciously. 'Don't tell me you don't know what a *plane* is?' She pushes me gently. 'Get out! You're having me on again, aren't you? Marcus, you are so odd.' She meets my puzzled gaze. 'Maybe you aren't kidding, after all.' She studies my face, then looks away into the distance, shielding her eyes from the sun. 'Wait, there's one now. See the plane there?' She points to the sky, but I see nothing. 'Can't you hear it?' I *can* hear the very faint humming sound. 'There! See?' In the distance, high in the sky, a silver glint catches my eye.

'Plane? Flying machine?' I ask.

'Yes. Ha ha flying machine, what are you, from the twenties?' I follow the plane's course across the sky. It looks like a tiny silver dagger, knifing through the air.

'It carries people?'

'Duh! Yes, silly. It's a passenger plane. The only way to travel these days. Pretty much the only way to go overseas, anyway.'

It draws closer, and I can hear it. This machine must be driven by great engines, to hear it at such a distance. A flying machine! Are there no bounds to this people's ingenuity? I press her for details.

'It is made of iron, no?'

'Mmm, aluminium, I think.'

'So, very heavy then. Why does it not fall? What holds it up?'

'It's like, well, air pressure and, um, the wings they, well I don't know. It's the engines. They keep it flying. They're very powerful.'

'As I thought. These planes, they fly across the continents, across the seas even?'

'Yes, they can fly thousands of miles in one go.'

'Thousands of miles!'

'Of course. See how fast it goes?' True, the plane has passed from horizon to horizon in scarcely a minute. But how could humans survive such speeds!

'I think I prefer to take a ship.' I would not dare fly in one of those things. For don't the sky and the heavens belong to the gods, not mortal man? Would not the indignant gods swat these silver insects from the skies? I ask Sabina, 'These planes, does one ever fall from the sky?'

'Yes, once in a while, but we don't like to think about that. It's really a safe way to travel, especially long distances.'

'It will anger the gods, the sky is their domain, not man's. I could not do such a thing. It would surely bring a curse on me.'

She shakes her head with an exasperated smile. 'You are a funny man. Still, I shouldn't say that. There's plenty of people who are afraid to fly. So, tell me, when are you leaving? Going soon?'

'Yes, soon. But I need help from you to get home.'

'Oh Marcus, for sure! Are you short? Do you have enough money?'

I nod, 'Yes. I have money. I don't need money.' I pat my jacket pocket where my coins are still hidden. 'It's just that I don't know the way home from here. To take a ship to Italy, I must get to a port. Pray tell me, how can I travel to a port? Is there one in Queensland?'

'By ship! You're kidding, right? I mean, I don't think you can travel that way anymore. Well, I suppose you could go on a cruise ship or something. You know, like the QE2, but really, you ought to fly. We have an airport here in Quilpie, if you could call it that. More like a field and a shack. But there's flights to Mount Isa and Brisbane. From there, best you get to Sydney or Melbourne. You'd have the most options from there. Qantas has flights to Europe every day. Paris, London, Rome.'

'Quintus? Who is this Quintus?'

She rolls her eyes. '*Qantas*, not Quintus. It's an airline company.'

'I see. It matters not, for I won't take a chance angering the gods in one of those things.'

'Okay I get it, you're afraid of flying. My aunt Donna was afraid too. She had a panic attack on a flight to Sydney once and was never the same again. She'll only go by train now! It was so weird. Well, you'll have to get to Melbourne or Perth; there wouldn't be any ships going to Europe from anywhere in Queensland.'

'So, I go to Perth or Melbourne? And take ship there?'

'Yes. Well, I don't know for sure. I would say try Melbourne first. There's a huge port there. I know my grandfather landed in Australia there in the fifties. Yes, go to Melbourne and ask around at the harbour. Maybe a ship will take you to Europe.'

'Melbourne,' I repeat, 'to Europe.' At last, I have a destination, a plan.

After the exhausting conversation, we sit quietly for a time. The silence becomes too awkward, and I get up to go.

'Walk me home?' she asks. We amble through the town together but say little. Halfway home, she takes my hand, and we walk hand in hand the few blocks to the house. Her hand is soft and warm, a comfort to me. Just before the front steps, she pauses.

'Visit me before you go, hey? Promise, Marcus?'

'I promise.' She kisses me, and bounds up the steps, into the house.

Later that evening, I approach the little yellow house one more time in the darkness. Reaching the porch, I overhear Shirley and Sabina speaking, or rather shouting.

'But Mum, he's afraid to fly. You know him! He's lived a very sheltered life. He didn't even know what a mobile phone was!'

'More likely he doesn't have the money. That's why he doesn't want to fly.'

'But he said he has plenty.'

'He could be just boasting.'

'Or just being modest. I like him, Mum.'

I tap on the screen door. 'Salve, Shirley! Sabina. Tony!' I call out.

The shouting stops abruptly, and Shirley greets me. 'Please come in,' she says, somewhat embarrassed. I take a seat in the parlour. Sabina makes her appearance and, with her mother watching, embraces me briefly.

'Mum, you don't need to hang around.'

'Careful girl, remember whose house this is.' Shirley disappears into the kitchen.

Sabina talks quietly. 'Marcus, I'm allowed to see you, but not alone. Dad isn't so happy about us seeing each other. They think, well, you're a little bit crazy. As if I'm still a child! It's just stupid, I know. I can take care of myself. I'm old enough to have a boyfriend. I'm seventeen. Can you believe it!'

'I can. The duty of parents is to safeguard their children, and I am a stranger from a faraway land.'

She sits next to me on the couch. 'You're not a stranger. This is what I've been telling my father. I know you pretty well. I like you.'

'I like you too, Sabina.' Awkwardly I try to find the words. 'You are beautiful and charming. And full of kindness—'

'You think I'm beautiful, do you?' She flicks her head and swirls her hair.

'I do! You be good wife for young man.'

'Ha ha, Marcus, you crack me up.'

'Crack up? I don't understand.'

'Do you understand this?' She reaches behind my head, pulls me towards her lips, and we kiss. Her lips are sweet and soft.

'Sabina. I ....' I look into her dark eyes. She looks playfully up at me and wets her lips. I stroke her velvety hair, and kiss her again, this time longer. Words it seems, are not necessary.

'Getting awful quiet in there, you two,' her mother says from the kitchen. She clears her throat loudly before entering. 'It's almost dinner time, young lady. Have you done your homework?'

'Well, no but I don't have much, just my essay for Mrs. Long.'

'Well then, you'd better get started. And I want you to help me with dinner.'

'Mum!'

Sensing it is time to leave, I rise to go. I ask Sabina to meet me after her lessons at the little park tomorrow, and head out.

Soon after lunch I reach the park and wait for Sabina at my favourite spot by the river, under the willow tree. The day is fair with brilliant sunshine and puffy white clouds. I pull out the image of Juno from my pocket and set it on the table. I speak softly to the goddess, begging for courage, not only to say farewell to Sabina, but for my journey ahead.

'Hey sailor!' Sabina bounces up in her school uniform and backpack. She swings it off and flings it on the table. She greets me with a long embrace.

'Sabina, angel. I must tell you something.'

She draws back and brushes the hair from her face. 'Don't tell me. You're an axe murderer. I knew it.'

That takes me back. 'Funny. No, not a murderer. It's just, that it's time for me to go.'

'You're going home now? To Italy?' she pouts. 'I wish you'd stay. But I know, you have to go home too. I mean, to be with your family and stuff.' She holds me tightly. 'Oh Marcus, I'm going to miss you terribly! You are so wonderful and, well, everything.' A tear falls to her cheek.

'I must return to my home. I miss my family, my mother, my father and my sister. I'll leave for Melbourne tomorrow and begin my sea voyage from there.'

She brushes away her tears and squares her shoulders. 'Still afraid to fly? Well by ship it is, if you must. I suppose it will be scenic. All that water.'

'There is another reason I must go.'

She looks at me seriously. 'What is it, Marcus?'

'I have not told you everything about myself. About how I came to be here.'

'What, did you come by rowboat or something?'

'No. It's, well, I was caught up in some evil business back in Italy.'

'What business?'

'It started when this man, this powerful man, tried to take the farm from my father. How you say, extorquere?'

'Extortion? What, you mean like the mafia or something?'

'Mafia?'

'Never mind.'

'When he not sell farm to them, at low price, some men came to the house to do him harm.'

'Oh my God!'

'It was terrible. We are peaceful, law-abiding family. There is no more honest a citizen than my father. But that didn't stop them. The day men came, he not home. So, they seized me instead, as a hostage. They threatened to have me killed if he didn't give in to their demands. But they must have not been satisfied, for they took me away to Rome.'

'They kidnapped you! What did they do to you?'

'They handed me over to the Imperial guard on a phoney charge of treason.'

'You mean like treason against the mob? Did they hurt you?'

'I took a beating or two, but nothing serious. Considering I was destined to be executed, I am most fortunate.'

'Oh my God, Marcus! But you got away. How did you escape?'

'There were four of us imprisoned together. One of us, a big man from Gaul, attacked one of our guards, and in the melee that followed, I escaped with my friend Lucius. But they caught Lucius and killed him, while I got away.'

'Killed him! I can't believe it. What a close call. Is that why you're in Australia? So they won't find you?'

'No. I didn't intend to come here. Although I wished for it, I didn't expect the gods to answer my prayers and send me here.'

She looks up confused, then shrieks with a sudden realisation. 'Are people still after you? Are they going to kill you?'

'If officers of the Praetor find me here, they will take me prisoner and return me to Rome in chains. After I escaped, there is no doubt a warrant for my arrest.'

'Arrest? But you've done nothing wrong. That's awful. But surely you are safe here, no one knows you are in Australia?'

'Not a soul knows I am here. I am not even sure how I got here, except by the will of the gods.'

She shakes her head. 'What about your mum? Have you called her since you got here?'

'No, she hasn't got a phone. My mother, she …' I can feel tears in my eyes, as I recall her face when she called out to me as I rode away with the soldiers that horrible day. 'I don't know how to get word to her.' Sabina takes my hand tightly, and we sit in silence.

'Marcus, don't go back to Italy. The mafia or the Praetor,

whatever you call it, will catch you. And torture you again. Your life is in danger!'

'I know. Yet I must go, I cannot remain here. I must return, to learn the fate of my father, to help my mother and my sister. And to let them know I am safe. For they have heard nothing of me since I was taken.'

'Of course, I understand that. Why don't you call your parents? Or write them a letter? Surely, they can help you. They can get a lawyer and go to the Italian police. Wait, maybe that's a bad idea.'

'They have no phone and I cannot trust a letter, for I fear it will be intercepted. Government agents regularly seize letters from abroad. The emperor always fears conspiracies. They will know where I am and send soldiers to find me. Roman law reaches every corner of the world. They will stop at nothing to lay their hands on me.'

'I don't know what to say. I never imagined. I mean, I do believe you. Of course, I believe you.' Thank the gods that somebody does. 'So, you're lying low in Quilpie. Well, you're safe here in this dust heap. No one even knows where we are, no one in the city certainly.' She puts her arm around me. 'Poor Marcus. I had no idea you were in trouble. I am afraid for you. What if something terrible were to happen to you? I would feel awful, not knowing.'

'Yes, I know, my angel. But I must return home. Consider my family, they must be worrying about my fate too.'

'Yes, you must go, I see that. I can't believe you are mixed up in all of that. You are such a, well, naïve young man. I will miss you terribly. I mean, I never had a boyfriend before. Can I call you my boyfriend? You've been so wonderful to me. You must call me! Won't you get a phone? You could get a pre-paid. But I don't know if that will work overseas. But you can use a pay phone. You *better* call me when you get to Melbourne. Call me every day, okay? Or every week at least?'

'I will. I promise.'

'Marcus, I have something for you.' She reaches into her pocket, and from it hands me a little paper pouch.

'For me?'

'Of course for you, dopey!' Inside is a tiny golden ring. It just fits on my little finger. 'It's an elephant hair ring. See, there's hairs coiled around it. I got it at a market in Mount Isa.' Sure enough, there are tiny black hairs woven within the body of the ring, that show at various points around it.

'Hair, from the elephant?' I had thought these creatures mythical. As children, we learned of Hannibal and his army crossing the Alps with elephants, but none of my generation has ever seen one.

'Yep, it's the real thing. To help you remember me. Coz the elephant never forgets, right?'

'It fits well. I am pleased to have such a gift.'

'Consider it a friendship ring.'

'Yes. I understand. I love it.'

'I mean it's not like we're engaged or anything.'

'Thank you, my sweet girlfriend. It is a gift of love. I will treasure it always.' We kiss, and I fight back tears.

'How will you get to Melbourne, boyfriend?'

'I will take a bus. I inquired at the Imperial. It will take me to Melbourne, passing by Roma, Toowoobola and Dumbo. It will take two days, Lucy says.'

'I think you mean *Toowoomba* and *Dubbo*,' Sabina corrects.

We linger, knowing it is our last evening together. The sun begins to set, and we must go. We walk together, hand in hand in the warm evening. At her gate, Sabina embraces me.

'I gotta go to school tomorrow. I probably won't see you. You look after yourself. And come back to visit me! If you don't, I swear I'll come to Italy myself and track you down.' She chokes back her tears.

'Goodbye, Sabina. May the gods bless you with good fortune, my beautiful angel.'

She manages to laugh. 'May the gods give *you* good fortune too, my beautiful, quirky Marcus.'

'Sabina, dinner time. No dawdling now,' her father calls from the open door. I turn away and leave, unable to hold back the tears.

I take my last meal at the tavern in a quiet corner, not wanting to speak to anyone. Later, in my room, I pack my meagre belongings into a new backpack that Sabina had bought me. There is not much: a few sets of clothes, my razor and comb. I count my money. To pay my board and lodgings, I have had to visit the bank every couple of weeks, selling a coin to the man in the spectacles. When I offered my best coin, a freshly minted gold aureus of Tiberius as Pontifex Maximus, he could hardly contain himself. I managed to extract nearly $3000 for it; I overheard him tell his workmates this was a bargain price. A few days ago, I exchanged several silver coins, he was most keen to acquire them too. I now have more than three thousand dollars. I am sure this will be enough for a long journey.

If only sleep would come. I see my home, my family. I see Sabina with her darting brown eyes and carefree laugh. I miss her already. I see the dungeon, running for my life in the corridors, Lucius being attacked …

At sunup, I depart the Imperial, which has been my home for the last two months. I settle my bill and give my farewells to the kind people that run the place. Just outside the hotel, a sign marks where the bus will come. A handful of people are already here with their cases. Others arrive and I witness a few tearful farewells. I pace, unable to sit still.

The bus arrives with a roar and cloud of dust. I follow the others aboard. There are plenty of empty seats, and I take one by the window. It is very comfortable, even the air is chilled. After a few minutes the door snaps shut and the bus lurches forward. Farewell, Quilpie. I hold my hand up to the window.

CHAPTER VIII

The bus stops briefly in several little towns, nearly always just outside a small restaurant. Alas the quality of the food is highly variable. Many of the passengers on the bus doze off in the afternoon, and I join them.

'Roma! Next stop Roma,' the driver bellows, waking me with a start. Through the window I see we are in another Queensland town, not dissimilar to Quilpie. Roma! The new Rome. Surely it was my people that founded this place. If there are any Romans in this nation, this is where they will be.

The bus rumbles through the heart of the town. It is a larger settlement than Quilpie, with more substantial buildings, more road traffic, and less dust. There are many curious trees with bottle-shaped trunks lining the roads. At some crossroads, the bus comes to a stop behind a queue of cars. After a time, they continue ahead. The bus repeats this puzzling action at the next intersection, waiting to cross for no apparent reason. The driver seems to be observing a bank of coloured lights, displayed above each intersection. How civilized! I am impressed that everyone, in any sort of vehicle, obeys these signals regardless of whether there is any traffic or not. Our Roman cities would do well to copy this invention; at busy crossroads one takes one's life in one's hand to cross.

The bus finally comes to a halt at the town centre. Determined to explore, I grab my backpack and disembark. A few others end their journey here too, most are greeted by family members with warm embraces. Not I, alas. One by one the passengers drift away, and I'm alone in New Rome.

I look for a hotel. There is undoubtedly one nearby. It is mid-afternoon and hot but not unbearably so. A handful of shops occupy some antiquated buildings on the main street, but many have closed early, as is the case in country towns everywhere. There is nothing here that makes this town any more or less Roman than Quilpie. In the distance something catches my gaze, a tall, pointed spire rising high above the surrounding houses. I head towards it; perhaps I will find Romans there. I come to a vast building of weathered sandstone with a high vaulted roof of iron. At one end, a spire with a large bell hung inside reaches at least sixty feet in the air. It is quite unlike any building I've ever seen. It sits in a large, manicured garden with borders of flowers and more of the curious bottle-trees. A signboard reads "St. Paul's Church".

A wooden cross is fixed above the imposing timber door. How odd! For it looks exactly like the sort of cross used in our Roman executions. I back away, puzzled and slightly fearful. What is this place? A place where judgment is passed on criminals? A place of death? An elderly couple burst out the great door. As they pass, they call out to me.

'Peace be to you, young man.'

I return the greeting. 'Peace to you.' A few others file out too, all giving me warm greetings as they pass, which puts me at ease.

My curiosity overcomes my anxiety, and I try the heavy timber door. It is not locked. Inside, past a small foyer, I find myself alone in a vast, dimly lit hall filled with rows of timber benches. The only light is the diffuse sunlight coming through the tall windows, which are made of coloured glass. The sublimely beautiful windows show human figures and geometric designs. I pass down the broad central aisle. Below the windows, in little niches, are sculpted figurines. At the end of the aisle is a sort of altar, bearing flowers, candles, and a large book with a gilded cover. Above, on the back wall, another great wooden cross is fixed, with a life-sized figure of a man tied upon it. He is clearly dying—being crucified in the Roman manner, *Romani mortem*.

Is this a shrine to this man? Is he worshipped by these people? At his feet, an inscription in Latin, "Iesus Nazarenus Rex Iudaeorum". Who is this Jesus of Nazareth, called king of Judaea? I know that King Herod had long ruled over the province of Judea, but on his death it was divided among his sons. How curious for there to be a shrine to one of Judea's kings, so many thousands of miles away.

I examine the windows; they are a kind of mosaic, formed by many pieces of coloured glass held together by strips of lead. Each window comprises a scene of human figures. I recognize this bearded man, Jesus, in all of them. In one, he is addressing a mass of people; in another, dining at a great table with a dozen other men. In another scene he is stripped of his clothing and kneels before a judge in Roman garb. In the next he is crucified. What was this man's crime? Was he falsely accused, as I was? On a large painted panel, behind the altar, is a scene of Jesus in heaven with a halo around his head, and angels paying tribute. He is surely being deified. This must be his temple.

I feel uneasy. I know nothing of the gods of this land. They must surely be powerful, having blessed these people with such marvellous abilities and prosperity. I fear I may have insulted their gods, by trespassing in this temple. I drop to my knees before the altar and mutter my apologies. *Forgive me, Dominus Jesus.*

A door opens near me, and the dim temple is flooded with sunlight. An elderly man in a white robe enters. He sees me kneeling and greets me.

'Bless you, young man, may God hear your prayers.'

I stand. 'Good evening, sir.'

'I apologise for interrupting a man at prayer. You're welcome to join us for mass tonight at 8 pm, or tomorrow morning at 11 am. Are you just passing through Roma?' There is kindness in his voice.

'I am from Italia. Marcus, from Campania.'

'Ah, buongiorno, Marcus. Parlo un po' di Italiano.' He is speaking the same dialect as Sabina's father, which I can make out with difficulty. 'I am Father George.' He holds out his hand. 'I learnt some Italian when I studied at the seminary in Rome, many years ago.' A man who has been to Rome! I ask him in Latin if he has lived in Italy.

'Pater George, nonne habitas in Italia?' This startles him. He looks at me closely.

'Did you address me in Latin, son?' he asks. 'Mi hai parlato in latino?' he asks haltingly.

'Latine loquor!' Yes, I do speak Latin!

'How extraordinary. Ita me—No wait. Ita me paululum Latinae.'

So, he does speak Latin too. I fire questions at him. Where is this place? Are there other Roman citizens here? Why is it called Roma? But I speak too fast for him, and he shakes his head, uncomprehending.

'Loqui tardius,' he tells me.

'Yes, I will speak more slowly.' *Marcus, calm yourself.* I tell him my name, and that I am a Roman citizen.

'Marcus Junius Corvus vocor. Romanus sum civus. Cogitesne?'

'Yes, I understand you, a little,' he answers in English. 'My Lord above! I haven't heard a man speak Latin like that since I studied in Rome. Not long after the war. But you speak it so well! Did you go to Oxford or Cambridge? Tell me, wherever did you learn to speak Latin?'

'From my mother and father, of course.'

'A clever child you were. Were your mother and father scholars?'

'No, agricolae. Farmers.' I tell him my family has been raising horses for years, since the time of the Republic.

'I am honoured to meet a traveller, so far from your home,' he replies.

'Father George, are there Roman people here in this town? I must know. Please. Are my people here?' He seems confused.

'If you mean Italians, then yes there are a few families. Many come to hear mass here. But I am not sure if they are all from Rome, particularly.'

'Does anyone else speak Latin here?'

He smiles. 'Oh, I would doubt that. Long gone are the days when all students studied Latin.' This place is evidently not an outpost of the Empire, as I hoped.

'Please, Father George. Why is this town called Roma? Was it not founded by Romans?'

'No, Marcus, not at all. It is named for the wife of Governor Bowen, Lady Diamantina, whose maiden name was Di Roma.' He shrugs when he sees my crestfallen face. 'Sorry to tell you, but no Romans founded this place.'

'I understand. Thank you. I am sorry.'

'Don't be! For any of us, there's always more to learn.' I try a new tact.

'Father, have you been to Roma, in Italy?'

'Oh yes of course, many years ago, as I said.'

'And you learnt to speak Latin there?'

'Yes, it was mandatory at the seminary. You know, for the liturgy and all that.'

'Who was your teacher? What school? Was it at Gaius Fruggi's academy?'

'Well, I don't remember. I had many teachers. I even met Karol Wojtyla there one year. I was studying for the priesthood.'

'Did you preach at one of the great temples in the Forum?'

'No, but I served for a short time at Santa Maria Maggiore.'

I haven't heard of any temple by that name. 'Father George are you the high priest of this temple, in which we stand?'

'Yes. I am parish priest here, for twenty-two years.'

I point to the imposing cross and the man being crucified. 'Please, tell me about this man, Jesus, who was put to death. I am sorry, I am an ignorant barbarian. This man, was he king in Judea? Is he god, or man?'

'That is a complex question, son. I would say he is both,' he tells me, carefully choosing his words. 'We know him and worship him as the son of God.'

'Son of which god?'

He smiles at this. 'The one God. The God of Moses and Abraham. The Christian God. His son Jesus walked the earth ages ago. He was a great prophet, healer, and saviour. He was crucified under Pontius Pilate and ascended to heaven.' His words explain well the scenes that adorn the temple.

'Crucified under a Roman? This Pilate, was he governor? Under Herod of Judea?'

'Yes, that is so. You do know your Bible, after all.'

'And when was this? Under Augustus? Or our Tiberius Caesar?'

'Well, according to scholars, under the reign of Tiberius.'

I understand now. This Jesus must have been recently martyred, and his followers have raised this temple to him. I've heard the peoples of the eastern nations are known for their unusual religions and cults, many of which have found followers in Rome. Why just last year, a group of troublemakers following the Egyptian cult of Isis had to be expelled from our province.

'Father George, are there many temples dedicated to the worship of this man, who is the son of your God?'

'There are. In every town in Australia, pretty much.' I don't remember seeing one in Quilpie.

'Do all Australians worship him?'

'Well, they used to. But not so many today, as there once was. Some worship Buddha, or Mohammad, or the Hindu gods. And sadly,' he shakes his head, 'many worship no god at all.'

'Your God must be all powerful. Has he not given your people such wonderful skills: to tame lightening, to move about in cars, to speak to each other at great distances.'

'Well, I hadn't thought of it that way, but that's true, we are very blessed here.'

'Do any men here worship the gods of Rome? Jupiter? Juno? Minerva?'

He laughs. 'No, not anymore.'

'Tell me Father George, why did you learn Latin, the language of my people?'

'Part of my priesthood training. Latin has been the

language of learning and scholars for centuries. The liturgy of the Catholic Church gave up Latin only in the last century. By which I mean the rites we say in this church.'

'And you learnt Latin as a young man?'

'As I said, I studied in Italy. When I was training to become a priest. But hardly anyone speaks Latin in Italy now, outside the clergy and better universities.'

This troubles me. 'You studied at Rome when you were a young man? So, you were resident in Rome at the time of the Julius Caesar, Marcus Antony, and Pompey the great? Did you ever see these great men?'

He furrows his brow. 'Marcus, are you mocking me? Do you think me a fool?'

'No sir! I have great respect for priests, of any temple. I just want to understand your ways, your religion. And to find other Romans like me.'

'Marcus, Julius Caesar has been dead for over two thousand years.'

'Now you are mocking me, sir! Why say you that? I was at Rome not three months ago, where Tiberius himself was at the Colosseum, presiding over the Games.'

'Tiberius, the *Roman* emperor?'

'Tiberius Caesar Augustus. Son of Livia, and adopted son of the great Augustus. Is there any other Tiberius?' He shakes his head and runs his hand through his thin white hair.

'Son, I don't know how you come to believe that Tiberius Caesar is still alive. Perhaps you are having a good joke at my expense. Yet I see honesty in your face. Perhaps people have been telling you these things and you have led a sheltered life. But let me assure you, Tiberius Caesar has not walked this earth for two thousand years. I have seen the mausoleum of the Julio Claudians with my own eyes in Rome, it fell into ruins centuries ago.'

Again, I feel my throat tightening. Caesar has been dead for 2,000 years? But he was slain in my grandfather's time, a mere sixty years ago. Surely this man would not tell me such a fabrication! I try to make sense of this. When I was dumped in the desert, could I have been unconscious for weeks, months, even years? I had once heard of a slave who, taking a blow to the head falling from a horse, slept for a month before coming to his senses. *But twenty centuries!?* I take the priest's arm tightly.

'Tell me sir, qui est imperator Romae nunc?' I ask again. 'Who is the emperor of Rome now? Who?' He flings off my arm and backs away, slightly frightened. 'I am sorry. I mean you no harm, Father George. Forgive me.'

'Think not of it, son. I see you are a little distressed. To answer your question, I don't know who the emperor is now in Italy, as you call him, they change their prime ministers so often. Conte, I think it was, at the last election.'

I am confused. 'And by your reckoning, what year is it?'

'What year is it, huh? Are you having me on again?' Seeing the pleading look in my face, he sighs and continues, 'It is AD two thousand nineteen.'

'AD?'

'*Anno Domini*. The Year of Our Lord.'

'Of which lord do you mean?'

'Lord Jesus Christ of course. The son of God who was crucified under Pontius Pilate.'

'The man-god to whom this temple is raised?'

'Yes. Young man, you have a very confused view of history. You seem to know a great deal about Roman history, yet I believe your teachers fooled you into thinking these things took place recently when they actually took place centuries ago.'

'That's impossible! I remember well my history lesson, being taught of our great heroes: Pompey, Caesar, and Augustus. Why my father, Gaius Junius Corvus himself was a patron of Tiberius Augustus and met him in person! He is a horse trader, and one time in Neapolis ...'

The priest shakes his head and waves his arms in disbelief. 'Okay. Let's not argue over it. Marcus, would you do me the pleasure of having tea with me? My house is just behind the church.'

'Yes, I will take tea with you.'

'Excellent. Come with me.' I try to calm myself. I follow him down a short path to his home, a small sandstone cottage behind the church. It is set in a pretty garden overflowing with vines and flowers. It is pleasantly cool inside. He beckons me to sit at his kitchen table. He sings intermittently while he prepares a hot drink of infused leaves. It has a bitter flavour, but I find it invigorating.

While we drink and take sweet biscuits, he asks me polite questions: where I live, about my family, and how I came to be in Australia. Though my English is poor, I can fill in the gaps with Latin words, which he seems to know and take great pleasure in hearing.

'Marcus, let me show you something.' He leads me into his library, the walls lined to the ceiling with books. After searching for a moment, he pulls one down. *Lives of the Twelve Caesars,* by Suetonius Tranquillus. 'Here. This volume is in Latin and English. It is a biography of the twelve Caesars: Augustus. Tiberius. Caligula. Claudius. Nero.'

'Did you say the *twelve* Caesars?'

'Yes, it just covers the first twelve emperors of Rome. But there were many more, over a hundred, I think.

'A hundred emperors!'

'Yes, until the Goths overran the empire and sacked Rome.'

I clap my hands over my eyes. 'Sacked Rome! The barbarians? When did this calamity occur?'

'I think it was around four hundred and ten AD.'

'AD? From the year of Lord Jesus?'

'Precisely.' He pulls out another volume, *The Decline and Fall of the Roman Empire* by a man named Gibbon. 'This book tells of ten centuries of Roman history, from the time of Trajan until the fall of Constantinople in the fifteenth century.'

'Fifteenth century reckoned how?'

'From the birth of our Lord, as before.'

The awful truth is coming to me. 'So, Tiberius really did reign two thousand years ago?'

'I swear by it. It is God's truth.' Father George hands me the volume of Suetonius. 'Marcus, please take this book, as a gift from me. I hope it will fill in the gaps in your knowledge of history.'

I leaf through the book. "An account of the life of Julius Caesar. An account of the reign of Augustus. Tiberius. Caligula. Nero. Vespasian." I flick through the pages faster and faster. It is as he says, a history of the Roman emperors, one after another, their reigns spanning centuries!

I think back to my dash through the Forum; it seems like an eternity ago now. What did I pray for? *Take me away. Take me away to the other side of the world. Take me a thousand thousand years away.* This is exactly what I prayed for. The gods answered my prayers. Not only I am at the end of the earth, but twenty centuries from my people, my time, my family. I am truly, hopelessly lost. I struggle for words.

I choke out, 'Thank you Father George, for answering my questions. I have learnt a great deal. But I am sorry, I must go. I go.' I thrust the book into my backpack and rush out of his home.

I pace about the grounds of the temple, unable to come to grips with what I've just learnt. I look through the book again. "Tiberius reigned for twenty-three years before his death at Capri, whereupon he was succeeded by Gaius, called Caligula, who ruled for six years ..." I squeeze my head in my hands and fall to my knees. Could there be a more awful truth. No wonder these people are so different! Their dress, manners, their language, their fabulous inventions—mortal man has had 2,000 years to improve himself. Twenty centuries to learn all the secrets of the universe! To harness fire and lightning, to project their voices and images over vast distances, to build flying machines. We Romans rose from barbarism and created a thriving civilisation, but what could we accomplish if we had 2,000 more years? Here I see the results in this strange and distant land.

This sun is setting now. I sit on a weathered timber bench, agonising over my fate. Mother, Father, Sister! I see your faces. I see the sun-soaked hills around our farm. The tears flow uncontrollably. *I am lost.* I will never see my home and family again. Anger grows within me. I pound the bench with my fists. 'Gods! Why? Why do you punish me so? Whatever have I done?'

In the dying twilight, a bird lands noisily on a branch above me. It is grey and brown, with the size and figure of a Kingfisher. It eyes me, cocking its head from side to side. I call out to it.

'What now, Kingfisher? Where am I to go? What is my fate? To die here, lost and alone, twenty centuries and thousands of miles from home?'

The bird cocks its head upwards and lets out a long, laughing cry. It stares at me closely again. It is mocking me. Is it laughing at my wretchedness?

'Laugh all you want!' I shout. 'I laugh at you! Where do you fish in this wretched desert? You are as lost as I am.' It raises its head and laughs again. 'What are you telling me?' Are you a messenger from the gods? Are you telling me to laugh despite my misery? If only I could. *Courage Marcus. Be not a coward. Whatever magic brought you here, can get you home.*

There is but one way home, I am sure. That is to return to Rome and once there to pray in the great temples of Jupiter, Minerva, and Juno. They sent me here, so surely my gods can bring me home, back to my world, my time! To the Forum, to Rome I will go. By the trio of the greatest gods I swear I will return to Rome or die trying.

I dry my tears, pick myself up, and fight the urge to wallow in self-pity. *One day at a time, Marcus.* The bird flies off into the darkness, calling loudly as it goes, and others match its mocking laugh.

CHAPTER IX

It is easy to spot the tavern at the centre of Roma, for it displays a brightly lit sign advertising beer and rooms. There are many people and cars around it. It is a welcome sight, as I haven't eaten for hours. At the entrance, there is a signboard bearing the image of a woman; it reads "Live Music—Fri–Sat–Sun. Camilla Robinson". I've seen the face before—it's the singer I saw in Quilpie.

I take a room, wash, and rest on the bed for a time. I think of my conversation with the priest. Did I imagine that? Was it a dream? He said Caesar has been dead for 2,000 years. I am no longer in the time of the emperor Tiberius, but far in the future. *My present is Rome's future.* It makes my head ache, and I cannot think. I lie in this little room, as if in a nightmare that I cannot awaken from.

Eventually, hunger drives my thoughts back to the present. This hotel is larger than the Imperial and has a separate dining room. But it is nearly empty, so I follow the sounds of people to the main bar. Here are a few dozen people engaged in animated conversation, like in any tavern.

I take a table in a corner. My meal takes some time to arrive, which is irritating as the place is not very busy. I down a large glass of ale and immediately order another. I am exhausted from my journey and traumatised by the revelation at the church. The drink soothes my troubled mind a little.

Camilla, the singer, takes the stage along with her guitar player and drummer. She is garbed in a provocative black dress. A few of the male drinkers whistle at her, but most of the patrons pay her little attention. She begins to sing. I cheer her performance loudly, which she notices and thanks me with a wave and a smile. When the band takes a break, she comes over and sits at my table, where I've just finished my meal.

'I know you. You're the guy with the weird get-up over in Quilpie.'

'Yes, I stayed at Quilpie. At the Imperial. You do singing there.'

'Yep, I do singing.' She looks me up and down. 'I see you you've hired a stylist. Looking good, young man.'

Not being sure what a "stylist" is, I change the subject.

'I like the way you sing. Your voice is very pleasing. And you are very beautiful.' Should I have said that? I suppose the drink has made me bold, or foolish, or both.

'Why thank you, nice of you to notice. Not many others in this bar seem to know I'm even here tonight. I'm Camilla.' She offers her hand.

'Yes, you are Camilla.' I close my eyes and wince for a

moment. *Idiot. As if I have never spoken to a woman.* 'I am Marcus. Where is your home, Camilla?' *Better. Keep calm and talk like a normal person.*

'I grew up in Mount Isa. Queensland born and bred. How about you? Getting the feeling you're from out of town.'

'I am Italian.'

'Oh really. You don't sound Italian. You have a funny accent, I mean, I like it. It's really sexy.' She smiles, and I catch her eyes, looking at me lustily. I start to sweat. *Why is it so hot in this room?*

'I speak the English poorly. But I learn.'

'Good enough for me. I'm just a country girl, no need for fancy words. Will you buy me a drink?'

'Yes, a drink. I will you buy a drink.' I jump up a little too enthusiastically. 'What is your desire?'

'How about a bourbon on the rocks?' I'm not sure what this is, but on repeating this to the bartender he nods and tells me he'll bring it over.

Camilla tells me a little of her life as a singer, visiting one town after another, all over Australia. When her drink arrives, she kisses me on the cheek.

'Thank you, sweetie,' she says. We clink our glasses together and continue our chat. I learn that the older man accompanying her on guitar is neither her father nor husband, but an acquaintance from her hometown of Mount Isa. She tells me the three of them have chosen to earn a living as musicians, rather than work in the mines there. To me, a reasonable choice, for mining is a slave's work. The guitar player appears behind her.

'We're on, Cam,' he tells her curtly.

She sighs. 'Gotta go, Marcus. Time for my set.'

'Yes, you must go. I will enjoy to listen.'

'Thanks honey. We'll talk later, I hope.'

The band resumes playing. The tavern is quite full now and has become very noisy; it is difficult to hear her sing. But she perseveres. So full of confidence! And she is very attractive. I order another glass and, engrossed in the music, watch the people in the bar. After a time, the musicians take another break and Camilla returns.

'Singing is thirsty work,' she says, picking up her glass and draining it. I ask her if she has ever been to Melbourne. 'Melbourne? Oh yeah. It's a big, big city, mate. A place that will eat you alive.' Before I can ask what that means, she is called away by a woman who appears to be the owner of the tavern. After a few minutes, the musicians again resume their playing. The serving girls, well trained by their employer, make sure my glass is quickly replaced as soon as it is empty. I drink far more than is good for me. I feel restless and bold.

At last, just after midnight, the music is finished for the night and the band say their farewells to the crowd. The room lights are turned up bright, and the musicians pack up their instruments. The patrons slowly disperse. I stand unsteadily and go out to the veranda. The cool air is refreshing, and the lights of the town are beautiful against the dark sky. I feel a gentle hand on my shoulder.

'Lovely night, isn't it, Marcus.'

'Good evening, Camilla. Yes, a beautiful night. I love your singing.'

'Thank you! I try my best. Even when I can count the number of people listening on one hand.'

'Do you go to your home now? You go to Mount Isa?'

'No, not tonight. The others are heading back, but I'm staying on another night. I'm doing a solo show tomorrow afternoon. You know, acoustic.'

'Ah, acoustic. I hope it's comfortable.'

She laughs. 'You are a funny man. Will you walk me to my hotel? Not safe for a lady to walk alone at this hour.'

'Yes, of course I will. I will be honoured.'

'It's this way, just a couple of blocks.'

I try to make conversation. 'Is it a profitable living, being a musician?'

'Ha ha, that's a good joke. Well, it's a living, but not a good one. We'll make six hundred tonight, but split three ways, two hundred bucks ain't much. And there's travel and accommodation to pay for.'

'Is it difficult, being far from your home?'

'Not really. Since I split up with my husband, I'm solo. The further away from my ex, the better.'

She is very talkative on the short walk to the Athena Inn. I am anxious to ask her about Melbourne, but can scarcely get a word in. The hotel appears to be quite luxurious, judging by the grand facade. It is flanked by stone columns, reminiscent of a Greek temple. In the lobby, a fountain, with a poorly executed statue of Athena. Camilla takes me by the hands.

'Marcus, would you like to come in for a little while? For a drink? I would be very pleased if you could join me. I mean, if you want to. Just for a little while.' She looks longingly up at me. Such a forward young woman inviting a man to her chamber! Sabina had told me that women here are not shy of talking to men. The honourable thing to do would be to politely refuse. Still, she is *very* attractive. What harm could it do? Just for a little while, like she said. She is probably lonely, being on the road all the time, and she hasn't yet told me about Melbourne.

Her room is well appointed with tasteful furnishings. A large, neatly made bed dominates the room, clothes are scattered about the bed and floor. She quickly picks them up and tosses them on a chair. She pours us both a drink from tiny bottles in a little bar in the room.

'I'll be right back. Don't go anywhere.' She disappears into the bathroom.

A guitar is resting against the wall; I pick it up. It is similar to a cithara, the instrument I am used to back home. I begin strumming, trying to learn how it is tuned. After a few minutes, Camilla emerges wearing only a white robe. She sits cross legged on the bed, opposite me. The sight makes me momentarily speechless. *What am I doing here?*

'Do you play? That's wonderful! Sing me a song. No one ever sings to me.' I take a few minutes to tune the instrument and begin to play an old song that my grandmother taught me.

'This is called *A Bird in the Olive Tree*,' I tell her. 'It is a tender song, about love.'

I begin to sing. 'Illic 'a oliva avis in ligno.' She smiles and sips her drink. I continue, struggling to remember the words and the chords. After many stops and starts, I get through the song. She applauds.

'That's beautiful, Marcus. Come here.' She pulls me to her, and suddenly she is kissing me long and passionately. I set the guitar down on the floor, trying not to break it. I was not expecting this. I am torn whether to resist her advances or give in. She kisses me again and pulls me on top of her as she leans back onto the bed. The warmth of her body, the sweetness of her lips is irresistible. I kiss her, long and hard. The door bursts open, and a man enters. He shouts at me as it slams shut behind him.

'Hey, lover boy! What the hell do you think you're doing!' It is the guitar player. He lets out a string of curse words, only some of which I am acquainted with. He drags me off the bed and punches me hard in the chest, flooring me.

Camilla shrieks, 'What are you doing! Leave him alone! He ain't done nothing wrong!'

'Maybe not, but you sure as hell have. Leave you alone for five minutes and this is what you get up to!'

'I thought you were going back to Isa tonight!'

'Change of plan, sweetheart. I can't believe you'd do this.' He pulls her up hard by the arm. 'I ought to belt you, too.'

'Ian, don't! Ian! You're hurting my arm!'

Having recovered my wind, I get to my feet slowly. His attention is focused on the girl. I watch for my chance.

'Hey! Stultus!' I shout. Although he doesn't understand the insult, he turns and I land a good kick with my knee in his groin. He falls, writhing on the bed.

'Marcus! You decked him!' She crawls over the bed to him, trying to comfort the man.

'Miss Camilla, please answer me. You say this man not husband, not boyfriend?'

'He isn't. Well, most of the time he isn't.' She grins lamely. My father had warned me about the fickleness of young women. It's time to make an exit. Remembering my manners I say, 'Thank you for a lovely evening, Miss Camilla.'

'Wait, Marcus!' she calls out, but I am not stopping. At full speed I run back towards the centre of town. I am looking for my hotel but lose my bearings and end up wandering around a residential area. I stop to catch my breath. I feel exhausted and scared. I also feel dizzy. I bend over and am sick in the gutter. I sit on the curb, lost in my wretchedness. My stomach hurts, my body aches. I curse my own stupidity. I should have known it would end badly, drinking and womanising. What was I thinking, ending up in a strange woman's bed chamber! *This is not part of the plan, Marcus.* I can already picture my father scolding me.

My stomach settles a little. I get up and walk back to the centre of town, eventually finding my room at the tavern. I stand in the shower for a long time, letting the warm water flow over me. Flopping on the bed, I stare at the ceiling. My heart is still racing from the events of the day. *Please gods, watch over me.* Guide me not down such a foolish path. I promise to behave as my parents have taught me, to stay away from liquor and women.

I wake late the next morning. My head feels as if in a vice, my chest is sore, my stomach unsettled. The room is already uncomfortably hot. I find breakfast nearby, and drink two large coffees, being very familiar with the healing power of this drink. Soon the pain in my head subsides. It is time to get out of this town. But first, I must pay a visit to someone.

It's mid-morning when I knock on the door of Father George's cottage. There is no answer, and I start to leave, when his face appears around the side of the house. He is garbed in gardening clothes and carrying a short spade.

'Marcus, a pleasure to see you. How are you this fine day?'

It is indeed a bright, sunny day. Too bright for me, however, in my condition. 'Father George, may I speak with you? I am in need of some counsel, and you were very kind to me yesterday.'

He pulls off his gloves. 'Certainly son, I was thinking of going inside for a drink anyway. My back can only do so much gardening,' he says, rubbing it to illustrate the point. 'Besides, I'm to give morning mass at eleven. We can talk over some lemonade?'

'Yes, lemonade. Thank you, sir.'

In his cheerful kitchen, he tells me of the flowers he is planting around the grounds of the church. But I am not paying attention, and he soon realises this.

'What would you like to talk about, Marcus? Is everything all right?'

'In truth, I had a most troublesome evening. I drank too much ale at the tavern, and I got into a, um, disagreement with a man at the Athena Inn. I am not proud to tell you about it.'

'There is more evil caused by drink than anything else in this world. I know it as God's truth.' He folds his arm and looks at me intently. 'You can confide in me, son. What happened? Were you hurt?'

'A little. Only a bruise, in my stomach.' I am unable to confess everything I did the night before. But the priest knows without my telling.

'Were you in a fight? Did you hurt someone?'

'I, I didn't intend to, but I was defending this woman. She was being roughly handled by this foul-mouthed man. I felt obliged to disable him, lest he injure her. I feel ashamed for drinking too much and getting myself into this trouble.'

'I see. This other man, was he hurt badly?'

'No, Father, I think not. He was groaning rather loudly when I left.'

He nods. 'Well, if you were coming to the aid of a woman in distress, you have done the right thing. You have no cause to feel ashamed. In fact, you have shown courage and kindness to this woman.'

I hadn't thought of it that way. 'I believe you are right, Father.'

'Still, perhaps you have learnt a lesson about drink and the consequences.'

I nod sheepishly. 'I am afraid, Father. Will your law keepers come to arrest me? I fear being cast into prison.'

'Oh, I think not. This man is unlikely to make a complaint, for fear of his own deeds coming to the attention of the police. And you have the woman as a witness to your actions.

Assuming you have spoken the truth, you have nothing to fear from the police, son.'

'The gods be thanked! I am so worried, I fear being arrested again—'

'Again? Are you on the run Marcus?' He pauses. 'Are you here legally?' I don't know what this means. 'Pray answer me. You have my word, I will not betray you. I promise to help you, no matter what you have done.'

'It's a long story, Father George. To tell you all would take many hours.'

He glances at the clock. 'I have one hour, anyway.'

'I am a long way from home. I am desperate to go back to Italy, and my family.'

'You have overstayed then?'

'Yes, my stay here is far too long. I must return home, to help my father, my family. Some evil business has overtaken them. They need me and I miss them so.' Surely this man, if any, would believe my story. 'Father, if I told you I am not of this place, would you believe me?'

'Of course, boy. I knew at once, that you are not from around here. Your speech and your mannerisms gave you away. Mind you, Australia welcomes people from many nations, and a large share are new at speaking English. But in all my years, I've not heard any man or woman who could speak Latin as you did yesterday.'

'If I told you, I am not of this time, would you believe me also?'

'What do you mean? Not of this time?'

'I began my life in a village, far removed from the city, in the south of Italy. You see.'

He interrupts, 'So, you are from a backward village? There is no shame in that. It is not so unusual. Why here in Queensland, in the Outback, or in the Territory, they are years behind the times. I've heard there are even people who have never used a computer. Can you imagine!' *I could indeed.*

'No, Father, that is not my meaning. I am from a different *time*, a time twenty centuries ago. I was brought here by the will of the gods. Not the god of Australia, but the Roman gods. I was in the Forum in Rome, hiding from soldiers, when—' The priest holds his hand up, as if to interrupt.

'Hold on son. This is this same nonsense you spoke of yesterday. That you lived in the time of Julius Caesar. Why do you concoct such a story?'

'Sir, hear me out. I mean no disrespect. I do not lie, for if I did may Jupiter strike me down.' I look up at the sky, and the priest looks up too, but nothing happens. He frowns at me. 'I know it is hard to believe. I could scarce believe it myself when it happened.'

'All right. Tell me the truth. The truth, as you know it, Marcus. Speak your mind and I'll not interrupt.' He folds his arms, and I begin my tale. I tell him of my living on our family farm, of being seized by soldiers in my mother's presence, of being imprisoned and dragged to Rome to die in the Games. He listens, frowning and fidgeting with his hands, continuously stroking his chin, barely hiding his disbelief.

'A fine script for a movie – wasn't that from *Gladiator*? Did you meet Russell Crowe in the dungeon?' He laughs at his own joke. 'Sorry. Please continue.'

I recount my imprisonment below the Colosseum, our escape at the trapdoor, and my flight through the Forum. Father George seems more interested now and follows my words intently.

'How did you escape the soldiers? You hid among the temples?' he asks.

'My intention was to beg for asylum from the priests in one of the great temples. But they wouldn't take me in. So, I prayed to Juno, Jupiter, and Minerva. I beseeched them to save me and take me away to the other side of the world, a thousand thousand years away from the hell I was in.'

'And your prayers were answered, I suppose?' He stares deeply into my face. 'A fantastic story, but I am not sure I believe it. Have you told others this tale?'

'No, not my whole story. I can only relate the truth and pray that you believe me. As I said, it is hard to believe myself, but it is exactly what happened. I come from a time long past, before there were cars, before electricity, before phones.'

'Well, I know some villages in places like New Guinea had no contact with western civilisation until the 1930s, but ancient Italy—why it has been civilized for millennia! I cannot believe that a man could live in isolation from the rest of the world and all its advances for twenty centuries.' I shake my head. It was foolish of me to tell him. 'How do you propose to return to your home and your time? Will you pray to your gods to work this miracle a second time? In reverse?' he asks.

'I have already tried that, sir. But here in Australia, so far from home, my gods have no authority. They are gods of Italy, of the Mediterranean lands. They have no abode here on the other side of the world.'

'And you truly believe in the gods of ancient Rome? That they hear your prayers and can answer them?'

'Of course, Father! I am a Roman, my family have been faithfully praying to them and making the correct sacrifices all our lives. And they have always protected us. Well, most of the time, I mean.'

'I fear your gods have no power in the twenty-first century, regardless of where you are. My poor Marcus. It seems you are well and truly lost.'

'That I am. At least you grant me that!'

'Marcus, there is one bit of advice I can give you.'

'Yes, please sir, anything.'

'Have you thought of praying to the Christian God. To our saviour, Jesus? I mean, it is wrong to expect God to answer our prayers as though in return for payment. But if you open your heart, honestly, to Jesus and the Lord, He—they will hear your prayers, of that I am certain.'

'That could be so. But I know nothing of your religion, your rites and sacrifices. It would be foolish of me to attempt them. I would just make the Christian God angry with me, a foreigner. A barbarian.'

'All I ask is that you try it sometime. He *will* hear you, and that alone may calm your troubled soul. He could give you guidance and bring hope to your heart. Is that not worth trying?' I nod. 'So, what is your plan now? Is there anything I can do to help you?'

'My intention was to go to Melbourne and take a ship for Europe. Can you tell me anything about Melbourne? Does it have a large harbour?'

'It does indeed. But surely it is better to fly to Rome from Melbourne? Or Brisbane? Do you need money for your passage?'

'I have money. It's just that I cannot bring myself to take one of your flying machines. The gods—' I stop myself. 'I am afraid to fly. I will travel by ship, from Melbourne, if it can be done. Are there ships bound for Europe departing from there?'

'I am not certain of that. It is odd, that you don't want to fly. By ship, a voyage to Europe will take months, even if you can find one that takes passengers.'

'I have time.'

He grins. 'Passenger ships hardly exist anymore. Only a few cruise ships sail the oceans these days. But it's possible you could find a freighter that might take paying passengers if they have a spare berth, or you could sign on as a crew member.'

'Crew?'

'You know, to work on the ship. To pay for your passage instead of taking wages.'

'I see. But I am not much of a sailor. I don't know how to haul rope or work sails.'

'Sails indeed!' He laughs heartily. 'It wouldn't be a sailing ship. They are all driven by diesel engines these days. My brother-in-law worked on a ship for many years. Grew tired of the extreme boredom—long stretches at sea with nothing to see or do. There's always a man or two who leaves the ship at each port, and new men are taken on. They need hands to maintain the engines, to cook meals, keep watch and so on. I would think any man can do it.'

'I could do that. I could work for my passage.'

'Well, there you go. You head down to the harbour, at Williamstown in Melbourne, and talk to the ships' captains. You could find something. But it will be a long, slow journey, and very dull.'

'Dull is good.' A long sea voyage is just what I need now. 'Are the harbours guarded by soldiers? Do they watch at the ports for wanted men?'

Father George rubs his grizzled face. 'Soldiers, no. Border police, yes. I suppose they patrol the harbour and ask for passports. But I think it very easy to board ship, the authorities take little regard of people leaving. They are concerned mostly with those who are arriving.'

'And the ships, they sail direct to Ostia?'

'I don't know about that. I don't think Ostia is a port anymore. More likely Genoa, or Antwerp, or Hamburg. My guess is after a stopover in Perth, ships would make for the Suez Canal.'

'Suez?'

'In Egypt. From there, I'm certain you could take a ship to any port in the Mediterranean. Including Italy. Perhaps Taranto, or Naples.'

'This is joyous news! I feel I have a chance now, of reaching my home. Thank you, Father George. Thank you. I will not forget you.'

'A word of advice, young man. Be careful. Don't trust strangers. Melbourne is a very large city, bigger than any you have ever seen, I suspect. It may be quite frightening for you. There will be scoundrels who try to take advantage of strangers not wise to city ways.'

'I am not afraid. I have been to cities before. But I take your meaning. My father always told me that cities harbour the best and worst of people. Give me a peaceful country village, anywhere.'

'You know it too! When you make it to Rome, and you need help of any kind, call in at the church of Santa Maria Maggiore. On Via Cavour. Father Ricardo is still a priest there, tell him you are a friend of mine and he will take you in. Here, I'll write it down for you.'

He returns with a small slip of paper. 'I wish you every success. Have a safe journey. I will pray for you.'

'Thank you, sir. I would be honoured if you would perform a sacrifice, even a small one, and pray to your great man-god Jesus to help me.'

'Oh, we don't sacrifice animals anymore. We speak to Jesus and to God from our heart. Would you like to pray with us, at our mass this morning? You can see for yourself how we pray.'

I nod. I wonder, would it be an insult to the Roman gods to pray to a foreign god? Surely there would be no harm in it. After all, I am here in Australia, a land where this Jesus has a strong presence. It would probably be a good idea to let him know that I am willing to honour him too. 'I will attend your Mass. Is that what you call your ceremonies?'

'Yes, that's right. Begins in an hour.'

'I have a bus to catch, just after five o'clock.'

'It will be completed in an hour, so you will have plenty of time to make your bus.'

'I will attend then.'

'Splendid! I'm sure you will feel better for it. And you will learn something of our faith.' *I hope so.* I must thank the man for his kindness, trust, and honest advice. I reach into my pocket and pull out a denarius. 'Please take this, for your kindness.'

'Oh son! I can't take money for helping a fellow traveller. It is the right and Christian thing to do.' He examines the coin and looks surprised. 'Oh wait, I thought you were giving me money. This is a beautiful little medallion. Thank you, Marcus. I will keep it in memory of you.'

I get up to leave, and he walks me to the door.

'See you soon, Marcus.'

'Goodbye, Father George.'

I tarry about the steps of the church, where after a time, people begin to arrive. I go inside and take a seat at the rear of the temple. There are few dozen people in attendance, seated on timber benches. From above begins slow dignified music, which fills the temple impressively. The ceremony is about to begin.

There is a pause in the music, and from behind us the priest and his attendants march in. The music begins again, louder and more majestic than before. Youths in white robes lead the procession down the aisle; one carries a golden cross on a staff, the others bear candles. Behind them is Father George, carrying a book which he holds high in his hands. They make their way to the altar, where the priest addresses the worshipers.

'In the name of the Father, the Son, and the Holy Ghost.' At these words, many of the faithful touch their foreheads, chest, then their sides of their bodies, making the sign of a cross. A song of praise follows. Though I can hardly make out the words, it is nonetheless uplifting. Father George leads the worshipers in prayers, at times kneeling, standing, or sitting. Readings are made from the great book, telling a story of Jesus and a rich fool. The priest then speaks at length on the meaning of the story: the foolishness of lusting for material things and placing them above the spiritual.

Then follows a most curious ritual. The priest takes a sip from a wine cup and tells the people 'this is the blood of Christ'. A plate of dry bread is produced; the people come forward in turn to take one, with the words, 'this is my body given for you'. After a final blessing, the priest and his followers depart down the aisle as they had come, thus the ceremony is complete. To my surprise no animals were sacrificed, which made the event less dramatic, but less malodorous, than a ceremony in a Roman temple.

The worshipers file out, engaging each other in warm and lively conversations. They disperse, and I find myself alone.

Inside, a young man sweeps the red dust from the floor. I feel awed and puzzled at what I have seen.

It is time to depart this town. I idle the remaining hours in a cafe near the bus stop. It eventually arrives and I take a seat in the nearly empty bus. As it pulls away, I say farewell to Roma, a place of pain and revelation. I look back, and see the spire of the temple of Jesus, a cross mounted on its peak. I whisper a prayer to this man-god Jesus, in hopes that he will hear and help me. Goodbye Roma, where I learnt the truth. Not of where I am, for I already knew I was on the other side of the world. But *when* I am. However impossible it seems, I have left my own time and arrived here, far, far in the future.

This explains all the strange and wonderful things I have seen since coming to Australia. I think of the achievements of us Romans, our engineering works, our great buildings and aqueducts, our art and literature. If we had achieved all this in just seven centuries since Romulus founded Rome, imagine what an industrious, ambitious people could have achieved in twenty centuries more.

CHAPTER X

The bus leaves the town behind, and we are again in the empty, sunburnt countryside. The hours pass. Small towns come and go. The terrain gradually changes. It is greener now, and we are in cattle raising country. I watch the passing landscape with interest. I spot a horse ranch with dozens of handsome animals grazing peacefully. We take on more and more passengers, the bus is nearly full when we finally reach the large town of Toowoomba. But I have no interest in exploring it. On to Melbourne!

As our sojourn here is over an hour, I step down and have a meal in the little station restaurant. The seats are hard and uncomfortable. I order a hamburger, which I have learnt does not actually contain ham, but a sort of stringy beef. It is not bad though, covered with cheese and served on soft bread. I idly watch the people coming and going. I fiddle with the little ring on my finger and remember my promise to call Sabina. I ask the station attendant if there is a phone I can use; he directs me to one that is operated with coins. After some time fumbling with the machine I finally get it to work, and dial Sabina's number. She answers.

'Marcus! How are you? Are you ok? Where are you? How was the bus ride?'

'I am well, Sabina.' I recount my adventures in Roma, leaving out the incident with the singer. I tell her of my visit with the priest of the church there, without mentioning what I'd learnt from him, of my voyage through time.

'Oh really? Are you catholic? I guess you must be, being Italian.' I tell her it was a chance visit, that I came to the temple accidentally, and asked Father George there for advice.

'What did you ask him?'

'He spoke some Latin, which was very comforting to me. He has also been in Rome, many years ago. We spoke of many things. He is a scholar and knows a good deal about Rome and the history of my people.'

'I don't get you. You talked about history?'

'Not only that. He gave me some helpful advice for when I get to Melbourne. He gave me a book too. He told me—' I was about to tell her how I learnt the truth of my travel through time when a voice interrupts us on the phone.

'Insert one dollar fifty to continue your conversation.' Having run out of coins, I am forced to say a quick goodbye.

'Bye my darling! You be careful when you get to Melbourne! Lots of bogans there!' Sabina says. Before I can ask what a 'bogan' might be, her voice is cut off. I return to the bus, happy and energised from hearing her sweet voice. I miss her a great deal already. I think of our walks in the town, our many outings together and our time talking quietly in her room. The loneliness begins to bite at me.

It is quite late when at last the bus departs for Melbourne. These vehicles are quite luxurious, the seats broad and comfortable, the windows made of smoked glass. The ride is quiet and smooth for the roads now are no longer gravel, but hard concrete. We leave the lights of the city behind. Many passengers are soon asleep. I try to do the same, but sleep is fitful; the bus stops occasionally, and the jolting awakens me.

Daybreak arrives, and not long after we stop at a cafe at a crossroads. I wearily disembark with the others, as I am badly in need of coffee. I wash the best I can in the tiny restroom. I take a quick breakfast, sitting near the window, anxious that the bus does not depart without me. A new driver, in a smart blue suit like his predecessor, stands on the steps of the bus.

'Moree. Dubbo. Shepperton. Melbourne. All aboard, please!' he shouts.

There is little to say of the remainder of the journey. The landscape becomes increasingly dry again, though most of the land is under cultivation. Our journey continues the entire day, stopping for food and toilet breaks every few hours. I begin to appreciate just how big this island of Australia is.

Finally, near nightfall on the second day, we approach Melbourne. The road widens into four, then six, then eight lanes. Thousands upon thousands of cars and all manner of vehicles travel at giddy speeds following one upon the other.

The road passes under and over other roadways via massive bridges; roads branch off on all directions, some raised high on concrete pillars. It is at once frightening and mesmerising. We are obviously approaching a great city. The sky darkens and it begins to rain, the first I have seen in this land.

'Melbourne weather,' grumbles the passenger in front of me. But it doesn't slow the traffic at all. We follow the torrent of cars to the city centre. The buildings grow taller. On the horizon are edifices of greater height, a forest of them, and we are heading directly for them. As we approach within a mile or two, the stupendous size of these towers becomes clear. Taller than fifty houses, one stacked on top the other. I can't take my eyes away from the window. I become increasingly uneasy; I must be mad to visit such a place alone.

Sabina had informed me that Melbourne was a city of four million inhabitants, and to accommodate so many citizens the people live in tenements stacked one upon the other, reaching into the sky. We pass many of these buildings of glistening glass and steel. I see lights in many of the tiny windows, and I wonder what sort of people live there.

It is dark when we reach the centre of Melbourne where the city lights make for a spectacular sight. The bus travels through the canyons between the great buildings. We pull into the bus station, lit brightly with harsh white lights.

'Southern Cross Station! Spencer Street,' the driver announces. We all disembark, relieved to be finally off this bus that has been our home for two exhausting days. The night is cool and the air damp. I sense we are near the sea.

Finding a room for the night is a priority. This is not difficult, as I discover numerous inns surrounding the station. I select one called the "Hotel Atlantis". It is a tall, elegant looking building, the lobby is well appointed with plush couches, a fountain, and marble floors.

I set my backpack down at the front counter and inquire the cost of a room. The young woman tells me they *start* at 150 dollars per night. City prices are something that Sabina didn't warn me about. It being late and my body weary, I accept. The clerk seems surprised that I don't possess a 'credit card', and I am obliged to leave a cash deposit of another 150 dollars. This leaves my purse considerably lighter.

Instead of a key, I am handed a small plastic card. I puzzle over what it might be for.

'Eighteenth floor, room 1803, first door on the right as you leave the elevator.' Eighteen floors above! So far above the ground! I consider asking for a lower room, but before I can, the desk clerk says, 'The pool and sauna are on the third floor, they're open until 10 pm.' If I take her meaning correctly, this hotel has public baths. Wonderful! Melbourne is indeed a civilized place. I ask her to direct me to the staircase. 'Lifts are that way,' she says, pointing down a carpeted passageway.

I trudge down the corridor. But at the end of it, there is no staircase, just two sets of steel doors, tightly shut. I try to pry them open, but they won't budge. I return to the front desk, to find the clerk busy serving an elderly couple. A young man enters the hotel from the street and heads down the corridor where I had just been. I follow him to see how he opens the steel doors. He pushes a little lighted button to one side, that I had not noticed. The doors slide open, he enters, and they quickly shut again. The rooms are protected by steel doors! A veritable fortress, this hotel.

I repeat the young man's actions, pressing the little button. After a minute, the left-hand doors open, and I enter. But instead of a staircase, I find only a tiny, cramped room, dimly lit. How do I get out of this suffocating box? How did the young man that entered just before me escape? In a panic, I leave the little chamber just as the doors close, almost catching me in their grip.

Back at the reception desk, the clerk is still helping the elderly couple, who have many questions. I pace impatiently. Finally, they complete their transaction, take their card, and head down the mystery corridor.

'Can I help you, sir? Did your key not work?' the clerk asks me cheerfully.

'Well, I do not know. Pray tell me, where is the staircase?'

'Stairs are just there,' she says pointing to another door at the opposite end of the lobby. 'But you'd want to take the lifts. Didn't you see the elevators?'

'Elevators?' I ask.

'Lifts? Ascenseur? Ascensore?' she says, but I don't get her meaning. 'One moment. I'll get someone to show you to your room.' She picks up a desk phone and speaks briefly. A young staff member comes over. I had seen him outside, greeting guests arriving by car and unloading their cases. 'Douglas, our guest is a little confused. Take him to 1803 please.'

'Sure, Liz.' The young man smiles at me. 'I'll show you to your room, sir. May I carry your bag?' I hold out my backpack for him. 'This way.' We head down the passageway one more time, and he presses the little button. The doors open, and we enter. The doorman presses a button marked "18" on the wall next to the door. I hadn't noticed the row of buttons before. There is barely perceptible lurch, and I can feel we are ascending. I look upwards, and then at the young man, who smiles back. 'Staying long in Melbourne?'

'I hope not.'

'Ah, just passing through are we? Flying out tomorrow?'

'No, not flying.' Our ascent slows. The doors open by magic and the man gestures to exit.

'To your right, sir.' I discover we are no longer in the lobby, but high up in the hotel. I should have guessed. An elevating machine. Ascensore, as the girl at the desk called it.

'May I have your key, sir?' the doorman asks. I hand over the little card, and he demonstrates its use. The room is large and luxurious with an enormous bed. He sets down my backpack and shows me some of the room's features. 'Your mini bar is here.' A private stock of liquors. How nice. But I have sworn off liquor after my experience at Roma. 'Here is your remote for your TV.' He draws open the curtains, exposing a magnificent view of the city through the large window. 'Enjoy your stay, sir,' he calls out, and departs.

I am drawn to the window. Stretching before me is the fabulous sight of the great city, reaching to the horizon. Thousands upon thousands of lights fill the view, like the stars of the heavens. I can see now how high up the room is: eighteen storeys above the earth! A weird, dizzy feeling rises in my gut. I back away from the window and shut the curtain.

There is a phone on the bedside table. I get out Sabina's phone number and dial it, but there is no answer. I leave her a short message, telling of my safe arrival in Melbourne.

It has been two long days on the road since leaving Roma, and I am tired to my very bones. I am also much in need of a bath. I discover a soft, white robe and a pair of slippers in the bathroom. I change into them, and take the elevator down to the third floor, where I was told the baths are. There is indeed a steam room, which I have all to myself. Afterwards, I bathe in the nearby hot pool. This is true civilization; the way man was meant to live. I reluctantly leave the warm waters and make my way back to my room. The large bed is the most comfortable I have ever slept in. As it ought to be, for 150 dollars.

In the morning, greatly refreshed from a long sleep, I draw the curtains and look out at the city. The view is not as frightening in daylight. So many grand buildings! Many reach much higher than even this hotel. In the distance, away to the south I see the glint of water, could it be the sea? At long last! I wash and quickly pack my things, retrieve my deposit, and venture into the streets of Melbourne.

It is a very busy place, people by the thousand crowd the footpaths, I presume they are on their way to their places of business. Most are dressed in long coats, for the climate here is far cooler than in Queensland. Many of the men wear smart, tailored jackets with a coloured ribbon of cloth around their necks. The women are mostly in long dresses, some in trousers and coats.

I feel the cold, for the concrete towers block out the sun and create tunnels of shadow and wind. There are cafes everywhere, indeed every second building seems to have one on the ground floor, and they are doing brisk business. I take an excellent breakfast. Thus fortified, I am ready to explore the city.

I pass by a large glass window. A row of young men and women, dressed in brightly coloured, tight fighting clothing, are running on some sort of treadmill. Running in place, going nowhere. Whatever are they doing this for? I recall a similar sort of treadmill in my village; slaves were made to drive a millstone wheel with their feet, walking forward, but never getting anywhere.

I head east towards the heart of the city. The streets are broad and filled with countless cars. It is a miracle there are no collisions! Crossing the roadway on foot is a dangerous undertaking, not only must I avoid the deadly cars, but there are also huge cumbersome vehicles running on steel rails which I later learnt are called 'trams'. They glide almost silently up and down the centre of the streets.

"King Street", reads the sign. To the north, nothing but traffic and buildings. But to the south I catch a glimpse of a river. It is only a short walk down the hill to its banks. The river is brown and muddy, about the breadth of the Tiber. Its banks are landscaped with trees, benches, and footpaths.

On the opposite side, the glass and steel buildings have a more moderate height. I can see the sky here; it is a grey day, foretelling rain. Numerous bridges cross the river, but there are no vessels on the river itself. Observing the current flow westerly, I follow its course downstream, my purpose to reach the sea for there I am sure there will be ocean going ships.

After half a mile, the river broadens for I am getting close to its mouth. The riverside parklands end and I am forced to take to the streets. I try to keep to the river's course, though access to it is blocked off by fences. The urban scene changes, there are no more glass towers here, just vast warehouses. The traffic is different too; nearly all the vehicles are trucks, carrying large metal boxes, the size of a small house.

I pass a small road leading directly to the water. On the opposite bank, I see ships tied up at concrete docks. They are made of iron! Can such vessels float on water? There is no doubt about it. But there is no way to cross the river here. Another half mile further I reach the river mouth where a great bay stretches away far to the south. The banks of the river here are lined with rough stone blocks. There are steps leading to the water. I kneel at the water's edge, scoop some water in my hands and taste it. Salt. The sea at last!

Far off to the right, I make out a complex of piers and ships. It will be a long walk to get there, but in the cool weather, an easy one. The docklands comprise a vast area of warehouses, cranes, dusty lots full of the big steel boxes, and ships. Ships large and small, rusty and new. But how to know where they are bound? I approach the nearest ship, a large one near 100 yards longs, moored at the wharf. A hatchway is open, and a rickety timber ramp leads from it to the pier. In front of the ramp, a young man in uniform sits idly under a makeshift canopy. He is working his phone, as does everyone in this nation whenever they are alone.

'Good day, sir,' I say cheerfully.

'Can I help you?'

'Your ship, where will it go?'

'Not my ship buddy. I'm just doing security here.'

'But where ship go? To Europe? I buy ticket?'

'One second, sir.' He talks into a little device mounted on his shoulder. 'Rudy, this is Vince. Could I have an officer to the gangway please? Yeah. Yeah. A gentleman has an enquiry. Dunno. Best you ask him. Out.' He turns back to me. 'Officer will be down in a minute. You can talk to him.' He goes back to stroking his phone.

Shortly, a man dressed in a smart, white uniform and cap emerges from the ship and descends the ramp.

'How can I help you, son?' he asks.

'Please, captain. Where does your ship go?'

'I'm not the captain. Second officer. This ship, *Sunflower IV*, is going to Hong Kong and Vancouver.'

'Ship not go to Alexandria? Europe?' I ask hopefully.

He shakes his head. 'No sir, we just do transpacific runs. Are you hoping to get on as crew?' Father George told me that ships seldom take passengers but may take on men to work the ship.

'Yes, crew. Or passenger. Good. But I must go to Europe.'

If I could just get as far as Alexandria, it will be easy to find a ship bound for Italy.

The officer shakes his head. 'Not many vessels out of Melbourne use the Suez Canal these days, except the odd container ship. And that business isn't what it used to be. Sorry.' He can see the disappointment in my face. 'Wait. Vince, is your team working any Greek ships? Didn't one come into Williamstown last week? Has it sailed?'

'Yeah, it was due to depart Sunday, but I think it's still here. Held up by a wharfie strike. One sec.' Vince speaks into his shoulder-phone. 'You're in luck mate, it's still here, Pier forty-one. Round at Williamstown. Head down there and talk to an officer. If you're lucky, you could get on as crew. If they ask, "Can you cook?" you must answer, "Yes." Understand?'

'Yes, I see. Williamstown? Is this far?' I ask.

'Not far, but across the bay.' He points it out across the water. It is hard to make out anything other than the distant shoreline. 'Best take a taxi.' The officer turns and heads up the ramp.

'Thanks, Rudy,' says Vince. The officer waves and disappears inside the ship.

'Pier forty-one, buddy. Look for a vessel named *Anastasia*.'

'*Anastasia*, yes.'

'Do you want me to call you a taxi?' he asks, seeing me standing there dumbly.

'Yes, taxi. Please.'

He orders a hired car for me. Within minutes, it arrives. The driver, a brown-skinned man with a neat moustache, greets me cheerfully.

'Where to, sir?' he asks.

'Williamstown. Pier forty-one,' I tell him.

'Very good, sir.' He steps hard on the pedal and we speed away. At an unexpected turn the speed throws me over on my side. I suspect this man spends his spare time racing cars. We are there in minutes. I pay the fare, and he speeds off in a cloud of dust.

A huge ship stands before me, streaked with rust, badly in need of paint, its name on the stern in bold white letters, *"Anastasia – Piraeus"*. This Greek port is barely a week's sail from Italy. Whatever it takes, I am going to board this ship. For it will take me home. *Home, by the gods.* There is no one about however, and the gangway is barricaded by a wire gate. I rest on one of the great pylons holding the ship's lines. The ropes are as thick as my arm. I am hungry, but there is nowhere to buy a meal around here.

After a time, another taxi appears, and three young men in light blue uniforms spill out noisily. They are of short stature and speak an unfamiliar tongue. One unlocks the gate at the ramp, and I approach.

'Good afternoon, men,' I call out.

'Bakit?' says one.

'Sino iyan?' says another.

'Hello. Please, where does your ship go?' I ask.

The third man, apparently their leader, comes over. 'Nowhere for the moment, still waiting to load our last cargo. But eventually, Rotterdam via Piraeus. Why do you ask?'

'Piraeus? The Greek city?'

'There's only one Piraeus that I know.'

'Can you carry me there? I buy ticket to Piraeus. Please.'

He shakes his head. 'We are not a passenger ship, sir. Sorry.'

'Please, I must go to Italy. Please, take me on ship. I can work for you. I strong man.'

'Iwanan ang tanga, Alejandro,' says one of the others impatiently as he starts up the gangway.

'I'm sorry, we've all the crew we need. Besides, why would you spend two months doing the dullest job in the world, when you could fly?' They turn to leave, closing the gate behind them, and disappearing into the ship. Why won't they take me? I curse myself for not preparing a better story. If I had only explained to them how I am a stranger here, lost, homesick, and needing passage back home to my family. I forgot the advice of the guard at the last ship, to mention I could work as cook.

I wander around the docks, up and down the long empty piers with the dilapidated buildings. There are several other ships moored here and I approach them too. But few are bound for European ports. Those that are, the answer is always the same: not taking passengers.

The sun is getting low. Hunger drives me back to the city. I manage to flag down a taxi to take me back to Spencer Street. It is busy now. Workers spill out of the tall buildings, returning home after their day's toil. It is difficult to navigate the footpath, going against a sea of people walking the other way.

I find a dimly lit restaurant. I loathe the thought of spending another night here, for the prices charged at the inns will soon wipe out my cash. Night falls and I remain at my table long after finishing my meal. An idea comes to me. I order some extra food and drink, and have them pack it to take with me.

I head back to the riverbank, where many people are enjoying an evening in the park. A large, brightly lit shopping centre shines from across the river. I lay on a wooden bench, stargazing to kill time. Some hours later, the riverbanks are dark and deserted. *Time for action.* I walk back to King Street, to a corner where I have seen taxis congregate. I wait some time for one to arrive, for the city is nearly deserted, a fact that makes me uneasy. *I should have bought a knife this afternoon.*

The taxi driver winces when I tell him my destination is the docks at Williamstown. He agrees to take me, provided I pay the fare in advance. Soon I am again at the Williamstown wharves. It is poorly lit, and completely bereft of people or vehicles. *Just the sort of place to get robbed.*

I walk quickly, glancing about nervously. My pack is heavy with the provisions I have bought. I am soon at the *Anastasia*, still moored where it was. The ship is dark except for a few lights far above in the cabin. The gate is locked and I have no way of climbing it without making noise. I test one of the thick ropes that secure the ship to the pier. There is no doubt they will hold my weight. I secure my pack tightly and start to climb. At first the ascent is easy, but the incline increases. I am in danger of losing my grip and ending up in the water. I pause to catch my breath, my arms and legs clasping the rope tightly. I shinny my way up, a little at a time. Finally, I reach the deck of the ship, undetected.

The deck is broad and loaded with hundreds of large

containers, all the same size, stacked one atop the other. I creep towards the stern cautiously, ducking in the narrow passages between the containers. I dare not enter the ship's cabin, for fear of being discovered. But one of these boxes would make a snug home.

I try the latch on one, but it is sealed with a bolt and wire. Removing the wire takes some time and cuts into my hand. I slide out the bolt, and the door opens with a loud screech. I freeze, but no one has heard. The crew are all inside the cabin far above. The container is full of cardboard boxes wrapped in plastic and stacked on wooden pallets. I move them around to form a snug nest. Closing the door carefully, I await the dawn.

I stir to the sound of an arriving truck and deduce that cargo has arrived for loading. It is first light and I dare not leave the container. Other trucks soon arrive. For some hours I hear the clang of machinery and men's voices, as more of the containers are loaded onto the ship by crane. I take breakfast in my iron home but take care not to eat too much, for my provisions to last as long as possible.

The last truck departs. Suddenly the entire ship trembles. It has started its engine. I hear the gangway being hauled in. The smell of fumes filters into my hiding place. I hear shouts of men and hear them casting off the ropes. Soon the ship's engines roar ever more loudly, and I can feel us moving. We are putting to sea.

After an hour, I push open the container door and peer out. It is another overcast day. I feel a stiff breeze, for we are far from land now. *I did it! I'm on my way home.* Pleased with my cleverness, I close the door and wait for nightfall. Though desperate to answer nature's call, I dare not emerge in daylight.

Finally, the sun sets and I venture out on deck. The land is now nearly out of sight behind us but a bright glow on the horizon still marks the great city. I linger for a moment and climb on top of my box home. The stars are out. I lie on my back and give thanks to the gods for my deliverance. Goodbye Australia! Goodbye to you, warm, generous, clever people. I have never met men so free with their generosity, nor women who are so free spirited and forward. And so many women with yellow hair. Goodbye Sabina. Goodbye Tony and Shirley. Will I ever see these shores again? If only to visit my angel with the ponytail? I twist the little ring around my finger. It's the only memento I have of that sweet girl. I try to sleep atop the container, but the cold wind drives me back into my shelter.

I wonder what I will find in the next country we touch at. Will the people there have the same inventions, the same wonderful gadgets as these people? I smile when I think of the first time I saw the road train, appearing out of the desert like a great smoking phoenix. Yes, the taming of fire to drive their mysterious engines is a great achievement. Cars that move without a horse, ships that move without sails. My people consider ourselves great travellers, yet a man can walk but twenty miles a day, perhaps fifty by horse. But here I have travelled hundreds of miles in a single day. And their flying machines! Soaring above the earth, at great speeds. Invading the lofty world of the gods, high above the clouds. The noise and the intrusion of lowly humans in their home must surely anger them. No, not me. I'll happily keep my two feet on the solid earth. Or on a ship's deck. And their marvellous phones! The ability to talk to one another a great distance—how god-like! Sabina explained how this device sends voices on 'radio waves', not just for miles but thousands of miles. No one in Rome would ever believe me if I told them of such things. In my time it takes weeks for a message from Gaul or Antioch to reach Rome. And their extraordinary buildings! The achievements of Roman architecture are impressive enough, but who in the empire could imagine a building fifty storeys tall, let alone construct one. But their taming of lightning—what they call 'electricity', is their most astounding achievement. What wonderful power is harnessed from it; to light darkness without flame, to power all the gadgetry that obsesses the people: their phones, computers, and TVs. Sabina tried to explain electricity to me once, but even she did not seem to know how it worked, other than some nonsense about tiny invisible particles.

Still, there are many of their inventions I could well live without. The TV for one. Or as Tony called it, 'the idiot box'. True, some of the dramas were amusing, but the endless interruptions to sell soap or beer or insurance made the experience too tedious to bear. Give me real theatre with air-breathing actors.

Still, I wonder, are the people here truly different from those of my home and time? Take away their engines – why if they had no cars, no aeroplanes, or steel ships, then my people and our own ingenuity would be a match for them. If they could see our great Roman theatres, aqueducts, and temples—we built these, with nothing but rope, and muscle and determination. Yes, these Australians are like us in many ways. I felt this most strongly in Quilpie. I spent much time in the tavern there and discovered what Australians are like without their gadgetry. Friends greeting each other, sharing a drink, enjoying life's simple things: a fine meal, a song from a pretty songstress. Remove the electric lights and it could be a tavern in any part of Italy. Yes, there are ruffians but show me a place where there aren't!

I think of all the kindness shown to me, a stranger from a faraway land, ignorant of their ways and language. The young black men who rescued me from certain death in the desert. What were their names? Bardo was one; was Mick the other? And the kind man who drove the great truck—didn't it frighten me out of my wits! And of course, Sabina, Tony and Shirley, who took me into their home and treated me as one of their own. Would a family of my time have been as kind? I like to think so, at least away from the city. Here, as back home, city dwellers living one on top of one another are less inclined to help strangers. One can only wonder why.

These Australians *are* like us in part because they are descended from us Romans. For they use our alphabet and many of our Latin words. Father George hinted that Rome fell four centuries after my time to the barbarians from beyond the Rhine. What then became of the Romans? Why, there were fifty million of us! Surely we did not die, but bequeathed our culture to the people of Italy, Gaul, Hispania, and Britannia. I am certain their descendants survive and have left their mark here in the great south land, Australia. Did not Tony once tell me they call one of their houses of government "the Senate", as in old Rome?

I worry what I will find in Europe of the twenty-first century. Will it be even more strange and bewildering than Australia? Perhaps Europe has sunk into barbarism and ruin.

I drift off, and dream I was trying to call my parents on a phone, yet they could never answer.

Chapter XI

Another day passes, and the ship is now far out to sea. The waves grow larger all the time. The ship pitches and rolls slowly, making it difficult to stand without holding on to something. In the afternoon, it begins to rain hard. I open the door of my container a little and gaze at the sea. The huge waves rise, and crash far below; it is at once a majestic and frightening sight. How long will our voyage take? The officer said two months. I must keep track of what day it is. I fear I have not brought nearly enough food and water.

Later that afternoon I venture outdoors and sit with my back resting against the container. I believe it safe, for I am out of sight of the ship's bridge, and surely no crew member would venture out in this weather.

Staring, mesmerised by the endless procession of the waves, I am startled by something rubbing against my legs. It meows. The ship's cat has come to pay me a visit. It has a handsome coat of ginger and white stripes, and purrs loudly as I stroke him.

'Hello little friend, you are a sailor too? Good of you to keep me company.' He meows again. 'Sorry, kitten. I have no food for you, for I need every crumb for this voyage.' He lingers around me for a time, then wanders off.

'Kitty! Where are you?' I hear a man calling and whistling. I bolt upright and freeze. 'Ginger? Are you here?' he calls again, this time much closer. I duck around the side of the container and dash for my home, but he has spotted me.

'Puneta! What the hell!' he shouts. I curse my stupidity. *Why didn't I stay inside until dark?*

'Hoy! You! Come here.' Startled and embarrassed, it is pointless to resist. I stand fearfully before the crewman. Will he throw me overboard? But he just pulls out an oversized phone. 'Captain. Captain.'

'Rolando here. Kumusta?' crackles a voice from the phone.

'I have a surprise for you. Stowaway ito, isang lalake.'

'Dear God. Another one! Who was on watch last night? Okay, I'll send down Lito and Alex to give you a hand. Is he Greek?'

'Hey! Are you Greek?' he barks at me.

'No, sir, Italian.'

'Italian dao. Teenager I think,' he tells the captain. 'Where were you hiding? In that container?'

'Yes, that one there. The blue one.' He peers in the partially open door.

'Get your things and come with me. No funny business.'

I stuff my possessions in my backpack. He grabs it from me, shuts and bolts the container door. He motions to me. 'Follow me.' Halfway to the cabin we meet two more sailors. I recognise one from a few days earlier when I tried to talk my way aboard.

'Lito. Alejandro. Guess what, I found the cat. And this dog, too,' says the man, who I learn is named Paulo.

'Well, well, you again,' says Alejandro. 'This is the guy asking to buy passage in Melbourne. When we told him we don't take passengers he wandered off.'

'He came back', says Lito. He scowls. 'Skipper hindi na masaya.'

'He's going to be pissed for sure. We'll have trouble at Suez. Not going to be easy to unload him on to the Egyptians. Boy, what's your name?'

'Marcus. Marcus Corvus.'

'This way, Marcus.' They lead me up several steep metal ladders to the bridge of the ship, high above the deck. From here the officers keep watch and steer the ship, for it has a clear view all around through tall windows. A crewman has the wheel and is talking to a man whom I take to be the captain. He is my father's age, tall and with a weathered face. He is dressed in a neat, white uniform. He looks me over, his contempt obvious.

'Don't you know you are on this ship illegally? We could have you arrested and jailed at our next port.' I say nothing, too embarrassed to speak. 'Well? Do you have nothing to say for yourself? What is your name? And nationality?'

'I am Marcus Corvus, sir. I am sorry to steal away in your ship. I just have to get home.'

'Nationality? Where is your home?'

'Italy, sir, near Naples'

'He's just a boy, sir,' says Alejandro, sympathetically.

'How old are you, son?' asks the captain, his tone softening.

'Nineteen years.'

'Great. Well, at least he's not a minor. Damned if I'm going to waste half a day dropping him in Perth. I suppose we can unload him at Piraeus. What do you think Alex, can we ditch him there and let the Greek authorities worry about him?'

The other officer shrugs. 'Maybe.'

'Have you searched him?' asks the captain. Rolando shakes his head. 'Tanga! He might be armed! Do it now.'

A sailor searches my pockets and pats down my body, looking for weapons. Another takes my backpack and upends it, spilling its contents on the map table. He pokes through it, opening all the packages of food and pitching most of the clothing onto the floor.

'Nothing, sir. Not even a passport.'

The captain looks at me sternly. 'Marcus, consider yourself under house arrest. You will do as directed by my orders until our next port.' I nod. 'You will hand me your passport for the duration of the voyage.'

'My what? What is passport?'

'Documents! Papers! Identification!' the others call out.

'Sandali, men. I'll address the prisoner if you don't mind,' interrupts the captain. 'You mean to tell me you have no papers? How did you get to Australia?'

'No, sir. No papers. I came to Australia, how you say, by accident.'

'Accident!' He does not believe me. 'Did you jump ship in Australia from another vessel?'

'No. No I got there by, ah, the will of the gods.' The sailors are amused but the captain is not.

'Undocumented. Great. We'll have a hell of time getting rid of him at Suez or Piraeus. *Puneta!*' he curses. He looks over my belongings scattered on the cabin table. 'Is this all the food you brought? Do you think that will last you two months?'

'No, I did not think—'

'No, you didn't think at all. Stupid, stupid thing to do.'

The men confer among themselves in their language. Finally, the captain again addresses me. 'Lito will show you to your bunk. You will take meals with the crew, and you will have the run of the ship until we reach port, where I will hand you over to the local authorities at my discretion. Do you understand?'

'Yes. Thank you, captain. Thank you. You are a good man. I will be good helper.'

'You're damn right you will help. You will carry out duties on the ship that I or any of the crew may assign to you. Do you have a trade? Any skills?'

'I am good handling horses.' This amuses the men and even the captain laughs.

'Not really need for that aboard ship, is there? Do you know anything about engines?'

'No. But I know how to cook. I good cook.'

'Oh really? Well, that's something. All right then. Tonight, you will report to the galley at four o'clock. That means the kitchen,' he says, pointing it out. 'Now put him in cabin three and get him some linen.'

One of the crew escorts me to a tiny cabin, one deck below. It is very cramped and has a single, tiny circular window. Another sailor throws some bed clothes at me and I am left to myself. I sit on the bed, both ashamed and relieved.

Later that evening I join another man named Albert, who is the cook for the entire crew, which numbers fourteen men. So few to manage such an immense vessel! In my time, even a ship a tenth of this size would need two dozen men at the oars and rigging. Albert is friendly, and we converse a little as we work, cutting and peeling vegetables. I learn that he is from a nation of islands to the north of Australia, called Philippines, named for a Spanish king who conquered them 500 years ago. All the crew are of this country. They have a shorter stature than the Australians, black hair, and a complexion like my own. Their language is called "Tagalog", and I become tolerably familiar with it over the course of the voyage. The cook and I prepare a hearty stew of beef, potatoes, and vegetables. After it has simmered in a great cauldron for the requisite time, the crew are summoned to the dining table. They chat amongst themselves, mostly in their own language. My presence at the table is awkward for all of us. The captain is absent, and has his meal taken to him in his cabin. I eat quickly and return to my cabin.

After two days, we see land in the distance, which the crew tell me is the western coast of Australia. We do not stop, but round the tip of the land and steer to the northwest. It soon drops behind, and once again we are alone in the open sea. That evening I ask Albert if there is a phone on the ship.

'I need to call a friend. I promised her I would tell her of my progress.'

He laughs. 'Girlfriend, no? I thought so. Good looking man like you. Well, if we were in port you could borrow my cell, but we are long, long way from coverage here.'

'There is no phone? One with coins?'

'No, Marcus. The ship has a radio, we can contact shore stations, but in the middle of the ocean, forget it. Anyway, the captain doesn't like us to use it for personal calls.' Knowing the captain's low regard for me as a stowaway, it is unlikely he will consent to my using it anyway.

The days pass, one day being exactly like another. The view from the rail is nothing but sea and sky. But we are sailing at a good pace, for the crew reckons we travel more than 300 miles in a single day. Gradually the weather warms. After two weeks it is warm enough to go outside without a coat. Rain often falls in great torrents, but the ship ploughs on at the same speed, in the same direction, day after day.

The ship's cat, who betrayed my presence, is called Ginger after a famous actress. When I point out to the crew that the cat is in fact, male, they have a good laugh, but decide to keep his name. He is a gentle companion, often seeking me out in my cabin. In return for his friendship, he is content merely for a scratch behind the ears. I am grateful to have him.

I am thankful too, for the lenient treatment I have received. I work at my chores with a will around the ship, seeing this as my way of paying for my passage. Assisting with cooking and washing up in the galley, and keeping the living areas clean are my duties. Alex, the chief officer, seems pleased with my work.

We take meals together, all the crew save one who is on watch and mans the wheel, keeping a close eye on the compass and the way ahead. Slowly the men become friendly to me. All except the captain, who is polite, but declines to speak to me at any length. The crew are inquisitive. I tell them of my home and family, and my adventures in Queensland. They show great interest in our farm in Italy and our horses. They form the belief that I was holidaying in Australia and ran out of money; I go along with that. They can accept I am a man of Italy, but who would believe I am a man of a time twenty centuries ago?

The evenings after the meal are very agreeable. Most of the crew gather at the dining table to talk, drink, and play card games. Lito, a short, shy man from an island called Cebu, brings out his guitar some nights. He plays and sings softly, and those who know the words join in. Stories are told of ports they have been to, women they have known, and trouble they have gotten into and out of.

The days are sultry now, with the sun nearly directly overhead. The air is sticky and suffocating. Sleeping is uncomfortable, even with the porthole open. The sun beating on the metal deck makes it so hot I cannot walk on it without shoes.

One night the crew ask if I could cook a real Italian meal for them. I tell them I would be pleased to try, but lacking olives, garum and goat cheese, I cannot think of a dish I could make with the ingredients on board. They accept my answer, with some grumbling.

A week later, Alex gathers us together after the midday meal. 'Guess what men, we have just crossed the equator. And you know what that means? Who among you are sons of Neptune?' He looks from face to face. All the men nod, except for me, not knowing his meaning.

'Marcus isn't!' announces Albert.

'Marcus! Marcus!' the others agree, enthusiastically.

'What am I? Or what am I not?' I ask.

'If you have crossed the equator before, you are a son of Neptune. That is, if you've been through the necessary ceremonies,' explains Lito.

'He would have crossed the equator on his way to Australia unless he flew down.'

Alex asks, 'Did you come to Australia by sea?'

'No, I did not come by ship, but—'

'Dunk him!' shouts Albert, and they all roar, 'Dunk him!'

'Very well. Prepare for the ceremony, gentlemen.' The men scatter immediately, some towards the shed containing the cleaning gear. 'Please remain here, Marcus.' I become uneasy. What are they going to do to me?

The captain soon arrives, smiling for a change. 'So, you're to become one of Neptune's sons, are you?'

'I don't know, sir. Tell me, is the divine Neptune to be summoned? Is a sacrifice to be made to him? Am I to be cast overboard?'

'Certainly not! No, son, don't worry. It is something every new sailor experiences the first time you cross the line. You'll not be harmed, I promise you.'

'What do you mean, the line?'

'The equator. The line marking the centre of the globe.'

Alex returns. 'They are ready, captain,' he says, taking my arm firmly. We step down onto a broad section of the deck behind the bridge. The entire crew are arranged in a line, each carrying a bucket.

The captain presides over the ceremony. 'On this solemn occasion, we welcome Marcus of Italy to join the brotherhood of Neptune's sons!'

The men form a circle around me. 'Kneel, infant, and prepare to be baptised.'

'Don't worry Marcus, it's just good fun,' whispers Albert.

I kneel in the middle of the circle. 'Loose!' cries the captain. One by one they fling a bucket of cold sea water over me. After the last man performs his duty, they all cheer heartily and help me to my feet. 'Well done, son,' says the captain. He shakes my hand, as they all do in turn, before dispersing in a jolly mood.

'Am I now a son of Neptune?' I ask Albert, wringing out the sea water from my shirt.

'You are. Congratulations.' He slaps me on the back. They

still pay tribute to Neptune. One of our Roman gods! I find this reassuring. But this is not the proper way to address the god; I hope he is not offended by this undignified ceremony. Just to make sure, when everyone has left I go to the rail and offer a prayer to Neptune. I thank him for a safe journey so far and ask his blessing for the remainder of the voyage. I have nothing to sacrifice so I find an Australian coin in my pocket and flip it over the side. I head to my cabin to find some dry clothes.

A week passes, and another. The constant sameness of the surrounding sea and the same unfailing hum of the engines, make one day exactly like another. Even the food is monotonous, for the fresh provisions have long since run out, and our fare all comes from a can or the kitchen's enormous freezer. Even the stories told around the table in the evening start to sound familiar. One night I ask about the ship's name, *Anastasia*.

'Does it have any meaning?'

'It's a girl's name, popular in Greek families,' ventures Alex. 'Lots of Greek girls in Melbourne.'

'Was she named by the man who owns the ship?'

'I would think so, but I don't know who that would be. The ship is owned by a big company based in Holland.'

'Anastasia means resurrection,' says Lito, the quiet one.

'What is the meaning, resurrection?' I ask him.

'To conquer death and to live again.' *To live again.* A good omen.

Some evenings, when the weather is fair, I excuse myself from the nightly card games and lie outside on deck. Some nights the stars are incredibly bright. The whole sky seems ablaze. I think of my home and ponder what my family might be doing at that moment. My mother no doubt making the evening meal; my father, resting in front of the fire after a day in the paddocks breaking in new colts. My little sister Valeria, with her cheeky ways, how she used to annoy me! Will I ever see them again? I often spoke harshly to Valeria and feel badly for not treating her better. I feel sorry for my disobedience to my mother, and to my father for my laziness. I pray the gods will let me return to them to make amends.

When I reach Rome, just a few weeks from now, will the gods allow me to return to my world? To Italy in the time of Tiberius? *It must be so.* In Australia, the Roman gods are powerless, so far from the homeland. Yes, that's why my prayers went unanswered. Of this, I am sure. When I set foot on Italian soil, the home and hearth of Jupiter and all our beloved gods, surely they will hear my prayers. I need only go to the Forum in Rome, pray at the temples, and offer sacrifices. They brought me to the other side of the world, didn't they? Then they can bring me home.

I remember the little figurine of Juno that I took from her temple in the Forum. I feel for it in my pockets and realise I haven't seen it for some time. It must be in the pocket of my old tunic. Back in my cabin, I search my old clothes but it is not there. *Where could it be?* In a panic, I dump the contents of my pack on the bed, and search every pocket, every corner of my pack—but it is gone. How could I have been so foolish as to lose it? I try to remember the last time I had it. Juno will be angry with me! I beat my fists on the metal cabin wall. I've ruined my chance to return, to work the magic that got me here. *What have I done?* I apologise to Juno, tears in my eyes. *Merciful Juno, forgive me.*

After another week at sea, we are roused well before dawn by the man on watch. 'Land, mga lalaki! The Somali coast. Turn out, get up!' We bundle out onto the deck in our sleeping clothes and press to the rail. Far in the distance, lights are visible scattered along the horizon. We dress quickly and gather on the bridge.

Alex shows me our position on the chart. We have crossed the Indian Ocean and are soon to enter the Red Sea, bound for Suez in Egypt. I learnt from the crew that a canal has been cut through the sands east of Alexandria, joining the Mediterranean with the Red Sea, at the head of which is the city of Suez. How far we've come! More than eight thousand miles.

The captain addresses us. 'Makinig kayo. Listen up men. That's the coast of Somalia ahead on the port side. Dangerous place, full of crazies with guns. And these waters are swarming with Somali pirates in small boats. Four men with AK-47s in a Zodiac have taken even the largest ships hostage here, and they don't think twice about shooting uncooperative crew.' The men look at each other uneasily. 'The pirates attack by stealth, their modus operandi is to use small, fast boats with big engines. They approach from the stern, pull alongside, then climb on board with rope and tackle. 'I want four men on watch at all times, one on each side of the ship. The more eyes the better. Alex, you take the bow, bring your binoculars and keep a sharp watch. All of you, take your radios and report any vessel of any size. Watch out for small craft, especially Zodiacs. Dicko, check all the hatches are bolted. Alex, unlock the arms cabinet. I want all the firearms out, cleaned and loaded. If an unauthorised boat approaches within a quarter mile, we'll shoot the bastards.'

Some are disturbed by this and talk nervously among themselves. Others, having passed through these waters before, put on a brave face and go about their duties as usual. I ask the captain if there's anything I can do.

'After breakfast, you can join Alex in the bow. Watch for small boats, they can be full of dangerous men.'

Breakfast is served, though it is still dark, and we are asked to eat quickly and clear the dishes. The first officer has been below and returned with several weapons: three long arms, and a pistol. He lays them out on the table with several boxes of ammunition. I had first seen guns in the desert, carried by the two men who found me half dead, though at the time I had no idea of their purpose. This I learnt from watching TV, where it seems every program has at least one person killed with these things. I know these innocent looking tools can deliver death at a great distance. Another invention of questionable value to mankind. Only the captain, the first officer and Lito are permitted to handle the guns. I observe them cleaning and later test-firing them off the side of the ship.

The dawn soon arrives, and to our left we can see the land of Africa itself still many miles off. Soon land also appears on the right, which Lito tells me is Arabia. For the first time in over a month, the ship alters its course and steers to the southwest, to pass through the straits. By late afternoon the land gradually closes, and it is clear we are entering a channel no greater than twenty miles wide.

Everyone is on edge. The crew, normally quick to joke amongst themselves, are serious and quiet. Instead of lingering in the dining area, most join the men at watch on the rails. *The more eyes, the better*, the captain said.

I spend the morning at the bow of the ship, scanning the horizon, looking for any sign of small boats. I say a prayer to Neptune to protect us from the villainy of pirates. Hearing me pray, Lito too makes the sign of the cross across his body, as I had seen others do in the church; he says a prayer to Jesus asking for protection. As the day progresses, we see some large freight-carrying vessels like our own passing within a mile or two in the opposite direction. But no pirate ships, the gods be thanked!

By evening we are in the narrowest part of the strait; the land is only a few miles away, and we see lights on the shore clearly as the sun sets. A few hours more, and we are through the straits into the Red Sea. The land recedes, and we are again in open waters. The ship's routine returns to normal, though the captain still insists on four men on watch at all times. There is some grumbling over the loss of sleep, as some men must remain on watch throughout the night. But the night passes peacefully.

We steer northwest now, and the waters about us gradually change from the deep red wine colour of the open sea to brilliant turquoise. The sky is clear of clouds, and the sun burns strongly. The crew tells me the water in this sea is quite shallow and needs great care in navigation, especially for a ship of this size which sits deeply in the water. Occasionally we approach close to the shore to find a safe channel. The land here is nothing but desert; only sand and dry hills as far as the eye can see. This must be part of the great desert that stretches across Africa, south of the Roman provinces. Whether they are still under Roman rule, I cannot know.

Two days later, the channel has narrowed again and we are in the Gulf of Suez, with the land in plain sight on both sides of the ship. It narrows further, and I can see a large city at the head of this gulf. The captain calls us together after breakfast to addresses us.

'We are approaching Suez City, for those who haven't been through the canal before. We'll be boarded by Egyptian officials, who will want to see passports and may do a walk around. They'll leave a pilot on board for the length of the canal, which will take us all day to traverse.

'Our Italian friend here, being without a passport, makes things difficult for all of us. I could report you to the Egyptians as a stowaway. They'll seize you and put you in an Egyptian prison where I doubt you'll last very long. It's what you deserve, but as a Christian man, I cannot bring myself to inflict this on you. Since you came aboard, you've been nothing but helpful around ship and I'm quite sure you are very sorry for putting us in this situation.

'Marcus, you will hide in one of the containers aft, we will lock you in and make sure no one sees you. You must keep quiet until after dark, until we are through the canal and into the Mediterranean. Then we will fetch you out. Will you agree to this?'

'Yes, I will hide. I will keep quiet. Please, don't let them put me in prison.'

'All right then. You two, Lito and Paulo, find a container on the starboard side, which will be in the shade, so he doesn't roast to death. Bolt and reseal it, so it doesn't stand out. And for God's sake, remember which container you put him in. Albert, fix him some food and water. And give him a bucket for when nature calls.'

So, I find myself once again in a hot metal box. I can see nothing, but I can tell the ship has slowed as the vibrations from the engine are much diminished. Soon we come nearly to a halt, with the engine barely running. I hear the sound of a small boat approach. I hear voices of unfamiliar men. After a long delay, the ship moves again, very slowly, and I assume we have entered the Suez Canal itself. Though shaded by other containers, the heat is stifling inside this box. I strip off my clothes and pour water over my head for relief. The day passes disagreeably.

Hours later, it cools a little. It must be near sunset. We are still travelling at a snail's pace, slowing almost to a stop at times. Finally, at nightfall, the ship's engines roar to full power. I can feel the familiar pitch and roll of the ship, we are back in the open sea. Not long after, Albert comes to free me from my prison.

'Hoy, Marcus! Still alive in there? Or are you cooked like a roast chicken?'

'Alive, not roasted, just a little boiled. Kumusta, Albert?'

'Mabuti, Marcus. Come, let's go up. You don't have to cook tonight. I think you've suffered enough today.'

'Thanks Albert. I just need water. I could drink a whole amphora—'

'A what?'

I smile and shake my head as we head up to the cabin.

That night, I rest on deck, happy to feel the cool air on my body. With the land far behind, the sky is again black and brilliantly lit with stars. I study their patterns, they are once again familiar: the Bull, the Hunter, the Great Dog. Proof I am nearly home. Soon I will be in Italy. But I suspect not the Italy I know. Will anything be the same?

CHAPTER XII

Two days later, we pass the great island of Crete, and we are amongst the Greek Islands. Historic Greece, cradle of civilization! I have long dreamed of making a voyage here. The brilliant blue-green hues of the sea and the whitewashed houses, perched on dark cliffs, that glisten in the morning sun are strikingly beautiful. I am told that the world's wealthiest people build their villas here, as they did in my time. I am not surprised; to bathe in the warm waters of the Aegean and to drink the fabulous wine, could there be a better life?

It is night when the ship approaches Piraeus, the port of Athens. The waters are thick with ships of all sorts. Due to congestion, we are not able to approach the docks but must anchor a mile or two offshore. The bustling port is well lit with brilliant white floodlights. Dozens of ships stand at the wharves, while tall cranes work shifting cargo.

Over dinner, the crew excitedly discuss their plans for

when they go ashore the next day. It is their first time on land in nearly two months, and they can't wait for their leave. Much of the talk is around what they will indulge in first: food, drink, or women. The captain brings up the subject of what will be done with me. He points out the proper course would be to hand me over to the Greek officials, where they would likely hold me for a short time until they are satisfied of my Italian citizenship, before releasing me.

'Would they put me in prison?'

'Only for a few days, perhaps.' Seeing the pain in my face, he smiles. 'Another option is to invent some tale, that you are a crew member who has lost your passport and papers.'

'But they would hardly believe he is crew, not being Pinoy.' says Lito. "Pinoy" I know is their affectionate term for a man of the Philippines.

'Pinoy ako naman!' I tell them all that I am Filipino and they all grin. But I wish to be a burden on them no longer. 'Please captain, may I go ashore here? I will make my own way to Italy. I don't wish to cause you any more trouble.'

Everyone's eyes turn to the captain. 'Marcus, it is true you caused us considerable grief by sneaking aboard the *Anastasia*. But you have acted honestly since we discovered you, and you have pulled your oar as hard as any sailor. You have made friends of all of us. If it is your wish to go ashore here, then so be it. You are Italian by birth, so you are a European. No one can prevent you disembarking, papers or not. Just lay low when the customs officer arrives. You can go ashore quietly tomorrow, after we've unloaded.' The crew all nod in agreement. 'We will miss you, son.' The captain stands and shakes my hand.

Albert jumps up, drink in hand. 'To Marcus. A toast to you, kaibigan!'

'To Marcus!' they all shout, and drink to my health.

'Thank you,' is all I can say, lowering my head. I will miss my sailor friends.

I again conceal myself in a container when customs officers finally come on board near midnight. After the crew's identities are taken, and the ship's papers and manifest inspected, we are cleared to enter port. The officials depart promptly, and I emerge from my hiding place. I find some of the crew in the dining room, too excited to sleep.

Few of us get any sleep. By sunrise we are up and having our breakfast. Soon a small vessel brings the pilot aboard, and we are slowly pushed by small tugs to our mooring. Once made fast to the wharf, the hatches are opened, and cargo to be landed here in Greece is identified. Somehow, the crew knows which of the thousands of containers above and below decks need to come off the ship here. The ship's crane springs to life, picking up the containers, rearranging them on the deck, while a much larger crane ashore takes them off. All day I watch the unloading. Ashore, a convoy of trucks is queued up on the wharf. As each container is brought over the side, it is lowered onto a truck that drives off within seconds. It all proceeds very efficiently.

The unloading is complete by sunset. There are no more trucks waiting. The crew, eager for their shore leave, have emerged from below, washed, shaved, and dressed in fine clothes; the first time I have seen them this way. I follow their lead and put on my best Australian clothes. We say our farewells at the top of the gangway, with many embraces and shoulder slaps, wishing each other well. Albert, my closest friend onboard, embraces me warmly.

'Sige! Goodbye, Marcus. Safe travels, wherever you go. God bless you.'

'Thank you, Albert. May you have Neptune's blessing too, wherever you sail.'

'Thank you, Marcus. Keep safe.' Soon all but the captain have departed and disappeared into the night. He emerges from his cabin, wearing his civilian clothes. He looks much less formidable without his uniform.

'Well Marcus, I think it safe for you to disembark now. Thank you for all your help onboard these past weeks. You are a fine sailor.'

'Thank you, sir, for accommodating me. You all have been very kind and generous to me.'

'On a long voyage we all work together. It's the only way to run a ship at sea. Here, I have a small gift for you.' He presses a small pin into my hand. It is a silhouette of the ship with *Anastasia* in tiny letters across its hull. 'I give these to every crewman, so they may remember their time aboard. Look on the back.' Scratched in small letters on the back is "Marcus 2019".

'It is very pleasing. Thank you, captain. I won't forget you—and the ship.' But what could I give him in return?

'One moment, sir.' I rush to my cabin and collect my things. I present the captain a little gift. 'Here. Please take this.' I hand him a shiny, new silver denarius. 'It is a coin of my country. Please take it in gratitude, and as a remembrance of your Roman sailor.'

'Very impressive! Who is the portrait?'

'It is Tiberius, who is emperor of Rome. *Was* emperor of Rome.'

'Thank you. That's very, um, interesting. Okay then, you had best be off. Are you all packed up?'

'Yes, my bag is packed, just there.'

'All right. Goodbye now. Stay out of trouble. Easy to get into mischief in a foreign port.'

'I will. Goodbye captain.' We shake hands, and I head down the stairs and disembark.

Having learnt that Piraeus is but a short distance from the centre of Athens, I set off on foot. It is early evening, and the road is thick with traffic. Cars, trucks, and motorcycles zoom about, all spewing thick, choking smoke. I work my way along the shoreline, passing container yards and parking lots. I regret not taking a taxi to the town centre, for the noise, smoke and dirty streets are making travelling on foot hard going.

Little by little the industrial lands around the port give way to residential streets. I pause at a traffic light. Far away to the east, high on a hill, is a glistening temple. The Parthenon of Athens! It's a magnificent sight, with its stately columns bathed in soft, yellow lights. This temple to Athena was already ancient in my day, and it is still there, perched on the hill overlooking the city, as it has been for thousands of years. Here I am in Athens, where Plato, Socrates and Aristotle lived and preached. The land of the Greek heroes, of Olympus, Delphi, Sparta!

I press on, catching glimpses of the Parthenon from time to time, as I find myself in the middle of modern Athens. There are small eateries in abundance lining the busy roads. Unlike in Australia, the signposts are in Greek letters. I regret doing poorly at my Greek lessons last winter. The aroma of grilling lamb leads me to a small restaurant just off the main road. It has a few tables laid out in handsome white and blue tablecloths. Inside, several roasts of beef and lamb are mounted on metal spits, slowly grilling over charcoal. It looks and smells irresistible, so with signs I order a roast lamb roll. It comes wrapped in a sort of soft bread with garlic sauce and leaf vegetables. It is exquisite, and I order another.

I notice that people coming and going at the restaurant not only speak Greek, but other languages as well, English among them. This is as surprising as it is comforting. While I can't imagine how it came to be that people in Greece would speak the language of Britannia, it will certainly be useful to me.

I also discover my Australian money is not accepted here. The man behind the counter directs me to a kiosk across the road, advertising "Money Changer" in several languages. I dispose of my Australian dollars for a much smaller amount of European money, which they call "euros".

There is a hotel a few doors down. With my legs stiff from the long walk from the wharf I take a room on the spot. It is quite cheap, under fifty euro, but turns out to be rather dingy and noisy. The stink of diesel fumes combined with less than perfect sanitation is not pleasant. Sleeping is difficult; I resort to stuffing tissue into my ears and holding the pillow tightly over my head. At last, I drop off.

The din of traffic begins before dawn and I can sleep no longer. I decide that I must make the pilgrimage up the Acropolis hill. How could I miss the chance to visit the most famous temple in the world? I take breakfast of some excellent Greek sweets and a tiny cup of potent coffee. I order some extra food for the journey and to make an offering to Athena, then begin my ascent of the temple hill.

The climb is gentle at first, though as the morning progresses the road steepens, and the sun grows hot on my shoulders. The traffic is less dense here, and I feel the powerful energy of this place. I have a clear view of the mighty Parthenon now, its marble columns dazzlingly white against the clear blue sky.

On a spur of the mountain, a sign directs me to the "Theatre of Herodes Atticus", built into the side of the hill. A signboard declares this to be built by the Romans in AD 161. Built by my people! The first I have seen in this new world. It is in marvellous condition, with thirty or more rows of terraced stone seating forming a semi-circle about the stage. I rest for a moment on the top row of seats. A gentle breeze blows. There's a stunning view of the city and sea. *My people built this.* I am nearing home.

I continue up the hill to the Parthenon itself, where many tourists have already arrived. After paying a small fee, I join the crowds at the foot of the temple. How resplendent! Its tremendous columns reach skyward, in perfect harmony with the heavens. Worthy of the great goddess Athena, whom we Romans call Minerva. Though we are not permitted to enter the temple itself, the view of its exterior is unsurpassed, leaving a profound impression of beauty and endurance. It reminds me of the temples in the Forum at Rome, though none are so grand, or as ancient as this.

Though its roof is gone, the Parthenon still stands in the twenty-first century. Many generations of men have lived and died, yet these stones still stand. All around are ruins of other structures that have not survived the ages. The cylinders of toppled columns lie about, weeds grow between the stones.

I take a seat on an ancient stone and eat my bread and cheese. There is little shade here; the sun burns my arms and shoulders. I study the crowd of visitors, young and old from all nations speaking a hundred different languages, who have all made the journey here to the birthplace of civilization.

I know I will soon be back in Italy, for it is only a few days journey now. What will I find in Rome? For we were the inheritors of Greek culture. Are the great temples, monuments and palaces of the Romans still standing? I long to know, but fear to find out.

I linger on the Acropolis hill until late afternoon, exploring the ruins, resting often to take in the view. The port of Piraeus is visible in the distance. I imagine the *Anastasia* is still there, her men preparing to head to sea once more. I miss those happy evenings around the cabin table after dinner, singing and telling stories. I miss my galley partner, Albert, who first befriended me.

As the shadows grow long, the tourists depart. Soon there are only a few of us left, savouring the tranquillity. I return to the Parthenon and offer a prayer on my knees to Athena, Zeus and Artemis, the great and ancient gods of the Greeks. I scrape a small hole in the earth and leave a small offering of food. Such powerful gods, to have dwelt here for thirty centuries guiding and protecting the Greek people, to whom the world owes so much. A security guard in a blue uniform approaches and politely points to the exit gate. I descend the hill slowly, reluctant to face the smoky streets below.

I keep an eye open for a hotel, for I have no intention of staying another night in the same noisy hovel. There are many hotels at the foot of the Acropolis hill, serving the innumerable tourists who make the pilgrimage here. I select one called the "Marble Inn". The room is small but comfortable, and best of all it is on a quiet lane away from the traffic.

It has been many hours since my modest lunch. I set out on the narrow streets in quest of something to eat. The marvellous smell of grilling meat draws me to a nearby eating house. I order a couple of souvlakis, as the lamb rolls are called, and sit outside on a broken stool to savour them. It is the best meal I've had, in the twenty-first century anyway.

Before retiring, I inquire with the innkeeper, a helpful man named Nikolas, what is the best way to take passage to Italy.

He is not surprised when I tell him I do not want to take one of the flying machines; he too prefers to keep both feet on the ground. He sells me a bus ticket to Patras, where I can take a ferry bound for Brindisi on the southern tip of Italy. Ticket in hand, I bid him goodnight.

The bus departs early in the morning, and I am up at dawn to ensure I do not miss it. The bus station is only a few blocks away. The passage out of the city is painfully slow, the traffic chaotic. Finally, we leave Athens behind. The rest of the journey is very pleasant. Our route takes us along the Gulf of Corinth, its blue waters on our right, rocky hills on our left. Fields of olive and grape line the road. I feel a pain of homesickness, and anxiety of what I shall find when I finally reach Italy. Every mile, every hour, brings me closer to home and further from Australia. I see Sabina's face again, it seems an eternity since I last saw her, saying our farewells under the willow tree. Will she even remember me?

We arrive at Patras, an unremarkable town, in mid-afternoon. We disembark not far from the docks, where several passenger ships are tied up, painted blue and white. I am just in time to purchase a ferry ticket to Brindisi, which I learn crosses the Adriatic overnight. I have time for a quick greasy meal at one of the many restaurants near the wharf.

Upon boarding the ship I realise I have purchased a deck fare, which means neither bed nor cabin, merely a seat in the large cabin forward. I ought to have known this, for the fare was a mere forty euro. It takes a long time to embark all the passengers, and there is an annoying delay before it finally departs. In the twilight I watch the lights of Greece recede. Soon there is nothing to see but the dark sky. I prop myself up in the hard seat the best I can and try to sleep.

CHAPTER XIII

After an uncomfortable night, I purchase bread and strong coffee from the cafe on board. Ahead, there is still little to see except the green waters of the Adriatic. The day warms, and in the calm weather I venture outside to sit in the sun at the bow. Soon the land is visible. Many passengers come to the rail. *Italy!* At last! I can see the land clearly now, the brown hills of Apulia. As we draw closer, I can make out the dry hills and farms.

By mid-morning we have arrived off the port of Brindisi. It is a large town, centred around a prominent hill on which are perched pretty, whitewashed houses and many churches. Surrounding the hill is the modern town with its busy streets. Though I have never visited this place, called Brundisum in my time, it has a long and famous history. It has a fine harbour and a strategic position at the tip of Italy. There was a Greek city here for 200 years before it became Roman. We learnt as children that the great poet Virgil, who penned *The Aeneid,* lived and wrote here. Perhaps I could pay my respects at his tomb, but will it be here still after twenty centuries?

The passengers rush towards the bow as the ship turns and manoeuvres to the dockside. It takes some minutes to tie up. The passengers shuffle about impatiently. Finally, the gate swings open and there is a rush down the ramp. I follow behind and plant my foot on Italian soil at last.

The moment is marred by the appearance of dozens of hawkers, thrusting pamphlets in our faces, peddling their hotel and taxi services. I push through them, avoiding eye contact. They continue to follow, however, and telling them 'no' has no effect. One follows on my heels near a quarter mile, until I deliver him some choice curses in Latin. He throws his hands up and retreats, uttering some curses of his own.

I continue my walk along the waterfront, which is attractively lined with palms. Brindisi has a well-protected harbour, and boats of all sizes are moored here, including many small, private yachts. Around the harbour are the whitewashed buildings of the town. I head towards the hill that marks the centre of the old town. Before I reach it, I come to a broad stone staircase. It leads up to a small plaza surrounded by old stone buildings, one of which is a church. In the centre of the plaza is an imposing column in the Roman style, and the remains of a second, long since collapsed. A placard advises that this column marks end of the "Via Appia", the ancient road from Rome. A fitting place to begin the last leg of my journey.

Atop the column is a much-worn sculpture of Neptune facing the sea and images of Jupiter, Mars, and Minerva are carved into the faces of the column. *The gods of my people, welcoming me to Italy.* Nothing will stop me returning to Rome now. I put my hand on the cold stone of the column and whisper a prayer for a safe journey, not only to Rome but back to my time. All roads lead to Rome they say. I will take the Via Appia home, even if I must walk every mile of it.

I return to the harbour side, where mercifully the hawkers have now dispersed. There are many restaurants there; I venture into one specialising in seafood. I have an early lunch of grilled fish, shrimp and scallops. The fare is superb, but sets me back thirty euro, which is near fifty Australian dollars. I must economise if my money is to last until Rome.

I lazily explore the waterfront. In a shop window, I see a poster advertising cities: Taranto, Salerno, Napoli, Roma. The new names for our great Roman cities: Tarentum, Salernum, Neapolis, Rome. The shop is an agenti di viaggio, a travel agent, which is exactly what I am in need of.

Inside, I purchase a ticket for something called "Trenitalia". The agent tries to explain, in a mix of English and Italian, that this is not a bus, but a train, another form of transport. She tells me there are no more direct trains to Rome today, but I can book a ticket through to Naples. A small map guides me to the train station.

I soon discover that a train consists of connected carriages that travel on iron rails, pulled by an electric engine. Inside the station, there are many platforms for boarding, with difficulty I find the correct one. After a few minutes, the train creeps into the station slowly and majestically. The engine has beautiful sleek lines, and the carriages shine like silver. It rolls silently to a stop. The doors open automatically, and it disgorges its passengers.

A young man inspects my ticket and redirects me to enter further down the platform. The carriage is spacious and well appointed. The broad windows are tinted, the seats comfortable. Boarding continues for half an hour or so, but the carriage is less than half full. With a whistle and a shout, the doors close, and we begin to move. The train inches out of the station and picks up speed. Faster and faster we go, until we are moving at a dizzying pace. It is astonishing how quiet and smooth the ride is. For the engine makes no noise and emits no fumes. From time to time, a hostess comes around and takes orders for food and drink. How civilized. I have now found my new favourite way to travel.

In minutes the city has been left behind, and we are moving through rich farmland, green and prosperous. Out the big picture windows, the southern Italian countryside rushes past. We make a few stops at the larger towns: Latiano, Francavilla, Fontana. In a mere hour we have crossed the heel of Italy. A voice announces we are arriving in Taranto, a large city and the second great harbour of Apulia.

The train lingers for half an hour, and many passengers board here. Every seat is taken, and some people must stand in the aisle. A group of schoolgirls sit opposite me, engaged in loud conversation in Italian. I can make out a few words, they are discussing their classmates, teachers, and boyfriends. Soon I grow weary of the chatter, as do most of the passengers within earshot, judging by their frowns and sighs.

We pull out of Taranto and continue our voyage north. The schoolgirls disembark at the next stop, to the relief of all. The landscape becomes more rugged as we cross the centre of the Italian peninsula. After an hour we reach the sea once again and approach Salerno. We progress slowly through endless industrial suburbs, a depressing sight after the green of the countryside, and finally arrive in the city centre. I pace up and down the aisle, impatient to reach our final stop.

We arrive in Naples in the early evening. The train moves painfully slowly through the outer suburbs of this city, which I knew as Neapolis. By all appearances, it is now a vast city. I recognise no landmarks; the untidy city is a mad tumble of buildings of all sizes, its streets full of impatient traffic. After several pauses, the train arrives in the centre of the city at a station named Garibaldi.

As expected, there are numerous lodging houses in the surrounding streets, but none very appealing. I take a room in a shabby hotel with the grand name of the "Hotel Napoli Bellissima". An ironic name, as it turns out.

I am eager to call Sabina. The room has no phone but there is one accepting coins in the lobby. After inserting the requisite money and dialling many digits, the phone rings, and a sleepy voice answers.

'Marcus. Woo hoo! You finally called! It's been two months, I was so worried.'

'I am sorry, but I had no chance to call. Did I wake you?'

'Yes, well it's three thirty in the morning here.'

'Really?' She tries to explain 'time zones' but she completely baffles me.

'Never mind. Just call a little earlier in the day. So, where are you? Last time you called you were in Melbourne! Are you home yet?'

'I am in Italy, in Neapolis. I mean, Naples.'

'That's fantastic! Have you been to your house yet? Were your family happy to see you?'

'No, not yet. Perhaps tomorrow I go up there, to where their farm was. Where it is, I mean.'

'How was your trip? Did you find a ship to take you to Europe? Or did you end up flying after all?'

'I did take a ship. Though it was difficult to find one.' I tell her of my journey from Melbourne to Greece, leaving out the part where I stowed away. 'We were at sea many weeks, that is why I could not call you.'

'I get you. Well, that makes sense. Don't worry, I forgive you. Did you like Greece? Did you see the Parthenon?'

'I did! It was magnificent. So … eternal. I said a prayer to Athena, asking her for guidance on my journey home.'

'Okay good, not something most tourists would do. So, do you miss me, Marcus?'

'I do, very much. I think of you every day. Wishing you were here with me.'

'Oh! I *so* want to go to Italy with you. But my mum and dad didn't like the idea. Maybe in the July school holidays I could come and visit you. I took a job at the grocery store after school. To save some money for airfare.'

'Good! That's great. I would love to see you, my angel. But I am not certain if I'll still be here.' How can I explain to her—when I go home, to my *real* home and time, it will be impossible to see each other again?

'What, are you going travelling again so soon?'

'I am not sure. Time will tell.' *Only the gods know.* 'How have you been? How are you faring with your lessons? Is your school year completed?'

'School! Blah! Yes, it's all done in December. I got eighty in history and ninety-one in English Lit.'

'Is that good?'

'Ha ha silly. Yes, it's very good. One hundred percent is the best, don't you know that?'

'Yes, I know. I am, how you say, joking you. How is Futura? Have you been racing?'

'No, Mum wanted me to focus on schoolwork, and Dad thinks it's dangerous. But at Easter there'll be racing on at Quilpie and I'm going to enter, riding Futura.'

'That's great. You are a natural rider. I know you love horses and to race. Makes you very joyful.'

'You know me, don't you.'

'Yes, I truly do. My Aussie girlfriend, right?'

'I like the sound of that. My Italian boyfriend!' She falls silent. 'So, where are you off to tomorrow?'

'I will explore Naples. It is a great city with much history.'

'Oh, I'm jealous. I sure wish you could show me around. I wish I were with you.'

'I'll call you again soon and tell you my latest adventures.'

'I love you, Marcus.' Her words catch me by surprise. There's an awkward silence.

'I love you too, Sabina.'

'Look after yourself, you crazy man. Call me soon.'

'I will angel. And you too. Work hard at your lessons. It will stead you well in future, of that I am sure. Send my greetings to your mother and father.'

'I will. Bye Marcus!'

'Goodbye, darling.' I realise how much I miss this sweet, loving girl. She has touched my heart and leaving her behind pains me. I know if I go home to my time I will never hear her voice or see her smile again, and it troubles me.

Having not stretched my legs all day, I set off to explore the city. Though it is after sunset, the traffic, both vehicle and human, has not abated in the slightest. The warm smell of hot food draws me to a small eating house. A brightly lit sign advertises "Pizza". The menu board lists several varieties, I select "Pizza funghi". It soon arrives, hot from a brick oven; a sort of thin pastry covered in tomato sauce, cheese, herbs, and mushrooms. I have no difficulty devouring the entire plate. If only the rest of the world knew about this delectable dish.

Back in my room, I sit on the tiny veranda overlooking the busy square. Motorcycles rush down the road, spewing smoke and noise. How unpleasant to live in a city in the twenty-first century! It is a mystery why any man who has a choice would dwell here rather than on a farm or in a peaceful provincial village.

It is a sultry night, and I lie in the dark struggling to sleep. The little ceiling fan provides little relief. I see my mother and father, the familiar places of home. Here in Neapolis I am only thirty-five miles from my parent's farm. Or, *where it once was.* I could easily get there. But what would I find? I'm a fool to think that anything would remain. No, not worth the trip. Yet the thought haunts my mind. Could I even *find* the farm? I remember the route well. Surely the mountains and rivers, the eternal landmarks, will still be there. Only Jupiter himself could erase them.

I doze off, but awaken again with the thought still on my mind. *What is thirty-five miles?* I switch on the light; its brightness burns my eyes. By the gods, I will go to our farm. It is two hours before dawn but I can't wait any longer. I throw my possessions into my pack and leave the hotel quietly. I strike out to the east, following the dreary city streets which are deserted at this hour.

As the sky lightens, the great bulk of Mount Vesuvius emerges from the darkness, vast and stark in the clear morning air. Its sides are covered in vineyards and greenery nearly to the top. The summit is black and blasted, a small puff of steam rises from the top. My route passes north of it. The mountain seems to hardly move, though I walk at a brisk pace. The city goes on forever. Residential land gives way to industrial: factories, warehouses, weedy lots and car sellers. By mid-morning, the city finally peters out. The road broadens and the pace of traffic increases frighteningly. I realise I am the only one on foot, alongside thousands of speeding vehicles. I regret not seeking some sort of motorised transport. I curse myself for not bringing food or drink. I press on.

By late morning, Vesuvius is far behind. The signs advise I am approaching the town of Marigliano, a little village at the crossroads of two highways. A station selling fuel, food and drink is a welcome sight. Some doughnuts and a sugary drink revive me. I sit outside, where there're a few tables for travellers, and wonder whether I will make Abellinum before dark.

I return to the shop and fill my pack with provisions, for I am unsure where I may spend the night. I walk through the pleasant town. It has many well-maintained stone buildings on its main street and large, leafy plane trees give welcome shade. In the village square is a tall stone monument with a bronze eagle on top. Could this be a Roman monument? "Pro Patria", says the inscription, "1940–1945". On the column, a dozen men's names are inscribed. It is a monument to fallen soldiers. A few flowers, now faded, have been left at its base. "Pax" the monument reads. Peace. The scourge of war still exists, will it ever be otherwise? I follow the road leading east. Soon I've left the town behind, and a sign indicates the town of Nola three miles distant. Encouraging, for Nola is the halfway point on my journey.

The miles pass quickly. The terrain changes: the flat cultivated land gives way to rugged hills. The road runs up a valley between the peaks. After puffing my way up a small rise, the city of Nola comes into view. It looks as it did it my day. Whitewashed houses with red tile roofs and dark cypress trees shimmer in the hot Italian sun. This town is famous as the place where Augustus took his last breath before being taken up into heaven. I wonder if there is a shrine to him here.

As I draw near, the twenty-first century Nola reveals itself with many modern buildings, and streets filled with parked cars. Still, it is a pleasant town, with many parks along the main road where a traveller can rest his weary legs. The streets are tidy with numerous well-tended flower boxes. I come to a spacious square, a pretty plaza surrounded by fine stone buildings and a grand church. But nothing shows the Roman people were ever here.

I rest on a bench at one side of the square and scrounge in my pack for something to eat. Though well fed, my feet ache, and the thought of having to walk another fifteen miles is disheartening. I notice several buses stop on the opposite side of the square. They arrive, linger a minute, and drive off. I watch closely the destination signs, but none are bound for Abellinum. Most are headed for Napoli. At least I shouldn't have difficulty getting back to the city. At length I see a bus marked "Avellino". It dawns on me that this is the modern spelling of Abellinum. I rush across the square and board. I'll not have to walk the fifteen miles after all.

As the bus drives east out of town, the road rises sharply. The terrain becomes rugged with lofty hills on both sides, the vegetation on their tops is burnt brown but green in the valleys between. The towns slip by, Schiava and Biano, then there is the long trek up and over the summit of the Apennines. The land is now too rugged for cultivation. Descending, we reach

Monteforte, and just beyond it, at last I can see Abellinum. The red tiles of the neat little houses look just as they did in my day. In a few minutes we are in Avellino, and I disembark.

The main street, "Via Italia", runs the same course straight and true, but the buildings are unfamiliar. I arrive in the town square and stand in the exact spot I stood a few months ago. This is the old forum, now called "Piazza Liberat". It is incredible to be here again, where nothing and everything has changed. There, on the west side, was the fish market. Over there, the vegetable sellers. On the very spot where I stand, our family friends Gaius and Livia sold their fine cloth. And there, where a small stone building now sits, was the town hall. Here, in the morning twice a week, a line would form of aggrieved and over-taxed citizens seeking appointments with the magistrate.

I am so close to my home! And yet a staggering gap remains, not of distance, but of time; the men, the women, the children that I used to know, are gone. Dead and gone, so long ago their bones have crumbled to dust. Am I the only Roman alive? Have I been chosen by the gods to be immortal? Not likely. But if so, I have lived longer than any man ever has. What is to be my fate?

I buy an orange and grapes. The young raven-haired woman serving me, aside from her clothing and the phone in her hand, could be the same Roman farmer's wife that served me in my own time. From the piazza, it is easy to find the road north, leading to our family farm. But the modern road takes a bend away to the east. Now I will have to find my own way.

I take my bearings; the hills, the dry gullies, I have known them all my life.

The land is well cultivated, the hillsides covered with neatly tended groves of olive and grape, just as in my day. Fences bar the way in some places, which I am obliged to climb over. I keep out of sight of the farmhouses, wary of being caught trespassing. The land rises and grows more broken. It becomes drier and the groves give over to pasture.

After an hour's walk, I must be near our farm—yet I cannot find it. The boundaries of the properties have changed, the paths and tracks, the familiar trees and houses, no longer exist. I know our farm is close by, but not a trace remains of our house, barn, or fences. There is a small rise with a rocky outcrop not far away, perhaps the view will be better there. I ascend slowly. I am on my last legs. At the top, I rest on a large round stone. People have been here before; the ground is littered with beer cans. The afternoon sun caresses my face, all around, the long grass ripples and waves in the strong breeze, sometimes bringing the smell of cattle. I feel so close to home. Weary in body and spirit, I stretch out on my back and stare at the blue sky, dotted with big puffy clouds. At least nothing has changed in the heavens above. The land around me too, the burnt hills of central Italy are the same as they've always been. Yet I'm further from home than ever.

CHAPTER XIV

The day is getting on, and it's time to go. I start down the rocky hill, and head for the road I can see to the south. On my right, I notice a small depression in the land, filled with a copse of willow trees that I had not noticed before. Why, it looks just like the little pond on our farm! I rush over through the long grass.

The vision is one I have seen a thousand times: the shallow pool, weeping branches waving in the breeze, the little stone bench. I stroke the soft foliage. Are these graceful trees the descendants of those that stood here 2,000 years ago? If they could only speak. What stories they could tell, of my family and their fate, and that of a hundred other farmers who have owned this land since, raising cattle and horse, the olive and the vine.

I collect a handful of soil and let it run through my fingers. Fine, fertile, black. Cultivated, I am sure, since long before even we Romans came here. I kick at the soft dirt. I catch a glimpse of something, a flash of blue in the sunlight. I paw away the dirt, and discover a tiny shard of blue marble, no bigger than my thumbnail. The pattern on it—I know it. It is from the marble bench my father built here! Smashed by men, weathered by the ages, who can say what happened to it? Father! You left this here for me. I know it! Mother, Sister. Here we sat, on this very spot, countless times in hot afternoons, ages ago. I carefully pocket the tiny shard, with a little soil clinging to it. The soil of my homeland. I will carry it with me until I pass from this earth.

I poke about, looking for signs of our house, but not a trace remains. The shadows grow long, and it is time to head back to Avellino. I don't want to be out after dark. I hurry back down to the town, now buzzing with people. I easily find a bus bound for Napoli. Ten euro buys me passage and saves me thirty-five miles on foot, a good bargain. I slump into my seat and stare blankly out the window as darkness swallows the Campanian countryside.

Within an hour I am back in the centre of Naples. The bus disgorges its passengers not far from the train station. The Bellissima hotel is a short walk. Too exhausted to seek better accommodation, I again take a room. Though badly in need of sleep, I am more in need of food. A nearby pizzeria answers, though the wait is long, there being many patrons ahead of me standing about impatiently. At last, I am served my pizza in a little box. I take it up to my room, tear open the box, and gulp the food down greedily. I fall asleep, exhausted.

I sleep late the next day, then stare out the window, brooding. Out on the street, I peer in one or two shops, but nothing interests me. My legs are stiff from yesterday's trek. I return to my room to sleep away the afternoon.

As the room darkens, I make my way again to the streets. I soon find a drinking house. Inside, small knots of men converse loudly amongst themselves. Few are interested in speaking to a stranger, so I depart after a single ale. I make my way towards my hotel, but after a time I realise I have lost my bearings. The streets here go every which way and all look alike in the dark. I curse myself for my stupidity. *Marcus, you've done it again.* I ask a man for directions to the Hotel Napoli Belissima, but he dismisses me with a wave. After a few more attempts, I give up and search for a taxi. But it is late, and there are none to be found. I enter what looks like a small bar.

The room is quite bare, with only a handful of tables. A group of rough looking men are sitting on plastic chairs in the dim light, smoking and drinking. They glare at me.

'Please men, where to get taxi?' I ask. They all stare, one laughs dismissively. Another, a balding middle-aged man with a large belly, gets up.

'Taxi, why of course signor straniero! I get you taxi.' He converses with his companions in low tones. 'Sit, sit,' says the bald man. 'Taxi arriverà in cinque minuti. Five minutes, he come.'

I thank him and sit, relieved. Italians, I conclude, are good people. Back in Quilpie, were not Sabina's family decent and kind people? After considerably more than five minutes, a car pulls up outside. The driver exchanges loud greetings with the bald man. 'Bruno here, he take you anywhere you want to go. He best friend.'

'Take me to Belissima Hotel? Please, sir,' I ask.

'Of course. A Belissima!' He slaps me on the back.

'Andiamo! Come,' says my driver. He leads me to his car, opening the rear door for me. Curiously, there is no "Taxi" sign on the roof, nor the usual markings on its sides. We drive off, through the gloomy streets. We make many turns and are going further from the city centre, until we are many miles out. We are on a main highway, travelling at speed.

'Are we soon to arrive?' I ask.

'Si, very soon. I go special way. More quicker.'

We enter an industrial area, devoid of houses or shops. There are no people about, and I don't like this.

'Okay, sir. You stop here. I go here,' I say. I try to open the door, but it is locked. I feel a cold sweat. *Am I to be robbed? Or murdered?*

We arrive at a long low building. A single window is lit from within. Bruno drives around the back, where a roller door is open. We drive inside, and from the shadows a youth, barely a man, emerges and pulls down the garage door behind us. *Trapped like a rat in a cage.*

The room is lit with a bare bulb hanging from a wire. A man is seated beneath it, his face covered by his hat. Several ancient cars, wooden crates, and trash are barely visible in this dilapidated factory. Another man dressed in a white shirt with no sleeves nor collar opens the car door and drags me out by the arm. Yet another, a massive bear of a man, approaches carrying a metal bar.

'Your bag. Dammelo. Give it. Presto!' he barks. Surrounded

by thugs, the only door blocked by the bear-man, I have no choice. 'Presto! Or I break your skull.' Slowly and deliberately, I pull it from my shoulder and hold it out to him.

'Please, take my pack. It is yours, sir. Please don't kill me.'

The young man takes it and tosses it on the desk, where the seated man looks up and peers at me.

'Dinero. And your money. Give it now!' shouts the bear.

'I have only a little, in the bag.' But they don't believe me. The man with the iron bar thrusts it hard into my ribs. I fall, gasping for breath. I try to stand but cannot. I feel a searing pain whenever I draw breath.

The young man, his face pocked with acne, approaches. 'La giacca! Your jacket. Give it!' The other men laugh. He pulls the leather jacket from my shoulders, spinning me onto my back, then puts it on. My precious jacket! The one I bought with Sabina on our shopping day in Quilpie.

'Cowboy. Clint Eastwood!' shouts white shirt. The others find this funny.

'Empty your pockets.' The bear-man comes at me and raises the iron bar for another blow. I quickly roll away.

'Si, si! I give.' I turn out my pockets and watch the last of my money fall to the floor: a roll of notes, and a handful of coins that scatter about the room. The boy gathers them and brings it to the boss' table.

'Eight hundred euro. Rich boy, no?'

I slowly rise to a sitting position, my chest in agony. I have to take short breaths, for a deep breath hurts unbearably. 'You not kill me?' I gasp. The old man at the desk crosses his arms.

'Don't worry, amico. We will not kill you. Just doing a little business. Our government says tourists are good for the economy. And it is a proven fact.' He looks to the others and they share another laugh. 'Get him out of here.'

Bruno, the driver who brought me here, approaches. 'Come, we go now.' I try to stand but it is impossible. I collapse to my knees, clutching my chest. 'Luca! Aiutatelo.'

The bear-man drops his weapon. Together with Bruno, they lift me by the arms, drag me to the car and heave me into the back seat. Luca gets in beside me while Bruno takes the wheel. The engine starts with a roar, the warehouse door is raised, and we are once more in the shadowy streets of Naples. Wedged in the corner against the door with my knees drawn up, I try to keep motionless. I fear my ribs have been broken. We drive on through the deserted streets, the white streetlights casting weird shadows on the road.

After a few miles, the car lurches to a stop. Luca reaches over me and pushes open the door.

'Fuori! Out!' He kicks me in my side, and I tumble out into the gutter. The door slams shut. The car speeds off.

The fall has made the intense pain in my chest even worse, something I thought impossible. I struggle to remain conscious. The slightest movement, even drawing a breath, brings a stabbing pain and a pounding in my head. *Clementia! Goddess of mercy, help me. Ease my suffering.* I lie on my side, motionless on the concrete. Around me, silence. It is well past midnight, and no one does business at this hour. In this dark quarter, only a fool would go about alone.

Nearby, I make out a row of shops. A lighted sign above one reads "Villaricca Café", though half the letters are broken. In the dim light I see sturdy metal bars across its windows; the door is shuttered with a metal gate, as are the businesses next to it. Just like the rough quarter of Neapolis in my time. I crawl and limp over to the cafe, and collapse in the doorway. If I can survive until dawn, perhaps the shop keeper will help me. I wedge myself in the corner of the alcove, out of sight. I slip into unconsciousness.

'Hoy! Fuori!' a man snarls at me. The sun is up, its light blinds me as I try to see my new tormentor. I try to stand, but I am too weak. Instead I sprawl onto the footpath, clutching at my chest. The man steps over me, unlocks the iron grate and raises it. The shopkeeper has come to open up for the day. He mutters something and goes inside. Soon he re-emerges, wearing a long blue apron and carrying a sign board which he props up on the footpath. At the curb, a van pulls up. Another man, likely his son, begins unloading it, carrying trays of bread and milk inside. I struggle to get out of their way.

The elder man turns his attention to me. 'You! Fuori! You no understand? Go away, no begging! I call polizia!'

'Mi dispiace. I am sorry. Please, I am hurt. Some men, they beat me …' The son, a handsome dark-haired youth with a short beard, stoops to look me over. He speaks rapidly with his father in Italian.

'You need doctor?' asks the father, hands on his hips.

'Doctor. Si. Please. And water.'

'Raymondo. Acqua.' The young man disappears inside the shop, and soon returns with a plastic bottle. I gulp it down, every swallow causing pain. I notice for the first time, my clothes are bloodied and my shirt torn.

'Grazie. Grazie,' I whisper. They speak again at length. I hear the word 'medico' many times.

'My son, he bring you to hospital. You wait five minutes, okay?' They leave me alone while they finish unloading.

Raymondo comes over and offers his hand. 'Come. I bring you to hospital.' I hesitate. *The last time I trusted strangers …* But I have nothing more to lose. What could they steal from me, but the torn shirt on my back? I need to see a doctor, to cauterise my wounds and set my ribs.

'Medico. Si. I come.' The young man helps me into the passenger seat. The floor is littered with many discarded coffee cups.

'Sorry, it is, how you say, messed up,' says Raymondo.

It is not long after sunrise, and there is little traffic yet. I am too feeble minded to observe where we are going. After a short drive, we arrive at a large, modern building surrounded by green lawns and vast parking lots. "Ospedale S. Maria dela Pitea" reads the entrance sign. Smartly dressed men and women come and go from the building. We pause in the van for a moment. Raymondo looks around as though unsure where to go.

'Ah, ingresso di emergenza.' He drives slowly into the semi-circular driveway and stops at the entrance. Opening my door for me, he helps me out of the car. 'There. Go inside. Doctor.

Medico, si? You walk okay?' I step in front of the frosted glass doors. 'Si. Inside. Go.' He waves me to enter.

The doors open automatically and I shuffle in. I turn to thank Raymondo, but he is already in the van, and drives off in a hurry. I suppose he doesn't want anyone to think he was responsible for my beating.

Inside, a large sign "Ricezione" hangs above a desk where a woman in a white uniform sits, looking at her phone. There is a strange smell of spirits and ammonia here. The bright lights and sterile surroundings are not comforting. Adjacent to the desk is a large room with many chairs, all facing a TV set that is on, but no one is watching. I limp towards the woman, but she doesn't glance up. As I reach her desk, another woman in similar uniform emerges from a room behind.

'Come stata la festa?' she says.

The seated women turns and answers her enthusiastically. 'Anna era li! Con Arturo. Si puo credere che!' I look from one to the other, but they continue their conversation, oblivious to my presence. I clear my throat to attract attention. They both stare at me for a moment. The seated receptionist turns to me while the other disappears. 'Posso aiutarti?' she says in an overly loud voice.

'Medico. Doctor.' As if my being hunched over in pain, and the blood on my shirt does not answer her question.

'Si. Qual e il tuo disturbo?' she asks. But I have difficulty understanding. 'Parli Italiano?' she asks, 'Francais? Allemange? English?'

'Si, English. I speak a little.'

'What is your complaint?'

'I was beaten. My ribs, bones, they are broken perhaps.' I clutch my chest to help her understand.

'Hmmm. Tessera sanitaria? Your health card?'

I shrug, 'I have nothing. Men take everything. My clothes only, I have.'

'Un minuto,' she tells me, as she too disappears. She soon returns with a young man, who is pushing a curious chair mounted on large wheels. He beckons me to sit.

'Quattro?' he asks the woman.

'Si, quattro.' He wheels me to a large room, lined with beds along the walls, some occupied with patients. Behind them are curious lights, tubes and bottles. I feel uneasy. *What are they going to do to me?* The man helps me out of the wheeled chair into one of the beds. I try to lie flat, but the pain is too great. I sit hunched over, grasping my knees. A young woman arrives, carrying a board with papers clipped to it.

'Cós e?' she asks the young man.

'Sembra combattere,' replies the young man, as he takes away the wheeled chair. The young woman snorts, disapproving of something.

'You speak English?' she says to me.

'Yes.'

'Good. I am Daniela. Nome? What is your name?'

'Marcus Corvus.' She writes this down on her tablet.

'Data di nascita?'

'Que?'

'Date of birth?'

'September. Sixth day from the calends.'

'Year?'

'When Caesar Augustus was consul for the thirteenth time.'

She mutters something resembling idiot though I don't quite catch it. 'Quanti anni hai? What is your age?'

'Nineteen years.'

'Diciannove. Why didn't you say so? Are you taking any medications? Any drugs?' I look up painfully and shake my head. Having recorded my details, she asks me to remove my shoes and shirt. Seeing my pain, she assists. The centre of my chest is a sickening blue.

Daniela, who I realise is a skilled nurse, performs a number of curious rituals on me, first fixing a necklace to her ears and placing a kind of pendant on the other end gently to my chest, as though listening. She grips my wrist firmly and looks at the little clock on her wrist. Another instrument is stuck in my ear for a few seconds and withdrawn. Having recorded the outcome of these tests, she wraps a cloth collar around my upper arm and squeezes a little black ball that soon grips my arm very tightly, before gradually relaxing it. The result of this too, is written down.

'Doctor Santoro will see you shortly. Rest here.' She deposits her writing board in the slot at the end of the bed and departs.

I feel no better, but no worse, from her treatment. I examine the equipment around the head of the bed; the wall is covered with strange devices and lighted displays. Other patients are brought in from time to time, including an elderly man in a wheeled chair, who is treated in the neighbouring bed. After a long conversation in Italian, he undergoes the same rituals as I did then they leave him in peace. A wounded child is brought in, crying uncontrollably. Its mother tries in vain to comfort it. The ruckus attracts the attention of several other hospital staff, before finally they succeed in quieting the child.

A quarter hour passes. At last a woman arrives, smartly dressed not in the blue or white uniforms of the other staff, but a modest, long blue dress. She is tall and slim, of some fifty years, her hair tied back with a little ponytail to one side. Her name badge reveals her to be "Medico Santoro". She picks up the board from its slot and studies it closely. 'Buongiorno. Sono il dottor Santoro.'

I nod. 'Marcus,' I croak.

'Parli Italiano?' she asks.

'Si, ma solo poche parole. I speak English a little.'

'Okay, good. Tell me Mr Corvus, are you in great pain?

'Si, very much pain. Very much!'

'I can see that. We'll get you some medication straight away for your pain. Please tell me, how did you come by your injuries?'

'A man, two men, they took me and beat me. They took me in their car.'

'Took you by force? Took you where?'

'I thought it was taxi but was not. They brought me to this dark place, and robbed me and beat me with an iron bar.'

'Buon Dio! That is terrible! Well, do not worry, we will treat your wounds. If you wish to see a police officer, we can call one to come here and take your statement.' I nod. 'Now let me examine you.' She looks at the scrapes on my arms and side, then looks closely at my chest. She presses my ribs gently. 'Does this hurt?'

I flinch and cry out. 'Yes, it hurts much!'

'I think you have bruised or possibly cracked ribs. We'll send you for an X-ray. That will tell us if there are broken bones. We'll give you morphine for the pain too. Do you understand?'

'X-ray?'

'We will take a picture of your bones to look for fractures.'

'Ah. Yes, all right.' *A picture of my bones*, did I hear that right? She writes something on the board and leaves me.

Shortly after, the nurse, Daniela, reappears carrying a small tray bearing little tubes of medicine. 'I will give you morphine. In your arm.' Seeing my puzzled look, she continues, 'to ease your pain.'

'Yes. The pain. Please.'

'Your arm, sir.' She scrubs a little spot on my upper arm with a sort of ether. While I watch, she jabs a needle into my arm, which stings sharply for a moment. Treating pain by inflicting pain! This is how doctors in the new world do their healing: with strange instruments in the ear, needles in the arm, and foul-smelling medicines.

'You might feel warm or a little sick.' I pay little heed, as I feel so terrible already. But in an instant, a flush of warmth courses through my body. I feel hot and sweaty, as if to vomit. The nurse cradles my arm. 'It will pass quickly,' she reassures.

Within a minute, the hot feeling fades and the pain in my chest eases a little. After watching me carefully for a time, the nurse departs, promising to return soon.

Whatever medicine she put into me, it is powerful and wonderful. I feel lightheaded, as though drunk on wine. The pain continues to abate until I barely feel it. It no longer aches with every breath!

Daniela returns. 'Signor Marco, are you feeling better? Or still painful?'

'Better. Much better. Is good medicine.'

'Buono. Good to hear. Please let me dress your other wounds.'

'Yes. Thank you, Miss Daniela.' She efficiently washes my scrapes with a scented cloth, and bandages the cut on my side I took falling from the car.

'All finished. Now, you rest here for a time. They will come to bring you for X-ray soon.' With the pain greatly reduced and the lightness in my head, I feel sleepy. I realise I am a little hungry.

'Signor Corvus. Riesci a sentirmi? Can you hear me?' Two young men, in green garb have arrived. 'We take you to radiology now. Just remain there.' Efficiently they raise metal bars on the sides of the bed and wheel the entire thing, with me in it, out of the ward and down the hall. Through some double doors we enter a strange, dimly lit chamber. Sitting in the middle of the room is a monstrous machine, horseshoe shaped with a jaw-like opening in the centre. An eerie humming noise comes from within it. On one wall a window opens to an adjacent room. *Gods protect me. Courage, Marcus.*

With my head thick from the medicine, and weak from hunger, I care little what they will do to me. A woman comes in and tells me this machine will take a picture of my bones, through the skin, and that I must keep very still when asked. I am helped onto a narrow, bed-like tray which is slowly fed into the jaws of the machine. It comes to life, with a loud buzzing sound. I close my eyes. *Help me, Juno. Help me, Minerva.* A little voice speaks into my ear. It bids me to hold my breath, which I can do only with difficulty. This is repeated a few times, then it is all over. The machine discharges me from its jaws. The two men in green return to deliver me and my bed back to its original place.

From time to time the nurse visits to inquire about my level of pain. Thus far, I am still under the spell of morphine. I drift in and out of sleep. Other patients arrive as the day progresses, and soon all the beds in the ward are occupied.

'Pranzo. Lunch time.' A middle-aged woman is pushing a cart, stacked high with metal trays of food. 'Hai fame?' she asks each patient in turn. I respond in the affirmative and am given a plate of sandwiches and fruit juice.

An hour passes. I start to feel pain returning; the medicine's effect is wearing off. Doctor Santoro eventually returns and sits beside me on the bed.

'We have your results now. We took an X-ray of your chest, and you have two cracked ribs but nothing broken.'

'That is good?'

'Yes, it's good. It will heal on its own. Is there anything else you want to tell me about how you got your injuries? Do you know the men who attacked you? This is criminal assault.'

'No. I don't know them. Nor where they took me. It was a taxi—a red car, a small car.'

'Did you get the licence number?'

'Licence?'

'The number of the car?' I shake my head.

'Well, I am not going to judge you; our place is only to heal here. You are lucky. There are no broken bones and no need for plaster. The skin is not broken, so there is no need for antibiotics. You must rest, avoid hard work or activity. Just try to breath normally, not too shallow. I will give you medicine for the pain, which you can take with you.'

'Morphine? May I take some morphine?' I ask hopefully.

'No, Marcus, we cannot give you that.' Seeing my glum look, she adds, 'There are some who would try to buy it from you. Or steal it.'

'Oh.'

'I will get you two weeks' worth of Codeine tablets. Take one or two when the pain is bad, but no more than eight tablets in a day. If you do not heal in two weeks come back to the hospital or see your doctor. Do you understand?'

'Yes, doctor. Thank you.'

'Great. I'll get your painkillers.'

I like the name of this medicine. *Painkillers.* The nurse returns with a small bottle of tablets.

'You may dress and go home now,' she says. I pocket the

bottle, dress myself, and make my way out of the hospital.

The bright mid-afternoon sun stings my eyes. Nearby, under shady trees, are benches of black iron. On some, patients sit in their hospital garb, speaking with family members. I sit out of the hot sun. What am I to do now? Stranded in Naples, without a denarius to my name. My gods have abandoned me! *At least you are alive, Marcus.* Black and blue, but alive. How will I get to Rome now? What can I do without money for even a meal, let alone a train fare. Rome is near 200 miles away and I'll never make it on foot. If these woes weren't enough, the morphine continues to wear off and the pain in my chest bites anew.

A bus comes up the hospital drive and stops near the entrance. A few passengers disembark, then the bus pulls away. Perhaps, if I explain my predicament, the bus driver will permit me to ride without a ticket? It couldn't hurt to try. I hobble over to the bus stop to await the next one.

After a time, a bus arrives, bound for Piazza Garibaldi. I let two young men board and follow them. I plead with the driver.

'Please sir. I have no money, I am hurt, very sick.'

But the driver shouts at me, 'No biglietto, no ride. Out, out!' I back down the steps, and the door closes in my face. So much for compassion.

I rest a while, unable to even think. As the shadows grow long, the doctors and nurses of the hospital finish their shifts, and many of them crowd around the bus stop. A bus arrives, and to avoid the queue at the front door many passengers slip in by the rear door. I follow their lead and take a seat at the back, trying to blend in. The ruse works. The bus makes its way to the centre of Napoli. Traffic and people choke the streets at this hour. Our progress is painfully slow; the bus starts and lurches to a stop every few yards, each time making my ribs ache.

At last, the driver calls out, 'Piazza Garibaldi' as we enter the square, and halt in front of the train station. I follow the crowd of passengers getting off.

It is now twilight. The station, a vast cavernous construction, is full of people rushing about in all directions, some drawing large cases on tiny wheels. Everyone is in a hurry. It is still uncomfortably warm. I meander past a row of food stands to an enormous electric signboard, suspended from the roof. It lists many cities: Capua, Bari, Taranto, Roma, with times of departure. Every few seconds it changes by some remote means. *Roma.* The schedule says there are three more trains tonight. By Jupiter I will be on board one of them! But can I swindle a free ride on a train, as I did the bus?

First, I must eat. But without money? I stop outside a busy restaurant, its tables crowded with diners. Half-eaten meals sit on many tables. I sit nonchalantly at one where a handful of cold, fried potatoes remain, and pick a few of them out. Next to me, a large woman is devouring a fittingly large plate of pasta. I can't help but stare at her meal.

She glares at me and says something in Italian that I don't understand, then gathers up her bags and leaves. In a flash I am at her former seat, gulping down her leftovers. It is undignified, but a man must eat. I form a plan. I'll board a crowded train, where I can avoid having to show a ticket to the overworked conductor. There is no time to waste, the station is getting less crowded every minute.

Fortunately, drinking water can be had for free in the station; I gulp down as much as I can. Time to find my train. I soon find the one I am seeking: "Roma Partenza 18:40". Passengers are already boarding the sleek looking train. There appears to be no one taking tickets, at least on the platform. With the carriages filling rapidly, it is close to departure time. A bell rings, a whistle blows, the train starts to move as I jump aboard. So far, so good. There are a few empty seats; I take one and try to get comfortable.

The view is impressive as the city lights flash past the window. I take out the bottle of pills the doctor gave me. I try to eat one; it is foul tasting, and I just manage to choke it down. But the painkiller works. After a half hour, my aches and pains begin to fade away. The gentle motion of the train is soothing. I can't help closing my eyes.

'Biglietto! Ticket!'

I snap awake. At the front of the carriage, two uniformed women are taking tickets. I stretch and stand slowly, trying not to attract attention. I slide towards the back of the carriage where glass doors lead to the next. I buy a few minutes of time by keeping ahead of the ticket takers. There are no empty seats in this carriage, so I make my way slowly down the aisle and again pass to the next carriage, just as the ticket takers enter at the other end.

I can't keep this ruse going indefinitely, for I can hardly jump from the back of the train. I see a chance—the lavatory. I push into it, close the door and wait, stalling for time. I cautiously open the door and find with relief the ticket officers have passed. I slip out and go slowly forward, finding my old seat near the middle of the train. *You did it, Marcus.* Still, I don't feel comfortable with what I've done. What would my father say?

The train picks up speed, and the urban landscape flies past. We leave the city behind, and only a few distant lights are visible in the darkness. The train goes still faster, we must be travelling one hundred miles per hour, yet the ride is smooth.

I nap a little. After a time, I sense we are slowing. We pull into a little station where some passengers disembark and are replaced by a handful of others. Onward we travel, racing up the centre of Italy in the darkness, stopping every half hour or so. A glow appears on the horizon and grows larger and brighter as we approach. We leave the blackness behind to enter a vast city. Harsh white streetlights reveal the dirty outskirts, fences, factories, and freeways. We pass through several concrete tunnels with walls covered in graffiti.

The train slows, the city buildings grow larger and more substantial. The appearance of the cityscape improves as we pass tree-lined streets, lit with elegant streetlights. We are now among stately, stone buildings and must be near the centre of the great city. Rome! The Eternal City. I have returned.

CHAPTER XV

A voice announces, 'Roma! Roma Termini! Tutti i passeggeri devono uscire.' There is a rush for the train doors. Outside, the platform is already jammed with people and baggage. I make my way through the great hall of the station and into the streets of Rome.

The station faces a broad piazza. Though it is now close to midnight, the square is still lively with cars, taxis and people. I see an enormous colonnaded monument to the south, perched on a hill and lit up with floodlights. It looks like a temple in the Roman style, but it is no temple I know.

I am tired, hungry and the pain is biting again. I dread the thought of spending the night on the street. I take two of the painkillers and swallow them whole; they go down easier if I don't chew them.

I must try to find Father George's friend. What was his name? The slip of paper bearing his address is lost, along with all my other possessions. Was it Ricardo? Yes, that's it,

Father Ricardo. A priest at a Christian temple here in Rome. But which one? I struggle to remember our conversation in his garden, a world away now, in the little town of Roma, Australia. *Santa Maria*—that was it. I ask for directions from a passer-by but get only a shrug in reply. I ask others but get the same reaction or none at all. People are afraid of strangers at this hour and I don't blame them. I see three elderly women emerge from the station dressed in black robes, with a white hood wrapped tightly about their faces. I plead with them.

'Please, signore. Where is Santa Maria?'

'Santa Maria Maggiore? The Basilica?' one asks.

'Si! Basilica di Santa Maria.'

'Via Cavour. Quatri centinaio metres, signore.' She points down one of the many broad streets leading off the square. I am relieved to hear it is nearby.

'Grazie, grazie signore!' Via Cavour is a broad avenue, lined with many impressive stone-faced buildings. Some have seen more prosperous times though; their windows and doors are boarded up. Few people are on the street and this makes me uneasy. Thankfully the road leads downhill. I trudge slowly without much pain.

Halfway down the hill a broad plaza opens up on the left of the road. Trees line the sides and behind them is an enormous domed church. At the centre of the plaza stands a solitary stone column, rising to a great height. A sign confirms this is the "Basilica Papale di Santa Maria Maggiore".

I ascend the stairs, but the great doors are bolted. If there is a Father Ricardo here he would certainly be asleep. There are benches under the trees along the sides of the square. A man in beggar's clothes is sleeping on one. I follow his lead and take a bench nearby. I'll have to wait for dawn, as best I can, for it is a cool night.

Trying to sleep, I am startled to feel something thrown over my legs. I look up into the face of a young man, dressed in a simple black robe. He is placing a blanket over me. He smiles.

'Dormi bene.'

'Thank you. Grazie,' I say.

'You can return it in the morning.' He moves on to the other man sleeping on the bench and gives him a blanket too.

'Grazie, padre,' says the beggar. I drift off into an uncomfortable sleep.

'Hoy! Alzati!' I bolt upright, only to stare into the chest of a police officer. *Not again.* I wonder if Italian law is as forgiving as in Australia. 'Alzati! Get up,' he repeats. I struggle to my feet. The sun is up, but I still feel the coolness of the morning and shiver even with the blanket around me.

'I go. I go now,' I mutter, bowing my head in respect. I walk stiffly back towards the street. I glance behind me. The officer has turned his attention to the scruffy man on the nearby bench. They are arguing, and I suspect the man will soon end up in custody. I suppose sleeping in the square is permissible, but not after sunrise.

I draw the blanket close around my shoulders. My head throbs from lack of sleep. My chest aches, and my back too from the roughness of the bench. Plus, I haven't eaten since the scraps at the train station last night. Via Cavour is becoming busy; many citizens walk swiftly up and down the street, most likely to or from the station. A cafe is visible across the road, its doors open and a few small tables on the footpath. But without money it is of no use to me. I try to take a painkiller, but my mouth is too parched to swallow it. I badly need a drink.

I shuffle up and down the street until I am certain the policeman has left the plaza, then I return to the Basilica Santa Maria. Three men in blue overalls are working there now. One man sweeps leaves from the grand staircase, another picks up the detritus in the square, the third tends the small garden. They work slowly, without enthusiasm.

I ascend the stairs to the massive doors of the church. Still locked. I fold up the blanket neatly and set it by the door. I approach the man sweeping the steps.

'Buongiorno.'

He turns and tips his hat to me. 'Buongiorno. Posso aiutarla? Can I help you?'

'I look for Padre Ricardo.'

'Padre Ricardo? Hmm. No.' He doesn't know the man. He calls out to his companion tending the garden, who does seem to know him. 'Not here. But you go inside to office and make appointment.'

'Grazie, grazie.' I am not sure where to enter. I tug at the church doors one more time.

'No, other door. Door say, "Ufficio".' The man points around to the left of the main building. Sure enough, there is another doorway marked with a small sign, "Ufficio".

I enter a dim room with a very high ceiling. It is furnished with musty blue carpet, and old, darkened timber furniture. An unoccupied desk sits in front of another office with frosted windows. Its door is open, so I make my presence known by feigning a cough. A bad idea in my condition; I grit my teeth against the pain. From the little office, an elderly man wearing wire spectacles shows his head.

'Buongiorno. Posso aiutarti?' He comes to the desk. He appears to be wearing the garb of a priest: white robes, with a broad cross printed in red on his chest.

'Buongiorno. I am sorry, I not understand, sir.'

'Ah. Are you English?'

'I am Italian. But I cannot speak your language well. I come from Australia. I know to speak some English.'

Somewhat confused, he replies, 'I am Nicholas. How can I assist you?'

'I look for Father Ricardo.'

'Padre Ricardo Mariani?'

'Si! Ricardo Mariani.' Now I remember his name, from the paper Father George had given me in Australia.

'He is not here. He comes to Santa Maria only on Wednesdays and Sundays to preside over morning mass.'

'What day is today?' I have lost track.

He frowns. 'It is Friday, son. What is your business with Father Ricardo? Are you a seminary student?'

'No, not a student. My name is Marcus. I come to ask for help. Father George in Queensland said to me that I might call upon Father Ricardo if I needed help when in Rome.'

'Oh? Father George? An Australian priest?'

'Yes, he is Australian man. Father George Turner. We spoke at length about Jesus, about history and about Rome.'

'That is good. Again, what do you seek from Father Ricardo? You say you are in need of help?'

'Yes. I came here to Italy a week ago, landing at Brundisium. I mean, Brindisi.'

'And?'

'I came to Naples, travelling to my parent's farm. But there I was robbed. I have no money, and I am in great pain from my injuries.' He squints closely at me, examining my body up and down. 'My rib bones are cracked. Very painful.' I lift my shirt a little to show him the bruises.

'No need to show me, son. I'll take your word for it. But how did you get to Rome?'

'I ... I, well,' I stammer.

'You hitched a ride?'

'Yes, yes, I hitched a ride.' I could hardly tell a priest I had stolen aboard the train. He rubs his chin as he ponders what to do with me.

'You say you are friend of Father George Turner? In Queensland, Australia? What parish?'

'Yes, I visited him there, in the town of Roma. He was full of generosity and kindness. He gave me much useful advice for my trip to Italy.'

'Roma!' He smiles at the coincidence. 'And here you are, in the other Roma. Well, I have no reason to doubt you. I would be a poor Christian if I turned away a destitute man on the steps of my own church. I will help you, per grazia di Dio. Tell me, have you eaten yet?'

'No. I am very hungry.'

'I thought as much. One moment.' He returns to his office, where I hear him typing on his computer for a minute or two. He returns, folding some euro notes and handing them to me. 'Here is a little money to tide you over for today. I have sent an email to Father Ricardo telling him there is a Marcus, friend of George Turner, come to see him.'

'Thank you. You are very generous.'

'Don't mention it. Now, let's get you fed. Come with me.' The helpful nature of this Christian priest differs greatly from the cold indifference of the Roman priests in the Forum temples, who cast me out when I cried for help. He leads me out of the office and locks the door behind him.

'Come! We'll have coffee.' We cross the road to the cafe I spotted earlier. He treats me to a strong coffee and a bag of sweet pastries. I stuff them into my mouth even before we have recrossed the street. Instead of entering the office, we proceed to the rear of the church where Father Nicholas unlocks a high gate. We enter a beautiful garden, full of large shade-giving trees and ferns.

'Great spot, no?' he asks. 'You won't find much peace anymore, in Rome. At least, not in the last thousand years. I often sit here to pray and meditate.' I nod, as we sit on a low, stone bench. I finish my breakfast and sip the rich, milky coffee.

'So, Marcus, tell me your story. Where are you from again?'

I sigh. Should I tell him everything? How I am actually

an Italian, like himself? Of his nation, yes, but not of his time. Would he believe me? I keep the story short and stay as close to the truth as possible, to avoid catching myself in a lie. As my father once scolded me, 'there are many versions of a lie, but only one of the truth'. I tell Nicholas my family reside in the south of Italy, but I was away from them in Australia for some months. Eager to return, I took passage on a ship back to Italy. This he accepts easily. I mention going to the countryside near Naples, trying to find my family's ancestral farm and that I succeeded, but found only rubble remaining. And of my misadventure in Naples, being tricked, beaten and robbed.

'That is terrible. Such a misfortune for a young man! Did you receive much injury?'

'Not so bad, but my ribs were cracked and are still painful. A shopkeeper's son took me to a hospital. The doctor there said it will heal, in time, with no bandages needed. They gave me some medicine for the pain.'

'Well, that is something. May it heal soon and leave you with no scars. But I imagine you have mental scars.'

'Mental scars?'

'The fear of being hurt again. Were you very shaken by the attack?'

'Yes, that is so. I have bad dreams of that terrible night.'

'Naturally so. We Italians are a kindly people in the main, but, in every nation, there are others ...'

'I know what you mean. I was treated most kindly by everyone I have met, save one or two.'

'There are always those who follows the path of the devil to prey on the innocent. To take from others what they are too lazy to earn themselves. It is not right, but this is the world of the twenty-first century.'

'And any century,' I say. He finishes his coffee. I offer him the last sweet roll, which he accepts.

'How did you come to know Father Ricardo? Are you family?' Father Nicholas says.

'No, sir. I have not met him before. I was given his name by Father George in Australia, as a man who could render assistance.'

'Ah yes, you mentioned that. Let's see if he's replied to my email.' From the folds of his robe he pulls out his phone. Why even temple priests carry these! He squints and looks at it over the top of his spectacles. 'Yes, he answered just now. Here, let me read for you. I'll translate to English. He says he would be pleased to meet any acquaintance of Father George's.'

'Good, very good!'

'He can meet you this afternoon. He'll be coming here around noon.'

'Ah, that is good.'

'Well, Marcus, I must return to my duties now. I will show you out.'

'Thank you, thank you, Nicholas.'

'It is my pleasure young man. Say, have you seen the inside of the basilica?'

'No. I have not been inside.'

'I'll take you through. I think you'll be impressed.'

We leave the garden, and I follow him through the rear door

of the church, into the basilica of Santa Maria Maggiore. It is a vast hall, with massive, white stone columns on either side. The walls are covered with immense paintings. The ceiling high above is elaborately ornamented too, and everything covered in gold leaf! At the front of the church is a splendid altar within an ornate gilded canopy. In grandeur, this church is the equal of the temple of Jupiter in the Forum. I study the painted ceiling and the delicate paintings visible between the columns. My host is evidently pleased at my reaction.

'It is a sight to behold, is it not my friend. Come, I'll show you the domes.' He leads me to the first great dome, fully fifty yards above! It is covered in a delicate mosaic in brilliant blue and gold. Two huge figures dominate.

'Who are the figures?'

'The larger is Christ our Lord. To the left, the Virgin Mary, mother of Jesus. See there, he places the crown on her head. At their feet there's angels, flowers, birds. Around the dome you can see the saints. There is St. Francis, St. Peter, St. Paul ...' It is hard to tell which of the two of us is more excited. 'Not bad for the thirteenth century artists, no? They call those times the Dark Ages but look what they accomplished.'

'Dark ages? Why were they so called?'

'All the lands of Europe went through dark times where learning and knowledge went backwards. Where ignorance, war, and pestilence were normal.'

'For many years?'

'For nearly a thousand years. After Rome fell to the barbarians in the fifth century the whole of Europe was ravaged and plundered. The great Roman empire shattered into pieces, from which it never recovered.'

'Rome was conquered and sacked? By which peoples?' I knew this must be so, for I could see myself the great monuments from my time are long vanished, my people dispersed. I knew already the rule of the Caesars ended long ago, but to hear this learned man speak of it as a long dead empire hurts me deeply.

'Sacked it was. Alaric, king of the Goths, was the first to breach the walls, in AD 410. But by then the empire was a shadow of itself: Gaul and Spain lost, and the Vandals overrunning Africa. The empire of the east resisted the barbarians and stood firm for another thousand years, until it too fell to the Turks. Have you been to Istanbul? After Rome itself, there is no city more steeped in history or with more splendid churches. Constantinople, it was once called.'

'No, sir I have not been. You say it remained Roman, long after Rome itself submitted to the barbarians?'

'It did. Its churches and monasteries held on the Christian faith, and what little knowledge that remained of the ancient world was preserved in Constantinople. By the Greeks, the Romans, and the early Christians who lived there.'

'Who brought the word of this Christ to Rome? The northern barbarians?'

'No, quite the opposite. The worship of Christ began with a handful of followers, in Judea. The early apostles, such as Peter and Paul, brought word of him and his teachings by land and sea to Egypt, Greece and ultimately to Rome.'

'And the people of Rome adopted his worship?'

'They did, though it took many years. Christians were mocked, persecuted, even murdered by some of the early emperors.'

'Such as the divine Augustus? Or his successor?'

'No, it began later, under Nero I think. A cruel, vile emperor. Murdered by the palace guard, if I remember correctly.'

'The emperor, murdered! Can you imagine? Was such an outrage possible?'

'It was, and believe me, the populous were thankful. He was a tyrant, debauched, and cruel. Or so Suetonius tells us.'

'Was his successor kind to the Christ worshippers?'

'After Nero's murder, there was anarchy for a time, but a man named Vespasian eventually took the purple. He was indifferent to the Christians, but more persecution followed later. Many Christians were put to death in the Colosseum.'

'In the great amphitheatre? Why I almost met such a fate myself!' I blurt out.

'What do you mean, son?'

'Well, I mean, I *felt* close to death. When I was beaten up, in Naples ...' He smiles and leads me to view the other dome, also adorned with beautiful mosaics and stunning painted glass. Along the walls, great frescoes show the life and crucifixion of Jesus, as I had seen in the church in the lesser Roma, but in far greater splendour.

'This must surely be the finest temple ever built.'

Father Nicholas smiles. 'I am pleased to hear you say it. I love it with all my heart. But no, this is far from the greatest church. You must see Saint Peter's, across the river in the Vatican. Still, our church is grand isn't it! And very old. According to legend, Pope Liberius had a dream of the Virgin Mary telling him to build a church. The next day it snowed here on the Esquiline Hill for the first time ever. He took it as a sign and built it here.'

How deep is the faith of those that follow this Jesus, to raise such a magnificent temple as this that is still standing after eight hundred years. The people still honour him after so many centuries, and this is not even the greatest temple raised by the Christians! We finish our tour. I thank Father Nicholas and take my leave.

He asks, 'Have you been to the Colosseum yet? If not, it's a short walk. Head down Via Cavour. You can't miss it.'

'The Colosseum? Yes, I have been, once before. Tell me, does it still stand?'

'You have been living in the wilderness haven't you! Yes, of course it still stands. It is but a splendid ruin now, well worth visiting. Take a tour, see the interior dungeons if you can.'

'I've seen them, Father Nicholas.'

He takes my hand and shakes it. 'All right then. Ciao, Marcus. May God bless you on your journey home.'

'Thank you, you have been most kind. Grazie for the tour. And may all the gods favour you as well.' He smiles and leaves me on the steps of the church.

As I walk back to Via Cavour I consider whether I should visit the Colosseum. What would I find? Do I really want to visit this place where my life was nearly snuffed out, just a few months ago? I know I have nothing to fear. *Caesar has been dead for twenty centuries, right?* I know the Roman empire has ceased to exist, and I have nothing to fear from Caesar's centurions. But I do fear the wrath of the gods, if I tempt them by returning to the ruins.

I follow the gentle slope of the road, descending the Esquiline Hill. As I reach the flat at the bottom, the vast bulk of the Colosseum comes into view. The great amphitheatre. Its walls still stand after 2,000 years! I had glimpsed the exterior only briefly, when we were bundled out of our prison wagons to be dragged to its dungeons. The walls of the arena are nearly intact, the three rows of arches still visible around most of the circumference. Alas, the stone has been stripped of its marble cladding revealing the brick beneath, and the statues which once adorned the archways are gone. If these stones could speak! The stories they could tell of the animals and men who died by the thousand here.

Though only a skeleton, it remains a magnificent sight. Now, I come to see it as a tourist. Before, I came as a prisoner about to meet my death. It all comes back in a rush; being dragged through the streets of Rome in a cage, locked up in the dungeons, the vermin, the animals, the smell of death, my cell mates—Lucius. Brave Lucius! The Illyrian and the great Gaul who fought so hard for his freedom. Even his great strength could not save him.

A large truck passes by noisily, bringing my thoughts to the present. A busy road runs in front of the Colosseum. Vehicles pass to and fro, oblivious to the great edifice. I cross the road and approach its walls. Built to last for all time. A tribute to the skill of Roman engineering. I make a slow circuit around, awed at every step.

There is a queue of tourists lining up to enter. Do they know the fate of those who entered the arena in my time? There are hawkers selling food and drink, exactly as there were 2,000 years ago. There are men dressed as centurions too. On closer inspection their costume bears little resemblance to the real uniform of a Roman soldier. But they are doing a brisk business posing for photographs with tourists.

I want to see the Colosseum as the Roman people saw it, from high up in the stands. I join the long queue of tourists. I buy a ticket, getting only a little change from the twenty euro note that Father Nicholas gave me. After a long wait, I am inside, treading on the dark greasy stones. I walk the corridors at ground level, where the masses would mill about and buy refreshments. Today there are just as many people, wide-eyed, taking photos, amazed to be in this majestic building. I come to a great archway and follow it towards the centre of the arena. Suddenly I am in the bright sunlight and the floor of the arena is before me. Unwittingly I have followed the path of the gladiators, entering to the cheers of the crowds, eager to witness the bloodletting.

I make my way to the upper levels. The tiers of timber seats are long gone and it is hard to make out where they once were. I climb to the top level, where the plebs and slaves would have sat. The long climb aside, these are still great seats commanding a fine view. Most of the arena floor is gone too, but a section has been rebuilt from timber to show where it once was. Below the floor I can make out the tunnels and cells, that once housed the beasts and men that were about to die. The corridors where we ran, fleeing from the guards! The elevators— I can see their positions. There is one right there at the very place where the Gaul knocked over the guards, allowing Lucius and me to escape. It is as though it happened yesterday.

There are two of me, the Marcus of today, and the Marcus of long ago. I see the past and present, blurred together. For a moment I am back in the Rome of my time. The bloodstained sand, the howling crowds. The vision fades before my eyes. It has all decayed, all fallen to pieces just as my life has. Nothing but a ruin. My home, my people, as long dead as this stone amphitheatre. I sit a while on the terraces, wallowing in bitterness.

I return to Santa Maria at midday, in time to meet Father Ricardo. At the doorway of his office, a slender man stands talking with him with great enthusiasm in Italian.

'Ah, Marcus!' says Father Nicholas. 'May I present Signore Ricardo Mariani.'

Father Ricardo shakes my hand vigorously. I was expecting a grey-haired man, but he seems much younger.

'Please, come to my office.' He leads me up a flight of stairs, to a much more impressive office with deep blue carpets, beautifully ornamented ceilings, and a dark timber desk. 'So, young man, tell me how is my old friend George Turner in Queensland? I understand you spent time with him recently.'

'Yes, I was travelling in Australia and passed through Roma, the other Roma you know, where I met him in the church. We talk, in his house, of Rome, and history. He was very friendly. He give good advice.'

'He is a first-rate historian. You should see his library. He is a walking history book, that man. Tell me, is he well?'

'Oh yes, he is strong and healthy. He was working in the gardens of the church when I visited. He has much fondness for his garden, and much skill at tending it, from what I see.'

'That is good to hear. Did you attend the mass there?'

'Yes sir, I did. It was most ... impressive. I have much to learn of your faith and ceremonies.'

'Attend mass regularly and you will soon learn what you need to know to be a good Christian.'

'Christian? The worshippers of Jesus who is called Christ?'

'Yes, we call ourselves Christians.'

'Ah.' Time to get to the point. 'Father, the reason I came here is to ask for your help.'

'Of course. Nick's email said you were in dire straits. Some trouble in Naples I hear.'

'Yes. I had just come from Australia and was passing through Naples …' I recount my arrival in Italy, and of the thugs who robbed me.

'Were you hurt badly?' I pull up my shirt a little, showing the ugly black bruises.

'Cracked ribs.'

'Eeii! Have you seen a doctor?'

'Yes, I have, I was given some medicine for the pain.'

'Good. Did you report the incident to the polizi?'

'No. I could not give their names or describe their faces. Or where they took me. Also,' I hesitate, 'I am not eager to talk to police officers. The men in ship told me to keep my head low and avoid contact with the authorities. I have no passport. Being discovered might get me thrown out of Italy.'

'Ah. Your passport was stolen?'

'Well, not exactly. I never had one to start with.'

He pauses, puzzled. 'Well, there are far less crimes. You are not in need of a doctor, nor a policeman, so how may I be of assistance?'

'When they robbed me they take everything. My Roman money, and every last euro I had.'

'Ah.' He grimaces, and rubs his chin vigorously, not pleased to find a stranger begging for money. 'I take it you have no employment? With your condition I suppose that would be difficult.'

'I have no job. I have not even clothing or food to eat.'

'Why do you not visit the Social Security Board? It is their function to help people in need. They can give you payments to tide you over until you recover and find employment.'

'I do not think they would help me, for I am not Italian.'

'I thought you said your family is from Campania?'

'Yes, they are. I was born in Campania.'

'Then surely you are an Italian citizen? You would have travelled to Australia on a European passport?'

'No, I have no European passport. I have no passport at all.'

'But you have a birth certificate, baptismal certificate, something that proves who you are?'

'That is my problem, Father. I have no papers. My father, my mother, they are no longer living.' I realise, with bitterness, this is the first time I have said this aloud.

'I see.' He frowns. 'And you have no family, so you cannot prove who you are in any way?'

'Yes, that is so. You understand my situation.'

'Penniless and no ID. A man from Italy, who speaks poor Italian yet speaks some English with an Australian accent. Well, my friend, you are a bit of a mystery! But fear not, I think you are trustworthy. What I can do for you is give you a room and board in our seminary school. With classes just finished for the summer break there are many spare beds in the dormitory. You can get a bed there and take simple meals.'

'Thank you, Father Ricardo!'

'But it comes with an obligation.'

'Yes, anything.'

'If you are unable to pay, you must help with the daily chores: cooking, cleaning, laundry. And we expect all guests to attend service on Sunday.'

'Of course, yes. I help cook. I am a good cook. I cook on ship for two months.'

'Then you should fit right in.' He writes out the address and directions for me, then goes to his computer to tap out a message to the landlord of the residence he spoke of. 'All done. They are expecting you within the hour.'

'Grazie! Thank you!' I kneel before him, take his hands and kiss them.

'Please stand, young man. Visit the welfare board. Though they may seem unsympathetic, it is their duty to help the needy and the destitute in this country. Bless you, go with Christ and please don't be late, the midday meal is soon to be served.'

'I will. Thank you again, Father Ricardo. I'll not forget your kindness.' I take my leave and cross the piazza again to the now familiar Via Cavour. Following his directions, I walk a short distance to the seminary school dormitories, on a narrow street just off the road.

It is an old stone building, four storeys high, with regular small windows each adorned with little flower boxes. Inside, the tiled floor and walls have seen better days, but are clean. A desk indicates "Reception", where a young woman with long yellow hair is seated, looking idly at a computer. She greats me with a warm, 'Buongiorno'.

'Buongiorno,' I reply. 'I am Marcus. Father Ricardo sent word I come.'

'Si, si, it is a pleasure to meet you, Marcus. I am Paloma.' She offers her hand. 'I understand you are in need of accommodation, si?'

'Yes. And I am sorry to say, I have no money.'

'Don't worry about that. All are welcome here.' She notices me nervously rubbing my chest. 'Are you unwell?'

'Yes. No. I had an accident in Naples. My ribs are healing still.'

'Oh, that's terrible! You were in a car accident?'

'No, I was attacked by some men.'

'Mio Dio! Mugged? There are rogues in Napoli that give that majestic city a bad name.'

'Yes, it was unpleasant. I trusted a man who promised to take me to my hotel, but instead, he brought me somewhere to be robbed.'

'Mamma mia! Well, you are safe here.' She begins typing at her computer. 'What is your full name Marcus? For our register.'

'Marcus Corvus,' I reply.

'And you are alone? No companions?'

'None.'

'Okay. How long do you plan to stay?'

'I am uncertain. You see, I am trying to get home and if I don't succeed I will stay on, but—well you would not believe me if I told you everything.'

'That is okay. It is of no consequence. Shall I say you will stay for one week?'

'Yes, one week is good.'

'You can always extend if you need to. Do you wish to take meals here? If you have no money, I think it best.'

'Yes, please. I will need food.'

'We do not ask for any money if you have none. But all guests staying free are expected to help around the dormitories and kitchen. To clean the rooms, wash the linen, help with cooking and clearing up meals. Do you agree to this?'

'Yes, I am happy to help.' Not being too keen on cleaning, I volunteer for the job that is the least difficult. 'I am a good cook. I learnt some cooking on ship.'

'Excellent! Not many men are willing to help in the kitchen.' She types a little more into her computer then fetches a key from a drawer.

'You are in dormitory A, in the men's quarters, second floor. Up the stairs. It is share-space, four per room. There is one bed free there and some space beneath for your things. You also have a cupboard for your clothes.' She looks behind me. 'You have no luggage?'

'No, as I say, I was robbed …' She looks at me piteously.

'Don't worry. You'll get back on your feet soon.' She hands me the key and a towel. 'Up the stairs, Dormitory A. Please lock the door whenever you leave the room.'

'Thank you. You are so kind. I would be lost, without your help.'

'Don't mention it, Marcus. Everything will be fine. If you

need anything at all, please come back here. I am here until 4 pm, after that Angelo will look after you.'

'I see. Thank you, Miss Paloma.'

'Lunch is being prepared shortly, you can join them in the kitchen. You may have a look at your room first, and wash up, if you like.'

Inside my room are four beds, stacked two by two. Judging by the untidy mess of clothes, there are already three men staying here. One of the lower beds is unoccupied. I tear off my shirt and throw it on the bed, taking possession. At the end of the hall is the bathing room. I quickly scrub myself from head to toe, trying to remove many days of accumulated sweat and dirt.

I return to the main floor, where Paloma leads me to the kitchen. We pass through a common area, with a few well-worn couches, a TV, and a table with books and newspapers scattered on top. Adjacent to it is the dining room, with long sturdily built timber tables, already set for the meal.

'This way.' Paloma pushes open a swinging door into the kitchen. It is brightly lit. Along the walls are many polished steel cabinets; stoves and counters are arranged in the centre. Pots and pans hang from hooks around the room. Two mature women in white aprons and caps are busy preparing the meal. 'Sofia, Giulia, this is Marcus. Egli aiutera in cucina. E australiano, ma parla un po' italiano.'

'Buongiorno, Marcus,' they say. Both are engaged in the cooking, one cutting vegetables, the other busy stirring some sort of soup.

'They don't speak much English, but they are lovely ladies. I'm sure you will get along fine.' Paloma says a few more words in Italian to them, then departs.

'Grembiule. Apron. You wear,' says one lady. I take one from a pile.

'Please, may I help to cook?' I ask. Sofia, the elder of the two, looks around the room, considering what a man might be able to do.

'Si taglia il pane?' She hands me a long knife, and points to several long loaves of bread. She makes cutting motions. 'Cut bread. Capisci?'

'Si! Capisco.' I start cutting up the first loaf. Before I can ask, Sofia has produced three large baskets, and sets them before me.

'Un po piu grande,' she advises, and I cut the slices a little bigger. 'Molto bene!' she says. I am doing it correctly now. She returns to her work. I take my time cutting all the loaves, glad to be doing an easy job.

'Si prega di mettere sul tavolo.' Sofia points to the dining area. 'You put bread to table.' I obey.

'Marcus, metta la bevanda sulla tabella.' I am not sure which drinks she is talking about. 'En frigo.' She points to the enormous refrigerator, larger than any I have seen before. Inside, a dozen pitchers of water are chilling. I ferry these to the tables. The diners have begun to arrive, there are already four or five people seated.

'Buongiorno!' they call out, and I reply in kind.

Soup, salad, and bread make up the simple meal. The three

of us serve it out to the fifteen or so residents who are sitting in small groups. Our assignment complete for now, I toss my apron in the basket by the kitchen door. I serve myself and take a seat at the end of one of the tables. I eat slowly, listening to the guests' conversations. Some speak in tongues that I don't understand, most in Italian and a few in English.

With their meals done, the diners bring their dishes to the kitchen. It doesn't take the ladies and I long to rinse and stack them into the washing machine. Duties complete, Sofia grants me leave to go. They extract a promise from me to return by 5 pm to begin preparations for the evening meal.

Back in the dormitory, I strip and wash my clothes in the bathroom sink. I hang them out the window; they will dry quickly enough in the hot afternoon sun. I climb into my bunk to rest a minute. I am weary from the day's work and I soon fall asleep.

An hour or so later, a couple of young men enter the room, apparently my roommates. They introduce themselves. Both are from a place they call Firenze, in central Italy. I give them my name. An awkward silence follows, which I break with an exaggerated yawn and pretend to return to sleep. It works and they soon leave me in peace.

I awaken to the sound of traffic outside. It is late afternoon, and many motorcycles zoom up and down our little street. It must be nearly five o'clock. I quickly wash, retrieve my clothes, and head down to the kitchen for my evening duties.

There are many more guests taking the evening meal. More than fifty people gather in the dining room, mostly young men and a few women. We in the kitchen are hard-pressed to prepare the dinner in time. Under the stern watch of our matron Sofia, we manage it, with all dishes ready and hot, mostly. This meal is more elaborate: a hearty meal of pasta, meat sauce, bread and cheese. It reminds me of my first meal with my friends in Quilpie. Some have brought their own bottles of wine, which I eye thirstily. The guests all pause before partaking the food, to say a prayer of thanks.

Everyone having been finally served, I join them, tired and hungry. I take one of the few spare seats where three couples are dining. They are speaking English, but with a curious drawling accent. They introduce themselves as being from a city called Atlanta, in a land they call America. They are amused that I've never heard of it. They are happy, convivial people, and seem eager to get to know me. They ask many questions, which will become tiresomely repetitive during my stay here.

'Where are you from? Are you on holiday in Rome? Where are you going next?'

I am tired but join in the conversation with as much cheer as I can summon.

The meal finished, most guests depart. Some to their rooms, some to the common room, the rest out into the night. But one group lingers, finishing off their last bottle of wine painfully slowly. This is irritating, as we in the kitchen cannot leave until their dishes are cleared and washed. I am increasingly impatient to get out of here, so I glide over to their table, and quietly begin to take their remaining dishes anyway. I hear a few sharp comments, but it works—they finally disperse. The mountain of dishes is washed and stacked in the washing machine, and I'm dismissed at last.

So, my first week passes here in the new Rome. I renew my stay for another week, then another. My wounds heal, and I soon become used to the routine. One night, after dinner, I sit for a time in the common room, idly watching a mindless show on the TV. It is some sort of dancing competition. The contestants are dressed in outrageous glittering costumes. The night is hot, I feel restless, and I decide it's time for a walk. The streets are semi-deserted as darkness falls. I head for the Colosseum, drawn by what, I don't know. Its power over me?

The great amphitheatre is spectacularly illuminated by large floodlights. The stones are bathed in soft yellow light, a breathtaking sight. I stand before the walls and call out to the shadows.

'Where are you now, Caesar! Your box is empty, your hangers-on, your slaves and underlings are dead twenty centuries. Tiberius Caesar! Are you in heaven, with your divine predecessor Augustus? You wanted to see me dead! By Jupiter, you almost got your wish! But the gods took that away from you!' But for my fellow prisoners, the man from Gaul and Lucius from Ostia, I would have been cast up to the arena floor to be hacked to pieces.

I circle aimlessly around the great building. There! The very ramp where we were brought down into the dungeons. Kept like animals, caged with the beasts, until our appointment with death. Only a few stones remain. And there! At this very spot was the iron gate we forced our way through, thanks to Lucius and his quick sword. This is where I regained my freedom. Over there! That's where I fled into the marketplace, with the guards in hot pursuit. The market stalls are long gone, and a great triumphal arch now stands in their place. Its inscription, written in comforting Latin, "Imp Caes FL Constantino …" It honours an emperor named Constantine, whom I have never heard of. The arch is also beautifully lit and it rises defiantly towards the stars.

Beyond, the Via Sacre leads to the Forum. The gate I passed through is no longer there, today the Forum is surrounded by a high steel fence. I grasp the bars and peer through them, into a dim field. I struggle to recognise anything within. Where once stood the great temples of the gods, the Senate House, and the Imperial Forum, is now little more than a field of rubble. There are remains of a handful of buildings, and a few scattered columns stand in their original places. But in the main it is a ruin, littered with tumbled columns and collapsed buildings. It is deserted; this gives me an idea.

Down the road a little, away from the Colosseum, the streets are less well lit. After surveying the surroundings, I quickly climb the fence. Not easy, as it is a good twelve feet high. I drop to the ground and my knees feel as they've been shoved into my throat. I roll into the shadow of an ancient heap of stones. I keep still for a time, breathing hard, wondering if my presence has been detected. Nothing happens, so I steal away into the Forum grounds, keeping to the shadows.

It is wasteland, a shocking ruin. Shadows play in the

fallen stones and ruined columns. It has taken twenty centuries, but what man once built, has been torn down by man. Who would ever have thought it, that Rome would fall! The greatest empire the world has ever known. Greater than that of Alexander or Darius or the ancient Egyptians. Now a shattered ruin, along with the Roman people, most of them anyway. *Am I the last Roman?*

Over there—is that not the ruin of the Senate House? Only a few bricks remain. The very place where the powerful men of Rome met and ruled for five centuries even before my time. Over there, atop the Capitoline hill, should be the temple of Jupiter Optimus Maximus, but it has vanished. The entire hill has been rebuilt. Now a grand staircase leads to a plaza at the summit, where I see an impressive bronze statue of a man mounted on a horse. There are modern stone buildings around the square, but no sign of the temple to the father of the gods. Jupiter, the almighty, what has happened to your house? What has happened to your power over the gods and the world of men? What could have caused your downfall? Did the Romans cease to worship you, and fail to sacrifice to you according to the sacred rites? What sacrilege did they commit that caused you to abandon Rome to the barbarians and their gods? I kneel at the foot of the hill and whisper a prayer to Jupiter. But if his temple no longer stands, how can he hear me?

I prowl through the ruins under the Capitoline hill. Here, three joined columns are still standing. They are all that is left of a great temple. I climb onto the podium and realise this is the temple of Castor and Pollux. Only the floor remains, with three columns rising defiantly as if holding up the sky. This is where I first took refuge when fleeing my captors. Won't the Divine Twins help me again? There are two of me, are there not? Marcus of the first century and Marcus of the twenty-first.

I kneel in the centre of the dusty temple floor. The altar and the colossal statues of the twins are long vanished. I pray to the twins. *Can you hear me? Patron gods of horsemen? Please help me. Send me home where I belong.* But their house is ruined too. Nothing happens. No lightning, no thunder, just the distant intrusion of a motorcycle racing up a nearby street. The twin sons of Jupiter too have abandoned this place, it is their home no more. Where do the gods now reside? *Do they even still exist?* I halt myself from thinking such sacrilege.

The spring of Juturna is still next to the temple. The little pool remains; the stones and reliefs surrounding it are worn but still distinct. I climb down to it and kneel at the water's edge. I drink from it, scooping the water with my hands just as I did when fleeing for my life. But the water is foul and I spit it out. I think of the sustenance it once gave me after my time in the dungeons, when I was near dead from thirst.

Who else can help me? *Juno, divine goddess of the home, can you hear me?* I have your image—wait—I no longer have it, for I lost it somehow. Curse my carelessness! *Please Juno, hear me! Help me!* Bring me home to my time, to my family. *I beseech you, hear me! I am Marcus Junius Corvus. A Roman!* I feel drained, and powerless. I don't belong here in this world.

'Please bring me home!' I wail.

I notice the ruin of another large temple nearby, of which six beautiful, fluted columns still stand, rising to a great height. I try to puzzle out what temple this could be. I can just make out a partial inscription in Latin on the pediment: "The Senate and People of Rome restored the temple consumed by fire". I know this place; it must be the Temple of Saturn! I saw a painting of it in one of Father's clients' houses. Yes, it is Saturn's home, rebuilt after a great fire. I push my way through the rickety wire fence that surrounds it. I climb up onto the great slab that once was the temple floor. Long gone is the image of the god, the golden altars and the urns of burning incense. How the ages have brought down the greatest of the gods and their earthly homes. I weep for you, Saturn!

Behind the row of columns, a scaffolding of metal and canvas has been erected. I suppose it was constructed by the city's workmen in an attempt to save these last columns from falling. Well, ninety-nine parts of a hundred are already gone, stolen, or desecrated, and *now* you try to save it! Too little, too late, my friends.

A crude ladder ascends the scaffolding. I climb it; my angry energy propelling me upwards. I swing my body up on to the pediment at the very top of the columns. I rest for a moment to catch my breath. It is a fine view up here, more than sixty feet above the Forum. The ruins of the temples stretch into the distance and are washed in gentle, yellow light. Far to the west is the Colosseum, a ghostly shell of silent, yellow stone with nothing but blackness in its archways. Further beyond is the skyline of modern Rome. The buildings are not as high here as those in Melbourne. Still, there are a few glass and steel towers, cockily reaching towards the heavens. Oh people of the twenty-first century! You think you can reach to heaven, where the gods reside. Fools, all of you. Man belongs with his feet on the earth, with the beasts and the creeping things. Only the gods and the birds dare to visit the heavens!

I rest on the ancient stones, sitting high atop Saturn's pillars. How far I have come. Since the gods snatched me away, here in the Forum all those months ago, all I wanted was to return to Rome! To return to the Forum, to pray to the gods to bring me back. And I have failed. I see Sabina's face looking up at me as she lay on the ground under the big willow tree. Sabina! I miss you terribly, and the immeasurable comfort you gave to a lost traveller. You taught me the ways of these modern men.

How could I be so foolish as to lose her number! Why didn't I commit it to memory? What was it? It was 61, 4, something—I will never remember. I pound the stones with my fists, over and over, until they are raw. It is I who is the greatest fool of all.

What am I to do? Am I doomed to live the rest of my life in the wrong century, a stranger in a strange land? I will never fit in here. Even if I learn their language well, I will never be accepted. Their machines, their cars, their electric toys. I cannot use any of these things. To the people of this time, I am a helpless child. I thought I could learn a trade here. But what could I do? Spend my days cooking food for tourists? Join the men sweeping the stairs of the Cathedral? Is this to be my life? I miss Sabina, my parents, my sister, and my home. All of them are out of reach now.

Maybe I could return to Australia. Back the way I came: Brindisi, Athens, Egypt, Melbourne, Quilpie. To Sabina and her family. They helped me before. I could work for her father, tending their horses. I could! But how can I go back to Australia, a pauper? I have not a denarius to my name! The first time I left Rome, at least I carried much gold and silver coin. Now, nothing but a handful of old clothes given to me by sympathetic tourists. I am cripple, unfit to work anywhere save washing dishes.

I sit with my legs dangling over the edge of the stones. *I could end it now.* My father, incensed at my disobedience, once said I would never amount to anything. It hurt me to hear him say that. But he was right! Penniless, a fugitive, wounded, damaged, illiterate in this new world. What is the point of living! I am so alone, so lost. Tears come, and I wipe them away angrily. *Jump Marcus, jump.*

But I cannot do it. I see mother's face and feel ashamed for my thoughts. She would never forgive me, never forgive the hurt that would cause her. And Sabina too—she would hate me forever if I gave up. I curl up and fall on my side, weeping, wretched, angry. I start to shiver, though the night is warm.

I jump to my feet and call out to heaven. 'Gods of Rome why have you abandoned me? Is your power no more?' Again, I shout, 'where are you powerful trio? Divine Jupiter, sacred Juno, holy Minerva! Hear me! Take me home! Return me to my time! Take me a thousand thousand years away from this place!' From my knees, I shout again and again my prayers. But nothing happens. *Nothing happens.* There are no gods.

283

CHAPTER XVII

Someone *has* heard, apparently. Standing high atop the Temple of Saturn I see two uniformed men approaching, bearing electric lanterns. Should I flee? One is a large, stout man, the other is a thin, bald man. Neither are likely to outrun me. But lost in my pain and rage I am too numb to act. One shines his torch on me.

'Ehi tu! Vieni qui! You there! Come down! You are trespassing on this monument.' I might as well get this over with. I put my hands up.

'I come down,' I tell them with an unsteady voice. 'Scendo. I come down, now.' I shimmy down the scaffolding and present myself to the night watchmen of the Forum ruins.

'Il tuo nome è? What is your name?' calls out the skinny one, obviously the senior of the two.

'I am Marcus Corvus.'

'Are you English? American?'

'I am … Australian, sir.' The two exchange grins.

'I told you. Either Americano, or Aussie. Always the crazy ones,' the skinny man says to the other. 'What are you doing here? Don't you know the Forum is closed? And climbing on the monuments is forbidden. You may damage them. And injure yourself!'

'I am sorry sir. I am very sad, very angry. I am lost. I am trying to get home and nothing I do will take me home.'

'Do you think climbing up there will get you home?'

'It might get you into prison,' says the large man.

'I was praying to the gods.'

'Up there?' He snorts loudly. 'Cannot you pray at the cathedral?' He grins at the other man.

'I pray to *my* gods, Jupiter, Juno, Minerva.' They look at each other again, mouths open.

'A nut case, I told you,' the fat man says to his partner. 'Don't make jokes with us. You are in big trouble. We can take you to the central police station if you like. Be straight with us.'

'I meant no offence.' I think it better to stop talking. My mother always told me that opening my foolish mouth when I was in trouble always made it worse.

The bald man takes charge again. 'You say you are lost. Have you no place to stay in Rome?'

'Yes, I am staying at the Santa Maria school dormitory.'

The large man chimes in. 'I know that one—near Via Cavour. Seminary students stay there in winter. Tourists in summer, I think.'

'Come with us.' I follow the older man, who has less energy than his younger counterpart and follows a few paces behind.

'Watch your step boy, you may fall in the dark.' Slowly we pick our way over the stones, back to the pathway. After some time, we reach a white, timber shack. Inside are two desks, a few plastic chairs, and a bare white electric bulb lighting the interior. They beckon me to sit.

'I will write you this citation, as you are trespassing on City of Rome property. I'll do you a favour and forget that you were climbing on the monuments,' the thin man says.

'Thank you, sir.' The man writes on his notepad, looking over his glasses as if struggling to make out what he is doing. The other sits outside on a bench, sweating profusely, obviously tired from his exertions.

'Identification?' *Not this again.*

'I have no identification, sir. I was robbed in Napoli. They took my papers.'

'A bold lie!' cries the man outside.

'Seriously, young man!' He shakes his head. He hands me over a sheet of paper and a writing implement. 'Write you name here, family name first, then given names.' I do as directed. 'There, write your passport number.'

'I don't know my passport number. It is lost,' I lie. I can see he writes "Australian" in the nationality space. Through my half open shirt, he sees the bruising on my chest.

'How did you get that injury, Marco? Robbed you say?'

'Si. I was attacked and beaten in Napoli. Cracked ribs.' The large man pokes his head in to inspect me closely. He whistles sympathetically.

'Let him go, Tomasso. He's had enough trouble already. No

wonder he is half crazy.'

The senior man pushes back his chair and sighs. He tears off the sheet of paper and scrunches it up.

'You are more trouble than you are worth. I see you have had a hard time. My nephew was robbed in Napoli two years ago too. Hurt badly. I know how you feel. Did they capture your assailants?'

'No, I think not.'

'Ah well. That is a pity.'

They escort me to the gate. The fat man unlocks it after searching for the correct key for a considerable time. Tomasso grips my arm firmly. 'Go home Marco, go to bed. Don't ever come back here, understand me?'

'Si. Grazie,' I call out as the gate slams shut behind me. I quickly make my way back through the empty streets to the dormitory. I cast off my shoes, and fall into bed, exhausted.

I hear the gentle, angelic voice of the goddess of Destiny.

'Give me one hundred sesterces,' she says.

'Why should I, Minerva?' says Jupiter, his booming voice betraying anger at such a request.

'Because I have won the wager! I knew he would give up his faith in the gods!' says Minerva, her face bathed in golden light. She tosses her hair to one side.

'Ha! Has he now?' Jupiter looks down for a moment from his gilded couch, peering at the mortals below. 'So he has. I thought that boy had more faith. Our game is finished then. Here, woman, take your winnings!' He flings a handful of coins at her, which she catches in the folds of her robe. 'But what shall we do with him now?'

'Comfort him. Or better, let us send him home. I pray you, Jupiter!'

He snorts from beneath his great beard. 'You are soft, woman. Why would I do that?'

She comes to his couch and strokes his hair tenderly. 'It would please me, husband. He has a good heart and has suffered a great deal.'

He closes his eyes in response to her caresses. 'You know I cannot. But I will grant you a favour, wife. Go find Mercury and send him to speak to Marcus, to console him.'

She must have done as he asks, for the youthful god with winged shoes appears in an instant beside me. He reaches his arm around my shoulder.

'Weep not, Roman! The gods still watch over you.'

'I knew you would hear me! I beseech you, send me home to my own time. To my mother and father. Will you not pity me? Take me home!'

'Minerva would send you home if she could. But she dare not, for Jupiter forbids it.'

'Pray, tell me why?'

'The old gods no longer have a place in the affairs of men. Another god is lord over the land of Italy.'

'Will he help me if I pray to him?'

'Aye, he will, if you put your faith in him.'

'But how shall I ask him to bring me home?'

'You must go to Saint Peter's and pray.' Mercury turns as

if to depart.

'Wait, Mercury, divine messenger! Where is this Saint Peter's? And how may I please the Christian god?'

'That you must find out yourself.' In a flash of white light, he disappears.

'Wait! Wait!'

I awake suddenly from my dream. It is still dark, and I am still in my bed at the dormitory, wearing my street clothes. Did Mercury just visit me? Was it really a dream? I have a fleeting vision of the gods talking about me, yet I cannot remember what they said. But Mercury, he was real! Was he? Did he not say go to 'Saint Peter's'? I have heard of this church, mentioned often by the tourists in the hostel. I must remember that, at least. *Saint Peter's.*

The dawn arrives, and I rise immediately as I've had an unsettled night. I am not required for breakfast duty and have no obligations until noon. Downstairs, the meal is being laid out. I take a large cup of hot coffee then fill my plate with toasted bread, fried egg and tomato.

What am I to do now? What *can* I do? I went to the Forum, where the temples of the gods lie in ruins, and begged them to bring me home, but they heard me not. Am I stuck here forever? In this world of cars, and noise, and smoke. Among these strange people, with their phones, computers, and flying machines. I don't want to be here.

'I want to go home,' I blurt out aloud, pressing my hands on the table. This causes a sudden silence in the dining room. The other diners stare at me for a moment, then resume their conversations.

I finish my meal, and storm out on to the streets of modern Rome. I walk purposely, yet I have nowhere to go. Past the Colosseum, where a long line of tourists is already queuing up. Past the Vittorio Emanuele monument, its massive bulk pretending to imitate the ancient temples of Rome. I find myself on a little street named the Via del Corso. I soon notice that the women here differ from the typical Roman; they are immaculately dressed in expensive clothes and glittering jewellery. They strut tall and proud in high-heeled shoes. How do they manage not to fall over? The street is lined with shops selling fancy dresses and handbags. I press my eyes to a shop window. Eight hundred euro for a leather bag! At the next shop, a thousand for a woman's gown! I shake my head. I wander aimlessly about, feeling unsettled.

'What am I to do?' I realise I am speaking out loud. I get some nasty looks from passers-by. Does my plebeian clothing offend them? I take no notice. My mind races, my thoughts out of control. On and on I ramble. I cease to care where I end up. I find myself on the banks of the Tiber. I follow it downstream and soon come to a broad stone bridge. It is built in the Roman style, its five arches carrying foot traffic across to the left bank. It is a soothing sight, and I start to cross.

'Hey twenty-first century man! My ancestors built this! Not so bad, eh? Show me one thing as graceful as this, that you weaklings have built! Is this not more beautiful than your glass and steel towers?' I am talking out loud still. Others crossing the bridge give me a wide berth. *Control yourself, Marcus.*

I stare at the shallow, green waters, the midday sun glinting off the eddies and ripples. *At least you, old river, have not changed at all.* How many have stood on this bridge and stared dreamily at your turbulent waters? Men and women live and die, year upon year, century upon century, yet the river never changes. Take away the cars, the people in their strange clothes, the modern buildings, and I could be in old Rome in the days of Tiberius Caesar. So close I am to my mother land! Yet as far away as the moon. *Gods! Hear me!*

'Why don't you hear me?'

I feel something poking me in the ribs. I turn abruptly to find a police officer standing before me. I say a few curses under my breath.

'Hey! Stai bene?' he asks loudly, his arms are crossed and his nightstick cocked in his arm. I cannot find my voice. 'Sei ubriaco?' he asks.

'No, I am not drunk. Please don't hurt me,' I croak out.

'Why are you talking to yourself? You are frightening the people on this bridge.'

'I, I don't know, I ...'

'Do you need help? Are you lost?' Am I lost? *Am I lost!?* You have put your finger on it, il poliziotto. Lost I am, more than you can ever imagine.

'Yes, well, in a way. I ...' What am I to tell him?

'Listen, amico. You are on the Ponte Saint Angelo. Do you know how to get to your hotel? Where are you staying?'

'Near the Termini Station.'

'Ah. Well, that is not far. Here, listen to me.' He gives me directions to the Piazza del Cinqucento in some detail. I nod, but I am not listening. I know well enough how to get back to my residence. I thank the officer and walk back across the bridge towards home.

Days pass, then weeks. My days are spent in the sweltering kitchen, with my silent Italian ladies as my only companions. I watch a little TV in the lounge but prefer to walk the streets when not on duty. With no money there is little I can do in my spare time except pace about the city, watching the people. I feel trapped here for although I have a bed and three meals each day, where is my future?

I must find work. But my only skill, raising horses, is of no use in the city. As useless as a fisherman in a desert. I am unskilled in the engines, the machinery, the gadgets of these people. I can't drive a car, a skill acquired by even schoolboys! Phones and computers baffle me. How can I earn a living here? My only prospect is to earn a few euros as a kitchen helper.

I must get out of Rome. But how can I leave this place without a penny in my pocket? I could return to Australia. Sabina and her family would help me, as they did before. Or would they? Her father was angry with me after I ran out of the house that dark night. Even if I wanted to get back to Australia, how could I accomplish it? By stowing away, stealing meals, acts of theft that are repugnant to me. Has my law breaking angered the gods? Has my thieving caused the gods to shun me, and refuse to listen? I puzzle this over and over on sleepless nights, when wandering the streets, and while cutting vegetables in the oven-like kitchen.

I feel my mind wasting away from the killing loneliness and unending boredom. Pain and anger are so close to the surface. And still, I have no plan. I have no idea what to do.

CHAPTER XVIII

It is now high summer. I rise early with the sun, choosing to work the breakfast shift while the day is still cool. By mid-morning, the sun begins to burn the city. The concrete shimmers under the blue Italian sky. In the afternoons it has become my custom to lie shirtless on my bed, staring at the ceiling and sleeping when I can, sweat dripping off me.

To drive away loneliness I make conversation with Paloma and Angelo, who work the reception desk. I learn that they earn wages here, as employees of Santa Maria, as do the ladies in the kitchen, Giulia and Sofia. Sometimes I speak with my fellow guests. Most are students; they come from many nations, but the majority are Italian. Communication is not always easy, but my command of Italian and English is improving, and most of them know a little of one or the other. At mealtimes, when I'm in the mood, I'll take a seat opposite a single traveller, deliberately choosing them as they are often eager to converse. I ask them about the lands where they dwell, which fascinate me. One night, an elderly couple from a country called Canada told me their province was so cold in winter that the lakes and rivers become solid as rock, and a man can walk upon them! Such tales I am sure are quite exaggerated.

Most travellers love to talk of places they've been and adventures they've experienced on their journeys. Newcomers to Rome invariably ask about the Colosseum, and if I've been there. 'Oh yes, I have,' I tell them. 'More than once.'

One oppressively hot night, I sit outside on the steps of the hostel with Angelo, who smokes a cigarette. He is a young man, barely twenty-five, well-built and handsome. He wears a short beard and I know that woman find him attractive from the way they fawn over him, especially the tourist women. We have become good friends. From him I learn a great deal about Rome and modern Italy. He helps improve my Italian and although I make many blunders, which amuse him to no end, he is patient. With his help I find more courage within myself to speak Italian. He talks of his family, his girlfriends, his studies; for he attends a university and plans to become a doctor. He is a devout man and attends church every week without fail.

I confide to him my pitiful situation; lacking money, family, and a job. I ask how to get work in this city, but he shakes his head. I must have an identity card to work in Italy, or anywhere in Europe for that matter. How to get such a card? With proof of citizenship, he explains: a passport or birth certificate. Of course, without these I am back where I started.

So, I am dependent on the good will of the church, working a few hours a day in the kitchen to earn my daily bread. I fall silent and return inside.

A few days later, Paloma taps on my dormitory door as I take my mid-afternoon rest.

'Ciao Marcus! Guess what, I have a message for you.'

I bolt upright. 'Oh? Di chi e?' I ask. From whom?

'From your friend at Santa Maria. Father Ricardo.' She hands me a small square of paper.

'Grazie, Paloma.' The note informs me he would like to see me, at his office.

Later that afternoon, I make my way to the back of the basilica. Father Ricardo greets me warmly.

'How are you getting along? I hear you've been doing great work in the kitchen.'

'I am going well. Yes, it's true, I have prepared many meals. Thousands.'

'Molto bene! And how are your injuries? Have they healed completely?'

'Si, Father. They have.' In fact, the improvement has been so gradual, I barely noticed. 'The bruises disappeared weeks ago, though my ribs are still a little tender.'

'Thank God. Marcus, I need to tell you something. We have limited space in the hostel. This time of year a great many travellers are looking for lodging in Rome and by the end of August, the seminary students will be returning for classes.'

'I see, Father.' I knew this day would come. I will have to find other lodgings. 'Must I vacate my room soon?'

'Yes, I am afraid so. But not immediately. You may stay another week or two if you require it. Do you require it?'

'Well, in truth, I would like to move on, but …'

'Have you saved any money? Have you been working at all?'

'Well, no sir. You see, I can't work for money as I have no identity card.'

'Ah. And your family? Did you manage to contact them?'

'No, I have not.' He frowns, as though disappointed in me.

'Perhaps you could stay with a friend? Have you made any friends in your time in Rome?'

'I suppose, yes. One or two.'

'Good then, perhaps you could ask them. As I said Marcus, you have been an exemplary guest and Sofia herself told me of your reliability and good work in the kitchen.'

'That surprises me! She scarcely speaks a word to me. But it is kind of her to say so.'

'Please make arrangements for other accommodation and let me know when you will be leaving.'

'I will, Father.'

'Thank you, Marcus.' He stands and shakes my hand, and I know it is time to leave.

The next evening, I find Angelo sitting on the steps while smoking, as is his custom when there is little to do in the evening. I tell him Father Ricardo has told me I must depart the hostel, as returning students will soon be requiring rooms. He nods.

'I won't have anywhere to stay, especially with no money.' He looks at me, draws a long puff and blows it out slowly.

'Please, Angelo, could I stay with you?' He winces and rubs his chin.

'You mean, at mio apartemento?'

'Si, it would only be for a short time. A few weeks. Possibly a few months.' He looks away and draws another long breath. 'A short time,' I repeat.

'So, still no denaro, Marco? I assume not.'

'No, just a few euro. I have no identity card, as you know.' He pauses, and looks skyward, as if reluctant to speak his mind.

'Well, friend I suppose you can stay with me. But I'm telling you, it might cramp my style.' I'm not sure of his meaning.

'I will be a quiet guest and a clean one.'

He nods. 'Si, I expect you will be ok. Still no money, eh?' I shake my head. 'Well, I have an idea. Maybe you could work at my uncle's restaurant. They often need a waiter or dishwasher.'

'Angelo! I would be very happy to work there. What about papers?'

'You could work for cash money. No papers, no questions. But you may have to take a little less wage, you know, it all being a little risky.'

'Cash money. Yes! Very happy to work. I am good worker! I can cook many dishes.'

He grins. 'I know you can. That rigatoni you cook up on Thursdays is fit for the angeli in heaven. You won't be required to cook I expect. They already have a couple of good chefs. Just wait on tables, take orders, clear dishes, stuff like that.'

'Si, Angelo. And where is this restaurant of your uncle?'

'He owns a pizzeria in Pinciano. Near the Villa Borghese.'

'Great! Grazie, Angelo. Grazie!' I take his hands and hold them to my chest.

'Is okay, Marco.'

'So, I can stay with you? Until I save a little money, then find my own place?'

'Si, you can sleep on my couch. No problem.'

'Thank you.'

He pauses for a moment. 'But there may be a time when I require you to be, you know, absent.'

'Absent?'

'If I am bringing a woman to my flat, you need to, how you say, vamoose for a while. You know, take a walk?'

This time I get his meaning. 'Of course, Angelo. Just give me a sign and I'll take a walk. All night if that's what you need!'

He grins. 'And get yourself a phone! Mio Dio, Marco, this is the twenty-first century! You can get one at the post office for fifty euro.' *Angelo, I am not a twenty-first century man.* 'And I'll get you a key made.' He flicks his cigarette butt in the gutter and returns inside. I sit on the steps for a moment. Thank the gods for good men like Angelo.

I move into his apartment a few days later. On my last day at the hostel, when the guests have departed after dinner, the staff gather to wish me well. Giulia produces a large chocolate cake, to the delight of everyone. She speaks well of me, as do Angelo and Paloma. Even Father Ricardo is there and says a few kind words. I was not expecting this, and am moved by the little ceremony. I thank them all for their generosity in taking me in when I had nothing. I promise I will not forget them.

Giulia quickly serves the cake, and it is time to go. Father Ricardo takes my hand warmly.

'Salve Marcus, arrivederci.' *Salve.* I have not heard that word in a year, and it warms me.

'Addio a tutti!' I shout out to everyone. Goodbye everyone. They come forward in turn to embrace me. Even the elderly Sofia, who has scarcely spoken a word to anyone, does the same and kisses me on the cheek in the manner of the Italians.

'Off you go, Marcus. Don't worry about the dishes,' says Paloma.

I go with Angelo to the nearby underground train station, and soon we are at his apartment, in a small block in the Pinciano district of the city. It is a small place, with only a single bedroom, but mercifully on a quiet street. Though its couch is not exactly new, it is quite serviceable as a bed. The location, near the parklands around the Villa Borghese, is perfect. I will spend many quiet hours in the magnificent gardens.

I soon settle into a new routine. Angelo is often out, at work or at university, so I have the place to myself most of the day. True to his word, he speaks with his uncle Stefano about taking me on in his pizzeria. Within a few days I have my first job. I report for duty one afternoon and am put to work helping in the kitchen. Stefano is a nearly bald middle-aged man with a broad, grizzled moustache; he has the intense manner of one who runs his own business. Hard working and serious, he keeps a sharp eye on his workers, but seems pleased with my work. Stefano pays me in cash each night. He often says as he counts out the bills, 'Remember, if anyone asks, I've never heard of you and you've never heard of me, right Marco?'

'I've never heard of you, Stefano,' I always reply, and return his toothy smile.

It doesn't take long to learn everything that needs doing in a pizza restaurant. Though another man always makes the dough, the rest of the job of making a pizza is hardly a challenge. There are only ten varieties on the menu, and I learn them all on the first night. After that I can make any pizza with my eyes closed. In time I earn their trust, and learn to use the little machine that holds the cash, and the one that lets people buy on credit.

Most nights when I arrive home Angelo is there, often already asleep. I watch his big TV with the sound turned low for a time. Watching TV somehow makes me drowsy; my eyes invariably grow heavy. I unroll my little blanket on the couch, and quickly fall asleep. We keep a pact not to disturb each other when the other is sleeping. Angelo leaves in the mornings with barely a peep, for which I am very grateful.

CHAPTER XIX

Autumn arrives in Rome. The sun grows less strong and the leaves turn. Fewer tourists move about the city. It is wonderful to have a little money of my own. Now I can afford to buy a new shirt, dine in a real restaurant, and not live like a beggar, but most of my pay I save as I promised Angelo I would.

Living with him is not all plain sailing. Like most bachelors, his concept of cleanliness is close to that of a trash heap rat. The apartment is often piled high with dirty dishes, old pizza boxes and unwashed clothes. That is, of course, until he plans to bring one of his lady friends home, then it is all hands to cleaning. For a man can live in a cave, but a woman must live in a pristine house.

Often he warns me in advance, so I can clear out after dinner. Other times he arrives unannounced with a young woman on his arm. Introductions in such situations are brief.

'Marcus, Alina. Alina, Marcus. He was just leaving.' My cue to grab my jacket and hit the street. Though I find it annoying sometimes, especially when the weather is foul, I cooperate cheerfully. I know to stay away for at least two hours, after which I can return to the apartment and re-join them. Though often I see neither until morning.

One Saturday evening, we find ourselves sprawled, as usual, in front of the TV. Angelo's date has cancelled, leaving him with a fine bottle of red wine and no one to partake with. I propose we knock out the cork; he agrees. We fill and refill our glasses while watching a football game half-heartedly. Angelo is clearly upset that this woman stood him up.

'I think she is going to ditch me, Marco.'

'Ditch you?'

'You know, dump me. Leave me.'

'Ah. That would be tragic, amico. Are you sure of this? Perhaps she just has some illness.'

'Yeah, sick of me I fear.' There is genuine sadness in his voice. 'And you, Marco. Have you not found a girlfriend yet? A good looking boy like you!'

'No, Angelo. Well, there is this girl in Australia, she is very sweet. I miss her very much. And I fear the women here think I am, you know, strange.'

He laughs. 'Strange, no. Different, si. You are like no other Italian I have ever met.'

'How so, Angelo?' I am genuinely curious how others perceive me.

'For starters, you can barely speak Italian. I swear I taught you almost every word you know. And you are so, don't take this the wrong way my friend, backward.'

'Backward?'

'You don't even carry a phone! I've never seen you use a computer or drive a car. Niente. It seems you don't belong to the modern world. Did you live on a farm your whole life?'

'Yes, I did. Near a village in the south.'

'I thought so. It must have been a *very* small village. I'm pretty sure they have cars in the south. They even have internet, so I hear.' I look away. 'What *is* your story, Marco? What is your past?'

'You wouldn't believe me if I told you.'

'Try me. Don't worry. There's no harm in telling me of something you're ashamed of. Were you in carcere? Prison?'

'No! Well, yes, for a short time …'

'Ah! Well, there's no shame in that. You served your sentence, now you can move on.'

'I know, Angelo.'

'What did you do? Burglary?'

'No, I am not a thief. I was arrested by people trying to extort my family.'

'Oddio! Did the mafia come after you? And you beat up one of their goons?'

'No, they arranged that I be arrested on false charges; the evil doings of a powerful man trying to persuade my father to give up our farm.'

'And your father, he wouldn't do it?'

'I don't know, that is the truth. I assume he held his ground. He is an honest man.'

'You don't know? Have you not talked to your father?' I

could feel the truth writhing within my gut, trying to get out.

'No, I haven't.'

'Why don't you call him? You can use my phone.' I shake my head. 'What is his name? I'll look him up.'

'His name is Gaius Corvus. But I cannot call him, he is not, he is …'

'Morto? Is he dead?

'No, I pray not.' *Actually, he has been dead for at least 2,000 years.*

'What *is* your story? I'll get another bottle and you are going to tell me everything. Tutto.' He disappears into the kitchen, and I hear the pop of a cork. He soon returns with another bottle and pours a tall glass for both of us.

'Come on. Out with it. You are my friend. I'll not betray you. Where are you really from?'

I take a deep breath. 'Well, it's like this. Everything I said to you, is true. My family is from Campania, we owned a small farm there and raised horses.'

'Bene. Good. So far, I am with you.'

'And the praetorians did come one day, and seized me, and took me to Rome.'

'Praetorians? Who are they? A Sicilian gang?'

'No, they are Romans, troops of the imperial guard. In my time they were the private army of Tiberius and his black fist, Sejanus.'

'Tiberius who? Is he the don of the operation?'

'Tiberius Caesar Augustus, emperor of Rome.' He looks at me, his mouth wide open.

'Of Rome! What, you mean, *ancient* Rome? The emperor Tiberius?'

'The same.'

'You are crazy! Pazzo! You think the private soldiers of the Roman emperor arrested you? Like back in the first century?'

'Yes. I know, it is hard to believe—'

'Crazy is more like it. And you are still alive here, in the twenty-first century? Are you saying that you are immortal? You've lived for two thousand years!?'

'No, far from it. I am only nineteen years old. Twenty, this month. I travelled here from the past. I mean, to the present. To 2019.'

'Sure you did. Okay. Sure. And by what magic did you get here, time traveller?'

'No magic. I prayed to the gods, to Jupiter, Minerva, and Juno, in the Forum amongst the temples. They sent me here.'

'They answered your prayers? So, the gods sent you here to modern Rome?'

'Well, not to Rome. To Australia actually.'

He shakes his head and throws his arms in the air. 'Mamma mia! Australia? Why? Did you travel on a kangaroo?' He laughs at his joke.

'Because I prayed to the gods to take me to the other side of the earth, to take me a thousand thousand years away from those barbaric times. They heard my prayers.'

'And brought you to twenty-first century Australia?'

'Si, Angelo.'

He drains his entire glass of wine and pours another. He

gets up and paces around the room, mumbling to himself. I pick up the Italian words for lunatic, crazy, plus a few curse words.

'How did you get from Australia to Rome? Did you fly on a winged horse, I suppose? Or perhaps Neptune carried you?'

'No, nothing so easy, I assure you.' I recount my adventures in Quilpie, in Melbourne, aboard ship, in Greece, Brindisi, and Naples. At first sceptical, he listens with ever increasing enthusiasm. Tears come to his eyes when I tell him how I found the remains of our farm in the Campanian countryside.

'What a fantastic tale! If true, it certainly explains a lot about you. If you grew up in ancient Italy, I suppose you can speak Latin?'

'Scilicet. Latinae lingua mea mater.'

'Veni Vedi Vici! Fantastic! You know, I think I believe you, crazy Roman.' He studies my face. He begins to giggle and soon is laughing uncontrollably. When he regains his breath, he takes another deep draft of wine. He takes me by the shoulders. 'You *really* think you are from ancient Rome?'

'I *am* from Rome, ancient you may call it. But I've been living here in your world, your time rather, for the last year.'

'How do you find it? The twenty-first century, I mean?' As I try to answer, a group of motorcycles roars past outside, drowning out my words.

'It is very noisy.' He nods in agreement.

'I am curious about one thing. You say you met a girl in Australia. Tell me about her.' *That's Angelo.*

'Sabina comes from a farming family, in a village in

Queensland. She lives with her mother, and father Tony who is retired I think, but once raised horses. She has a brother who is away, studying at a university in the city.'

'No, I mean what does she look like? Bella donna? Is she hot?' I recently learnt the meaning of this phrase.

'Oh, she is hot, as you say. A fine-looking young woman. She has dark hair and wears it long. Beautiful brown eyes.'

'And her figure?' He traces an outline of a woman in the air with his hands.

'She is slim and well-figured. But she is still a girl, eighteen years old by now.'

He slaps me on the shoulder. 'Dolce! Sweet! She sounds magnifico. Why don't you call her? Wait, she lives in the twenty-first century, right?'

'Yes, she does.'

'Well then, ask her to come visit. Italy is full of Aussies; she would fit right in.' I tell him I lost her phone number with all my other possessions in the robbery. 'I see. Tragic, Marco. Is she on Facebook? Twitter? Surely you can find her there?'

Facebook. Sabina had shown me this thing on her phone once. It seems to be something people are obliged to look at for hours every day. It shows you endless pictures of dogs, cats, and food. Of what use this is, I know not.

'She may be, but I know not how to use it.'

'Crazy Roman. Here, I'll look her up myself. He picks up his phone and works at it for a minute. 'Sabina, you say? What is her last name?'

'I don't know.' *Why didn't I ask her?*

'Well, what town did you say she was from?'

'Quilpie.' I spell it for him. He works at his phone again.

'No luck. Maybe she's not on Facebook. Or maybe her profile is on private. Who knows.' He tosses his phone on the table. We fall silent, and Angelo tries to watch the football. But soon he grabs the remote and turns it off. He turns again to me. 'How do you intend to get home? Are the gods going to send you back?' There is a hint of sarcasm in his voice.

'I don't know, Angelo. I tried praying to the gods, but they did not hear me.'

'Maybe they heard you but decided not to help you this time. Where did you pray?'

'At the Forum, at the Temple of Saturn. I felt the father of the gods would surely take pity on me, for I am a lost son of my own father.'

He thinks about this for a moment. 'Maybe the old gods are dead. I mean look around the city. Their temples, their statues, all smashed and thrown down. Maybe they left Italy, forever.'

'Yes, I fear this too. Perhaps they no longer pay attention to the prayers of men, for no one honours them, keeps their temples or makes the sacrifices anymore.'

'I am sure of it, Marco.' Angelo's face grows long as he realises the implication. 'So, you are trapped here, in our world?'

'Lost in your mad, noisy world. Lost in Italy, even though it is my home—was my home.'

'What you have to do Marco, is give up on your gods. There is a new God in Rome now. The Christian God. The god of most of Italy's people.'

'Would he help me? Surely he will know I grew up ignorant of him and have never offered him prayers or sacrifices.'

'It's never too late. The preachers tell us this all the time.'

'Does the Christian god really intercede in the lives of men? Could he help me?'

'Of course he does! He has been working miracles on Earth since time began. Go to a church, Marco. Pray in silence.'

'To Jesus? The one that was crucified?'

'You know him already. The son of God, who died for us. Read the Gospels. Promise to follow his teachings: forgiveness, love, charity, all that. Maybe he will smile on you.' Our heart-to-heart talk lasts late into the night. He keeps prodding me, testing me, as best his liquor-soaked mind can. He asks absurd questions, like did I know Julius Caesar, or Romulus and Remus? I tell him what the city looked like back in my time, when the temples still stood in all their glory. When the Colosseum was newly built. I tell him about the bloody Games in the arena.

'It's true! Gladiators fighting to the death.' I assure him it was very true, and that I very nearly became a victim in the arena, myself. 'And did they butcher Christians? Like in the movies? Throw them to the lions?'

'Well, I had never heard of the Christians until I came here. But I believe this Jesus walked the earth around my own time, preaching in Judea, when I was taken prisoner.'

'Tell me, what year did you leave your time?'

'In the fifth year of the emperor Tiberius.'

'I mean which year AD?' I shrug. He pulls out his phone.

'According to Google, Tiberius ruled from AD fourteen to thirty-seven. So, you must have left your time in the year AD nineteen. Wow! Just like you said. Two thousand years, on the nose.'

We talk and drink until nearly dawn. Before he crawls to bed, Angelo tells me again to adopt the Christian faith. He says it will let me find peace, even if it may not be possible to return to my own time. I promise I will. Starting with attending church service with him this very morning. With that, we call it a night.

We manage to get to the church just as the service commenced; both of us suffering the effects of too much wine. Despite my pounding head and parched throat, I listen carefully to the service, and try to follow the rituals. There is some spirited singing, beautifully performed by a choir perched in the loft above the altar. In the middle of the ceremony, the high priest presides over the sacrament of bread and wine, just as I had seen in the little church in Australia. *Take, eat, this is my body and blood, shed for you.*

Following this, the priest speaks at length, telling the tale of a proud youth who demanded his inheritance from his father, then set out on his own to a far country. I follow the story earnestly. *Is he speaking to me?* The youth spent his fortune on riotous living, and when famine came, found himself destitute and despised. He returned to his father begging for forgiveness. The father rejoiced and ordered a fatted calf to be killed in honour of the youth's return. I think of my father and how he must be yearning for news of me. And how he too would weep with joy if he knew I was alive. I miss him terribly. He was a kind, caring man, who loved me, my mother and my sister. I wipe a few tears away. Angelo notices this but says nothing. We walk home in silence.

A few days later, I am resting after a long shift at the pizzeria. My back aches from being on my feet for many hours. I sprawl on the couch, watching some mindless trash on the TV, eating leftover pizza I took home after close-up. In bursts Angelo with a pretty, dark-haired girl on his arm, one I have not met before. She is wearing very little, in spite of the cool autumn weather. I hold out my hand to her.

'Buona sera. I am Marcus.'

She doesn't take it, but folds her arms and barks at Angelo. 'What is *he* doing here? You said you live alone!' She speaks with an unusual accent that I cannot place. She glares at me. Angelo looks at me with pleading eyes.

'It's okay, he was just leaving.'

'It's after midnight, where am I to go?' I rarely challenge Angelo, but this time his request is unreasonable. There is a tempest outside and I have no intention of cowering in a doorway somewhere, at this hour.

'Per favore, Marco. We won't be long.' The girl puts her hands on her hips.

'So?' she asks both of us.

'Angelo, amico you must be joking if you think I'm going outside in this weather. You and—'

'Jelena.'

'— can do what you want. I'll turn up the TV. I won't hear anything.'

'Oh my God, Angelo! Either he goes, or I go.'

Angelo takes my arm and pulls me aside. He half whispers, 'Please, amico. Just this one time. Look at her! She's so hot! She's half Serbian. How can you do this to me?' He reaches into his pocket and hands me a twenty euro note. 'Go see a movie or something!' He grabs my jacket from the hook behind the door and thrusts it into my arms.

'Fine. Remember, this is my home too,' I say, looking straight at the woman.

'Ciao!' she calls out sarcastically. I put on my jacket and storm out.

How could my friend do this to me? Throwing me out in the middle of the night so he can enjoy a tryst with this girl. A harlot no doubt, judging by her dress. I have had quite enough of this business. Angelo is a considerate man but loses his senses when anywhere near an alluring woman. Where am I to go? Are the cinemas open at this hour? I remember one near the Termini station, but that is a long walk from here and it is a brisk night. What if it is closed? The park is nearby, but unsafe at this time of night.

A few blocks away I find a bar that is still open, and use Angelo's twenty to buy a drink to calm my temper. But after a while the bar too closes, and we patrons find ourselves in the street. It's too soon to return to the apartment.

I wander about for a time and come to a small open square. At one end is an imposing building that looks like an intact

Roman temple. Built by my people?! Flanking the entrance are massive stone columns, forty feet tall. The inscription is still readable. "M. AGRIPPA L F COS TERTIVM FECIT". Built by the great Marcus Agrippa! A Roman hero, soldier, and right-hand man of Augustus. He died ten years before I was born, but was much revered. This must be the Pantheon. We learnt of this temple as children. Built by Marcus Agrippa to honour *all* the gods, to ask for their perpetual support for Rome and its people. *It still stands.*

The great doors are open and I venture in. It is a vast, round hall, its floors and walls ornately decorated in coloured marble. All around are niches with elegant statues and paintings. High above is an enormous dome, so high it is barely visible in the soft light. At the centre of the dome is an opening; I can see stars through it. From the paintings and the crosses, I know this temple is no longer dedicated to the Roman gods, but to the Christian one.

I linger inside, studying the paintings and warming myself. There are only a few people here: a couple of tourists are taking photos, and at one end of the hall, a priest is holding service with a handful of worshippers. I walk softly over and sit on one of the wooden benches. The priest asks us to pray in silence. I mouth a prayer to the old gods of Rome. For this is their home too, is it not? But just as when I prayed at the Forum, nothing happens. *Maybe Angelo was right.* A different god rules Italy now. I try praying to him. I tell him in whispers that I promise to follow Jesus, to learn the correct sacrifices and prayers, and to follow them devoutly. *Give me a sign. Take me home. Ostende mihi signum. Suscipe me in domum suam. Give me a sign. Take me home.*

Were my prayers heard?

'Go in Peace,' says the minister, and the little group stands to depart. A couple of security guards, stifling yawns, politely shepherd us and the tourists out into the square. The great doors are bolted shut behind us. I ramble slowly back to the apartment, my body stiff with cold. At home, the girl and Angelo are asleep, snoring loudly in the bedroom. I shut their door carefully, throw off my jacket and boots, and fall asleep on the couch.

The next day I am too weak to go to work, my throat is raw from my late-night walk. I ask Angelo to call his uncle to inform him. This he does, though he does not otherwise speak to me. There is little fodder in the house, so I set out for the nearby outdoor food market. It is my favourite place to shop. Here I can get fruit, vegetables, fish and meats from sellers within ramshackle canvas tents. The merchants are friendly, and the food fresh.

Today it is gloomy, wet weather, so I quickly buy a loaf, some cheese, and grapes, then start for home.

Around me, shoppers hurry about their business, their coats drawn up close. Across the street, I notice a young man with curly brown hair, dressed in a grey cloak, staring at me. When he sees me return his gaze, he turns suddenly and walks towards me.

I know that man! His face is familiar, yet I cannot place him.

Fearful of what he wants, I dash into a section of market stalls. I move steadily down the aisle, glancing back occasionally. There he is again! He looks at me for an instant, then dashes towards me. I dodge my way through the aisles. The wind picks up suddenly, the canvas tents covering the food sellers blow about madly, throwing off sprays of rainwater in all directions. I've lost sight of him. I scan the market in all directions and see no one but shoppers trying to keep out of the rain. I turn for home, and bump straight into him.

'Who are you?' I demand.

'Tu ad acum,' he says quietly, and turns to leave. *Go to the needle.*

I ask him to wait and to tell me his name. 'Exspecta! Amica. Quid est nomen tibi?'

'Lucius. Decii filio.' *Luicius, son of Decius.*

He takes me by the shoulders. 'Go to the needle,' he tells me again in Latin.

'What is the needle?'

'Go to the needle in the square. It will take you home.' He turns and runs off.

'Home? To my own time?' I ask desperately. 'Wait!' I call out. I try to follow, but he has vanished. What does he mean?

I hurry back to the apartment, getting a good soaking on the way. It is thankfully deserted, and I fling my shopping on the table. I stare out the window to the dreary street, trying to comprehend what I have just seen. Who is this Lucius, son of Decius? A Roman like me, surely! Did he not speak perfect Latin? And he wore a cloak, instead of the modern style coat.

Who sent him, with this puzzling message? Could *he* be a messenger from the gods? Lucius—a common enough name around my village. I hold my head in my hands, trying to place his face.

Wait, I know now. It was Lucius from the dungeon! The man who escaped with me. But he was cut down and killed by the guards. I saw it with my own eyes. Did he not die? He couldn't possibly be alive! Surely, I was seeing a ghost! How did he get here? And what did he mean, *go to the needle in the square?*

CHAPTER XX

The next few days at the apartment are uncomfortable. Though Angelo apologised for tossing me out into the street that night, there remains an uneasy tension between us. I know I will have to move on soon, for I have again worn out my welcome. Although I enjoy Angelo's company and his interesting lifestyle, I need a place I can call my own.

One evening, when I'm not working and Angelo is out on the town, I pull my hoard of euros out from their hiding place in the stuffing of the couch back. I count it on the table, the crisp notes making an impressive sight. I have saved nearly 2,000 euro. Plenty enough, one would think, to obtain my own flat. On my meagre wage, I know it would be nearly impossible to pay the rent on an apartment in Rome. Still, if I could obtain a room in a shared house, it might be affordable. But it would still be someone *else's* house.

How I miss living in my own home. My family home, on

our sunburnt acreage. I miss the smells of the country, the sounds of birds welcoming the dawn and dusk every day, as they did on the farm and in peaceful Quilpie. I detest city life; the noise and never-ending fumes of cars is offensive to my country senses. I start feeling sorry for myself again. Alone, rootless and still with no way to get home.

The sound of Angelo unlocking the door brings me out of self-pity. I sweep up the pile of cash, fold the notes and shove them in my pocket.

'Salut Marco. Quid agis?' he asks. I taught him a few phrases in Latin, which he uses when he is in a good mood.

'Bene, Angelo. Just thinking of going to sleep.' It is a lie, as it is barely 9 pm, but I am anxious to avoid speaking to him.

'Oh, so early? Had a busy day?'

'Not so busy. Little to do.'

'Bored eh. Say, why don't you stay up. Juventus are playing Napoli tonight.' I know Juventus is his favourite football team. Every Italian male of any age is required to religiously support a football team, and I felt obliged to choose a team of my own. As a southern boy, naturally I picked Napoli. I am pleased to hear the warmth in his voice again, which I haven't heard for some time.

'Your boys had better look out! We Campanians play rough in everything we do,' I boast.

'You haven't a chance! Anyway, it will be a good contest. Why don't I get us some snacks.' He returns from the kitchen with two bottles of beer and some packets of salty, greasy snacks that I confess I've become very fond of. We chat a little, both relieved that the tension of the past few days has evaporated.

We follow the match intently. An early goal by each team gives us both something to cheer about. It is still one goal each at half time. Angelo turns down the sound.

'Marco, old friend. I want to tell you something. I'm sorry about the other night. It was disrespectful of me. It's just, when I am with a woman—'

I hold up my hand. 'I know. I know. It is all right.'

'No seriously, amico, you have a right to be angry.'

'Si, Angelo. This is your home after all, and I am only a visitor. I need to find my own place. You have been a fine host allowing me to stay here for so many weeks. I am taking advantage of your kindness.'

'Not at all, Marco. You've been a fine guest. I know you buy food for us, and cook, and keep the place tidy. I am such a pig to live with.'

'You are no pig. Well, since you cheer for Juventas, perhaps.' He laughs. 'But thank you for taking me in when I was at my lowest.'

'Anything for a friend. Hey, you can stay as long as you need to. Have you been saving a little money?' I tell him I have, and that I will soon look for a room to rent somewhere.

'That is fantastic, Marco. I wish you well, wherever you go.' The awkward silence is ended, fortuitously, when the football resumes. We are both relieved to have resolved our differences and we watch the rest of the match in high spirits. Juventas wins by a goal, which sends Angelo to bed whistling.

I ready myself for sleep and turn the TV low. There is some sort of cooking competition, where stern faced and rather rude judges pillory what, to me, look like well cooked dishes. I drift off, feeling better than I have in a long time.

I am in the Colosseum again, chained to a pillar in the centre of the arena floor. Thousands upon thousands of spectators shriek at me from all sides. A pack of lions circle me, moving ever closer. They eye me hungrily, their mouths dripping. I tear at my chains, but they budge not an inch. A lion lunges towards me, his jaws open! I wake from my nightmare with a start.

It is dark and silent, it must be well after midnight. As the pounding in my heart settles, I cover my head with my pillow. *Why gods? Why can't I even sleep in peace?* Caesar and your barbaric games, will you never let me be? I am no longer your prisoner. Yet still you torment me!

As I struggle to sleep, I half remember my dream from months past, where the gods determined my fate. They sent Mercury to tell me how to get home. *Go to Saint Peter's Square,* he said. Piazza San Petro. I have never been there, but I know it is on the other bank of the Tiber.

The next day, unsettled and irritable from a poor night's sleep, I leave the flat early. It is another blustery day with much rain. The gusty autumn wind rips the remaining leaves from the trees as I make my way through Borghese Park. The smell of damp leaves fills the air, for winter is almost upon us. I come to the river. Its waters are low at this time of year. The banks here are lined with tall plane trees, bare and gaunt.

Nearby is a desolate lot, closed off by an ugly wire fence. Inside it is a large brick building in disrepair. A tangle of weeds grows on top of the ruins, as do a few forlorn cypress trees. A tourist signpost reads "Mausoleum of Augustus". Augustus! The resting place of our divine emperor, restorer of peace! I walk around the ruin, but the site is fenced and deserted. No doubt desecrated centuries ago, the golden urns overturned and stolen, the ashes cast on the ground. I pick up a handful of dust in my hands and let it trickle through my fingers. *Oh father of the Empire, I hope you are not as lonely in heaven, as I am on earth.* I pray his soul in heaven is resting easy. It begins to rain.

I continue along the river and cross the Tiber at the Vittorio Emanuele bridge. A broad avenue, Via Della Conciliazione, leads to an enormous domed cathedral in the distance. A sign points the way to Piazza San Pietro.

I push against a stiff breeze and draw my coat closer. The avenue opens onto a square of truly awesome proportions. On either side, a curved gallery of enormous marble columns wraps around the sides of the plaza. Opposite stands a church larger than any I have seen, dwarfing even the great temples in the Forum. Father Nicholas told me Saint Peter's was the grandest church in the world, and here it is in all its majesty.

I am drawn to the white pillars flanking the square. They are more than sixty feet high and two yards broad at their base. A covered passage runs between them, and I move through it to keep out of the weather. The stupendous size of the colonnade is overwhelming. The sun emerges, and briefly lights up the gallery of columns opposite. On the roof of the colonnade stands a row of colossal statues, glowing brilliant white in the sunlight. I wonder what gods or men these are who stand watch over this place.

I reach the steps of the basilica of Saint Peter. Its facade of limestone is vast but has little decoration. It too is topped by a row of statues, the figures gazing out across the square, many holding crosses in their arms. An inscription begins, "In honorem Principis Apost ..." *In honour of the prince of the apostles.* A broad staircase fronts the entrance. In front of that is a series of rope barriers, much like those I have seen at tourist attractions where visitors must queue to enter. On this wintry day there is no one waiting.

The interior is far more magnificent than the facade would indicate. A long hall recedes into the distance; a jumble of archways and massive gilded columns hold up the vaulted roof far above. Along the walls are little chapels containing diverse altars and statues. The floors, walls, and ceilings are all laid in fine marble patterns and mosaics. All about the basilica are Latin inscriptions. My people's language! Did my people build this church? The Romans must have become Christians.

I stop beneath the great dome. Inscribed around it, "Tu es Petrus Et Super Hanc Petram ..." *You are Peter, and upon this rock I will build my church and to you I will give the keys to the kingdom of heaven.* This cathedral was dedicated to this man Peter.

There are tourists and worshippers here, but the place is so vast it is not crowded. Tourists are snapping photos, which seems disrespectful in a sacred place such as this, but the temple priests tolerate it.

Off the main hall I find a large altar sitting under a sort of canopy, held up by black twisting columns of bronze, its purpose a mystery. As I study it, an old man in a beggar's garb approaches.

'Do you repent? Do you ask forgiveness of all your sins?' He thrusts a bony finger in my face. 'You must for your prayers to be heard!' Before I can answer, he drifts away to repeat his message to another.

I enter a small alcove devoid of people, save one old man who is kneeling. His eyes are tightly closed, he prays softly in Latin.

'In nomine patris, et filii et spiritus sancti.' His face is thin and gaunt. He wears a sparse robe of what looks like sackcloth; his wrinkled hands clutch a silver cross and a string of beads. The alcove holds a simple altar, behind, a mosaic in coloured glass shows the crucifixion of a man. I notice the victim is upside down. The image is frightening and grotesque. By the inscription, I learn it depicts the death of Saint Peter himself.

I kneel near the old man, trying to hear his prayers more clearly. Perhaps, if I know how to pray to the Christian God, he will hear me. I listen, but I can barely hear him with the echoes in the vast church. I edge closer. He looks up with a start, and looks me in the eye, saying nothing. I ask his forgiveness.

'Peto venia,' I whisper, bowing my head to him.

'Filius, Quad vis?' he replies in a weak, croaking voice.

'Can you teach me to pray to God? The God of Jesus, and Peter?'

I fear I have offended him, for he snaps back:

'What, in this sacred place? Where Peter himself was taken up to heaven! Who are you, asking me to teach you to pray?' His response takes me aback. My troubled soul can bear no more and I can't help but shed tears.

'I am sorry. I am just a lost man. Forgive me.' He softens.

'There, there, son. Dry your eyes. I am sorry for my harsh words.' He closes his eyes, looks upwards. 'Forgive me, Father,' he whispers, then he takes my hand in his. 'Forgive me, boy. I beg you.'

'I forgive you. It is nothing.'

'How could I help you, brother? Please tell me.'

'I am lost, sir. Lost and far from my home. I have nothing. I am sure only God can help me, but I don't know how to pray to him or how to make sacrifices. Could you teach me a prayer? A simple one? I don't want to offend God.' He studies me. I feel ashamed to have disturbed this pious man. 'I am sorry, I am not worthy.' I stand to go, but he stops me.

'A lost traveller, are you? Well, show me a man who has never been lost in his life. Why, when I was a young man I, I …' he whispers, lost in thought. 'Of course, God can help you. But you must *believe* in him. As for a prayer, there is no need to say a particular one. Say a prayer in your own words. Speak from your heart. He will hear you.'

'But I have prayed, and I fear I was not heard.'

'Because you didn't see results in an instant? God does not

cast favours about like a rich man running for office.'

'No, you are right. I was wrong to expect that. Please help me to pray.'

'Believe me, I am no teacher. Just a humble Christian. But I could give you a little guidance, perhaps.'

'How do I become a Christian?' He thinks for a minute.

'Well, for most people it starts with being baptised.'

'Baptised?'

'A ritual washing away of sins. A simple ceremony to initiate you to the faith.'

'Besides baptism, what else must I do?'

'You must confess your sins.'

'Sins? Crimes I have committed?'

'Not only crimes, but the ills you have done to others whether in anger or not. And most importantly of all, forgive those who have sinned against you.'

'Even those who have wronged me?' *Sejanus.*

'Especially those! You will never be at peace with yourself, or with God, if you hold hate and vengeance in your heart.'

'Oh.' This turns my thoughts upside down. 'And God will accept me if I do those things?'

'He will! Of that, I am sure. You said before, you have nothing. Is that *really* so? Pray to God and thank him for what you have. A strong body, a good heart, food to eat, a roof over your head. Do you have these things?'

'I do. All those things. In that light, I am not so poor.'

'There you go. You are on your way to becoming a Christian. Peace be with you, boy.' He stands and shuffles off.

I sit for a time, trying to remember what he taught me. A man of such age and wisdom must be speaking the truth. I make my way out of the great basilica slowly, lost in thought. Outside, it is foul and damp. It is getting close to sunset. I cross to the centre of Saint Peter's Square to better take in the magnificence of the plaza. In the precise centre stands a slender granite pillar that I hadn't noticed before. It is a hundred feet tall and tapers to a point. Strange figures are carved in this gigantic needle of stone.

A needle! Is this what Lucius spoke of? Did he not say to go to the needle in the square? I study the foot of the obelisk. It is of Egyptian make, for the figures are hieroglyphs. Everyone knows the Egyptians were civilised centuries before the light came to ancient Greece or to Rome, and their gods the most ancient of all the gods.

A simple iron cross is fixed atop the obelisk, high above. The symbol of Christ. I circle the monument and study the inscription on its the western face. "Christvs Vincit, Christvs Regnat …". *Christ conquers, Christ reigns.* The new God of Rome! Even the ancient gods of Egypt are subservient now.

The sky darkens, and rain falls. The wind blows hard, driving everyone to take shelter. The wind rips at my clothing, and I am quickly soaked. I find myself standing alone in the square before this great obelisk of granite. *I suppose this is my baptism.*

The wind blows stronger. I can feel the raindrops burning the skin of my face. *Forgive all my sins, great Lord.* I feel something rising in my chest. I feel warm despite the tempest around me. A bolt of lightning flashes, illuminating in stark white light the statues perched around the square. It flashes again and it is as though all these holy men and women of marble are staring directly at me. I pray to Jesus, and I feel a touch on my shoulder. I turn in fear but there is no one there. I pray to Saint Peter. Lightning flashes again and I see in the clouds a bearded man, Peter himself, nailed to a cross upside down! The image terrifies me but vanishes in an instant.

There is one more thing I must do. *Forgive,* the old man said. *All* those who have wronged you. Can I forgive those who robbed me, and beat me in Napoli? Those young thugs! Living in an impoverished neighbourhood, perhaps this is the only life they know. I can forgive them. And those men who seized me in my home, dragging me from my family. They were in the pay of Lord Sejanus; did they not do what they must, to satisfy their ruthless master? I forgive them too. And Sejanus? No! I could never forgive this heartless man! It is he who caused all this pain, to me and my parents. His insatiable greed caused the ruin of not only my family, but so many others. Forgive, the man said. If I ever met him, try to keep my hands from his throat! Sejanus would not even recognise who I am. He likely does not even know the plight he has caused me. He is a sick man, cursed by the gods with an insatiable desire for wealth. He brought about my delivery to the twenty-first century, which has not been *all* bad. Did I not get to see the future of mankind, in a way no Roman ever has seen? To see such wonderous things. *And I would never have met Sabina.*

My body trembles from the icy wind. I look up at the cross

atop the obelisk. Forgive, the man said. Can I cast out the hate in my heart for him? *Sejanus, I forgive you, even for what you have done to me and my family.*

Tears come as I think of all those I have wronged too. I wish I had been a better son, to help my father in the farm chores, and not shirk whenever I could … I am sorry mother, for mouthing off at you, when I knew you were only trying to teach me to lead an honest and responsible life. And my sister Valeria, how could I have been so unspeakably mean to you. Forgive me all of you, for my lapses and wickedness. The pain of missing them is so strong I feel it tearing me apart.

'Take me home, great God! Take me home to Rome, to my family, to my time, a thousand thousand years ago!' A gap in the clouds appears on the horizon, and I see the sun, huge and blood red. A ray of light touches the obelisk, and it smoulders. The sun vanishes again. A bolt of lightning strikes the great obelisk and throws me to the ground.

CHAPTER XXI

I try to raise myself but cannot. I struggle to draw breath, for it feels as though an enormous weight is resting on my chest. Again, I try to stand, but fall flat on my face for all my strength has left me. I lay still as feeling slowly returns to my tormented body.

Finally, I sit up, wipe my eyes, and a bright blue sky greets me. *Where am I?* I am certainly no longer in Saint Peter's Square. Before me is a field of golden wheat, waving and rippling in the breeze. Behind, a muddy road leads to a little village a short way off. I see nothing I recognise. Is this a dream? Are the gods playing games with me?

My body is shivering. My clothes are soaking wet. How can this be, on a cloudless day? The intensity of the last minutes in the square comes back to me. The storm, the hand on my shoulder, lightning striking the obelisk.

I struggle to my feet and plod slowly into the village. The road passes mud brick houses with thatched roofs. I pass a knot of people, who stare in silence at me. I stop a young woman in a simple robe and shawl, carrying a basket.

'Dove sono? Where I am?' I ask in Italian. She glares at me in fright. 'Please, domina,' I plead. But she dashes away. I look for some sign as to where I am. *Or when I am.* There is not a car to be seen. I come to the village square, where there is a little market. A handful of women sit before their baskets of goods, idly gossiping. A sight that could be any place, in any century. I go over to them, trying to hear what language they speak. But they abruptly cease the conversation, and stare, fixated on my clothing. I ask them what year it is.

'Quid anno est hoc?' They look at me as if I am crazy. I ask again, louder, 'Quid anno?' But they are afraid to speak now. Not wanting to create a disturbance, I move on.

I soon reach the end of the village. Far below to the east, I see a river. But which river? In an untilled field, a group of children are kicking a ball about. It rolls to my feet and I pick it up. A boy of about ten years runs to fetch it. He is dressed in a ragged tunic.

'Domine, quaeso mihi pila,' he calls out politely. He is asking for the ball in Latin! I hold it out to him and ask him what year it is.

'Filii, quid anno est hoc?' He looks at me strangely and tries to take the ball away, but I grip it tightly. I ask him the question that will tell me everything.

'Quis est imperatorem Romae?'

Though puzzled by the question, he answers calmly. 'Tiberius, domine.' I ask him to repeat it. 'Tiberius Caesar,' the boy says again. I heard him correctly. *Tiberius!* I fling the ball in the air.

'Tiberius is Caesar in Rome! Thank the gods! Tiberius is Caesar!' The child retrieves the ball and runs back to his mates, no doubt wondering who is the strangely dressed man asking odd questions.

Could it really be true? I am home. *Home.* The gods have sent me back to my own country and my century. After a year of toil and pain, I have returned to Rome! I kneel and touch my forehead to the warm earth. *Thank you, gods, old and new, for answering my prayers.*

I jump to my feet and gaze towards the river again, my vision sharpened by the exhilaration I feel. To the west, it snakes its way through fertile farmland. To the east, it appears to flow out of a large town; I can just make out the tiled roofs. It must be a great city, for the settlement stretches nearly to the horizon. Could it be Rome? Or perhaps Capua? It couldn't be Neapolis, for this city is nowhere near the sea. Straining my eyes, I can just make out the outline of a monumental building, gleaming white, standing above the horizon. The Colosseum! Not the ruin I had seen in the twenty-first century, but the original in all its splendour. I am in Rome. Thank the gods! This little hill where I stand must be the Vatican hill. How humble it is today. There is no basilica here, no Saint Peter's Square, just fields of wheat, a muddy road, and a nameless village.

It is mid-afternoon, and I need to find food and a bed. I check my pockets; I have a few hundred euro, but this paper money is worthless here. I fling it into the wind. *Penniless again Marcus, what else is new.* I have no friends in Rome, and the thought of running afoul of imperial guards makes me uneasy. But how to get passage home? I am surely not going to walk to Campania. *A ship.* I must get to the harbour of Rome, at Ostia, for I remember something I must do there.

I trot down the hill towards the Tiber. Along its bank runs a well-travelled road, all the way down to the sea, about fifteen miles away. I walk downstream, setting a good pace, and after a few miles I leave the village behind. There is much foot and oxcart traffic passing in both directions; I hope I can beg a ride when my legs give out. As I round a bend in the river, I spot a small barge, firmly grounded on a sand bar. It is about ten yards long, three broad, and is carrying a load of amphora. Two boys are on the raft struggling to free it with their poles as the water level is low. I call out a greeting to them.

'Salve, pueri!'

'Salve, domine,' they reply, without enthusiasm. I stand at the bank, taking in their plight.

'Will she not budge?' I ask in Latin.

'Not an inch sir. We have tried everything, and we are quite spent.'

'That is most unlucky.' I have an idea. 'Are you bound for Ostia?'

The older one calls out, 'We are indeed making for Ostia wharves, we must land this load there by sundown.'

'Could you use another crewman? I am headed that way myself.'

'By all means! We are in need of another pair of strong arms. Will you take a denarius?'

'That I will. Agreed!' I pull off my jacket and shoes, tie them around my neck, and plunge into the river. Thankfully it is scarcely three feet deep, the bottom sand and pebble. I wade over and climb aboard the raft.

'I am Linus,' says the older boy, who extends his hand. He is slim and wears his sandy hair long. 'This is my brother, Felix.' The other boy is short and a little stout; his chubby face is pink from the sun. Both are clearly tired from their exertions. From their quality garments and well-spoken manner, I assume they are from a well-to-do family.

'I am Marcus!' I say cheerfully. 'Thank you for letting me aboard.'

'We are pleased to have you, sir,' says Linus, while the other wipes sweat from his brow and looks forlornly downstream. 'I can tell by your manner of speech, you are a Campanian.'

'I am. From Abellinum. Here, young Felix, rest a while. I'll take your pole.' He is relieved to hand it over, and immediately flops down at the rear of the barge, his feet dangling in the water. With a minute or two of hard pushing, Linus and I manage to free the barge, and we are soon working our way downstream. Though we ground softly from time to time, we make good progress. In the sun it is hot, hard work, for the current is swift and much effort is needed to keep us off the bank.

I try to make conversation. 'May I ask what is your cargo? Wine?'

'Olive oil, for the warehouses of Vibius Rufus.'

'Ah. From your family farm?'

'No, we bought it at the market in the city. My family are traders; we purchase oil from all over Latium, and ship mostly to dealers for Africa.'

'That's great.' I can think of little more to say, and we fall silent again. After a mile or so, Linus tells Felix to relieve him at his oar, but the young boy refuses.

'I am too tired, brother!' he whines. I see a look of anger in Linus' eye; he sighs but doesn't chastise the youth.

After another few miles, we pause in the slack water of a broad bend in the river. We pull to the bank and ground the raft under a shady copse of oak trees. The boys offer me water from a terracotta vessel wedged in the bow. It is cool and sweet. The older boy digs into a leather bag, and produces a loaf of bread, and little jar of olive oil and fish paste. A fine Roman meal. Linus shares it out, a packing case forms our table. I remembered how the residents in the dormitory in Rome said a prayer before partaking. *Thank you, Lord for this food, and all our blessings.* And just to be sure, *Thank you, Vesta, for this food.*

We tuck in. How I have missed real food!

'This is fine garum,' I tell them. 'Did you buy it in the city?'

'No, it is our mother's recipe,' says Felix, who has cheered up a little and is busy stuffing himself.

'It is excellent, isn't it,' says his brother. 'She adds some garlic, and lets it mature in a little cellar at our house.' I nod, and gulp down another slice of bread, with a thick coating of the salty paste.

'So, what brought you to Rome, domine? Did you have

business in the city?' asks Linus, who stretches out to rest in the shade.

'No particular business. I came up for the Games in the amphitheatre,' I say quite honestly, though I do not mention my participation was not as a spectator, but as a victim.

'The Games! Did you see the gladiators?' Linus asks excitedly.

'And the beasts? Did you see the great cats?' asks Felix, wide-eyed.

'Yes, I saw them all. Lions, tigers, and many angry, frightening beasts.'

'Tell us more! We wish we could see the Games! But our father won't let us go. He says it is too bloody for children. Can you believe it! "Children" he says. I am fifteen years old!'

'It is a bloody and terrible spectacle, I will not pretend otherwise. The cruelty to the poor wretches torn apart by beasts, or forced to slaughter each other like pigs, I found unbearable.' I see the frightened awe in their faces. 'And the butchering of innocent animals I found most repugnant of all.'

'Perhaps, when we are older we could go, brother,' says Felix.

'I tell you, young men, I would watch the chariot races at the Hippodrome, any day. Now that's a spectacle worthy of the emperor!'

'Oh yes! The races! Father took us twice last year. Our seats were right across from the palace. It was a grand sight. Why in the very first race, there was a great crash, half the riders spilled out! Do you love the races too, Marcus?'

'I love them dearly. My family breeds horses on our farm.

Some of the swiftest horses ever to come out of the south have come from our farm,' I boast.

The sun is getting low, and Linus reminds us we must get moving to make Ostia before dark. I break off a stout oak branch and strip it smooth, so that all three of us may oar at once. We shove off and push into the current. The water is deeper now, and the current steady, so working the barge is much easier. For some long stretches, we merely rest on our poles and let the current do the work.

The sun has just set by the time we get to Ostia, but the evening twilight is bright enough to see by. We are near the sea, for the winds bring the salty smell to our nostrils. Along the river's edge, more and more buildings appear, lining both shores. We float past warehouses and docks. We have arrived at the port of Rome.

'There, the dock with the bold red letters.' A sign marks the wharves of the Vibius Rufus Company, "Exportatores Olei: exporters of olive oil". We give a last few tugs on our poles, and we bump into the dock. Our wearisome journey is over.

Two men approach; one, a slave, steadies the raft and makes it fast to the wharf. The other is a tall, middle-aged man in fine clothing.

'Linus! Gods be praised you are here at last. Pray, why are you so late? Felix, were you not pulling your weight?'

'Our father, Gaius Vibius Rufus,' Linus tells me.

I jump off the raft onto the wharf. 'Honoured to meet you sir. I am Marcus Corvus.' He takes my hand and shakes it warmly.

'Salve, young Marcus. Am I to guess, Linus, that you have signed on a hired hand for the journey?'

'Father, it was so slow, the river so shallow. We grounded just above Tellenae and couldn't get off.'

'We couldn't do it on our own,' says the younger boy.

'The water is so shallow, Father, we took to grounding so many times I barely had the strength to pole off,' repeats Linus.

'It is as the boys say, sir, I could see they were stuck fast, so I offered to assist them,' I tell their father.

'Very well. I feared you might have had a difficult passage, there has been so little rain yet this winter. I was quite worried that ill fortune had overtaken them when they hadn't arrived some hours after their expected time. Marcus, I am exceedingly grateful to you for looking after them. Boys, have you paid the young man?'

'Not yet. We were going to give him a denarius.'

'A denarius? Here son, take ten for your gracious deed. Marcus, you have been too kind, to help my sons.' He presses a handful of silver into my hand.

'Thank you very much. It was no trouble at all. Any decent man would have lent a hand to the young gentlemen.'

'Aye. But decent men are few in these times. Tell me, are you passing through Ostia? Do you have lodgings for the night?'

'In truth, I do not, sir. I am bound for Neapolis to return to my family home near Abellinum. I was hoping to take passage from Ostia.'

He shakes his head. 'You'll find all the south bound ships have departed already. With the strong westerly blowing, no ship will take the chance on a night departure. Pray, stay with us. My home is close by.'

I accept, and whisper thanks to the gods for my good fortune. I know what my mother would have said: kindness to strangers reaps its reward, many times over.

Torches are lit as darkness falls. After supervising the unloading for a time, Rufus beckons me to join him and his sons. We leave the dockside and walk a few blocks through the dark, narrow streets of Ostia. We come to the gate of a high-walled compound, and pass into the grounds of a large villa, their family home. Torches light the path to the entrance of the grand house, where servants greet their master and lead us into the atrium. It is a beautiful room, colourful frescoes on the walls depict the gods and goddesses resting in fanciful scenes. A shallow marble pool of water is in the centre, strewn with flower petals.

I greet his wife, Poppaea, and father, Quintus, who welcome me warmly. I am invited to share dinner, and to take a bed for the night. A few words to the house slaves and all is arranged. A fresh shirt is offered to me after a bath, and soon we are all sitting at the dining table where a fine meal has been prepared: baked fowl, fresh prawns and cockles, coarse bread, olives and fruits. We oarsman recount our voyage down the Tiber.

'Darling, you should have known the river would be low and too troublesome for a heavy load at this time of year,' says Poppaea.

'I know, dearest, there is no need to remind me of it,' Rufus says, somewhat irritated. 'But we were thirty amphora short of a full load for tomorrow's shipment.' The talk turns to the olive oil business, of which I learn a great deal. The unpredictable price of oil in Ostia, Carthage, and Alexandria is discussed at length; the cost of transport and insurance is lamented. The villains who insure ships, collect duties, unload at foreign ports, all come in for a prickling denunciation by Rufus while his father stabs the table with his bony finger in agreement. Rufus complains just how hard it is to run a business in these times.

'But enough talk of business, we are boring our guest,' announces the mistress of the house.

'Lady Poppaea, it is most fascinating. I have grasped in a single meal all the finer points of the olive trade.'

'Many years of hard work it took to get to where we are, right Father?' says Rufus, as he pushes back his chair. The old man does the same.

'How we got through those hard times during the last war, I will never know. Why hardly any ship could take to sea without pirates seizing it!'

'Yes, Father, those were trying times.' Rufus looks at me and rolls his eyes.

I push back my chair too. 'Domine, that was a superlative meal, I must thank you. I have not eaten so well in all my twenty years.'

'Please Marcus, address me as Gaius.'

'Thank you, Gaius. And you too, my lady, it was superb.'

Poppaea agrees. 'Our new cook knows her craft well; she is a great acquisition. The gods know how many cooks we tried before we found her!'

'Come, recline with us,' say Rufus, as he and his father rise. The children are packed off to bed, and the four of us move to a nearby sitting room. Silently, a servant lights some oil lamps, then sets a goblet of sweet wine and a small bowl of figs next to each of us.

Rufus takes a long draft of wine. 'Do tell us about your family, Marcus. I understand you breed horses in the south.'

'We do indeed.' I tell him of our little farm, and our horse business. Rufus listens intently, quizzing me on the cost of feed, transport, and the price of a good horse in Naples. When I speak of my parents and sister, emotion begins to taint my words, and betrays me.

'Does something trouble you, son? Is your family all right?'

'I … I pray so. It's just that I have not seen them for a year. When I left, there was great turmoil. I have struggled to return all this time.'

'Do tell us, Marcus,' says Poppaea. 'You are among friends here.'

'I do not wish to trouble you. You have been too kind already.'

'Speak freely, boy. We'll not betray your confidence. We are in your debt, perhaps we can help you,' says the senior Rufus.

'Well, it all started a year ago at our farm at Abellinum.' I relate how I was seized and taken to Rome.

'An outrage!' cries Rufus. 'What business did your father get caught up in?'

'I did not know of any dispute, with anyone. My father was an honest man. But I am mainly ignorant of my father's business. He wanted me to learn his trade, but I was, well, a shirker by my father's own words.'

'Speak not ill of yourself. By your own deeds this afternoon, you cannot be called a shirker. But tell us, what became of you?' I continue, telling them of my escape to the Forum.

'Where the high priests hid you?'

'Well, no, they ordered me to leave. But, the gods, our gods, preserved me. Of that I am absolutely certain.'

'Thanks be to Jupiter! And the divine Vesta, mother of the innocent! Of course, she is to be thanked,' says Poppaea.

Rufus calmly agrees. 'Truly the divine gods are to be praised for your deliverance. This was a year ago? You have been in hiding since?'

'Yes, I went away, across the seas. To the end of the earth in fact.'

'And you've not been home to Campania since? Did you send word to your family that you are well?'

'No, I could not. Until just recently I was not even in Italy. I admit I should have made a greater effort.'

'The time has come then to return to your family. I assume you are departing at once?'

'Yes, I am most eager to go home now. I will sail tomorrow for Neapolis as soon as I can find a ship.'

The others return to reclining on their couches, shaking

their heads. They talk among themselves for a time, amazed at my story. They pronounce a curse on Sejanus, who has so corrupted the honest emperor Tiberius, successor of Augustus.

I take a long drink of wine, before interrupting. 'Gaius, pray, may I ask you something?'

'Of course, Marcus.'

'Do you know of oil merchants named Sufinius? I am told they trade out of Ostia.'

'Decius Sufinius? Yes, certainly, we are well acquainted. We often charter a vessel together.'

'Yes, Decius. Did he mention a son?'

'The boy, Lucius. A gentle, intelligent young man. He suffered some tragedy, I hear. Decius is reluctant to speak of it.'

'He did, and that is another reason I have come to Ostia. I must speak to his parents. I have knowledge of his fate which I must communicate to them.' Rufus sits up, pulls his couch closer, and looks at me gravely.

'Do speak directly, Marcus. Decius is broken-hearted this past year, wondering what happened to his gentle son. Even now, he cannot speak of Lucius without tears in his eyes. What do you know of this? Leave nothing out.'

'When I was taken to Rome and condemned, I was taken to the dungeons. Cast in the same cell with me, was Lucius, son of Decius.'

'Oh! To share a common fate? Did he say how he came to be condemned?'

'A brief word only, that criminals from the city in the name of Sejanus tried to usurp their family business. His father refusing, they delivered him a savage beating; when this too did not alter his mind, they seized his son and daughter-in-law, as they did me.'

'Decius never spoke of this. I knew he was troubled; his mood was dark, his manner nervous and agitated for some time last summer. Then, in the month of Sextilis, he told me he had some accident and was confined to his house for many days. And that his son and his young bride had disappeared.' Rufus stares out the window for a moment, then back at me.

'Where is Lucius? Did he escape with you?' They all look at me, dreading what I am to say.

'He did not survive. He fled through the tunnels beneath the arena with me, pursued by the guards. We got as far as the Forum gate together. But they caught up with him.'

'He was recaptured?'

'He was not. They, they …'

'Out with it, boy!'

'They cut his throat. I saw the blood and I saw him fall.' Poppaea shrieks in horror.

'Gods help the poor boy!' The elder Rufus is speechless and ashen-faced. 'Poor innocent soul. Such a fate!'

'It is a tragedy. A fine young man full of potential to be wasted, for nothing. For the greed of that monster,' says Rufus. 'What of his young wife, Julia? Do you know her fate?'

'Lucius said she was taken to be sold in the slave market.'

Rufus stands, and paces about. His wife tries to calm him. The old man sits, lost in thought. The silence is broken when

Linus, Felix, and two younger children bound into the room with their nursemaid.

'Good night, Father!' they say as one. 'Good night, Grandfather! Good night, Mother!' They all kiss the cheeks of the elders.

'Our daughters, Livia and Cassia.'

'I am honoured to meet you, Lady Livia and Lady Cassia.' They blush and giggle.

'Say goodnight to Master Marcus, children,' says their mother. One by one, they give me a peck on the cheek too, and run down the hallway giggling, followed by their nurse.

Rufus returns to his couch and sits, facing me. 'Marcus, I can only wish you godspeed to your home and family to bear the good news that you are alive and well. But first, we will go to the home of Decius. I will take you there tomorrow, after breakfast. It is late, and I can see you are tired from the day's labours. Cato! Come Marcus, Cato will show you to your sleeping quarters.'

A servant shows me to my room. In bed, alone at last, I gaze at the ceiling. By the light of the flickering oil lamp, I see the ceiling is painted with mythical scenes. There is Hercules, capturing the Cretan bull. Many labours too I have performed, but one yet remains. With the troublesome image of Lucius' last moments in my head, sleep comes with difficulty.

I am awakened by a servant, who taps gently on the door. He brings me a cup of fruit juice, and a vessel of warm water to wash. He tells me breakfast will be served shortly. In the house, there is much bustle as the morning meal is served to the children and the contingent of slaves, which number around a dozen. I am guided out the back of the house, into a magnificent garden. There are fountains and statues, flowers and pathways, with palms, olive and lemon trees. A long porch, decorated with elegant columns, frames the courtyard where a table for four is set. Rufus is already there, looking intently at some parchments.

'Good morning, Gaius! I think I am transported to Arcadia. What a lovely garden.'

'Thank you, Marcus. It gives us all great pleasure. It truly helps me to regain my nerves and attain peace after a troublesome day.' The elder Rufus, and Poppaea join us. We exchange greetings of the day and take our breakfast. There is little talk; the thought of our lamentable task ahead brings little cheer to the table.

'Let us be on our way, Marcus. I have sent word ahead to Decius at sunrise, he will be expecting us.'

'I do not envy you, Marcus. To bring such bitter news is as painful a duty as could be imagined,' says his wife.

'Too true, Lady Poppaea. I had no wish for this burden. But Lucius and I, we took an oath in the dungeon, to inform each other's families of the other's fate should one of us survive.'

'And so you must. Come, Marcus,' beckons Rufus.

We are soon in the streets of Ostia, which are lively at this hour; street sellers, ox carts, sailors, hawkers and merchants are everywhere, making travel tedious. After a few blocks, we arrive at the house of Decius Sufinius. Their family home is also within a walled compound, though of smaller dimensions than that of Rufus.

A servant boy shows us in. We find Decius waiting in his study. He rises and takes Rufus' hand.

'Decius, I thank you for making time to meet me. Pray, how is your wife, is she well?'

'Yes, she is well enough, though she is much vexed these days. A new cook to train, you see. The house has been close to burning down three times!'

'Ah, the poor thing. I don't envy the mistress in a family of means. Such a burden, to deal with the never-ending trouble of slaves and servants. May I present Marcus Corvus, of Campania.' Decius shakes my hand warmly. 'He was of some assistance to my sons yesterday, in getting a barge downriver from the city,' Rufus says.

'Marcus, a pleasure to meet you. Are you staying long in Ostia?'

'No, I hope to depart this very day for home, in fact.'

Rufus intercedes. 'Please, Decius, can you ask Marcella to join us? It is of the highest importance.'

'Certainly, Gaius,' he says, and beckons a servant to fetch the mistress of the house. A woman of small frame, dark hair and eyes, in a simple white dress arrives.

'Ah, you have guests, husband,' she says softly. 'Gaius, how do you fare? Is the family well?'

'We are all exceedingly well, Lady Marcella. May I present Marcus Corvus, a friend from Campania.' She takes my hand and nods.

'What is this about, darling? Has something happened?' she asks her husband uneasily.

Rufus steps forward. 'Please, can we sit somewhere quiet? Marcus here has come to Ostia to see you. He brings word of Lucius.'

'Our son Lucius?' cries Marcella.

'The same. Please, let us speak in the sitting room.' Decius takes his wife by the sleeve and guides her into an adjacent room; we follow.

When we are seated, Marcella fires questions at me. 'Sir, who are you? What do you know of Lucius? Who sent you here? Gaius, do you trust the man?'

'Patience, good lady. Yes, I feel this man is trustworthy. He performed a brave act of kindness to my children just yesterday. And he stayed under our roof last night.'

Decius speaks calmly. 'Forgive us, son. Since Lucius disappeared last year, we trust no one and fear everyone. Do tell us what you know of him. Is he alive?' They both stare at my face intently, their faces frozen in fear. I pause, and look Decius in the eye, unable to bear the gaze of Lucius' mother. I shake my head.

'He is not, domine. He is dead, killed last September, at Rome.'

Marcella cries out. 'No! It cannot be so! No!' Decius puts his arm around her, and she buries her face in his shoulder. 'No! My poor sweet boy!' she wails. Decius comforts her, brushing her hair aside, and whispering in her ear. With tears in his own eyes, he tells her to hush.

'We knew it to be true, dearest.' He wipes his own eyes with his sleeve. 'We thought as much. With over a year gone and no news, we could hardly expect otherwise. That boy would cross through Hades itself to get home, if he could.'

Decius sits with his wife's head now in his lap, her tears uncontrollable. He calmly asks me to tell what I know of Lucius' death. I recount the story that I told Rufus, of the agents of Sejanus coming to the house, my seizure, and journey to Rome and the dungeons.

'Why that evil swine! He tried the same evil ruse on me! He sent his goons to me to buy my business at a pitiable price with threats of violence if I did not sell! I knew that man was behind Lucius' disappearance. It is his habit to rob the better families of their hard-earned wealth. And with threats, beatings, and death, if thwarted!' says Decius. 'How did you win freedom? Did you defeat the gladiators?' Realising the incredulity of his question, he continues, 'Or did you escape before being cast up?'

I recount how I was imprisoned with Lucius and the others, and how we escaped, leaving out nothing. Even Marcella, wretched with grief, dries her tears and studies my face in silence, taking in every detail. I tell how we surprised the guards at the gates of the Colosseum and fled for our lives towards the Forum, with the guards in pursuit.

'I cannot bear to hear of it! They caught up with our son?' cries Marcella.

'They did. He fought to the end, but they struck him down and put him to death on the spot.' Both his parents turn away in horror, their faces wrenched with grief.

'Come, Marcus,' says Rufus. 'It is best we leave them to grieve.'

'Pray friends, give us just a moment!' says Decius. Rufus and I stand outside the door. We look at each other, but neither know what to say or do, with the couple sobbing together inside. After some minutes, they regain their composure. Decius calls out, his voice cracking, 'Please Marcus, tells us more. Is there anything else you can tell us of his final hours?'

'That is all I remember. He did not die like a wild beast in the arena. He died without shackles on, fighting for his freedom to the last.'

'Perhaps you can take a little comfort in that,' says Rufus.

I continue. 'He kept his good humour to the end. Even with death but minutes away, he spoke with a clear mind of his home, of his family, of you two. He enjoined me to take an oath, there in the dungeons, to inform each other's families should one of us live beyond the day.'

Decius nods. 'I thank you for coming here to tell us. We are forever in your debt, young Marcus.'

'It was my duty to you both, I could not do otherwise. I apologise for taking so long to get here. I was forced to flee, and ended up far from Rome, across the seas. I only just returned to Italy this month.'

'Think nothing of it. What of his wife, Julia? They took her the same night they came for Lucius. Is there word of her fate? Her parents have been enduring the unendurable, as have we.'

'Lucius mentioned only that they threatened to sell her in

the slave market, but of her fate, I know nothing.'

'The poor child. Such a lovely, sweet girl,' whispers Marcella. Decius rises, and clasps both of my hands.

'Thank you, son. May the gods be ever merciful to you and deliver you good fortune and happiness for the kindness you have shown us.' Marcella embraces me too, but can say nothing, her tears flowing freely again.

'We will take leave now. For young Marcus plans to take ship this very day for his home,' Rufus says.

Decius accompanies us out into the bright sunshine. 'May Neptune calm the seas for you and may all the gods protect you on your journey.'

'Thank you, sir.'

'If you pass this way, I pray you pay us a visit. You will always be welcome.' I promise that I would.

'Decius, please come and dine with us tomorrow night, if you and your wife are up to it. Grief is always easier to bear when suffered in the company of friends. Farewell for now,' Rufus says.

As we leave, I notice my shoulder is damp from the tears of Lucius' mother. I shed a tear or two myself; Rufus sees this but says nothing.

We return to the house where Rufus asks me to sit in the garden, while he excuses himself to take care of some business. I sit comfortably for a time, well attended by servants who ensure I don't want for food or drink. After an hour, Rufus returns.

'I have arranged a passage for you this afternoon. The ship sails an hour before sundown.'

'Thank you, Rufus! You needn't have done that. I am very grateful to you.'

'Not at all. I am most happy and honoured to do this for you, to set you on your way home.'

'Thank you, from the bottom of my heart.'

'Come, we'll take lunch before you sail so your food is well settled before you put to sea. Have you sailed before? River rafting, excepted?'

'I have, Gaius. I have spent some months at sea just this past year. On a very large ship. The ride was gentle and I did not fall victim to sea sickness.'

'Good. I wish you well. When the time comes, Cato will bring you to the ship.'

Rufus takes his leave; business requiring him at the wharves. I am left to take lunch with Poppaea and the four children. The boys come in noisily to take their seats, and without a pause start pawing at the piles of food. Their little sisters take their seats too, opposite me. They are much engrossed in me, and their mother chastises them for ignoring their food. The elder, Livia, watches me intently while I eat.

'Are you married, Marcus?' she asks, tipping her head to one side.

'What a dumb girl question!' announces Felix.

'Felix! Show some courtesy to our guest and your little sister. She is merely inquisitive.'

I turn to Livia. 'No, little one. I mean, not yet.'

'Are you promised?' she asks.

'Well, there is this girl ...'

'What does she look like?' asks Cassia, her younger sister.

Poppaea smiles patiently. 'Girls, do not be so inquisitive, perhaps Marcus does not wish to speak of private things.'

'It is all right, domina, I don't mind.' I turn to Livia. 'I do have a lady friend. She is two years younger than I.'

'Will you marry her?' asks the girl, and all look at me intently.

'It would be difficult. She lives very far away.'

'In the city?' asks Livia.

'No, not in Rome. She lives across the seas. But she is an Italian girl.'

'What's her name, Marcus?' asks Poppaea, now interested.

'Sabina.' I have not spoken her name aloud for months. 'To answer your question, little Cassia, she is tall, slender, and has long dark hair, like yours. But I fear we may never be together again.' Poppaea sees the sadness in my eyes.

'If the gods wish it, you will be reunited. I will pray to Venus that it is so. Now, let us not speak further of sad things. Tell me, will you go directly to your parents' farm?'

'Yes, lady. I expect we will arrive in Neapolis just after dawn, two days hence. From there, I will make for Nola first, a journey of about twenty miles. Then to the farm near Abellinum, a few miles beyond.'

'You have money for provisions and your passage?'

'I certainly do, thank you, domina. Your husband most graciously paid my passage.'

Poppaea admonishes the children to finish their meals. The table is filled with grilled fish, fresh breads and fruits. Soon the children excuse themselves and dash off. Poppaea suggests a short rest in the courtyard of the garden. Uncomfortably full of good food, I agree. I am shown to a large daybed, covered with cushions. The hot afternoon soon brings on a comfortable nap.

I am awakened an hour or two later. Cato, the head of the house slaves, asks me to prepare my belongings as we will be departing soon. I have only the clothes on my back so I wash quickly then return to the atrium of the house, where the family has gathered, save Rufus. The children each take both my hands in turn and wish me a safe journey.

'Such lovely, well raised children,' I tell their mother, who beams proudly.

'They are our pride, and all that we live for. Soon you will be back with your family too. Do send word when you reach home, whether the news is good or bad.'

'I promise, domina. I am touched by your kindness.' A female slave comes forward and hands me a basket filled with food and drink.

'For your journey. Ship's fare is not usually fit for rats, I understand,' Poppaea says.

'Thank you again.'

'Farewell, Marcus.' The others call out their farewells as Cato and I head out into the bustling streets of Ostia.

It is now late afternoon. We reach the harbour, where hundreds of ships are moored, with many more coming and going. It makes a grand sight. I wonder where all these great ships are bound for? By the winds to Spain, Africa or Egypt?

How wonderful a sailor's life would be. Some distance along the wharf we reach a stoutly built single-masted sailing ship, already heavily laden, its crew busy stowing cargo and coiling rope. Cato speaks with a deckhand, who soon returns with the captain.

A well-built man steps off. His long hair is nearly white and his weather-beaten face eyes me intently.

'I am Marius,' he says with the authority of his station. 'You are Rufus' young charge, are you not?'

'I am. Marcus Corvus.' He shakes my hand firmly.

'Welcome aboard. I owe much to Gaius Rufus, I would not be in business today without his patronage, especially during the last war. Marcus, there is a spare hammock for you in the cabin. Stow your things in the chest below your hammock.' I nod. 'Very well then. Come aboard, there is much to do if we're to get away before dark. Unless you're handy with a rope, I suggest you keep clear of the sailors.'

'I will. Thank you, Captain.' I climb aboard and find my hammock.

As dusk falls there is much shouting as the ropes are heaved aboard and stowed. We push off, and the vessel heads for the harbour entrance. Near the sea wall, the mainsail is bent. The breeze blows strongly; the ship lurches forward. We pass the harbour entrance, its beacon fires now lit. I move to the stern deck and watch the lights of the harbour fade in the distance.

CHAPTER XXII

Night falls and the ship pushes on at speed. As the seas grow heavy it takes effort to stand in one place. I wedge myself in a corner, out of the breeze. The land is now barely visible behind. I nibble at the food I was given, but my belly is uneasy; I am not only unused to being at sea in a small craft, but apprehensive of what I will find when I reach home. *Home.* It is so close now.

The captain comes to speak to me. 'Come Marcus, dine with us. Bring your rations.' In the centre of the little cabin, a table is fixed to the deck; four sailors are seated. After introductions, Captain Marius slaps me on the back.

'So, tell us your story, son. What brought you to Rome? Seeking your fortune, no doubt?' The sailors eat with their hands from rough iron plates. Each man has a wooden cup gripped in his palm. They gaze at me by the soft light of a flickering oil lamp.

'Judging by his clothing and lack of possessions, fortune he did not find!' says one sailor.

'Too soft for the city no doubt,' says another.

The captain interrupts. 'Leave off! Marcus here was in the service of my friend Gaius Rufus who spoke highly of him. Go on, Marcus.'

'I am Marcus, son of Gaius Corvus. We are a family of horse breeders. Our farm is near Abellinum, in Campania.'

'Ah, horse traders, eh! An honourable profession, like that of the sea, right men?' says the captain. I tell them of my family, our peaceful life on the farm, and my being seized and taken to the arena. They stroke their beards, straining to hear every word over the roar of the sea and wind.

'By Jupiter! What a fate!' shouts one. 'How did you survive?'

'Fool, he slaughtered the lions and won his freedom! That's how the games work,' says another.

'A boy, barely a whisker on his chin, slaying lions? With his bare hands! You are full of dung, Titus!'

'I'll show you who's full of dung,' Titus says and slams his mug on the table. The captain intervenes.

'Silence, let him tell the tale himself. Aye, go on, Marcus. How did you get out of the arena? Did you kill the lions?' I tell the tale of my escape.

'Incredible. And where did you flee to?' says the captain. I pause, reluctant to answer.

'It was far away, in the desert to the south. And now, I am finally going home. I have not seen my parents this past year.'

'Poor creature!'

'Neptune will steer us a fast course, I pray for it. We are

already making good time.'

'Thank you. Thank you all for hearing my story.'

'A fine tale. Who would have guessed, a mere boy having endured such things. A toast, to Marcus!'

'To Marcus!'

'To Marcus, the unbreakable!' The sailors continue to tell yarns, and drink until midnight, when the captain orders our little party to break up. We take to our hammocks. It has gotten quite cold, so I help myself to a coarse canvas blanket. The rocking of the ship is soothing and I am soon asleep.

I wake to find the crew already up. The coastline is in sight a few miles off. The breeze is still strong from the northwest, and the captain is pleased with our progress. The rest of the day is uneventful.

The following morning, we are roused before dawn by the man on watch, for the lights of the port of Neapolis are in sight, a few miles ahead. The wind falls a little as we approach the land, and the sun is well up by the time we reach the harbour entrance. We stand off for a short time, eventually the harbour master's vessel rows out and comes alongside. Marius arranges a tow in. As we come to the wharf the crew spring ashore and tie us up. I climb onto the dock; my legs unsteady after two days on the pitching boat. The hold is already open, with Marius standing above it, giving orders for the unloading. I get his attention.

'Thank you, Captain! I'll take my leave now.'

'Farewell, Marcus. I expect we'll not cross paths again. Keep away from those lions, eh.'

'I will, Captain. May the gods be with you!' He waves and disappears into the ship's hold.

So, here I am, in Neapolis again. Home is but a day's journey away. I feel a knot of anxiety in my gut. There is no time to lose if I am to reach the farm by nightfall. The city streets are as busy as ever, and it is only with difficulty I weave my way through them towards the east. I find the Via Argine, broad and straight, the first road that will take me towards Nola. I walk with purpose, and soon reach the city walls. It is astonishing how quickly I reach the countryside; today the city is but a tenth the size of its twenty-first century counterpart. Many travellers on foot, and all manner of animal transport share the roadway. I have little trouble obtaining a ride for the twenty miles to Nola on a wagon pulled by two sturdy horses. The owner is quite happy to take two sestertii as fare.

I climb into the back of the wagon. It is carrying crates of fowls and geese, sheltered from the sun by a canvas awning. I wedge myself into a spot at the rear of the cart, resting on soft hay. My host drives the horses at a brisk trot, and the city recedes swiftly. The ground gradually rises. We are soon in green fields and fresh air. I had forgotten how beautiful the southern Italian countryside is. *So close to home.*

The pace of the horses is steady, and the gentle motion makes me drowsy. I sleep a little, but the smell is unpleasant, and the geese squawk loudly at every bump in the road. By midday we have arrived in Nola. We stop near the town forum, exactly where I stopped to rest on my way to Rome so many months ago. I thank the driver, and clamber down.

Unlike Neapolis, two millennia have not changed Nola. The forum, the market and the narrow streets, are just as I remember them. At the marketplace I spend lavishly on food, not only for myself, but to bring as gifts to my family. Cheeses, seafood and garum fill my little basket.

I prepare a sandwich, a snack I learnt from modern man, and eat quickly. I drink deeply from the public fountain nearby. I hunt for a ride to take me over the mountain to Abellinum. This road is less well-travelled, so it takes me some time and a denarius to arrange passage on an oxcart. My luck is holding. It seems I will not have to walk the last few miles.

The journey is painfully slow, and I get down as soon as Abellinum is in sight. With fresh energy, I hurry to the town centre. It is late in the day. The market has closed and there are few people about. No matter, I devour a quick supper from my basket.

Now, the road north is clear and familiar. There! The farm of Lucius Flaccus. And there, on the rise, the farm of my childhood friend Septimius! I almost run the last mile. There, in the soft light of dusk, is our farm. *Home!* I run down the path to our front gate and push it open. I hurry past our little pond and the willow trees. Oddly, there are no horses in the front paddocks. Where is my colt, Phoenix? He is always grazing here.

I reach the house and burst through the door.

'Mother! Father! Valeria!' I shout. In the kitchen, steam rises from a pot on the stove, but mother is nowhere to be seen. 'Mother!' I shout again. *Where is everyone?* I dash to the sitting room, but no one is there. I rush to my parent's room—it too is empty. Fear rises in my heart. Where could they be? And why are there no horses in the fields? Has something terrible befallen my family? I rush back out of the house.

'Mother, Father!' I call out, now frantic.

'Marcus?' I hear a shout from behind me. My mother emerges from the barn, a basket of eggs under her arm.

'Mother! It's me!'

She shrieks, drops the basket, and grasps her face in her hands. 'Marcus! Gods be praised!' I rush to her and embrace her. She holds me so tightly it hurts. She pushes me back and looks me over. 'Dear sweet boy! Are you hurt? Are you in one piece?'

'I am, mother, I am fine. Thank the gods you are safe too!'

'Valeria! Come quick. Your brother is home!' My sister appears from the barn and stares at me, her mouth open. I pry myself from my mother's grip, and go over to embrace her, but she does not return the gesture. As I pull back, she slaps me hard in the face and returns to the house without saying a word. My mother wipes the tears from her eyes. She hugs me again, gently.

'What is wrong with Valeria?' I ask.

'She has been like this for many months now. She barely speaks to me, either.'

'Why is this so, Mother?'

'It pains me to say this. She blames you for what has happened.'

'What has happened? Pray tell me!'

'It's your father.'

'Where is he?'

'He is not here. He has been gone for nearly a year. They took him not long after they took you. We have had no word of him since.' Stupefied, I fall to the ground at my mother's feet.

Father, where are you? Where are you?

'For heaven's sake stop your whining, child!'

'But why doesn't he call, Mum? He has my number. Not even a text. All these months! He must be in some sort of trouble.'

'More likely he's just moved on, Sabina. You better get used to the idea. He's gone and I dare say he's not coming back.'

'But I miss him so much, Mum! I loved him.' I bury my face in my hands.

'I'm sure you had a crush on him but, love—you hardly knew him. It was only a few weeks. Takes a lot longer than that to fall in love with someone.'

'You don't understand. You and Dad, you're so old!' I storm out of the house, letting the screen door slam behind me. What do parents know anyway? I'm a grown woman, eighteen years old! Yet she still calls me a child.

I head towards the centre of Quilpie. *I can't wait to leave this town.* I'll go to Melbourne for uni. The further away from my parents, the better. Although, I don't know anyone there and I hear the crime rate is pretty high. I kick a stone down the road and stub my toe in the process. 'Damn it!' I curse. 'Why doesn't he call?' I try to hold back the tears but they flow freely.

It's early evening and the warm night is still. The smells of the Queensland outback, the red earth and eucalyptus trees, are strong. I walk aimlessly past the shops in the main street, all shut for the night. Past the clothing store. *That's where we went shopping together.* I look in the window and sigh. *He was so handsome in his new clothes.* Past the cafe, where we had so many coffees together. He loved coffee as if he'd never had it before. I miss him so much.

I continue to the edge of town, to the little park by the creek. *We spent so many hours here.* There, beneath the old willow tree, is the derelict picnic table. It has been a wet summer and the creek flows with a gentle murmur. I climb up on the table and sit, legs drawn up, resting my chin on my knees. *This is where he held my hand the first time.*

Tears come again. *That strange, wonderful man.* Is he alright? I wouldn't be surprised if he fell victim to some low-life. He was so trusting. How on earth would he survive in the big city? Could Mum be right? No, no there's no way he could have a new girlfriend. No woman would fall for such an odd man. Something must have happened to him. I cry uncontrollably. He promised he would call, but he didn't – something *must* be wrong. I wish I had given him my email address. Except, I doubt if he even knows how to send an email.

Did he love me? He said he did on the phone! He was such a strange, quirky man, yet so sweet and gentle to me. And so naïve! He didn't even know what a phone was, or how an aeroplane stays in the sky! Well, I don't exactly know that either, though they did teach us in grade seven science, I think.

I take my phone from the pocket of my jeans, and scroll through my photos, looking for pictures of Marcus. *This is my favourite, taken the day before he left.* A selfie of us together, sitting on this very spot. The pain bites hard. *Has he forgotten me already?* True, he was a couple of years older than me – was I too young for him? Has he found a new girlfriend back home? I cover my eyes at the thought, and the tears flow anew.

The shadows grow longer. The colours of the outback fade. I look up towards the setting sun, and at last my tears begin to dry. *I hardly have any mementos of him! Except this old ring.* I twist it around my little finger. *I don't care if it's a little rusty. It's so pretty! Two hands joined, mine and his.* I twist off the ring, to examine it more closely. Is it a man's hands and a woman's hands? It must be. This is comforting. As I try to put it back on my finger, it slips, and falls to the picnic table. It rolls through a crack, onto the ground.

'Sabina, you idiot! Why am I always so clumsy?' I shout at myself. I crawl under the table and spot the glint of metal among the dried leaves. *There you are. Oh my God, I'd die if I lost that ring.* I bang my head on the bench of the table as I get up. *Ow! Idiot again.* I notice something half buried in the leaf litter. I pull it out and dust off the dirt. It's a little statue, about three inches high, seemingly made of ivory. Under the base the word "Juno" is inscribed in tiny letters. *Well, the day's not a total loss after all. Where did this come from?* I turn the statue over and over in my hand. The last ray of sunlight catches the ivory figure. I look up at the flame-red sky. A gust of wind blows a shower of leaves from the trees nearby, then is still again.

www.ingramcontent.com/pod-product-compliance
Lightning Source LLC
Chambersburg PA
CBHW060735190726
48285CB00001B/215